WARLORD
THE GIFT
BOOK 5

MARC STAPLETON

Copyright © 2024 by Marc Stapleton

All rights reserved.

No part of this book may be reproduced in any form or by any electronic or mechanical means, including information storage and retrieval systems, without written permission from the author, except for the use of brief quotations in a book review.

To my wife… yet again

"Fear not for the future, weep not for the past."

PERCY BYSSHE SHELLEY

CHAPTER 1

"So, this is it?"

"This is it," Baynes confirms with a proud grin on his face.

I'm standing on a blank, almost featureless street corner in upstate New York. Baynes is beside me, buzzing with excitement, gesturing to the building before us with barely concealed enthusiasm.

"It's a vape shop," I say out loud.

At least, it sure looks like a vape shop. I'm staring at a small retail unit, occupying the corner lot of a square office building. Despite the size of the shop, its name is grandiose: 'The Vape Megastore'.

It's just turned evening, but the shop is drenched in bright, gaudy light. There's a pink neon sign that hurts my eyes in its intensity; a kitschy, ostentatious LED banner below it flashes a series of brands and prices quicker than I can read, and everything is bathed in the orange glow of a nearby streetlight like a second sun.

"We're downstairs," he replies, rubbing his forehead with one hand and pointing to a sad, lonely black door with the other. It stands just beside the vape shop, secured with no less than three locks.

"An underground lair huh?" I ask him as we stroll to the door, and he picks a large set of keys out of his pocket. "Here I was thinking we were the good guys, while you're channeling your inner Bond villain?"

He smiles at me – a sarcastic, acidic grin – before adding a loud, cackling, maniacal laughter, evidently his best impression of a supervillain. I smile awkwardly in response, and he turns back to the door.

Baynes, Alessia and I left Thailand shortly after our peculiar backstreet bar rendezvous; we had to make a choice to either follow Vincent to Malaysia and try to heat up a cold trail, or come back home to meet the others and put a more detailed plan in place.

I don't know if it's my grating sense of sentimentality – the fact it'd be nice to see Dante, Jude, and their outfit – or some tiny, imperceptible amount of homesickness within me, but I picked the latter option. Alessia, on the other hand, traveled to Europe and promised me she'd join us in a week.

Baynes and I only got off a plane seven hours ago, followed by a five-hour car ride that I happily slept the entire way through, mostly so I could avoid Baynes' collection of classic rock and roll. I woke up here, a small town in upstate New York called Enderton; the sweet suburban setting for Baynes, Dante, and Jude's post-*me* career.

After he's done with the locks – each seeming to take longer than the last – he opens the door, revealing a dim corridor with awful, blue-painted walls, and another lonely door at the end of it. There are paint cans stacked to one side, and bundles of newspapers at the other. It might not be Baynes' garage, but it sure has the same vibes.

We walk to that door and open it, before walking down a set of damp, gray steps beyond, our paths lit by a flickering lightbulb overhead. At the bottom, Baynes, me, and our flickering shadows meet yet another door, this one protected by a cage and a keypad.

"It ain't Langley, but it's good enough for me," Baynes says enthusiastically as he thumbs in a combination.

"Lots of security," I point out.

"Lots of secret work!" he barks back, as the cage door opens and we step through the door behind it.

I walk into a brightly lit space, with a strange smell of dampness hanging in the air. I'm in a room with three desks, upon which sit four laptops, and more loose papers than I can count, along with a behemoth of a printer situated in the center – enormous monument the rest of the furniture is gathered around in worship.

The walls are a drab white, complete with black scuff marks and yellowed stains; the only windows are a couple of grimy slits at the tops of the walls – tantalizing openings to the world outside, too high to reach – and the floor is a hard blue carpet, stained in more places than I care to count.

There's an open door, beyond which I see stacks of cardboard boxes, seemingly a decorative favorite of Baynes'.

"Huh," I murmur, looking around the room. Well, I guess it *is* an improvement from our previous setting: saving the world from a lock-up garage.

"Jude!" Baynes calls out, just as I lock my eyes onto a blackboard nailed lopsided on the wall, filled with chalk lines that connect articles and printed photographs. I turn my head again to see a dainty figure in that doorway, with effervescent blonde hair by her shoulders.

"Kris?" she asks, smiling warmly, her eyes lit with a hopeful spark.

"Jude," I say, smiling back at her.

"It's really you." She takes a couple of slow, tentative steps towards me.

"It's really him," Baynes says drolly, crossing his arms.

"New face, right," I say, sheepishly. "It's useful, but isn't exactly helpful for keeping frie—"

She interrupts me, running over to embrace me, wrapping me in a warm hug. I'm taken aback; I stand frozen for a few moments too long, before easing my shoulders and hugging her back.

"Where have you been," she says, not quite a question. After a few moments, we part, and I gracelessly smile at her again, pretending to be someone who hasn't eschewed human contact for the last two years.

"Ohh, you know," I dumbly reply. "Hiding, I suppose."

"Hiding," she says, turning her head to look to Baynes, who looks back with an expression that says he doesn't understand either. "For more than two whole years?"

I feel my cheeks begin to flush red with embarrassment. Jude is the first person I've reunited with who hasn't tried to kill me, whether by bullet, knife, or classical rock album. Instead, she's asking me the questions any normal, rational person might ask; questions I don't really have a satisfactory answer for.

"I think there will be plenty of time to reminisce about old times later," Baynes says, probably sensing my unease. Jude crosses her arms and furrows her brow, but doesn't protest.

Her expression is one of concern; she wants to enjoy the reunion with me, but the fact I'm wearing a wholly unfamiliar face probably makes that difficult. Her eyes shine a deep blue, and there's the undaunted persistence of a smile creeping in at the corners of her lips. She wears a neat blue shirt and a black skirt with white sneakers.

Her hair is shorter than I remember, cut to the shoulders, and a far brighter shade of blonde than it previously was. Then again, maybe that's just my flawed recollection; a reflection of the darker times back then, and a testament to the rare optimism I feel today.

"I know it must be strange seeing me again," I tell her, taking the initiative again. "But I'm back, and I've got work to do."

"Where's Dante?" Baynes asks, a question aimed in Jude's general direction.

"Where do you think?" she asks sarcastically. I find myself smiling, and soon realize that I can't stop. It's strange and heartwarming seeing them both interact like this; I brought them together as misfits, in a 'save the world as we know it,' and after two years of my absence, they're still together.

Baynes turns back to me and points past the doorway Jude came from.

"Let's sit down," he says, just as I hear a faraway door slam shut. The three of us turn our heads, hearing labored footsteps, and Baynes speaks once more: "Oh, well, speak of the devil."

The office's front door opens, and a stout figure appears within the open frame, his face obscured behind a stack of small cardboard and plastic takeout boxes adorned with Chinese lettering. I recognize those arms though; his dark skin bearing a patchwork of tattoos, and maybe there are more of them than I remember.

"Dante," I say, just as he dumps the boxes on a desk beside him and looks up. His hair isn't the frizzy mess it was before – it's cut shorter now – and his facial hair is gone. He wears a set of black, thick-rimmed glasses and a surprised expression, like he didn't expect to see me here yet.

"Kris, is that you?" is the first question from his lips, a familiar refrain.

Like Jude, he bounds over to me, clumsily chest bumping me and wrapping his arms around me, seemingly studying the contours of my back and arms. After a few moments, he steps back and looks me up and down.

"It's me, all right," I say to him, smiling nervously. He's

still studying me with his dark eyes, darting from my hands to my face.

"Goddamn, it really is, isn't it?" he says, before holding a solitary hand out for me to shake. I reach forward and shake his hand. The smell of that Chinese takeout he just dumped beside us fills my nostrils, provoking a rumbling from my stomach that I hope no one notices.

"It's him, it really is him, he is really here, he's real," Baynes says dryly, evidently growing tired of the same words, over and over. "Get the food, let's sit down."

We move to the next room, filled with cardboard boxes and plastic containers – all of them full of stationery or other junk – with a distinctly out-of-place wooden dining table in the corner. There are four wooden seats – each a different size, and a different shade of brown – which we waste no time in claiming.

Dante distributes the food – greasy cardboard boxes and plastic Tupperware with flimsy wooden chopsticks – as, to my surprise, a strange silence descends upon us. It's been two years, and evidently no one quite knows how to break all that ice yet.

"You know," Dante finally says, drawing everyone's eyeline from the food to his face, "I didn't think you'd come back."

"Yeah, it's been a while," I say to him, a beaming smile across my face now. He goes in for one more chest bump-hug combination, and I oblige.

"Where the hell have you been, man?" he asks, shaking his head in disbelief. "It's been years!"

"Tell him, Kris," Baynes says, a noodle dangling from his mouth. "Tell him about the vampire."

"The vam… I'm sorry, what?" Dante splutters. His eyes are wide, twitching as though he's expecting the punchline to some bizarre joke, while betraying a certain amount of fear that it isn't a joke at all. I see Jude lean forward intently, positioning her chin on her fist.

"Well," I say, prodding a glob of rice around with a chopstick, "you wanted to know what I've been up to all this time? Buckle up, and I'll tell you."

CHAPTER 2

"Huh," Dante murmurs with a vacant expression, his mouth buying time for his brain to process everything I just said. The food on the table before us goes largely untouched. It's probably cold by now. "Well, how about that."

I don't think I left anything out. My two years of self-imposed punishing labor; the purple-eyed stranger in the alley; the heartless pharmaceutical megacorporation and its blood-obsessed mad scientist, and the piles of bodies, some of them clones, and most of them people.

I try my best – with Vega's occasional whisper in my ear – to explain the science of it all: the gene editing, Vincent's thirst for blood, his ruthless strength, and the spark of madness seeing himself cloned thirty-two times lit within him. I don't know how much of it filters through, other than one important thing.

"So, he's out there, right now?" Dante asks, before I see his Adam's apple move within his throat; a visible, nervous gulp.

"Malaysia, we think," Baynes adds, his expression cold and unmoved. "But in reality, by now he could be anywhere. Matriel Pharmaceutical has facilities all around the world.

Their products – drugs, cosmetics, medical equipment – are popular on every continent. Who knows what his next target will be."

"Jesus," Jude says, shaking her head, before chuckling to herself nervously. "I thought it'd be sweet to see you again. Now we find out you're bringing Dracula to our doorstep."

"He isn't coming here," I tell her, waving my hands dismissively. "He doesn't know anything about you guys. He just wants to seek revenge on Matriel, the people who murdered his dad and made him like this."

"I guess it's more exciting than stalking cheating husbands on social media," Dante says, finally beginning to smile. "Or finding runaway daughters, or background checks, or any of the other crap we do here."

"Wait," Jude says, leaning forward again. "You want us to help find this guy, this vampire?"

"If you're willing," I reply. "Baynes says he'll help, and I've already got a kick-ass Italian commando on the case, and I wouldn't ask you to put yourself in harm's way. Not after what happened to –"

I pause, not quite brave enough to finish that sentence. I've been in this room for half an hour or so, and haven't spoken his name once yet. Somehow, despite all those crazy words I spewed out about vampires and blood and bodies and gene editing, I haven't been able to say the hardest one: Jack.

"It's okay," Jude says, rescuing me from my own momentary cowardice. "We speak of him from time to time. We wouldn't have succeeded without him. On a terrible day, he did a wonderful thing."

"We run this whole thing in his memory," Dante says, leaning back in his chair before looking around at the cold food and the cardboard boxes. "And, we don't really have any other choice."

"It was tough at first," Jude says. "We had the FBI on our

backs. Lots of questions, lots of interview rooms and men and women in suits. But after a while, Dante and I realized they had nothing to link us to the airport raid."

"As the weeks went on, Silas McCaulay's plans were exposed," Baynes says while prodding his lips with a napkin, as I realize he's the only one of us to finish his meal. "The suspicion on us died down – I believe they came to see us more as extrajudicial vigilantes than terrorists – and we were able to get back together and open this place."

"This job is all I have," Dante adds. "I can't get any other kind of job. No cybersecurity firm wants a guy with my kind of heat."

"It's the same with me," Jude says. "I'd just got out of a cult, and jumped straight into a conspiracy to kill Silas McCaulay. No one was going to put me on their reception desk, considering the FBI kept sweeping me up for questioning."

"Hell, technically I'm still dead," Baynes says, shrugging to himself. "I mean, everyone at the CIA, FBI and any other agency that matters knows that isn't true by now. They all know I'm still out here, and that I was involved at the airport somehow, but no one can prove anything. So here we all are, in the big, wide, gray area. Not quite fugitives, not quite free."

"And Jack is the only one of us who ever got called a hero," Dante adds. "After the truth about Silas McCaulay came out, they only had one man to pin his death on: Jack. The public don't really know and don't really care, but his family knows he saved the world."

"Yeah, Baynes told me," I tell them, seeing Dante smile warmly in response. "It's nice to know that some people appreciate what he did; some people who matter."

There's another few moments of pointed silence between us, before Baynes speaks up again.

"I've taken the liberty of looking into the business side of things," he says, idly tapping a finger on his temple. "The government of Thailand are offering a bounty, roughly 40,000 dollars for the apprehension of Vincenzo del Clemente."

The business side of things huh? I lean back and listen, crossing my arms as I patiently wait to find out which sponsors' brand names we'll be engraving on our silver bullets.

"But that's nothing compared to the eight million dollars Matriel Pharmaceutical itself is secretly offering for his capture, dead or alive."

"Hah," Dante laughs, almost falling backwards on his chair. "Now that's real money."

I snort, loudly; an implicit expression of my distaste at accepting any sort of financial reward from that company. Baynes looks at me with a pair of guilty, anxious side-eyes, before moving on entirely.

"I think if we use all of our resources – our investigative knowledge, our computer skills, Kris's ability to disguise himself – we can find this guy, this wannabe vampire, and bring him to justice," he says, excitedly. "This will put our company on the map. Worldwide recognition and world-class resources."

He goes on, and I put my head in my hands. This hasn't turned out anywhere near what I had intended. I wanted to reunite with my old friends to fight a virtuous battle against a dangerous foe, the only superhuman in the world besides me.

Instead, we're sitting at a dining table in a slum office, talking about all the ways in which taking down Vincent will increase revenue this quarter. And that's not even considering the bitter, acidic taste I get in my mouth when I think about accepting a single dime from Matriel.

"Look," I say, planting my palm down on the table loud enough to shake a couple of mugs, ending the idle chatter around me. "I have to say this: I'm not doing this for money, or status, or any of that. I'm doing it because he's going to kill a lot of people. I've seen him leave more dead bodies behind than I can count, and I want to see no more."

Baynes straightens his posture, pursing his lips slightly. If I know him, he'll want to have his cake and eat it too, but the others might be slightly purer of heart.

"I'm going after Vincent no matter what," I go on to say. "Because I know I'm the only one who can fight him and win, and because if I don't, he'll keep killing, or even worse, someone will figure out how to create more of him. I'm asking for your help, but like two years ago, there will probably be no riches and no recognition. Just a thankless, good deed."

Dante nods resolutely, while Jude stares into a corner of the room, apparently deep in thought.

"Hell, man, you know I still owe you," Dante says, nodding ever more emphatically. "I'd still be stuck in that jail cell if it wasn't for you. I'd hunt tigers and lions and werewolves and dragons for you man."

"I'm in," Jude pipes up to say, surprising me slightly. "It'd be nice to do something that feels good again. I don't want to spend all my waking hours photographing cheating spouses. I want to save lives."

I smile at her, and she goes back to quietly eating the remnants of her meal.

"You know we can do both, right?" Baynes says, asking what's good about having the cake if he can't eat it, just as I predicted. "We can kill the vamp, win the day, and still collect the money."

I don't say anything back to him; his lip quivers, and I can tell he's not done yet.

"And besides, we *need* money. This will be an international investigation. There are travel costs, surveillance, translation, even bribes to think about. It's not as simple as staking out the local blood bank."

"Baynes, we're not returning him to Matriel," I tell him sternly. He opens his mouth to protest, but soon folds, and sinks back into his chair. "We're not taking him back to some laboratory where they can clone him and bleed him and make a thousand more of him. It's not gonna happen."

He takes a deep, exasperated breath, and then nods.

"We'll see what we can do," he then says after a couple moments of fraught silence. "He's powerful, but he's got to eat. He'll leave a telltale trail of assaults. We'll keep our ears to the ground and hope for the best."

"So, what," Dante says, a devilish smile on his face while shrugging his shoulders. "We're a supervillain-hunting agency now? Van Helsing Enterprises?"

We all laugh, and I sit back in my chair, smiling appreciatively at the others. As the rest of them discuss other fanciful agency names, I find myself looking to the lonely, drab wall beside me, and see my own photograph there on a noticeboard, beside a bunch of newspaper clippings. The evidence of another worldwide search for one weird, weird guy.

"I've got faith in you," I tell Baynes, nodding to the noticeboard. "After all, you found me."

CHAPTER 3

It's cold. I hate the cold.

Another cold takeout, sitting on the table before me, slowly soaking through to a muddle of printouts below. Another cold day, in this climate I still haven't adjusted to after years of hot and sticky Thai sun, in this damp office which refuses to retain any warmth.

And, of course, the same cold, surprisingly bloodless trail; no Vincent, and not even the thinnest thread to pull at that could reveal his whereabouts.

As it turns out, tracking a vampire is surprisingly difficult. Every culture has its own mythical vampire, and Hollywood depictions of bloodsucking demons reach far and wide.

It's been three weeks. Three weeks I've sat in this office, listening to Baynes reading out incomprehensible machine-translated news stories from far-eastern news sites, stories that turn out to be about motorcycle clubs, fat-cat bankers, anime-inspired emo bands, or fictional movie villains that just happen to call themselves vampires, or anything remotely close.

I'm watching Dante balance on the back two legs of his chair, hovering in place with no small amount of skill. Still though, one of these days he's going to fall. I feel like I've spent three weeks waiting for it.

"How about this?" Jude asks in a booming voice from across the room, shaking me out of my fascination at Dante's chair.

"Huh?" Baynes grunts, looking up from his laptop.

"A story out of Shanghai," she says, her eyes reflecting the clinical white light of her laptop screen. "Someone apparently stole a shipment of human blood."

I jump to my feet – and see Baynes do the same – and navigate around the myriad desks, paper bins, and errant takeout boxes that obstruct my path, until I dart behind Jude, close enough to read the laptop screen. Baynes joins us, stroking his chin.

"Human life blood?" he asks, reading the translation with suspicious eyes.

"Yeah, I guess that's the translation," Jude replies. He reaches down to the trackpad and scrolls down, before finding another translated word and pointing at it.

"Sperm bank," he says, drolly, before straightening his posture again. "The authorities are looking for a man who stole from a sperm bank. It's a bad translation."

"Ohh," Jude says, embarrassed, before closing the browser tab and wiping the back of her hands across her eyes, as though to expunge a troublesome vision.

I pat her once on the shoulder and quietly amble back to my seat. I think we can rule out the notion of Vincent robbing a sperm bank, unless of course he's really lost his mind.

Something catches my eye; I glance up at a small flatscreen TV bolted onto one of the blank walls here. It's set to a business channel, and the name 'MATRIEL PHARMA-CEUTICAL' in bold, domineering lettering fills the screen, along with a bunch of numbers and a graph with splashes of red and green.

Matriel's share price plummeted with the news of their

brand-new, hydrogen-powered facility going up in flames. Vincent and I managed to stay out of the news, but the deaths of a bunch of workers – including Thammai – sure didn't.

"Look at that," Baynes says, pointing up to the screen, and that graph of the company's share price – a line that falls precipitously, before recovering just as fast – looking like a horseshoe. "It's like nothing ever happened."

After the insurers opened their checkbooks, and Matriel managed to tamp down the news of the death of one of its star scientists with some glitzy new drug announcements, the stock price shot up again.

The rebuilding of the Bangkok research facility is already being planned, and Baynes tells me security has quietly been tripled at every Matriel Pharma property. Business as usual, and Vincent nowhere to be seen.

"Are there any other leads? Anything else at all?" I ask, shuffling through the papers in front of me and fidgeting in my seat.

"Well, we've got a bunch of things," Baynes says defensively, leaning back in his chair, perhaps sensing my aggravation at spending the past three weeks doing nothing. "I've got a chat with an old contact at the CIA soon, and we've got a number of other promising sightings."

"Baynes, none of these leads are promising," I tell him, rifling through the papers before me one more time. "An Indonesian man who filed his incisors down to get on TV; a teenager in Japan who killed his teacher and drained his blood because he saw it in an anime; an Australian billionaire who bathes in blood because he thinks it'll grant him eternal youth."

I carelessly throw the papers across the table; they go flying halfway across the room, something I didn't intend, but a fine way to make my point regardless.

"None of these people are Vincent. None of these people

are even close to being him," I tell him. "I feel like we've wasted three weeks."

"Kris, I'm sorry you feel that way, but you have to understand it's difficult," Baynes says. "We barely have any money here. It'd be great to be able to hire investigative teams – to get boots on the ground all around the world – but it's just not possible on our budget. He's a needle in an earth-shaped haystack. One person in eight billion."

I take another frustrated breath, and Baynes goes on.

"He's lying low, trying not to draw attention to himself. He's waiting the spotlight out, probably feeding from poor and disadvantaged people, in one of the most densely populated regions in the world. He knows that he can't afford to make too many assaults in one area, so he's moving around. We likely won't find him until he makes headlines again."

Suddenly, Dante makes a noise – a panicked, animalistic yelp – and I see him finally fall backwards off that chair, hitting the floor behind him with a bump and sending a few more loose papers flying.

"I'm okay!" he yells, as Jude hops off her chair to tend to him.

"I need to get some air," I murmur, taking the opportunity to sneak out. I make my way over to the door and open it, finding that grim concrete staircase on the other side isn't quite empty; the eye-catching figure of Alessia stands at the top of it, heading down into the office.

"Where are you going?" she asks as I pass her on the staircase. She barely gives way, and I have to sidestep my way past her.

"I need to collect my thoughts, I'll be back," I tell her, before closing the door behind me.

Alessia came here from her sojourn in Europe one week ago. To my surprise, she hasn't stabbed anybody's eyes out, or shot anyone in the spine quite yet, but if she's anything like me, all this mundane office work is surely tempting her.

I make my way out of the building and into the streets of Enderton. It's lunchtime or thereabouts – the vape megastore is closed, its usual clientele not quite awake yet – and the sky is a pallid gray plane.

It's a dull day – a day where the sun can't pierce the clouds; a day when every color is dampened by the pervasive grimness of it all, and that grimness permeates your soul, convincing some far region of your brain that no day will be as bright as the ones you remember, ever again.

Or perhaps I'm just not enjoying the return to this climate.

I cross an empty road, sliding my body between two parked SUVs, and walk down the block, heading for a bodega a short walk away. A pair of sneakers hangs from a telephone cable that stretches from building to building above me, swinging quietly in the wind. The mere sight makes me want to run again.

"Vega," I murmur to myself, seeing that the block is deserted other than some faraway traffic. "Talk to me; where do you think our teenage vampire is hiding?"

I think Baynes' appraisal is accurate, he says. *Vincent is smart enough to evade capture, he's proved that so far. He knows to stay in densely populated areas where he can feed on a population that won't attract headlines. He's lying low, and could be planning his next move.*

"I should never have returned here," I say, dodging an oily puddle in the sidewalk. "I should have stayed in Asia. We could have followed his trail, investigated it all in person. We could have had our noses to the ground, following his trail of blood. Instead, we're stuck in a basement, making paper airplanes and swapping scary stories."

It was never going to be easy, you know that, Vega says. *He's no longer the dazed and confused teenager who hopped off a train and doesn't understand his nature. He's now a determined killer, desperate to avenge his father, and the people who took his humanity away. He's ruthless and won't be captured easily.*

"Well, at least I'd feel useful," I reply, before heading into the bodega. After a couple minutes of idly walking up and down its aisles – the bright fluorescent lights above stinging my eyes – I bag up five cold coffees for the others, probably the most important work I've done all day.

I'm barely halfway back to the office when my right leg begins to twitch around the upper outside thigh, a strange sensation that takes me right back to the times I've taken a bullet there. After a confused moment, a ringtone begins to sound out alongside the vibration, and I realize it's no bullet, but a call on the cellphone Baynes gave me.

I take it out of my pocket and take the call, trying to put the notion out of my mind that I'm so out of touch I'd mistake a phone call for a bullet.

"Yep?" I say.

"We've found something, something promising," Baynes says, three words that make the drab streets of Enderton suddenly seem so much brighter. "Get back here, and we'll tell you all about it."

Here's hoping this isn't another horror movie fan trying to make it big on reality TV…

CHAPTER 4

"Monaco."

Baynes leans back in his seat after saying it, a sly smile on his face.

"Monaco?" I ask, feeling everyone else's confused eyes dart to me. "Like, in Europe?"

"Yes, well, Monte Carlo to be exact," he says. "An old contact of mine at Langley has been tracking someone there; someone who's been making waves, so to speak. Someone who's already on the radar of numerous spy agencies throughout the world. Someone who's said to be very dangerous."

I close my eyes and take a deep breath; the high-rolling casinos and extravagant hotels of Monte Carlo aren't exactly where I expected Vincent to show up. In fact, it's perhaps the furthest point from it.

"This person is Swiss," Baynes says, perhaps sensing my skepticism. "Speaks French and Italian, supposedly in their early twenties."

He leans forward now, excitedly knocking the plastic bottle of coffee I bought him all over the table, which he momentarily scrambles to soak up with a bunch of papers, before looking back to us with bright eyes.

"And get this, this weirdo is claiming they're a vampire."

I look across the table to see Dante and Jude smiling; Dante nods slowly, and Jude scrawls something on a notepad. Alessia, on the other hand, has the same coldly cynical expression I know and love.

"You're saying he traveled across the world to the richest tax haven in Europe?" she asks, her arms crossed. "He gave up drinking blood and took up blackjack?"

"I'm saying there could be former Matriel executives living there," Baynes says, nodding to himself. "Multimillion-dollar houses, fabulous casinos and beaches, it's exactly the sort of place your evil drug company executive would hang out."

"What else did you learn?" I ask him.

"They think he's an arms dealer. He's living on a yacht moored in the Monte Carlo marina, with a bunch of armed guards, and –"

I laugh, throwing up my arms in an exasperated, exaggerated motion.

"Baynes, that obviously isn't him!" I cry, as I feel the mood in the room begin to deflate. "He's a blood-hungry superhuman who sleeps rough in derelict offices and stows away on freight trains. He doesn't own a yacht, or require armed goons, or know the first thing about dealing weapons. And he'd never in a million years tell anyone he's a vampire!"

"Wait a minute, I haven't gotten to the best part yet," Baynes says, retaining a sly glint in his eye. "There's a massive, wealthy hospital in Monaco, decked out with all the latest high-tech medical equipment, and a huge storage facility for human blood."

He takes a deep breath before continuing.

"A few days ago, a bunch of armed robbers broke in and

stole a huge shipment of that blood, some forty gallons or so. This man – this mysterious Swiss arms dealer – is the prime suspect. They're calling him the vampire of Monte Carlo."

I hear some shocked breaths from beside me, and look to see that even Alessia's expression has softened. Her lips are still pursed, but her eyebrows have lifted, seemingly receptive to the possibility that Vincent has taken up a new career in weapons smuggling.

"Sure, some things don't check out – I don't know why they're claiming he's an illegal arms dealer – but perhaps the intel is muddled," Baynes says, clasping his hands together, almost in a prayer-like pose. "Perhaps Vincent and the arms dealer are working together. Or perhaps the arms dealer stole the blood to sell to Vincent. What if they have a deal?"

I must admit, it's the closest thing to something even resembling a lead we've had in three weeks. The stolen shipment of blood, the unfinished business within a millionaire's playground, the language, the nationality, they're all hits.

"No picture?" I ask.

"No picture," Baynes confirms. "No one even knows what he looks like. He came out of nowhere, and now he's dominating the Mediterranean arms trade."

"Alessia," I say, turning to her. "What do you think?"

"That skinny kid ain't an arms dealer," she says, shaking her head, her eyes angled downwards. "But there's only one villain I know who's weird enough to steal forty gallons of blood. It might be worth putting boots on the ground over there."

"There's just something about that place," I say, putting my head in my hands, and raking my fingers through my hair. "Sure, he grew up affluent, but it's not like he's a rich kid, or like he's addicted to the trappings of wealth, you know?"

"You'd be surprised at the sort of criminal underbelly that

exists in a place like Monaco," Baynes says, veering dangerously close to one of his meandering CIA career stories. "It's only rich and glamorous on the outside. Deep down, it's a lawless black market for everything your immoral billionaire boss could dream of. Here, I was once in Toulouse, and –"

"He's got a point," Alessia says, thankfully interrupting before he could joyride our meeting down memory lane. "These tax havens exist as hubs for all sorts of sketchy people. If Vincent is planning something big – something terrible – then he'll find everything he needs right there."

I look to Dante, who shrugs as soon as we lock eyes, and then Jude, who stares into the corner of the room again, still deep in thought. Baynes, on the other hand, wears a gigantic, proud grin; he looks like a man who can't wait to get on the roulette table.

"Hmph," I groan, looking up to the ceiling. "It just doesn't feel right."

The entirety of the ceiling fills my vision: three white spotlights set into the plaster, only two of them working; a series of damp water stains forming ambiguous shapes like clouds; a scratch, perhaps a meter long, browning at the edges. The more I stare at it, the more it feels like it's coming down on me. Crushing me. Suffocating me.

"But when has anything ever felt right, I suppose?" I say to that falling ceiling, to which Baynes chuckles.

"All right," he says with glee. "Dante, shall we put a plan together?"

I lean back in my chair as they both spend a few minutes hashing out some plans; how to find this undead arms dealer, and how to get me an introduction. They bat ideas between each other like a proverbial blood-soaked ping pong ball, until they come up with something sturdy enough to call a plan.

"We say you're the security apparatus leader for a, uhm,

private pharmaceutical business, from…" Baynes says, before drumming on the table with his fingers in a faux anticipatory drum-roll. "From the nation of Madrevaria, since you're already familiar with that part of the world."

I look to Alessia, who stares back at him with hard, skeptical eyes. I think she'd prefer him to keep Madrevaria out of his mouth, but he's on a rampage here.

"Private pharmaceutical business? Security apparatus leader? What the hell does that mean?" I ask, sick of trying to decipher Baynes' euphemistic riddles.

"He's saying you'll pretend to be a Madrevarian drug lord's head honcho," she says through gritted teeth, a role she too is entirely familiar with. I see her clenching her knuckles tightly beside her, and aiming to move things speedily and innocently along, I speak up once more.

"How fast can we set this up?" I ask.

"I can create some fake professional history for you online, ex-Navy SEAL, current private security, that sort of thing," Dante says.

"We'll create a fake passport and a burner bank account tonight," Baynes adds. "We can have you booked onto a flight tomorrow. I'll ask a favor or two from some old contacts in Europe and hopefully will be able to get you an introduction, otherwise you're investigating on your own."

I nod at him and try my best to put a smile on my face, still uneasy with this whole thing, but feeling a warm embrace of relief that we're *doing something* at last.

"Wait a minute," Alessia says, in a shrill, stern tone that strikes a small amount of fear into me. The four of us stop what we're doing and turn to her. "I'm going too."

Again, another wave of relief washes over me. She didn't reach across the table and rearrange Baynes' face, I feel like we're all making progress today.

"I'm the drug lord's former head honcho; I know how to

speak, how to act, and I know Madrevaria as well as anyone, I'll go with Kris," she says, resolutely.

Baynes looks to me receptively. All I can do is nod my approval.

"Okay, no problem," he announces, triumphantly. "We'll create two fake passports, and set you both up as business partners."

As much as I like to work alone, I have to admit that going as a double act makes sense. Trying to ingratiate myself with an arms dealer's minions is almost as fearful a prospect to me as trying to fit in with the wealthy; doing both at once, I'd fool nobody. At least Alessia looks the part.

"So, we're sending our two most capable undercover agents to Monaco, are we all agreed?" Baynes asks.

I look around the table as everyone nods, or says their agreement. Finally, I nod my assent too.

"Beautiful," he says.

"I'll get the travel and accommodations sorted," Jude says before jumping to her feet and heading for the other room.

"I'll start on those fake histories," Dante says, joining her.

"How's your poker face?" Baynes suddenly asks me, a wry look about him. I don't quite know how to answer; I sit clueless for a few too many seconds, until Alessia pipes up.

"*Madonnah mi*," Alessia sighs, smirking at me. "I bet he's never even played."

"Oh, I'm sorry, I thought we were going there to find Vincent and jump into this stolen blood mystery. I had no idea you wanted me to bring home the poker jackpot too."

Alessia laughs, putting her hands to her mouth as though she's trying to stop. Baynes looks at the papers on the table before him with a knowing grin on his face.

"Does poker have a jackpot? Is that even a thing?" I finally ask, getting the impression they're mocking me.

"Make yourself a new face and we'll get some

photographs taken for a new passport," Baynes says, standing up from his seat and leaving the room.

Alessia smiles at me, the world's most naïve secret agent.

"We're talking arms dealers, and the city with the richest casinos in Europe," she says, drolly. "You're gonna need to know how to play cards…"

CHAPTER 5

"You didn't bring sunglasses?"

She stares at me from behind her pair, two mirrored aviator lenses, in which I see my new face, warped to monstrous proportions. I didn't even see her put them on.

"No," I reply. "Funnily enough, on occasions like this they usually don't last very long."

Her eyebrows quickly rise above the rims of her sunglasses – a quizzical look – before she quickly gains some understanding of the point I'm trying to make and drops them again, resuming her silence.

The same of course goes for the cellphone in my pocket, the clothes on my back, and the luggage we're currently both waiting for at the carousels – all typically assured to be blown apart in a mission, and all generously given to me over the past few weeks by my friends back home.

We hit the ground in Nice – in the south of France – an hour ago. The flight was largely unremarkable; a crying toddler beside Alessia didn't stop me from getting the sleep I needed, thankfully. The fact she's wearing her sunglasses inside perhaps suggests she didn't get the same amount of rest, however.

"What do you think of all this? Like, really?" I ask Alessia, who barely even turns her head to look at me. There are smatterings of French tourists around, but no one who cares to listen in. "An arms dealer? A wannabe vampire? Gallons of stolen blood?"

It's just past 8 a.m.; perhaps I should have saved these questions for after she's gotten her first coffee inside her, but I'm feeling brave.

"Isn't it a bit late to be having second thoughts?" she asks in a dry, low tone, before continuing on. "If you really want to know, I think it's probably nonsense, even if it is the best lead we've got. These rich guys are weird; someone calling himself a vampire and stealing a load of blood wouldn't shock me."

I see our luggage emerge from the bowels of the luggage carousel – two small, black suitcases, full of Monte Carlo-appropriate clothing Jude thankfully picked out for us.

"But maybe we get lucky, maybe it's connected to Matriel somehow," she says, grabbing her suitcases off the carousel as they pass. "And besides, even if it's all completely unrelated, I hate these arms dealer types; they're the lowest of the low. Merchants of death."

She charges ahead, leaving me to grab my own suitcase and catch up to her as we make our way outside.

"There are worse ways to spend a weekend than enjoying the Mediterranean sun, sipping a couple of martinis at the casino, and smashing an arms dealer's teeth out with your bare knuckles," she adds, still pacing ahead.

When we make it outside, I pull out my cellphone and call Baynes to tell him we've landed, all the while marveling at the clear blue sky above me, and the sun above us appearing almost white. I feel myself smiling, reunited with the optimistic sun.

Baynes tells me there's a taxi waiting to take us the half

hour or so across the border into Monaco, as well as a twin room in the cheapest Monte Carlo hotel they could find, booked for two nights.

"I'm still working to secure that introduction to our target's organization," he says, lapsing back into agency talk, just as I see Alessia flag down our car. "Until then I'd recommend you get settled in. Also, I know I'm a broken record here, but money is tight."

"I'll try not to charge too many cocktails to the room, my man," I tell him, before saying my goodbyes and hanging up.

Our ride is a stuffy four-door sedan, with darkly tinted windows that block out a lot of the day's beauty. Alessia sits beside me in silence as I look out onto the coast – a gorgeous deep blue sea, dotted with the white crescents and upright masts of yachts and fishing boats, stretching all the way to the horizon.

I'm so entranced by the sights I barely notice us crossing into Monaco. My unobstructed view of the sea gives way to a series of downward rolling hills, scattered with trees and vineyards, and trailers selling flowers by the side of the road.

"It's been a while," Alessia says as we draw closer to Monte Carlo, and the hills slowly become populated by quaint, pretty apartment buildings and sprawling parks.

"You've been here before?" I ask.

"Twice. First was when I was in the forces, and despite the drinking, it was uneventful. The second, Gerard and I came to meet a client. A sketchy one; a bad guy."

And she leaves it at that; her work within the shadowy criminal underbelly of this place, left unsaid.

When we get to Monte Carlo, I'm seized by a strange feeling. The city is beautiful; a thriving bay, comprised of cascading vistas of pretty sand-colored apartments and houses, most topped with red-tiled roofs, and surrounded by roads that wind and coil around them. Within the bay, the sea is calm, appearing a sapphiric blue.

Each row of buildings climbs another foot of the hills and cliffs that surround the bay, until the homes and hotels end, and a thick forest tops the surrounding peaks. It's a full spectrum of color – vibrant sports cars, golden-tipped towers, and gleaming windows reflecting the blue sea beyond, and the huge array of yachts in the marina.

But I can't help but shake a certain, troublesome feeling – or perhaps, a memory. All these wondrous sights – the rolling hills, the cascading streets of colorful homes and towers, no two the same – remind me of another place from my past: the favelas of Madrevaria.

Sure, it's prettier here in some ways – the greens are greener, the roads are tidier, and every facet of every building is kept proudly clean – but to an unprejudiced eye, the settings look similar. A dense city built into the side of a mountain; a populace unafraid to express itself. The only difference is the ostentatious, shameless display of wealth at every turn.

Every turn brings a new sight; a new gleaming tower, or deafening sports car thundering past us. It's a stunning, obscene monument to humanity's avarice; a brazen tally of our most revered material possessions, etched into the mountainside for the world to gawp at.

Our car slowly rounds the corners, descending to sea level by the bottom of the bay, and finally comes to a stop at a small hotel, by the side of a busy four-lane road, adjacent to the area.

Alessia says a few words to the driver and we get out. Alessia goes to get our suitcases from the trunk, but I can't resist a moment in the sun. I walk to the edge of the pavement, put my hands on the railing – the heat burning the tips of my fingers – and close my eyes.

"Hey, come on," the predictably terse voice of Alessia says, just as I hear the trunk slam shut. "Don't get too comfortable, these streets aren't as clean as they look."

I open my eyes and slowly follow her into the hotel, wheeling my luggage as I go.

If Vincent really is here – if he's really caught up in this outwardly pristine and brilliant, but shadowy, anarchic city – she's right: the streets won't remain clean for long.

CHAPTER 6

"How do you like it?" Baynes asks, his nasally voice – carried across the Atlantic Ocean, and broadcast on small, tinny cellphone speakers – sounding almost demonic.

"This was the cheapest place?" I ask, looking around me. The room is gorgeous – red and black wallpaper in regal patterns, fine wooden furnishings, and a couple of luxuriant single beds, with fluffy white pillows. We even get a balcony, sunlight streaming through a set of white net drapes.

"The cheapest place that offered some discretion, yes," the demonic voice booming from the cellphone says. "It was either this, or put you both up in a hostel with a bunch of drunk students."

"What about the intro?" Alessia says as we both stare down at Baynes' pixelated, occasionally frozen face in the cellphone screen.

"There's a woman, a German, named Ada-Maria Kitzler, she's got arrest warrants all over Europe for all sorts – smuggling, possession of deadly weapons, sale of prohibited items, loan sharking – and she's supposedly neck deep in this stolen blood thing. My contact says she's got a private poker room at one of the larger casinos."

"She's in partnership with this mysterious arms dealer?" Alessia asks.

"Yeah, we think so," he replies, after a maddening delay. "Dante found some pictures, as well as a criminal record a mile long. There's even some stuff we unearthed on some previous identities. We'll send them through."

"This doesn't sound like much of an intro," I add. "I thought you were arranging a sit down with her?"

"Kris, you can make any fleeting encounter a sit down if you kick hard enough," Alessia whispers to me with a sly smile. She shouts to Baynes, "It's fine, send us the details and we'll handle it."

"There's one more thing," Baynes says. "There's a buy-in at her private room. A large one, potentially."

"Uh-huh," I murmur.

"And we're all out of money," Baynes replies.

Ah, oh yeah. My status as the world's deadliest and yet most impoverished secret agent comes back to bite me again.

"If you're going to take the polite route, you'll need to find some money, or a backer, or something," he says. "And if you take the impolite route, well, Alessia is our in-house expert on that."

Without missing a beat, she reaches down and hangs up the call, with all the force and ferocity of poking a man's eyes out, before rolling her own eyes.

"I really hate that man," she says, with a derisive snort.

I laugh and go to begin unpacking my luggage.

"He's useful," I say to her, looking through the clothes Jude bought for me. A gray suit with a black shirt, all my size, and smart too, given the money restraints that we're so frequently reminded of. "Even if he is utterly unbearable."

"Hmph," she grunts, before going through her own suitcase.

"I always thought you'd want payback for what happened in Madrevaria," I tell her, neatly unfolding my clothes, an action that seems somewhat dirtied by our reminiscing of that time and place. "I'm relieved you get along as well as you do."

She doesn't say anything, at least, not at first. After a few audible breaths, she speaks.

"It was a long time ago, and it's not as if Randall Baynes did it all himself," she says, emotionlessly. "He was part of the agency, and now he isn't. We all do work we live to regret."

I pause, thinking about what she said. I feel I've a lot more regrets than most. In fact, the five of us might be the same in that regard. Misfits, thrown together by bloody circumstance and rotten luck, sticking together in pursuit of a greater evil.

"Besides," she says, taking a purple dress out of her suitcase, and holding it against her tall, sturdy frame. "I might still change my mind."

———

After an hour of staring into a laptop screen going through the details Baynes sent through – photos of Ada-Maria Kitzler, arrest warrants, news articles, and previous identities – my eyes begin to hurt. All the while I hear the muffled cries of seagulls outside, and the distant chatter of tourists passing below our balcony.

I spend the hour trying to absorb as much as I can, while having Vega resculpt my face slightly enough to be able to commit crimes with impunity, so long as I can change back to the one on my fake passport later.

Alessia is engrossed by it all, memorizing every smallest morsel of information in tense silence. She flicks between images like some utterly consumed, hard-boiled detective seeking a murder suspect, only I know it isn't exactly justice we bring.

Ada-Maria Kitzler is forty-two, though her newer identities are all claiming to be in their early thirties. She has a shock of short, messy red hair, presumably dyed that color, considering in her older images she's brunette. She's somewhat short and stocky; wide, but not overweight. And she has a scar below her ear, origin unknown.

"How do you think we do this?" I finally ask her, tearing my aching eyes away from the bright light of the screen. "How do we introduce ourselves to Ms. Kitzler here?"

"Well, as I see it, we've only got one option," Alessia says. "Unless you can think of a way to make twenty grand overnight, we're taking the more direct route. Find her, capture her, make her talk."

I should have known. Between charm and harm, Alessia is always going to favor the latter to get what she wants.

"What if she doesn't talk?" I ask, a question that finally has her turning to face me, with a bemused expression slapped across her face. "Like, she's a hardened criminal, working for a fearsome arms dealer, or even worse, Vincent himself. What if she's going to keep her mouth shut?"

Alessia looks like she's going to break out in rapturous laughter. As it is, she manages to restrain herself.

"Kris, c'mon now, they *all* talk."

And with that, she turns back to the laptop screen.

I can't even argue. I believe producing a twenty-grand diamond overnight is way beyond the capacity of the nanomachine network, and it's not like I have any other foolproof get-rich-quick schemes at the back of my mind.

Still, the prospect of mounting a make-or-break kidnap of an experienced criminal – within one of the wealthiest, most secure cities in the world, full of snap-happy tourists and nosy businesspeople – doesn't exactly excite me like it does Alessia.

I walk to the screen doors, with the balcony just beyond, and look out at that gorgeous blue sky again – an endless realm of optimism and opportunity – and get the sense of hope I've been looking for, albeit from an unorthodox source.

Why don't you go to the casino, Vega says, suspiciously close to taking the role of the devil on my shoulder. *Tell her you're scouting out the venue. Who knows, with the right guidance, you might win something.*

I smile to myself before turning to Alessia and telling her exactly what Vega told me to say. She barely seems to notice, waving a hand dismissively while the bright light of the screen continues to fill her pupils.

I take my suit and shirt to the bathroom and change into it, and then make my way outside. The sun is bright – almost as bright as that laptop screen – and again I wish I'd brought sunglasses, but I go on. I make my way up the sandy, cobbled pavements and sidewalks, and round the twisting, winding roads slowly climbing the hill, with only one destination in mind.

CHAPTER 7

Maison de Joie Hotel and Casino is supposedly Kitzler's gambling den of choice; a sprawling crystalline tower, some ten stories high, standing alone on the hillside like a gleaming silver sword, embedded within the rock.

Even from a block away, it dominates my field of vision; a great, nauseating monument, like the mythical siren on the rock, drawing travelers to their doom, or in this case, mere bankruptcy.

A set of open doors soon greets me, along with a dainty, friendly faced woman behind a reception desk, itself adorned with hundreds of flashing LEDs, welcoming me with a Mexican wave of reds and oranges.

She speaks to me with soft words in a language I can't speak – French, I'm guessing – and I say a few awkward words in English, to which she smiles and waves me through, no doubt assuming I'm yet another rich American on his way to lose his shirt.

I stroll to another set of glass double doors, guarded by two blank-faced heavies, wearing black suits and shirts. One of them looks upon me with unkind eyes, before opening the door for me to enter. I show him how to smile, and go inside.

The first floor of the casino is like something out of the set of a Hollywood movie, one about coked-up billionaires and cool-as-ice special agents, quaffing cocktails and throwing dice at a table.

The walls are covered in a splendid black wallpaper adorned with golden patterns, and the occasional television showing soccer games or some other European sport. There are no windows – not a photon of natural light is allowed here – with the only illumination coming via a series of domineering golden floodlights above.

It's only midday, but already I see it's busy – dozens of bodies dressed in smart, gaudy colors surround a series of tables with their utmost attention. The tables themselves – the few I can see between the crowds – are large and distinctive, their green and red fabric upholstery giving the space a needed splash of color.

In the middle of the room is a statue of sorts; a hideous golden figure – perhaps the owner, or perhaps the man who's lost the most money here over the years – locked eternally in some outlandish pose. His arms are stretched upwards, as though he's beckoning the sun to appear.

There's an indistinct chatter filling the air, an unintelligible chorus of laughter, whispers, idle conversation, and commiseration, all sounding out against the soft backdrop of some cheesy europop song.

I stand at the periphery of the room and drink it all in. I can't remember ever going to a casino before. It's like a room out of time and space; a little nook outside of reality itself where the normal laws of physics don't seem to apply. A dark corner where no natural light can reach, a small universe governed only by one guiding principle: luck.

Over there, behind that big wheel, Vega says, drawing my attention to the gigantic, colorful wheel full of numbers and surrounded by a group of hooting and hollering women, like the worshippers to some strange deity. *There are blackjack tables. You should try your hand at that.*

Sure enough, at the very end of the room – some fifty yards away, hidden away behind the wheel and the crowds – sits a row of crescent-shaped tables, upon which I see a collection of white cards.

I walk over there – smelling both the sickly sweet alcohol on the air and the stench of despair emanating from the roulette table, and a man who sits with his head in his hands – and think to take up a seat at the first blackjack table, only for Vega to speak again.

Wait here, and watch the game for a few minutes. If we are to stand any chance of winning, I need to create a running total of the cards that have been played.

I do as he says, leaning against a drinks table, watching the blackjack table before me. There's a short, brunette woman of maybe forty years of age dealing, and a strange collection of characters quietly sitting around the table.

I try to follow the action – seeing a fast-paced exchange of cards, and a largely emotionless audience – but find my attention wandering to the people sitting around the table, an uncomfortable collection of humanity's strangest specimens.

There's the pale, middle-aged man with black, slicked-back hair and giant purple rings around his eyes. He looks like he offed his wife a week ago and hasn't slept a wink since then, content to fritter away his time gambling until they inevitably find the body.

And then there's the bronze-skinned, energetic old man in the middle, fizzing with an uncertain energy, so much so that he can't keep his leg from vibrating below him, to the annoyance of everyone else at the table. He has the air of a man who's so, so close to rescuing the family business, if he can just win one more hand…

Finally, there's the wife; the thirtysomething French

woman wearing a resplendent gown and conspicuously large wedding ring, with a permanent state of bitter resentment locked on her face. Despite continually winning hands, her expression only grows darker; a woman whose husband went out on the yacht a week ago and has barely called her since.

Okay, it's time, Vega says, snapping me out of my people-watching reverie. *Take a seat and play as casually as you can. I'll tell you what to do.*

I do as he says, taking a small wad of bills from my back pocket – the remnants of whatever paltry money was left for our mission – and placing them on the table, before taking my seat. The dealer takes one look at me – a brief, nonchalant glance – and grabs my money, exchanging it for a stack of green chips.

Right out of the gates I'm hit with two troublesome cards – a seven and an eight – but Vega doesn't seem fazed.

Hit it, he says in my ear. I do as he says and tap the table for another card, a move I anticipated feeling vaguely cool – a move I imagine myself acting out in some Hollywood movie – but ultimately feels exactly how it looks: like I'm tapping my finger on a table. I guess my cool casino moment will have to wait.

The dealer flips another card and slides it over to me – another eight – before taking all my cards from me and declaring me bust.

Don't let it worry you, Vega says, right on time. *The card count is currently high; the odds of you winning that hand were favorable, but not insurmountable. Play again.*

I remember watching a documentary on card counting. I can't remember how it all works, other than the nebulous objective of keeping a running count of everyone's cards going, so I leave it to Vega, and place another chip on the table, receiving another couple of cards for it.

Sure enough, I win the next hand. And then the next one. And then the one after that. Before long I'm attracting venomous glances from the others at the table, and growing my pile of chips ever larger.

A couple of hours soon pass in this ethereal place – time losing all meaning when you can't see the sun moving across the sky; just the cards moving across the table – and after losing a bunch of hands, but winning a whole lot more, my pile of chips is three times the size it was when I started.

Order yourself a drink, Vega suggests. *Pretend to be a little bit drunk, even though I will ensure the alcohol won't ever reach your blood. Better to look like a lucky, cluelessly drunk gambler than a sober card counter.*

Again, I follow his suggestion, scoring a couple of free cocktails. I even aim some cocky banter around the table, telling the suspected wife-killer that his luck will turn around soon. He gives me a bitter snarl back – an almost animalistic growl – that I can't help but smile at.

Another couple of hours pass, and I pretend to get a little drunker, all while growing my pile of chips ever larger. Part of me begins to really enjoy this; following Vega's suggestions for hit or stick feels like playing with cheat codes, a thankful guarantee that no matter how little I understand this game, I won't lose.

My friends at the table leave me – the bored housewife and the others – replaced by a procession of other faces, some young and some old, but most of them awed by my wins, and agitated by my pretend drunkenness.

A dissonant thought briefly occurs to me – should I feel bad about this? I'm cheating, after all. Then again, I think of the casino and its boundless riches, and the fact I'm using Vega and the nanomachine network for something other than brute force violence and growing back new limbs. Hell, anything feels saintly compared to *that*.

By the time the fourth dealer comes around – the fourth face to look at my pile of chips with distrust – I can't even count my winnings. I'm on my seventh cocktail, which I take from the waitress with a grin and a wobble, before I catch something in the corner of my eye.

Bright red hair, cut neat and short, a couple of tables away. I try to remain cool, looking back to the table, before taking another casual glance in that direction after winning the next hand.

Sure enough, it's Kitzler, sitting at another blackjack table some twenty yards away. She's flanked by two burly men in black shirts, each sporting a crew cut and rippling muscles, barely contained within their clothing, and each looking as ugly and out of place as the golden statue in the middle of the room.

I finish my drink and turn my attention back to my mountain of chips, asking the dealer to exchange them for something smaller. She gives me a suspicious look – the look that wonders whether me, tipsy as hell, can really win that much – before taking them all away, and exchanging them for a couple of different colors, each labeled '10,000'.

"Whoa," I say out loud upon seeing that number for the first time.

Act cool, Vega tells me, noting my wide-eyed, child-like wonder at seeing five figures of winnings. *Remember you're being watched.*

I mumble an awkward thank you to the dealer and leave the table. I find a comfortable place to stand beside roulette, where I can ostensibly watch the action on the table, but instead keep a close eye on Kitzler.

She's sitting at a blackjack table, with her two heavies sitting on either side of her. She looks different from the photos; smaller, somehow. She sits almost perfectly still, only moving one hand to react to the dealer. I don't know what I expected from her, but in some intangible way, this hardened criminal disappoints me.

She sure loves to gamble, doesn't she, Vega says.

I decide to head to that table, but I stop as soon as I see

another man, standing on another side of the room, staring in her direction, just as I am. He's middle eastern, with thick black eyebrows and intense eyes, and a square jaw that twitches as though he's struggling to keep the lid on an explosive tension within him.

He sees me – our eyes briefly meet – before he looks away from me, like I've caught him in some guilty, unseemly act. I look back to the roulette table before me, and when I glance up again, he's gone.

"More security?" I ask under my breath.

Perhaps, Vega replies.

"Here you are," another familiar voice says. It's Alessia; I spin on my heels to see her behind me. "What, have you been watching tables this entire time? Haven't felt brave enough to sit down yet?"

She laughs to herself before putting a hand on my shoulder in a show of bashful condescension. She's wearing that ankle-length purple dress, with a small amount of make-up on, bringing out her large brown eyes.

"Don't worry, I'll show you how it's done," she says cockily, her lips curling into a devilish smile.

I don't say anything. I just take the two chips from my pocket – 10,000 euros apiece – and hand them over to her. She coolly takes them from me, takes a quick glance, and looks back to me with an expression of utter shock and horror.

There's the cool casino moment I was looking for.

CHAPTER 8

"I suppose we'll do it the polite way after all," Alessia says, her voice tinged with disappointment. Whether that disappointment stems from the fact she won't get to commit a violent kidnapping, or that I won twenty G's and she didn't, I don't know.

"Now we just need an invite, right?" I ask her. We're standing outside the casino in a small smoking area where Alessia holds a lit cigarette, never putting it to her lips.

"That'll be easy enough," she replies. "We've got the money. Or, rather, you got the money."

I smile at her. She looks at me with an envious fire in her eyes – that, and perhaps a little admiration.

"I'll head inside and ask around," she says, putting the cigarette out against a glass ashtray. "I don't think these goons are particularly discreet about their private rooms. If they think we've got the money to burn, they'll let us in. After that comes the tricky bit."

"Convincing her to introduce us to the arms dealer?" I ask, rather naively.

"Convincing her you're a hard-as-nails enforcer to a drug

lord," she curtly replies, before winking at me and walking back inside.

She paces away to grease the various wheels of criminal enterprise that'll hopefully buy us into that game, and I'm left alone to mill around like a sad puppy, much like how she first found me.

I go back inside, and head straight for the blackjack table Kitzler was sitting at, but see that she's already moved on, as has her security. I go back to the bar – an array of taps and bottles, accompanied by an ever-moving bartender – and order another drink, before reprising my whole drunk ignorant American act, and wait for Alessia to return.

I'm barely halfway through my first cocktail when I sense a figure beside me; tall, wearing a long purple dress. I turn, murmuring something about the private room, when I lock eyes with a pair of blue eyes, not the brown eyes of Alessia I'd expected.

"Oh, I'm sorry, I thought you were—"

"Someone else?" the woman asks. She's blonde, with two large blue eyes, set within a large amount of black eyeliner and mascara. Her lips are painted dark red. her skin is a pale white – as if she's never left this sunless building – and her hair falls in neat, shiny curls, like she arrived here straight from playing a 1950s housewife in an advert. I'm no expert, but her accent sounds French.

"Yes, I mean, kinda," I stammer, before wiping the stupid look off my face with a smile. "Sorry, am I bothering you?"

"Not at all," she replies, staring into me with those deep, intense eyes, eyes I could lose myself in if I had the time. Without breaking her gaze, she speaks again: "I heard you're the king of this castle."

I stare back at her blankly – my smile twitching slightly – until I finally grasp the meaning of what she just said; rather than mistake me for actual royalty around these parts, she's surely referring to my exploits at the blackjack table.

"Oh, blackjack?" I ask. "Yeah, I guess I got lucky."

She's maybe in her mid-twenties, probably around my age. She wears a long dress, resembling more a ball gown you'd see in photographs taken on the Titanic than anything modern. Her entire style looks like it's from that era. In an opulent, tawdry den like this, she stands out as a lone star of class.

"It's Delphine," she says, holding her dainty hand out to me. I take it, shaking it awkwardly, before enduring another moment of panic when I can't recall my fake name.

"Well, my name, my name is—" I casually say, stalling for time, trying and failing to produce another cool casino moment. "Carter. My name is Carter."

"No first name?" she playfully asks. Of course, I haven't gotten around to remembering my first name yet.

"Not right now," I answer, truthfully and stupidly. Rather than roll her eyes at my goofiness, though, she giggles – her red lips curling into a warm smile.

"Wow, chilling," she says, still giggling to herself. "What, are you some kind of secret agent?"

"Hah, no," I say, shaking my head. "I'm here on business. How about you?"

"I'm adaptable," she replies. "Business, pleasure, it's all the same in a place like this."

She narrows her eyes at me – her pale skin and deep blue eyes a gorgeous contrast – and I can't help but feel like she's flirting with me.

"This is a strange land," she says in that French-sounding accent, looking around the venue at the various oddballs, misfits, and weirdos. "Everyone is rich, and everyone is alone. Everybody wants to advertise their wealth, but nobody can hide their loneliness."

I look behind her, at a poker table filled with sad-faced men deeply embedded in their cards, none of whom look like they know each other. Likewise, the rest of the bar is full of lonely men and women, dressed formally, reading their cellphones or newspapers and nursing their cocktails like baby birds.

"Wealth isn't everything," I say, looking back to her. "Not in my experience, anyway."

Finally, a statement I can believe in; I think my first time holding five figures of cash was right this very afternoon. I have the power to generate priceless diamonds from my very fingertips, and yet I rarely do.

"So, Mr. Blackjack Genius, if wealth isn't the most important thing in this world, what is?"

She takes her drink from the bar beside her – a dark-red, ambiguous liquid – and sips it through a straw, leaving tiny imprints of lipstick behind as she does so.

As for her question, I couldn't even begin to answer that. My mission here is to pull a teenage vampire out of hiding and bring him to justice, or failing that, investigate why someone would steal forty gallons of human blood. I'm not exactly your average business traveler.

"Maybe I'm the wrong person to ask," I say, before taking a swig of my drink. "But I'd just like to leave the world a better place than I found it. I was a sickly child; we never had any money growing up. So, money doesn't mean a lot to me now, you know?"

She nods – her eyes staring into me – but doesn't say anything in reply. Instead, I see the purposeful figure of Alessia walking towards us from the other end of the casino. I take a deep, disappointed breath, knowing she'll tear me away from this strange and alluring conversation.

"Mr. Carter," Alessia says drolly, before looking Delphine up and down with skeptical eyes, sizing her up; an action she seems to repeat with every suspicious stranger she sees in public. "Let's go, we're done here."

"Done, here?" I repeat, before looking back to Delphine,

who smiles at me and puts the straw of her cocktail back between her lips.

"We've got business to do, come on," she says coldly, putting her hands on her hips. Slowly and reluctantly, I slide myself off my chair and look back to Delphine.

"Don't let yourself get too lonely," Delphine says to me, a collection of vague words that provokes Alessia into tensing up; I see her fists clench at her hips, and her head turn ever so slightly sidewards, as though she's cracking the bones in her neck in anticipation of violence.

I say a brief goodbye to Delphine before following a still-tense Alessia out of the casino, and to the streets of Monte Carlo outside. The sun is down, replaced by the wondrous lights of the city, filling the air with the same brightness and intensity.

There's an electricity in the air; a febrile, uncertain atmosphere, as the now-fierce wind from the bay brings the taste of salt water, and the dark clouds – far above the mesmeric lights surrounding us – could unleash furious rain and deafening thunder at any time.

"We've got two seats at Kitzler's poker table," Alessia says, pacing ahead so quickly I have to practically hop and skip to keep up with her. "Three p.m., tomorrow. We should spend the night ensuring our backstories are watertight, and a plan for every eventuality. We need to be prepared."

"Yeah, sure, but –" I shout, weaving past a couple of tourists on the sidewalk trying to keep up with her. We make it back to our hotel, charge through the lobby, and up a set of stairs to our corridor, and finally, to the door to our twin room.

"Hey, wait a minute," I say to her, seeing her finally slow down. "We don't need to rush around, do we? We've got all evening here."

She looks back at me with a scornful expression, her jaw

tense, and her eyes conveying the sense that she's far from pleased by my attitude.

"You mean, so you can waste your night flirting with French flapper girls?" she cruelly asks, a sarcastic question that feels like a stiletto between my ribs, and makes me wonder exactly what's going through her head.

"Ouch, there's no need for that," I tell her, before grinning and pushing my conspicuous luck a little too far: "Jealous, are you?"

She looks back at me with those coldly intense eyes – two roaring, freezing cold portals to the cruelest Antarctic blizzard – and slowly moves her body closer to mine, pressing me into the doorframe of our hotel room. Then, in one sudden movement, she hits me with the flat of her palm in the chest, just below my sternum.

"Oof," I groan, feeling winded at the blow. The pain shoots through me; a cruel, stinging pain I haven't felt since the last time we fought back in Thailand. I move my hands there defensively, and as she withdraws her palm, I feel her leave the keycard to the room behind, embedded against the fabric of my shirt.

"Open the door," she barks, stepping back.

I gather my breath and move the keycard to the door handle, which unlocks with an audible *click*. She pushes past me and through the door without another word.

I can't help but smile to myself before following her inside.

CHAPTER 9

"Okay. Game day," I say to myself, echoing those same words I heard from Mikey, two years ago.

"Huh?" Alessia grunts. She's standing on the other side of the room by the balcony, as I stare into the bright glare of our open laptop. She's already changed into her dress, a black ankle-length gown, the same design as the purple one from yesterday.

"Just something I say to myself before the big ones," I tell her. "Call it a ritual, I guess."

We've spent the last evening and all of this morning reciting our cover story: that we're both former special forces, now providing security services to a South American drug lord.

Sure enough, it comes easy enough to Alessia, who furnishes our story with minor details from her own travails with Charles Forrest, all without mentioning his name even once.

"Never thought you'd be the superstitious type," she says, looking out of the balcony window, a few shards of sunlight emerging from the drapes, illuminating her face in a shade of gold. "Until I saw you win twenty large at a blackjack table, that is. Clearly you must be doing something right."

I close the laptop and throw my suit jacket back on, before going to the bathroom and catching a moment of fright when I see my latest face staring back at me in the mirror.

"How's your poker revision?" Alessia calls out to me from the other room, as I rake my fingers through my hair one last time, ensuring I'm at least halfway presentable.

"I know there are fifty-two cards, and they're all different. Does that help?" I say to her with a grin as I walk back into the hotel room. She looks at me with a pained, unamused expression. "No, but for real, I'll do fine, just wait and see."

Of course, I don't tell her that I'm a gambling genius; the host to a super-intelligent AI that will ensure I make the most of every hand and adeptly scrutinize every other player to ensure I always win. Hell, why do I even spend my days punching bad guys in the face, when I could be sitting on my ass at a poker table?

"Well, you'd better hold your own out there, because we likely get one shot at this," she says, cracking her knuckles. "We'll play the game, get to know her, and then when the rest of the table is out, we'll tell her we want to do business, and meet her boss: this blood-stealing arms dealer."

"Sounds good," I answer, closing the laptop.

"This table might have some of the sketchiest miscreants in Europe – a real rogue's gallery of murderous generals, wanted criminals, and sleazy businessmen. We'll have to stay on our toes."

I nod at her.

"And we'll likely be frisked as we go in," she adds. "That means no weapons."

"My body is a weapon," I cockily tell her.

"Maybe," she replies, with a sly grin. "But your mouth is a liability. Let me do most of the talking. You just concentrate on not losing us our stake."

Well, I can't argue with her there.

We pack up the laptop – preparing to toss it, and all evidence of our mission into the bay – and leave the room.

———

Alessia speaks French to a dainty woman at reception, who smiles receptively – the sort of smile you get when you're frittering away twenty grand – and gestures for us to go to a small door beside her, guarded by a tall, slender man, wearing all-black and indoor sunglasses.

The man steps aside as we approach, and opens the door for us, revealing a small elevator, furnished with black wooden panels and a polished, marble-effect floor that I can see my own reflection in.

We both step inside and the tall guy joins us, justifying his presence by pushing the only button on its control console – a large red button, labeled 'limité'. The doors close with a cold rush of air, and we're quickly ascending the crystal tower.

When the elevator slows to a stop, the door slides open and we walk out into a corridor decorated much the same as the lift, with a series of unassuming black doors. We follow our guide – our footsteps echoing out on the mirrored flooring – until he directs us to the final door.

He says a couple of words to Alessia in French, before patting her down – her droll eyes looking to me, silently recounting my cheesy line about my body being a weapon from earlier – and gives me the same treatment. When he's happy we're not taking guns and knives to a card fight, he steps out of the way of the door.

"Good luck," he says, as we pass him and enter.

The room is a large, hexagon-shaped space, with six black-paneled walls, and six different paintings hanging on each. It's surprisingly sparse; there's a dark carpeted floor, and a simple black ceiling with a dozen small gold floodlights shining upon the centerpiece: the massive poker table, dominating the room.

It's a rectangle with curved corners, upholstered in dark-red fabric that immediately makes me think of dried blood. There's a dealer sitting there – looking at us both with a welcoming smile, if slightly inattentive eyes – and ten other empty chairs.

"I guess we're the first ones here," I say to Alessia. We both take chairs beside one another on the left side of the dealer, and wait.

It doesn't take long for some interesting faces to show up. First is an Austrian cowboy – a man named Hans, dressed in a leather jacket, denims, cowboy boots, and a Stetson, which he appears to be wearing the wrong way around. He has a cheery demeanor – greeting each of us – which I can only imagine won't last long at a table like this.

Next up is a Russian man, calling himself a former public prosecutor in Moscow. He's dour-faced, wearing a funereal black suit, and immediately orders a drink from the dealer, who radios his order downstairs. He has the look and mood of a man who just buried his mother, and for some reason came straight here.

"That's Denis Karpov, he's a dissident Russian police chief," Alessia whispers to me. "Half the governments in the world want him either behind bars or dead. Just make sure that you don't accidentally drink his negroni."

I look back at her with wide eyes, and nod.

Over the next fifteen minutes, the table fills out with more faces, some nervous, some excited. There's a couple smiling men from sub-Saharan Africa – one a former president, one a former general – a Canadian businessman in a garish pink smoking jacket, a British woman calling herself a Lady, and a Chilean mercenary with a gnarly scar above his eye.

"Hector Chavasse," Alessia whispers, gesturing at him. "They say he was a government-sponsored torturer. Not the kind of man I'd normally want to humiliate on the poker table, but here we are I guess."

"I suppose we play the hands we're dealt," I murmur back to her.

I think of asking her how she knows so much about these people – a murderer's row of the world's worst war criminals, crooked politicians, and skeevy businesspeople – but I decide to keep that question to myself. Better to wonder how many of these people she's worked for, than to ask and learn some horrifying truths.

Finally, Kitzler's security arrives – those two burly men I saw at the casino, with square jaws and expressions like they've spent the past hour chewing hemlock – and with no small amount of pomp, the small, wide figure of Kitzler herself.

"Afternoon, everybody," she says in a stern, German accent. "Is everyone feeling lucky?"

She wears a black turtleneck sweater, and black denim pants. Her hair is a brighter shade of red than the table, cut short and neat, and her eyes are small and beady, set within a perpetually suspicious face.

"Yes ma'am," the faux Austrian cowboy says, rising to shake her hand, before taking a second look at her two heavies and deciding against it. The rest of us make slightly less awkward greetings to her, and she finally takes her place at the table, exactly adjacent to the dealer.

"Let's play," she says with a sly grin.

CHAPTER 10

Fold, Vega says. I do as he tells me, laying my cards on the table beside my already-substantial pile of chips.

Alessia glances over at my cards, before looking to her own, slightly smaller pile of chips, and making the decision to fold as well.

We're several hours into the game already, and we're both still holding our own. Some faces at the table have disappeared. The Africans and the English Lady quickly went bust, said a few awkward goodbyes, and left. Even the Chilean torturer departed with a wounded smile. Perhaps there's a bellboy he can waterboard to cheer himself up.

On the other hand, the pink-clad Canadian businessman – growing ever drunker and ever more friendly with the dealer – was forcibly removed by one of Kitzler's heavies, serenading all of us with a chorus of insults and vague threats as he went, like a singing, leaping salmon. As entertaining meltdowns go, it wasn't bad.

Kitzler, however, has remained oddly quiet throughout. Her attention has been entirely on her cards – scrutinizing them with those small, piercing eyes of hers – while remaining tight-lipped as the others engage in superficial, mundane conversation.

Despite my success on the table, I'm starting to lose patience. I may be slightly richer, but we're no closer to Vincent, the arms dealer, or the trail of stolen blood that brought us here.

We play another hand, just as the cowboy runs out of chips. Just as I predicted, that joyous smirk he brought to this room is gone, replaced by a tired, bitter acceptance that it's over. He rises from the table, his Stetson falling backwards off his head in the process. He turns and madly scrambles across the floor for it, before making an embarrassed exit.

The Russian is bluffing, Vega says. *His face twitches every time he looks at his cards. He's a terrible liar.*

I act on his advice, and up my bet. The Russian gives me a cold look, before revealing his hand and surrendering the remainder of his chips. He makes a quick departure, and just like that, another adversary is defeated. Only Kitzler, Alessia and I remain.

"I love to gamble," Kitzler suddenly says, a deep drawl that surprises me. It's the first meaningful thing she's said yet. "The luck of the draw, the fact that no two hands are ever the same."

She pauses, before chuckling to herself.

"And, of course, what it does to men," she says with a smirk.

"You're clearly good at it," Alessia tells her, gesturing to the pile of chips she has, as large as my own.

"Yes, it's a useful skill," she replies, acquiescing to Alessia's flattery. "When to up the ante and when to lay down your arms. The ability to manage risk and make good decisions."

If I were a career criminal, with arrest warrants all over Europe, I perhaps wouldn't brag about my ability to manage risk.

"This game introduces you to all sorts of people," she goes on to say. "Interesting people, powerful people, terrifying people. People who'll kill you over a four of spades; people who'll open massive doors for you. And do you know the best part?"

She looks to me, as though I'm supposed to know the answer. I briefly consider piping up with a sarcastic remark and pointing to my winnings, but decide against it.

"The best part is that everyone at this table starts as equals," she says. "Everyone is only worth the sum of their chips. It doesn't matter if you ate breakfast at the Four Seasons or from a dumpster. Here, you're only as good as your winnings."

I look at the table – the battlefield upon which seven other participants fought, and bled – and throw another couple of chips in. The dealer shuffles the deck, and Kitzler – who can't stop opening her mouth now that it's just us and her – speaks up again.

"That shuffle the dealer just made, did you know that sequence of cards is perfectly unique? Each shuffle will produce a series of cards that has never been seen before, and will never be seen again."

I scoff, snorting to myself with disbelief. She notices, and glances over at me with dubious eyes.

"I find that hard to believe," I say to her. "You can't honestly say that that sequence of cards will never be seen again ever? In all the decks in all the world?"

"It's true," she says. "The probability of a perfectly shuffled deck occurring on this planet, or any other, is so astronomically massive as to be negligible. Some mathematician told me that at this very table. He lost everything, incidentally."

She's right, Vega says, never missing an opportunity to highlight my ignorance. *The probability of a perfectly shuffled deck recurring again is fifty-two factorial. That's fifty-two, times fifty-one, times fifty, times –"*

"I'll have to take your word for it," I say out loud, to both Kitzler and the aggravating voice inside my head. She grins, nods sagely, and goes on.

"You can create almost perfect exceptionality with that deck. Like the sorts of people who come to this table – each unique, with their own desires and crimes and fears and abilities and weaknesses – each shuffle is one of a kind."

That phrase – one of a kind – is one I heard from Vincent himself. Are we getting closer to him?

We play the hand– I fold again, and Kitzler calls Alessia's bluff, winning the pot.

"And yet, there must be one victor," Alessia says. "Everybody leaves this table empty handed, everybody but one."

"That's right," Kitzler says, grinning to herself.

"Survival of the fittest," Alessia adds, perhaps trying to move the topic onto weapons and death and destruction and all that jazz. "Only the strongest survive, on this table, like in life."

"I suppose that's right too," Kitzler says before looking around the table, first to her goon squad standing at opposite corners of the room – their huge frames hugging my peripheral vision like hideous stone statues – and then at the dealer, who freezes in place, partway through a shuffle.

"Why don't we take a break?" Kitzler then says, clenching her fists and then stretching out her fingers as though she's endured a tough day manning some antiquated, Dickensian cotton-spinning machine.

The dealer immediately stands and makes a quiet exit – the door held open by one of Kitzler's goons – while Alessia and I look at each other with frustration.

"You said before that people from all walks of life come to these tables," Alessia then says, as Kitzler rises to her feet. "Well, we came to this one specifically, to meet one person."

I take a fast, surprised breath. I didn't expect Alessia to go for the jugular quite so soon, but maybe she's as impatient as I am.

Kitzler on the other hand is unfazed. She stares at Alessia with an expectant, confident look on her face.

"You," Alessia says, crossing her arms. "We want to speak to the international businesswoman. The woman who can facilitate sales of important defensive measures, and move items across the world."

I flinch a little; it's like Alessia inserted into the back of her head an SD card of *Baynesisms* – dull euphemisms all gleaned from the big, boring man himself – but I understand why she's doing it. Ostensibly, we're looking to buy guns for a drug lord. Probably shouldn't say those things out loud.

"Can I speak candidly?" Alessia asks. Kitzler looks around the room before nodding in her direction. Alessia then spends the next couple of minutes explaining our cover story – that we need weapons for our client's 'self-defense'. Kitzler, though listening, doesn't appear moved, however.

"You're too late," she says with a small, sly smile at the corner of her lips. "I'm out of that business."

"That's not what we've heard," Alessia says, with a determined steeliness that makes me glad she's doing the talking and not me. "We've heard you're working with someone new. Someone who calls themselves a vampire. If you're not willing to help us, can you at least refer us to someone who will?"

Kitzler seems to recoil a little – she looks down to the table, and then at the two goons of hers that still stand menacingly at the different corners of the room – before taking a visible breath, her shoulders rising and falling.

"No," she replies, a word that feels like a bitter blow; a word that suggests we wasted precious time sitting at this table, with nothing to show for it other than a pot of ill-gotten winnings.

"No?" Alessia asks.

"No," she says again. "If my boss wants to do business with you, you'll know about it. Until then, you'll have to wait."

I exhale, loudly and deeply enough to draw Kitzler's attention. What a waste of time; all of this – the flights, the hotel, the gambling – just to submit ourselves to the whim of a German gambling addict who may have nothing to do with Vincent anyway.

"I heard you were powerful, that you could make things happen. I must say, I'm disappointed," Alessia says, an insult that fills me with nervous adrenaline. Kitzler looks up at her, but rather than appear offended, she seems to take it on the chin.

"You know, I've done a lot of bad things in my life. I'm wanted all over the world," she says to a stern-faced Alessia. "Police, drug cartels, smuggling gangs, human traffickers. Everyone wants me either dead, or locked away so that I never see the blue of the sky again. I thought I was done for. That is, until I met my new boss."

She leans on the table with both hands, slowly looking between Alessia and me.

"Now, I can travel freely. No one but the police dare mess with me and even they have second thoughts, and it's all because they know who I'm working for. Before, I had a tiny organization; a pitiful little enterprise I had the gall to brag about. Now, I'm the right hand of something new; something great and fearful. A monster that could rule the world."

A monster? Kitzler leans forward and drums her knuckles against the fabric of the poker table.

"So, don't pretend you came here to meet with me," she says, "because I know that like everyone else, you're really just enamored by the one above me."

I glance over at Alessia, who still wears that stern, unflappable expression, but I know that deep down she's probably seething.

"We'll resume play in an hour," Kitzler says, walking over to the door. One of her heavies opens it for her, while the other begins to stride across the room. Alessia suddenly bolts upright from her chair, makes a sidestep, and clatters into him, knocking them both off balance.

"I'm sorry," she says, removing her hand from his hip, "my mistake."

He shakes his head and resumes his path, joining his fellow goon by the door, and the two of them follow Kitzler outside.

"Well, that was a bust," I say to Alessia when we're left alone.

"Oh, I don't know about that," she replies, holding her hand up beside her head. In one rapid movement, she turns her palm around, showing a plastic card concealed within.

"What's that?" I ask.

"A keycard, for a room in this very building," she says with an artful wink. "I lifted it from one of those lumbering dinosaurs just a moment ago."

"Whoa, that's amazing!" I cry, "How'd you learn to do that?"

"You don't grow up an orphan without learning a few survival tricks," she says, before gesturing to the door. "Let's get out there and do some real work."

I glance back at the chips on the table – tens of thousands of euros, won from some of the meanest SOBs in Europe – and turn back to the door.

Enough of Texas hold'em. Now, the *real* game is on.

CHAPTER 11

We go back downstairs and take another elevator, this one up to the hotel complex on the higher floors.

"How do we know which room is hers?" I ask Alessia as the doors slide shut, and the elevator hums into action.

"I made sure I learned that yesterday," she says. "I managed to trick a dealer downstairs into calling through to reception and then giving me Kitzler's room number. Told him some crap about transferring a bar bill from her room to mine; these dealers aren't paid enough to care about discretion."

The elevator doors slide open again, unveiling a hotel lobby with two massive, attention-grabbing chandeliers, and a lonely, spotlessly white grand piano sitting below them, with no player and no music. Only after a couple of moments do I notice the reception desk, a smaller, quaint feature of the room.

There are marble columns on one side of the lobby – large enough to nail up a card cheat or two – and on the other, an enormous fish tank, illuminating that side of the room in a marvelous aqua blue. I see dark forms darting from side to side within it, but Alessia has already charged ahead of me before I can get a chance to admire the contents.

I catch up to her and we find ourselves within another corridor, with a plush, endlessly long rug beneath our feet, and a series of doors at irregular intervals to either side of us.

"This new boss she talked about," I say to Alessia in hushed tones. "Someone powerful, and fearful. Do you think that sounds like Vincent?"

"I don't know about that," she murmurs back. "But whoever it is, she's right about one thing."

"What's that?"

"I really can't wait to meet them," she says with a diabolical smile.

I think of her self-professed hatred of arms dealers – the lowest of the low – and it all starts to make sense. Some folks gamble, other folks race cars or play sports to feel alive. Alessia, on the other hand, smashes her fists into people's faces, and this week arms dealers are at the top of her list.

We walk on, until Alessia comes to a sudden halt.

"This one," she says, gesturing to the closed door before us. I take a look up and down the corridor, while Alessia puts her ear to the surface. "It's quiet inside. Shall we do this?"

I nod at her, feeling a spike of excitement through my veins, more intense than any winning hand at poker could grant me.

She swipes the keycard by the handle, and after the quiet *click* of the unlocking mechanism, she pushes down on the handle, plunging herself into the darkness of the room within. I take one final look to ensure we're not being watched, and then I join her.

I let the door slowly close itself behind me – a quiet creak, followed by a loud slam – enclosing us both almost entirely within silence and darkness. I see Alessia's form just before me – shadowy and tense, and remaining perfectly still, as if she's having misgivings, or senses something that I don't.

After a few moments, I see her slowly begin to move again, reaching over to a barely visible light switch on the wall beside us. I hear her take a slow breath before she flicks the switch, and a dim amber light fills the room.

It's a hive of decadence, all right. It's more a luxurious, resplendent lounge with a bed conspicuously thrown in than any hotel room I've seen before. Despite the visible luxury that pours out of every wall, it's a mess.

There's a massive, crescent-shaped couch, upholstered in black leather, decorated by what are presumably Kitzler's discarded clothes. A champagne bucket sits beside it, filled with numerous empty bottles, and the bed is strewn with clothes and papers. Poker chips adorn every surface like confetti at a wedding, and there's a sticky wine stain on the hard wood floor.

Alessia looks back to me with an amused expression – enjoying the notion that our power-obsessed adversary lives like the casino's pet pig – and then slowly walks to a solid oak desk at the center of the room, where she's evidently attracted to a laptop.

I wait by the door and look to the wardrobe beside me – a huge wooden structure, composed entirely of mirrored doors – and see a safe inside. I crouch beside it, but find it open, and empty.

I'm slowly picking myself up to my feet again when I hear a curious noise: the sliding creak of a door on its hinges, perhaps. I glance up to see Alessia focused on the laptop, and open my mouth to warn her, but by then it's too late…

"Arrêtez-vous!" a voice yells out, deep and severe. "Stop!"

Alessia freezes in place – her arms lingering by her sides, trembling slightly with nervous energy – before she tenses up, looks behind her, and slowly puts her hands up, and to her head.

The unseen man spits another mouthful of words in French – words that Alessia understands and I don't – and I watch as she slowly drops to her knees. I stay frozen in place, with my heartbeat racing in my ears, and realize one thing: this man – whoever he is – hasn't seen me yet.

I wait, and soon hear footsteps – slow, deliberate, careful steps on the hard wood floor – and see a gun emerge from an unseen corner of the room, and with it, a dark figure, masked by shadows, walking slowly towards her. He's tall, and visibly edgy – the gun shakes in his hand – and what's more, he doesn't have the presence of mind to check if she's alone.

Alessia says a couple more words in French, just as he makes it across the room to her. I see him reach for his waistband, and I seize my opportunity. I run forward, provoking a thunderous noise that turns his head instantly, and in a split second, realize that I recognize him from somewhere…

I pick up a clenched fist above my head. He sees it – a panicked expression on his face, the unspoken admission that he made a big mistake – and begins to swivel his body to aim his gun my way, but he's not quick enough. I land a punch to his forehead, and he folds over, his torso falling sideways before his legs can follow.

Before I can collect my breath, it's all done. He's an unconscious body on the floor, and Alessia's hands are already off her head.

"Nice work," she says, in a tone of relief I can't remember ever hearing from her.

I look behind me and see the ensuite bathroom door wide open; a nook in the spacious suite that I couldn't see from my position by the safe.

"I'm guessing he was hiding in there," I tell her, nodding to the door. She looks over, before biting her lip with barely concealed frustration.

"I guess he was," she says, her tone deflated.

I turn my attention to the lifeless body beside me – the

poor man I just sent to the shadow realm – and put my hands on his face, turning him to the light. He's olive-skinned, with thick eyebrows, and I remember him now.

"I know this man," I tell Alessia. "He was in the casino yesterday. I saw him watching Kitzler from a distance."

"More security?" she asks, before crouching beside him and rifling through his pockets. She pulls out a wallet and opens it. "Oh, crap."

"What?" I ask, seeing her expression change to something between amusement and horror. She plucks a small, plastic card out of the wallet, and holds it up to the light.

"It's a French police warrant card," she says. "Seems you just assaulted an officer."

I look at the card and see a photo of his unkind face staring back at me, alongside the name Ahmed Rabiot.

"What the hell was he doing in here?" I ask. I run my fingers along his neck to check for a pulse, and to my great relief, I quickly find one.

"He was probably doing the same as we were," she says, crossing her arms. "Anyway, we shouldn't stick around here."

"Yeah, right," I say, seeing the cop begin to stir, his arms twisting, and his legs shuddering like he's emerging from the most brutal hangover anyone has ever seen. After looking to her blankly, I remember the very reason we're here. "What about Kitzler?"

"We'll have to improvise," Alessia says, taking his gun from the floor before hopping over the cop and past me. I follow her to the door, just as that word sprints to the forefront of my mind.

Improvise? We just knocked a cop unconscious, and as soon as he regains his wits and invites his buddies, this entire casino is going to be hotter than the surface of the sun. Our options are dwindling by the second, and Alessia wants to wing it.

"You know, I always preferred the impolite route anyway," Alessia says with a knowing grin.

CHAPTER 12

We briskly walk down the corridor and back into the hotel lobby, attempting to look more like business travelers late to a meeting than what we really are: dangerous, wanted criminals, escaping the scene of a cop thumping, and wasting no time to commit our next crime.

We ride the elevator down, and head to the next elevator up to the private poker room, agreeing that it'd be best to intercept Kitzler there, and then delicately 'persuade' her to come with us.

The elevator door slides open, and we're back in the liminal space of that anonymous corridor with the polished, mirrored floor. But this time, it's different. There's shouting – frantic yelling, echoing between the walls – the soft consonants of the French language, shouted with terror and malice.

Alessia looks back at me with wary eyes before we slowly make up the ground to the poker room's door, which lies slightly ajar. She flattens her back to the corridor wall, sneaking a glance through the crack in the door, while keeping that handgun concealed behind her.

After a couple of seconds – and more frenzied shouting

from within – she turns back to me with an uncertain look, her eyes cagey and calculating. She hands the gun to me, grip first; I take it from her, holding it by my side, and she leans in to whisper to me.

"It's the cops," she says in my ear. "They're trying to put the cuffs on her."

"What do we do?" I ask, dreading the possibilities that must be going through her head.

"Hide that gun, and follow my lead," she says, before turning back to the crack in the door. I quickly stash the pistol in the back of my waistband and pull my suit jacket over the top of it.

In a decisive movement, she opens the door and clumsily strides through it – attempting to appear every bit the sort of happy-go-lucky half-drunk gambler this casino is filled with. I take an anxious breath and follow her, trying to put the sort of grin on my face that suggests I didn't just punch out a cop.

"Hey, what's th—" Alessia says dumbly, skipping right into the middle of an armed police situation. She's met by a volley of angry, wary shouting, and after she freezes on the spot – just beyond the doorway – I can see the entire scene.

The first thing I see are Kitzler's heavies – those big, doddering Easter Island heads – face-down on the floor, their hands clasped on the backs of their heads. One of them looks up to us, a newly earned bruise above his eye.

Kitzler on the other hand kneels in the corner with her hands on her head, her eyes following every motion with an unamused, wearied look about them. She barely stirs when she sees Alessia and I; she wears the face of a woman who just wants to hurry up and get inside a room with a lawyer.

The last, and entirely new feature of the room is the pair of red-faced armed French policemen – one of them aiming his gun at Kitzler, the other aiming at Alessia – who haven't quit yelling for even one moment. A pair of cacophonous bobbleheads, trying to assert their dominance, but only appearing out of their depth.

"Okay, okay," Alessia says, taking a purposefully clueless step towards the first cop, provoking a litany of French swearwords. The man behind him lowers his gun and glances towards us – aiming away from Kitzler for the first time – and I can practically hear the gears in Alessia's mind turning.

"Sorry, sorry, I didn't realize something was going on here," Alessia says, shaking her head and waving her arms like a dumb tourist. Now both of the cops are looking our way, evidently appraising us as a couple of drunk distractions, rather than the true dangers we really represent.

As soon as both men are looking our way – their guns lowered – Alessia springs into action. She throws an arm, grabbing the closest cop by the wrist, and bends it behind him, provoking a shriek of pain. He lets go of his gun, and I get my signal to make my move.

I feel myself propelled by a surge of adrenaline; I reach behind my back, finding the grip of that handgun, and aim it towards the second cop, whose face turns from annoyance to fear in an instant. The shouting stops, and the only noise is the sound of the gun clattering against the floor.

The four of us stand there, seemingly frozen in time; the two cops a panicked tangle of anxious limbs and open mouths, a contrast to the resolute, determined postures of Alessia and me.

"Okay, let's be cool," Alessia says. I keep my eyes – and my aim – on the cop, whose frightened face sits behind the sights of his gun, aiming directly at me, an uneasy standoff.

"Put your gun down, buddy," I tell him, just as I see a bead of sweat gather at the bottom of his hairline. "We're all getting out of here alive."

As soon as that last word escapes my lips, I'm shaken out of my skin by a deafening sound – an eardrum pummeling blast – that wipes my mind clear of any focus I ever had. I blink and see a strange pattern on the wall beside him – a deep red scribble, like a toddler was let loose with crayons – and he slumps to the side, falling to the floor.

Only now do I see it for what it is: blood and brain matter, glistening in the light.

I look to Kitzler, who stands there in the corner, aiming a handgun in the cops' direction. She pivots slightly, adjusting her stance, and I see a flash of orange, and another deafening *bang*.

The man closest to Alessia falls limp, his body falling facefirst onto the poker table, as Alessia still holds onto his wrist, which hangs above him like a gravestone. She drops it, and it too falls by his side limply.

"Nice distraction," Kitzler says to us, as I look back to the red bloodstains on the walls and the twitching corpses before me. I glance back at her to see her – the remorseless cop killer – putting her gun away, and then, with a sense of profound regret, I lower my own gun.

Alessia begins to speak, but I don't hear her. I realize I'm still holding my breath – holding my last, fearful gasp of air in my lungs – and allow myself to exhale. I look back to Kitzler, who smiles.

"C'mon, let's get out of here," she says, walking briskly around the poker table. She paces past her two heavies still kneeling on the floor, provoking a grunt and an unintelligible word from one of them.

"What about your boys?" I ask in a voice that doesn't even feel like my own – a shocked, sickened voice that seems to come from another place within me.

"These guys? They won't talk," she says, as I drop the gun I'm holding. She says a few words to them in German, and with overawed faces, they nod. "They'll clean up and get out of here."

Alessia – who still has barely moved a muscle since those two men were shot – loosens her shoulders and turns to face me with a guarded, hesitant expression. She's undoubtedly seen plenty of people killed in her life, but seeing Kitzler so casually execute those cops – as coolly as she'd shuffle a deck of cards – seems to have perturbed even her.

"You want to meet my boss, do you?" Kitzler asks, a question which wakes Alessia from her slumber; she spins to face her attentively. "Well, let's go do it."

Alessia's eyes light up again; I guess we're back on the trail, despite an ultraviolent, tragic hiccup.

Kitzler charges past us, and Alessia quickly follows her out of the room. I take one last glance at the scene – the blood on the walls, the lifeless bodies and the puddles of blood growing beneath them, and the two blank-faced goons looking between each other with hapless expressions – before I too turn and follow them both.

We cross the corridor outside, and Kitzler opens one of its many featureless black doors, before disappearing inside. Alessia and I – after sharing a wary glance – join her, entering a gray stairwell; a ghostly, liminal space, composed of dusty concrete and steel handrails that impart sharp flecks of paint into my skin as I grasp them.

We descend a couple of floors, finding ourselves in another gray tunnel beside the kitchens, with the jubilant chatter of the casino audible from the corridor beyond. Kitzler looks left and right, before making a beeline to a fire escape.

Without a word, we follow, and leave the scene of our latest crimes – and a couple more bodies – and embrace the cleansing, cool sea air of Monte Carlo.

CHAPTER 13

"Oops?" Alessia asks, as the engine of Kitzler's vehicle kicks into a higher gear. I look over to her before looking back out of the window beside me, and the dancing lights of the bay – whites and reds and yellows spinning across a black sea – that provoke bright, dazzling halos in my eyes.

Suddenly, I feel like I'm a kid again. I have a distant memory of a car journey back from the lakes, back when my mother was still alive. My Dad was driving, bickering occasionally with my mother, who mostly hid behind a map, and I was sitting in the back, staring at the yachts on the lake.

I remember feeling exhausted, but knowing I couldn't sleep because I was so transfixed by the beauty of it all: the dark blue of the dusk sky, the pitch-black waters, the white sails swaying gently in the wind, and the warm, bright lights of the yachts, like faraway stars in the night's sky.

It felt like a perfect, enlightened moment in a dark, uncertain childhood. A snapshot of time, frozen within my memory, when just for one dark evening, everything seemed far brighter.

"The dead guys?" Kitzler answers, bringing me crashing

and burning back to today's reality. "Maybe. They looked like pigs, and they talked like pigs. But maybe we got lucky, and it was a couple of gangbangers playing pretend, trying their luck."

I'd almost forgotten about the two corpses from before; another couple of dead bodies to add to the list of traumas I should one day tell a therapist about.

"It doesn't matter anyway," Kitzler says, as I feel Alessia's eyes burning into the back of her head with disdain. "I think we overstayed our welcome in Monaco, time to go somewhere else."

The hue of the streetlights changes ever so slightly as we speed away from Monte Carlo, from a bright white to a warmer amber. A few more words are exchanged up front – another language, between Kitzler and the driver, an ashen-faced man I haven't met before, with glasses and an earpiece.

I turn back to the window just as we speed behind a hillside, entirely blocking my view of the bay. Maybe I should be making small talk right now – attempting to keep up the pretense that I'm a hardened criminal, working for the baddest drug lord around – but I realize I can't quite find that level of boldness within me.

"Alright, we're past the border," Kitzler says as we navigate a single-lane road, behind a quaint, brick building and a sandy hill. "If you're going to meet the boss, then you're going to have to follow some rules."

"Oh?" Alessia says, subconsciously – or not – clenching her fists. "What rules?"

The driver pulls the car over by the side of the road and turns the engine off. Kitzler reaches into the glovebox, and then turns to us from the upfront passenger seat with an item in her hands. Black fabric, wound around her knuckles.

"Wear these," she says, throwing the first to me – which I catch between my fingers – and the second to Alessia.

"You've seen firsthand there are men with guns out to get us. We can't be too careful."

I run the material between my fingers, sensing that it isn't just mere fabric; there are stitches and patches of thicker textiles. It's a blindfold.

"We're not wearing these," Alessia says. "If we're going to do business, you need to respect us as equal partners here. That means sitting at a table, man to man, woman to woman. No blindfolds."

There's a silence between us as the cooling engine ticks over, and the driver turns the interior light on, letting me see the blindfold in clearer detail.

"But we're not equal partners, are we?" Kitzler says, in her impish Germanic accent. "If you're serious about wanting our services, you'll respect our security protocols. We can't just invite *anyone* into our castle."

Alessia gives me a side-glance – full of frustrated eyes and bared teeth – ready to argue back, but I speak up before she gets a chance to.

"We're serious. We'll do it," I say, provoking another annoyed glance from Alessia beside me, but thankfully, no more resistance. We're already in this as deep as the hole in a cop's head; surely we can endure a little more darkness.

I see Alessia take a deep breath, and slowly fasten her blindfold around her eyes, and I do the same. It fits perfectly – there being two thick fabric blinders stretching across my vision – and I'm deprived of all my sight. No pretty dancing lights on the bay, no furious Alessia, nothing.

"Good," Kitzler softly says. "I'm glad we can respect each other."

I feel Alessia move beside me – a quiet and petulant breath, or a defiant flinch – as the engine starts up again, and the wheels beneath us turn, audibly crunching gravel before we make it onto flat, quiet asphalt again.

The rest of the journey passes without event or conversation – perhaps half an hour of patiently listening to every smallest, almost imperceptible change in road texture, every frustrated breath from Alessia, and the passing of every car or truck as we drive into the night.

"Okay," Kitzler says as the road texture changes yet again, provoking a harsh, pebbly sound as the tires struggle to gain traction in the dirt. "We're going to get out of the car, and onto a small boat."

"A boat?" I hear Alessia remark.

"A boat," Kitzler drolly repeats. "We'll lead you every step of the way, but we'll need to restrain your hands."

The car comes to a halt, and sure enough, I feel hands on me, easing me out of the car by my shoulders. I follow along, clambering out, and feel my boots touch grass once more.

My hands are bound behind my back by what feels like a cable tie, and I'm led forward in the dark once more, feeling something like sand beneath my feet, and then the unmistakable booming of my footsteps against the wooden planks of a dock.

"Big step," a male voice says in a French accent, and I do as he says, striding forward, landing on a floating, uneasy surface. I'm gently pushed into a seated position, and feel Alessia beside me, needing neither eye to sense her tense, seething body joining me.

"Hope you know what you're getting us into," she whispers beside me, just as I hear a high-pitched engine roar to life and feel the spray of salty sea water against my face as we begin to sail.

Do I know what I'm getting us into? Why of course, we're pursuing a loose lead on the teenage bloodsucker we're seeking, investigating the theft of dozens of gallons of blood from one of the richest cities in the world. And now we're blinded and restrained, accompanying a murderous cop killer to meet her boss, who could be several magnitudes worse. It's simple.

The speedboat picks up the pace, and soon my lips are

chapped from the cold breeze. I lick them, tasting a layer of salt that reminds me of pointlessly sinking tequilas in Eastern Europe some two years ago. From one dark, self-destructive path to another.

We bob up and down on the waters – I feel like my stomach and intestines disconnect from my gullet and drift around inside my thorax, sickeningly banging against my ribcage and turning upside down and inside out – until after twenty or so minutes, we begin to slow down again.

"Well, this is it," Kitzler says, an ambiguous tone that sets my heart racing. Part of me – the wary, anxious feeling in the back of my mind - expects to feel the cold steel of a gun barrel pressed against my temple. She could kill us both here and dump our bodies in the sea; perhaps it was a mistake to entrust our lives to a mad, murderous gambler.

"We're here," she then says, as a deep, relieved breath leaves my lungs. The boat stops bobbing and weaving, and settles into a tender rocking from side to side. I hear something else – the straining of coarse fabric against steel – and realize we're being tied up.

Another hand guides me to my feet – I follow along, and take another guided step onto the hard, trusty sternness of dry land. No more waves, no more bitter taste of sea salt and burned off diesel, and no more jumbled up guts.

I'm led another few steps – up a small staircase, onto another wooden decking – and placed on what feels like a leather-upholstered stool. I hear Alessia stumbling around beside me, and feel another gust of wind on the side of my face.

"Here they are," Kitzler says, in a decidedly different tone of voice from the one I've heard from her so far; deferential, and careful. "Supposedly they're the security team of a merchandiser in Madrevaria."

"Thank you, Ada," a high-pitched, feminine voice says. I

immediately feel like I recognize it, a strange and faraway memory from before the bodies and the darkness.

"Can please we lose the blindfolds?" Alessia says, her words polite, but her tone lacking in sincerity.

"Take the blindfolds off them," the feminine voice says again, in a delicate French accent. I know her, but I can't quite place her yet...

I hear footsteps behind me, and feel the hair on the back of my neck brushed by the cuff of someone's shirt. The blindfold is lifted from me, and after battling a sharp, painfully intense light, I see that we're not on dry land at all. We're in the open deck of a yacht – a large one – surrounded by those same dark waters as before.

"You've already met, I think," Kitzler says as I move my eyes to her, seeing her leaning against a railing with the black of the nighttime sea behind her.

"Yes, we have," the other voice says. I look to the other side of the deck and see a female form – skinny, pale, wearing an elegant white dress, with golden hair by her shoulders. In this light – a warm, amber glow, evocative of those ships on the lake all those years ago – she looks stunning.

It's Delphine, the woman from the casino bar. Evidently, she did her research on us.

"You know me," she says, taking a couple of slow steps towards us, removing one hand from behind her dress – a hand that holds a gun. "I like to work in the shadows."

CHAPTER 14

"You're the woman from the bar, aren't you?" Alessia asks, as I straighten my posture. My wrists are still bound in the cable ties, but I think I could break out of them easily enough. To my relief, though, Delphine's gun remains by her side.

"Delphine," I say, seeing her eyes light up when she hears the name.

"My middle name," she replies. "My real name is Rose. Rose Delphine Delissalt."

I feel a strange change in Alessia beside me – she flinches or recoils in her seat, seemingly reacting to that name. She knows her, or at least, she knows the name.

"You're the arms dealer everyone's losing their minds about? The one they're calling a vampire?" Alessia asks, her expression turning from heated aggravation to hesitant unease.

The black water of the Mediterranean lies behind them both, with only a single series of lights – an oil tanker, or a procession of smaller boats – visible in the distance. I see stars in the sky, and a couple of long, thin clouds, illuminated by moonlight.

"And I know who you are too," the woman says, taking a couple more tentative steps between us, that gun still menacingly dancing beside her. "Alessia d'Alessandro; warrior, bodyguard, assassin. You're quite the legend."

I quickly turn my head, looking to Alessia sitting beside me – her arms still bound behind her – and see her mouth hanging open slightly, with her eyes wide, and a few errant strands of hair flowing behind her in the breeze. She looks as surprised as I am to see our false identities go up in smoke.

"What does all this mean?" I ask, a dumb question, but the only one I can think of asking that might grant some clarity.

I see Alessia's throat move – she takes a loud and visible gulp – before speaking.

"Ms. Delissalt here is a member of the Delissalt family of uhm, how do I put it, discreet entrepreneurs."

Rose smiles gamely, as though she approves of the description.

"I used to deal occasionally with Mr. and Mrs. Delissalt, whom I presume were Rose's parents," Alessia says, in a careful, unsure tone that suggests her dealings with Rose's parents weren't exactly peaceful.

"We've met," Rose says, crossing her arms, while keeping that gun very noticeably in view. "A few years ago, on a yacht very similar to this. I was a lot younger, a student, maybe. You and my papa didn't get along. There were cross words, hot tempers."

Oh man, what have I blindly walked us into here? I thought we could get back on Vincent's trail, but instead, we're dredging up historical insults straight from Alessia's tongue, the mafioso version of Family Feud.

"Look, I just want to say that –" Alessia says, before Rose cuts her off with a *tsking* noise that, to my surprise, silences her.

"I recognized you in the casino," Rose says. "I did my research – had Ada take some surreptitious pictures of you and your friend here – and there you were, the famous Alessia d'Alessandro, but under a false name, trying desperately to meet me."

Alessia is quiet; she stares back at Rose with two wide, cautious eyes, as though she can't work out her intentions, and perhaps, has a lot of reason to fear them.

"Let me just say," Alessia says after several fraught moments of silence. "I heard what happened to your parents, and I'm very sorry for your loss, and if you think that had anything to do with me, then you're mistaken."

Okay, *what*!? I stare at Alessia, unable to contain my sense of astonishment and dread. It's bad enough to find yourself bound and at the mercy of ruthless, murderous arms dealers. When you have to deny having anything to do with their parents' deaths too, it's maybe time to consider an early exit strategy.

"You did threaten to kill them, don't you remember?" Rose asks, as I strain my wrists against my restraints while trying to remain visibly still.

"It was in the heat of the moment," Alessia says in return. "I didn't have any problems with your parents, and I had no reason to kill them. It was just an insult."

"You know, if I may, I can attest to that," I say, speaking up, and immediately regretting doing so. Alessia looks to me with a cold-faced look of bemusement, and I go on. "She threatens to kill people all the time. And she very rarely goes through with it."

"I remember thinking you're a bold woman; fearless even," Rose says, as I lean forward slightly, trying to give myself a little more leeway to break the ties. "That day, I remember thinking one more thing."

"Okay," Alessia says back, blinking for a second too long, readying herself for whatever Rose has planned for her.

"That you're a great judge of character," Rose says, a sentence that surprises me again. Rose uncrosses her arms and looks back overboard to the dark sea. "My mother and father were awful, awful people. My entire family was built on death and blood and lies."

Kitzler nods to herself, and Alessia glances at me with a quizzical look on her face.

"I was sick when I was a kid. Aplastic anemia, a really serious illness," she says wistfully, as I think about that car journey with my own mother and father again. "I had long stays in the hospital. Many painful, lonely hours. And they didn't care. They didn't visit, even once."

Alessia takes a deep breath beside me, her chest rising, and then falling as she waits to see where this sob story takes us.

"After all that, they sent me to a private school. A boarding school in Switzerland. I had to have weekly blood transfusions, so naturally, all the other kids said that I was a vampire. I was bullied. I didn't matter that my pale skin was caused by my condition, or that the blood was needed for me to survive."

Another criminal mastermind, stealing people's blood to survive. She's no Vincent, just a garden-variety outcast with childhood trauma and a desire to make the world pay for it.

She passes the handgun to Kitzler. I take the opportunity to look behind me, seeing two men – one, the glasses-wearing driver from the car, and another taller, thicker man, whose pug-face I don't recognize – and the assault rifles in their arms, held delicately across their bodies like ancestral treasures at a royal funeral.

"You said you heard what happened to my parents?" Rose asks Alessia, turning back to her and approaching slowly.

"I heard they made a lot of enemies," Alessia says, her tone deep and unflappable. "It was a group of rivals that got them. That's all I know."

"You're half right," Rose says, walking up to Alessia – who still sits there motionless, her hands tied behind her back

– and kneeling on one knee before her. "It was indeed their rivals, but they weren't alone."

She points a finger into Alessia's leg, just below the knee. Part of me wonders if that's the part of her leg with the burns, and if Rose knows about that; Alessia's own bitter memento from an abusive parent.

"It was me. My idea, my plan," Rose then says, before bounding up to her feet again. "I'm the one who gave my parents' enemies enough information for them to take them out. A private jet crash over Patagonia. A clean cut."

"You killed your own parents," I say to her, still not quite believing that this is the sweet, soft-spoken woman I met at the casino bar.

"Yes, I did," she replies. "And then I took their empire from them. Their entire business – the arms manufacturers in Siberia, the secret shipping routes, the dealers in the middle east – I inherited it all. Even this yacht belonged to them. Or at least, a shell company of a shell company of a lawyer of theirs. I know where the bodies are buried and where the riches are stashed."

I feel myself shaking my head. I turn to Alessia, who stares into an empty corner of the deck, not quite able to summon the same sense of disgust that I do. Maybe she and Rose are alike; forced into a lifestyle tempting death, doing business with the devil, all because of the sins of the father.

"I don't blame you for threatening to kill my parents that time," Rose says to Alessia, walking around the backs of our seats. "Maybe you even inspired me, along with a hundred other terrible things they did."

"I don't even remember you," Alessia says defensively. She almost sounds hurt. She's accumulated two more bodies, and she didn't even mean to.

"Don't worry about it," Rose says. I look behind Alessia to see her untying those cable ties from around her wrists. "I was a nobody back then. A dumb little kid. Now, I'm somebody."

She walks behind me, and I feel her releasing my restraints – her cold fingers brushing against the backs of my wrists provokes a strange feeling in me. Part attraction, part horror.

I feel the plastic band around my wrists fall away, and I slowly draw my hands out before me. I look to see Alessia has done the same, and sits there quietly, watching Rose walk across the deck.

"Now, one of the newspapers here calls me the vampire of Monte Carlo," Rose says, her voice bolstered with an undercurrent of pride. "I ran with it. I decided to start signing off my messages that way. That word that was used to hurt me, I can reclaim as my own."

"We thought they called you a vampire because of the shipment of blood you stole," I say, a statement that attracts her attention. She looks at me – with two striking, endlessly blue eyes – and smiles.

"Yes, I should have known that job would attract headlines. Maybe the beginning of the end of our time here in Monaco."

"Job?" I ask. "I assumed you needed that blood for your condition."

"No," she says, giggling to herself as though I asked the dumbest question she's heard today. "I'm rich. I can buy any doctor and any medical treatment in the world. And besides, I've been healthy for a while. I'm not some freak; I don't steal blood for kicks. I did it for business."

She really isn't Vincent, or even anything close to a vampire. Nevertheless, the trail isn't yet cold. I scratch my head and ask the only question that makes sense.

"Then who did you steal the blood for?"

CHAPTER 15

Rose crosses her arms, and pushes her lips together in an exaggeratedly protective gesture. The wind picks up, and a large wave passes under the boat, rocking us from left to right for the first time I've noticed tonight. Perhaps a storm is coming.

"You know I can't tell you who my clients are," she says with another giggle, albeit this time a little more aggravated than the last. "You're only both here because Ada-Marie vouched for you; that you got her out of a spot with the police."

She looks at me with an amused disdain; a look she might give a beggar who asks for the entire contents of her purse, and doesn't even say *please*.

"For a start, I don't even know who you are," she says to me.

I smirk at her. Even the world's largest spy agencies don't know that I'm a nanotech freak who can change his face at will. The bride of Dracula has no chance.

"And you as for you Alessia," she says, walking back towards Alessia again as another wave flows beneath us. "I admire you. I've heard of a lot of the things you've accomplished in your life. The battles, the contracts, the dirty work. You're an inspiration to us."

I look to Alessia, who sees me glance her way and flinches, suddenly turning her head away from mine as if this is all some big revelation; that she's ashamed of her past.

"But, even for you, I can't talk about my clients," she says. "I know you understand. I think you're one of us, after all."

Rose turns to a grinning Kitzler and puts her hand on her cheek.

"I suppose you'd both better make yourselves at home," Rose says, looking back to us. "We can talk business at last."

"Business," Alessia says in a grave tone, standing up from her seat for the first time. "You think I want to talk business?"

I'm getting a bad feeling. The weather has shifted – there's a humid fullness to the atmosphere, that storm beginning to brew – and the wind now whips around us, blowing Alessia's hair out of place.

She doesn't seem the same woman who blindly boarded this yacht. Instead – hearing instances of her own ambiguous past dredged up and paraded as inspiration for Rose's ill-doings – something has altered within her, like the rising tempest.

"Why else are you here?" Rose asks, still smiling. "I heard you worked with that drug lord in Madrevaria – *El Bosque* – and now you're working for another. I feel like we can do business; like we can start a beautiful friendship."

Alessia takes another couple of slow, purposeful steps towards Rose and Kitzler, who stand next to each other. Rose adjusts her posture – widening her stance, repositioning her body as though she wants to shake Alessia's hand – and in doing so, the outline of a solid object briefly becomes visible by her ankle. A weapon, perhaps?

"A friendship?" she asks, imparting one brief glance to the couple of assault rifle-toting goons behind us. I look up at the sky, and see that the stars and the moon have disappeared. The clouds are setting in.

"I hope so," Rose says, undeterred, but perhaps wondering where exactly Alessia is taking this. Unfortunately, I have a pretty good idea; one that makes me think about the distance between me and those goons, and consider how many bullets I'd soak up trying to get over there.

"But you said it yourself. You're a vampire," Alessia says, walking another couple of steps so that she's directly facing Rose now, almost squaring up to her. "A merchant of death, a parasite. You suck the life out of families and communities. You take money from the worst people in the world and give them the tools to kill innocents at industrial scale."

Rose's smile slowly leaves her face, replaced by a look of wary bafflement. Kitzler, too, hardens her posture and repositions herself between Rose and Alessia, like she's the referee preparing to split them up.

I glance at the pair of armed men again – surreptitiously side-eyeing them – who both look between each other with dubious, perplexed expressions. They don't know what to make of this either, but they seem to sense the atmosphere deteriorating.

"I'm not like you, Rose Delissalt," Alessia says, just as I see Kitzler beginning to puff her chest out assertively.

I feel my heart begin to race – the pit of my stomach falls to somewhere around my ankles – and the adrenaline surging through my veins forces me to slowly clench my fists.

"In fact," Alessia says, moving her face ever so close to Rose's now, "I detest you, just as I detested your family."

Rose hesitantly opens her mouth to speak, but nothing comes out. For all of her grandstanding about being a dangerous, mythical beast from the very deepest pits of hell, she's wilting like a flower in front of a real warrior.

I look across to see those goons slowly changing their positions – re-adjusting their grips on their rifles and aiming them towards Alessia – and realize that I need to do something.

"Alessia," I say, in a venturing but stern tone.

Another quiet, fraught moment goes by, and I think I see something on the distant horizon; a bolt of lightning, a momentary flash of white that illuminates the sky for the briefest time, and Alessia makes her move.

I see her drop to the floor, aiming a spinning kick at Rose's legs. Rose falls in a heartbeat – her legs swept out from under her with enough force to make her entire hapless body airborne for a second – and in doing so, her dress rides up, revealing the holster by her ankle.

I find myself jumping to my feet, thinking I should get to work on the goons behind me, but no sooner have I landed on both heels than Alessia's already reached for Rose's gun. She grabs it, and fires four shots almost instantly – *one, two* in the chest of one guy, and *three, four* in the chest of the next.

Both men fall to the ground – not even having the opportunity to show any pain on their faces – and I turn back to the standoff, where Alessia is lying beside tonight's wannabe vampire on the ground, with Rose's own, formerly hidden gun pressed against her temple.

Kitzler stands there, frozen – her hand by her side, and her gun still in its holster – wearing a look of sheer horror on her face. That distant thunder – a loud, shuddering thunderclap – finally sounds out, provoking a jump from her. Between the first bolt of lightning and the following thunder, perhaps two seconds passed.

I take a fast, charged breath, and bound over there. With one hand I grab Kitzler's hand – pulling her fingers away from the grip of her weapon – and take her gun with the other.

Alessia – still lying on the deck beside an emotionless Rose – nods once more at Kitzler while staring me decisively in the eyes. I take the hint and frisk search Kitzler, finding another gun hidden on her. I aim it at her, and she despondently puts her hands on her head.

"You know, you should have hired female security," Alessia says, slowly dragging herself and Rose to their feet, while never letting the barrel of that gun leave her temple. "They're smaller targets, and they're better shots."

"My God," Kitzler mumbles to herself, as Alessia gestures towards the seats they had us sitting on mere minutes ago.

"Now then," Alessia says, in that authoritative, deep Italian accent of hers. "Maybe I do want to talk business after all…"

CHAPTER 16

Another bolt of lightning appears in the distance – a brief, bright white fracture in the pitch-black sky – bringing with it another sudden crack of thunder a few seconds later.

It's half an hour or so since Alessia turned the tables on our hosts. They're both now sitting down, with many loops of insulating tape wrapped around them, restrained entirely to a couch built into the sundeck.

All of that action before – our blind entrance, Rose's uncertain intentions, and Alessia's badass commando moment – was so intense I never really got a chance to admire the yacht.

It's huge; a great, obscene show of wealth and opulence. It's composed of three floors – an upper deck, featuring yet another sundeck with a hot tub – with empty wine glasses bobbing around in its waters – and the captain's cabin, with all the sail controls.

There's a dining room and kitchen on this deck – half-eaten plates of food and a massive refrigerator, whose contents I helped myself to – and a set of berths underdeck, with small, but fabulously appointed rooms. There are artworks: pre-modernist watercolors and oil paintings, which I wouldn't be surprised to find on some list of stolen masterpieces.

This is the kind of environment where dirty, deathly deals are agreed, away from the prying eyes – and laws – of the authorities. I can see why a budding arms dealer would make it their base.

There was even a small crew – three people we found cowering underdeck, including the captain. We let them take the speedboat, telling them to rush back to dry land and not to send anyone out to out to join us. They seemed scared enough to comply.

"It's true, I don't remember you Rose," Alessia says to her, kneeling by her captive body on one knee, in a mirror image of what happened half an hour ago. "But I do remember your mother, and her habit of keeping a gun holstered by her ankle. I remember, because she pulled it on me."

Rose turns her head away, breaking off eye contact with Alessia. I guess hearing a comparison between her and her own mother is too much for her to take.

"The apple doesn't fall far from the tree, huh," Alessia says, one last insult, before rising to her feet again.

I stand back, watching all of this with a beaming smile on my face. I'm more than happy to see Alessia in her element here; kicking arms-dealer ass was what she wanted, and kicking arms-dealer ass is what she's getting.

"What do you want? You can't just be here to talk about that blood," Rose says, defiantly spitting the words like they're laced with acid. "Is it money you're after?"

"No, not money," Alessia replies. "Some of us aren't in this for superyachts and stolen riches, you know."

"Then what?!" Rose barks, showing the first real outburst of emotion I've seen from her yet. "What the hell did you come here for?"

"The blood," I say, as I see another flash of lightning in the distance, with a thunderclap some few seconds later. "Tell us about the blood. Who you stole it for, and why."

"Oh come on, that's what you want to know?" she says, fighting against her restraints briefly – enough crudely spooled tape to suppress a leak – before looking back to me with desperate eyes. Her blonde hair is a mess, no longer the immaculately styled 50s pin-up it once was.

"That's why we're here," I say, as Alessia takes one of the borrowed guns out from behind her and aims it at Kitzler's head.

"Fine, fine, I'll tell you," Rose says. She takes a deep breath, straining against the gray tape binding her to the couch, before continuing.

"It was a contact in Africa. Nubalaya, to be exact. My parents used to do business with the warlords in the second Nubalayan civil war. Really big money. They sold hundreds of thousands of weapons. Billions of units of ammunition. My parents made their names on it."

I hear the rain begin to come down – a slow pitter-patter, slowly increasing in intensity by the second.

"Tell me about that contact," I say to her.

"I don't know much about him, they say he's a warlord who controls one of the disputed regions of Nubalaya. His name is David Faye."

"Why did he want the blood?" I ask, as the rain begins to pummel the decks.

"I don't know!" she yells, making her voice heard above the sound of the rain lashing down on the wood and the fiberglass surfaces of the yacht. "He got in touch through one of my parents' old contacts. He wanted 40 gallons of human blood, and he specified it had to be *rich* blood."

"Rich blood?" Alessia asks.

"Yeah, the blood of the rich. Blood from an affluent, wealthy nation. Blood from a clinic whose doctors were millionaires. You know, that kind of voodoo crap."

I sink my head into my hands. This isn't what I wanted to hear. I'd hoped for some tangible connection with Vincent – some wild, but firm lead that we could pursue. Instead, we've uncovered a strange and completely unrelated tale about a mad African warlord and his taste for wealthy blood.

"I thought a private clinic in Monaco would be the best place to steal the blood from, and make the client happy," Rose says. "He paid on time, we shipped the blood to him, and I've heard nothing from him since."

She struggles against her restraints again before looking back to me with defiant, angered eyes.

"What the hell is this all about?" she cries. "There's a priceless Rembrandt in my room downstairs, and hundreds of thousands of dollars' worth of jewelry in the suitcase, and all you care about is this stupid blood?"

I sigh – a deep breath that involuntarily escapes my throat in an irresistible act of disappointment – and turn to Alessia.

"What do we do with them?" I ask as another thunderclap sounds out, increasing in volume over the course of several seconds.

"Keep them tied up," she says in response before grinning to herself. "I've got an idea."

She sends me looking for a lifeboat while she heads downstairs. It doesn't take long for me to find what I'm looking for – a motorized dinghy by the other side of the boat. Small, but apparently seaworthy.

I walk back up to the deck to see what Alessia has found: reams of documents – massive stacks of papers of different colors, with inventory lists and client info, and probably a hundred other bits of sensitive information – along with a staplegun.

"What's that for?" I ask, gesturing to the staplegun held menacingly in one hand while she sorts through a stack of papers with the other.

"You've decorated a Christmas tree before, haven't you

Kris?" she says to me, as though it's the most casual thing in the world.

I watch in amusement – and a little bit of disgust – as she begins stapling the papers to Rose and Kitzler's restrained bodies, dancing between them, singing occasional verses from some festive Italian song as she does so. I can't even believe what I'm seeing, but compared to her killing two armed men in a flash just before, I suppose this is thankfully tame.

After a couple of minutes of this bizarre horror show, they're both covered in papers – the painful evidence of their wrongdoing – that flap and flutter in the passing wind.

"What do they look like?" Alessia asks me, as Rose turns her head away rebelliously.

"I don't know," I say, honestly. "A pair of IRS agents who tried to serve papers to the wrong household I guess."

Alessia laughs, her eyes wild and full of triumphant, avenging cheer.

"What are you doing, Alessia?" Rose asks, looking up at her while a pink sheet of paper flaps around her cheek. "This isn't you. You're not a cop. You're no angel. You're one of us: a hunter, a killer. I know the kind of person you are, the kind of person who my parents hated, but respected."

Rose's eyes are pleading – two clear blue windows to a desperate mind – but Alessia isn't moved.

"I'm not anything like you," she says, leaning in closer to her. "Maybe, a long time ago, I was. But I've seen things you wouldn't believe. Things aren't like they were. It's a different world."

"What now?" I ask, remembering that those crew members we set free may be calling the authorities by now. Alessia straightens her posture, waves a demure goodbye to Rose, and walks with me to the other side of the deck.

"Okay, this is what we'll do," she murmurs to me, satisfied the sound of the rain will keep her plans for our hosts a surprise. "We'll sail the yacht into the marina. They'll get picked up by the police; after all, we dressed them in all the evidence they need, and if we're lucky we'll damage a few other assholes' superyachts too."

She grins – her eyes lit mischievously by a brief bolt of lightning in the distance – and seems to expect me to congratulate her on that plan, as though it's some delicately constructed masterplan. It's bold, and very *her*, I can give her that.

"You get the lifeboat, I'll set the yacht on a course," she says before turning to go upstairs.

"You can pilot this thing?" I ask her.

"I was a bodyguard to the wealthy, of course I know how to sail!" she yells, never turning or slowing her ascent upstairs.

I turn to go back to the lifeboat, but I catch Rose's eye as I do so – those alluring, hypnotic blue eyes – and she notices.

"You know I'll find you someday," she says, emotionlessly. "I'll get out of this bind. I'm the vampire of Monte Carlo, after all."

"You're no vampire," I tell her back. "Honestly, I'd know, I've met a few."

She looks back at me with a sort of offended bafflement. I could clarify that they were mostly all clones of the first vampire I met, but I won't be doing that.

CHAPTER 17

We've only just made it out of the dinghy and onto shore – feeling the crunch of sand and gravel beneath our feet – when we hear the superyacht collide with the marina. We're perhaps half a mile away, but the sound still reaches us.

It's a grinding, enduring *crunch* of wood and fiberglass and steel, carried along with enough kinetic energy to sustain the noise for a few seconds.

"I guess that was it," is all Alessia says, continuing her walking pace step for step.

We find ourselves in a small French coastal town, with a name Alessia tells me but I forget almost instantly. There are a dozen holiday homes – lit in silver moonlight as the clouds begin to subside from the passing storm – and an empty, dilapidated lighthouse, whose spotlight I can see is broken even from here.

Beyond that, there's a quaint little rail station – the type you only see in Europe with pretty painted columns and a decorated canopy roof over each platform – and a café, barely still open at this late hour, whose dim orange light from indoors illuminates the scene.

"I'll call Baynes, you do the rest," Alessia says to me, taking her cellphone out.

"The rest?"

"Coffee, dark," she says with a smile.

I walk into the café, a small space with a mere handful of tables and chairs, and haplessly struggle to order two coffees from a woman who speaks no English.

When I think it's mission accomplished, I go back outside and sit at a small table, the only one guarded from the earlier rainfall. When Alessia is done with the call – a succession of bored-sounding *yeps* and *nopes* – she comes to sit down, with a tedious look on her face.

"He's just landed in Nice," she says, not exactly what I expected to hear.

"Nice?" I ask.

She gestures over the hill and the dark horizon, towards the west.

"Over there," she says, sarcastically. "The place we got off the airplane Kris, come on."

"I know where Nice is. I don't know why Baynes is there," I clarify, my tone slightly aggravated. "I thought the budget was stretched. Why is he meeting us out here in Europe?"

"God knows," she says, looking back at the open café door, no doubt wondering where those coffees are. "He says he's been trying to call me, but we were busy playing cards. My cell has been switched off."

I can't even imagine what would motivate Baynes to drop everything, rush onto a plane and throw himself into the action zone. An irresistible gambling addiction he's kept quiet up until now? European Elvis Presley convention? The possibilities are tragic, and endless.

"He's getting us train tickets," she says. "We should be able to hop on a train from this platform and meet him in Nice."

Before I can say another word, our coffees arrive – that

tired-eyed woman hobbles out, holding a tray of two tall, dark coffees, and then turns and heads back inside without a word, closing the café up for the night as she does so.

"That was all very weird, wasn't it?" I say after putting the cup to my lips and deciding it's way too hot. Alessia grunts an inquiring response, and I continue: "The arms dealer we were hunting. The stolen blood. None of it panned out like I'd hoped."

"Oh, I wouldn't say that," she replies. "Do you know how much better the world will be with one more member of the Delissalt family out of business? We did good – no – *great* work tonight."

"It was like some ghoulish family counseling session," I say, staring off into the dark night's sky. "But with guns and bullets and poker chips."

She laughs before burying her face inside her coffee cup.

"You met her parents," I say to her as she resurfaces; not really a question, but definitely an invitation to talk.

"Yeah, real nice, salt of the earth folks," she says, sarcastically. "What do you want me to say? They were terrible, as all arms dealers are. He was a Harvard psychopath with a taste for the finer things, she was the daughter of a bank robber with a hunger for drugs to feed. And as we found out, all their worst traits combined to create our little miss vampire."

She picks up her cup again, but quickly puts it back down again when she gets another inescapable urge to speak.

"The Delissalts were the types to be selling arms and ammunition to both sides of a war, no questions asked. They were evil, ruthless, cold. They'd screw anyone over for a dollar; they'd devour their own children if there was something in it for them. And, hell, their own parents, judging by everything we heard tonight."

She pauses, closing her eyes firmly as if banishing a bad memory from her mind, before opening them again and taking another sip.

"The last time I met them it was on a yacht just like the last one," she says after a few moments of silence. "It was an arms deal, it went wrong, and it became a horrible mess."

And with that one, ultra-ambiguous statement, she goes quiet again. When I hear Alessia talk about her past like this, she strikes me as a fascinatingly rich, if somewhat dark tapestry. Coarse, colorful, and fraying at the edges. I get the feeling that this recollection is one thread I shouldn't pull.

"And as for her, mademoiselle Rose Delphine Delissalt," Alessia says after a minute or so, "she was unique. A unique collector's item; a prototype monster that somehow escaped the lab, just like our friend Vincent. Don't feel bad about losing his scent."

She goes for her coffee again, and I make another attempt at drinking my own. Finding it merely intolerably hot, rather than like kissing the surface of the sun as it was before, I gulp down a mouthful and look back out to the stars. I hear distant sirens – the police descending on our handiwork at the marina.

"We did great back there, Kris," Alessia says, before grinning, and jokingly punching me in the arm. "And you didn't let us down, either with your mouth or your card playing."

I smile back at her, but I can't completely hide my disappointment.

"But he's still out there," I tell her. "And we're back to square one."

She takes a deep breath into her cup of coffee – I see a cloud of vapor exhaled out of her cup – before she takes a sip and speaks again.

"Why are we doing this? Why are we flying around the world, dodging bullets and risking our lives, Kris?" she asks me. "Aren't we trying to make the world a better place? That's why we're hunting Vincent down, and that's why taking out Rose Delissalt was an unambiguous good; a flawless victory for us. She'd have run that arms-dealing empire just as ruthlessly as her parents, if not more so."

She takes another sip – an animated, triumphant sip of her coffee, throwing herself back into her seat and casting her head back like only an Italian can.

"You know, if we go on like this and catch a few more supervillains," she adds, "the world will be a perfect utopia way before that kid wakes up out of his casket and resurfaces."

I laugh – a dejected, disenchanted laugh – and hear something like a distant train, sounding not too dissimilar to the thunderstorm that still echoes in my memory.

"I think that's our train," Alessia says, taking one last gulp of her drink and climbing to her feet.

I follow her – leaving half a cup of bitter, black lava behind – and follow her to the platform of the train station. It's a couple of platforms – one either side of the rails – and a small building that appears to be closed up at this time of night. The whole place is lit in sickly light that illuminates the brickwork a shade of green, like a dirty fish tank.

"And you know," she says, one more thing apparently being on her mind. "Even when we find him, and deal with him, it's not like either of us will ever go back to peaceful civilian life. It ain't us."

I don't say anything. The train gets ever closer, and ever louder, until it slows to a stop by our platform and we both get on, a bitter taste still lingering in my mouth.

CHAPTER 18

"Bonjour!" Baynes yells across the room to us, briefly rising to his feet and waving before dropping down to his seat again. He has a napkin tied into the collar of his shirt, upon which several dark-red stains are present, like bloody fingerprints. "Come join me!"

Alessia and I share a brief glance – a dreary understanding that it's going to be a long night – before walking across the empty restaurant floor and taking the two seats beside him.

We're in Baynes' hotel, a small and old building built from beautiful beige brick, with dark-green vines that reach around the walls, and bay windows composed of small panes of glass, held in by aging black frames.

This is the hotel restaurant – a picturesque little room with tiled floors and pretty amber lampshades – and it's empty. God knows how he – a brash American, holding a takeout bag – convinced the staff to let him in at this late hour.

"Great work, great work, guys," he says, putting a chicken wing to his lips and chewing the flesh off it. "Alessia told me about the Delissalt girl. I can't even believe it, it's an outcome beyond my wildest dreams. Like we hit a jackpot or something."

"A jackpot?" I ask, but he doesn't seem to hear me. Instead, he wipes a bead of sweat from his forehead, and his fingertips against his napkin.

"My God, they said these were spicy, but –" he coughs, interrupting himself. He looks terrible – a pale, panting, sweating wreck – reduced to goblin status by what appears to be twenty spicy chicken wings.

"Why did you come here?" I ask him, but again, he's suffering his own existential torment right now, and isn't listening.

"They never had this sort of spice when I was younger," he says, panting and fanning himself with the napkin. "This sort of spice is Prometheus' flame, it should be forbidden to us mere mortals. Maybe the world is in the state it's in because we stole the Gods' precious treasures, you know?"

"What the hell are you talking about?" I cry, as Alessia looks to me and rolls her eyes.

Finally, that gets his attention, and he stops blathering long enough to wipe his mouth with the napkin and look me in the eyes.

"I came here because I wanted to update you on the mission, and an added objective to consider," he says, tears streaming from each eye. "Your cell phones were understandably off, and I know you'd already destroyed the laptop, so I thought I'd come to Monaco in person to update you in person, and investigate myself whether anything had gone wrong."

"What added objective?" I ask, somewhat distracted to be asking this of a man with tears rolling down his cheeks.

"I managed to negotiate a bounty for the capture and incarceration of Kitzler and her mysterious boss," he says, still stumbling over each word like his tongue is laced with deep heat. "I wanted to tell you both to consider turning them into the authorities, you know, if it didn't turn out to be Vincent after all."

He takes his glasses off and wipes them too, before continuing.

"But then I landed here, and Alessia informed me that you'd already done it – Kitzler and the Delissalt daughter, delivered to the police in a nice, gift-wrapped package. Beautiful, beautiful work, you guys. This will prove very lucrative for us, and our efforts around the world."

Lucrative? I watched two cops get shot in the head today – their brains splattered all over the wall; their partners and children deprived of a husband and father – and now I hear that the true sum of all our accomplishments is a lucrative bounty? We didn't capture Vincent, but we did capture one big bag with a dollar sign on it?

"Did you know about this?" I turn to Alessia and ask her, my tone hard and terse, betraying how I feel about it.

"No," she says, before shaking her head nonchalantly. "But it makes sense."

I pause, feeling myself filling with a bitter, heated anger. He did it again – he made me a mercenary, throwing myself into storms of bullets on the other side of the world, all for a secretive reward, one I don't get to learn about until after the job is done.

Baynes, on the other hand, couldn't be happier. He reaches for his glass and picks it up into the air victoriously.

"Cheers to you both," he says.

I see those stains on his napkin – dark-red barbecue-sauce stains, looking just like the brain matter I saw sprayed across the casino walls – and feel I can't contain myself any longer. I smash my fist on the table – making even Alessia flinch – before reaching over and grabbing Baynes by his collar.

"The hell is wrong with you!?" he yells into my face, his spicy breath making me blink repeatedly.

"You did it again, didn't you!?" I cry. "You made me into a drone!"

"A what?!" he shouts back, looking to Alessia in confusion, and perhaps a little panic.

"A mercenary! A mindless worker ant!"

"What are you saying, man?" he asks, gently pulling himself away from my grip on him.

"This is just like Madrevaria all over again," I say as I relinquish my grip and he flings himself back in his seat, before adjusting his collar. "Sending us across the world for a big, secret pot of gold."

Alessia leans back in her chair and crosses her arms, no doubt thrilled to hear us digging up that old chestnut again. Baynes, on the other hand, is uncharacteristically quiet.

"Did you know about this bounty before you sent us out there?" I ask him, slowly and sternly.

"Okay, just listen to me," he says, his voice monotonal and measured again. "Yes, there was a bounty for Ada-Marie Kitzler, and another for the successor to the Delissalt empire, but I didn't know that we'd be able to claim those bounties. I mean, we are barely allowed out on the streets, let alone able to consider ourselves established bounty hunters!"

He goes to adjust his collar again, leaving a small, dark-red stain on it.

"As soon as you left, I looked into it, and negotiated a no-questions-asked-fee for Kitzler. That's when I flew out here and found out you'd bagged Delissalt too."

"Man, you're a professional liar," I tell him, feeling that heat and fury surging to my fingertips.

"We sent you here to look for Vincent because the intel was good!" he yells, leaning across the table at me. "The stolen shipment of blood, the Swiss education, the whole vampire thing, it all fits! It was a good lead – wrong, of course – but the intelligence was sound. *That's* why we flew you both out here."

He picks up another chicken wing, before taking a second look at it and throwing it back down in frustration.

"You took down a world-renowned arms dealer," he says, jabbing a finger at the table with each word. "Someone that civilians and governments alike feared. A true agent of chaos; a dealer of death and destruction, and as luck would have it, you earned some money doing it, and you're mad?"

I look to Alessia, who glances back at me with reasoning, understanding eyes, the sort of expression that quietly asks me to reconsider my anger. I suppose she's taken a few bounties in her time, and she doesn't appear at all disturbed by this one.

"I know, Kris, you're frustrated because we didn't find your guy," Baynes says. "Well, we are too. And we're not going to stop looking. I know you've also had bad experiences in the past; experiences where you've tried to do good, and it hasn't panned out that way."

I snort derisively. I don't much appreciate him referring to my experiences in Aljarran or pursuing the Quiet One, even though deep down, I know he's right. Perhaps that's why it hurts.

"But, please," he says, "take the win on this one. It was a great accomplishment, and it's yours."

I close my eyes and take a breath. When I open them again, he's sitting there right in front of me, reaching for the chicken wings again, covered in blood-red stains, salivating like one big, greedy pig with its snout in the trough. The sight nauseates me.

"I'm going to get some air," I tell them both, rising to my feet.

Baynes says something as I turn my back and begin pacing outside, and I don't hear it. I burst through a fire door, and feel the unwelcome embrace of the cold, but humid night; the kind of night that brings you out into a freezing-cold sweat.

I don't like waltzing out of there in some dramatic scene,

but I can take some alone time while I calm myself down, can't I?

Kris, Vega says, *we should talk about this.*

Maybe I spoke too soon…

CHAPTER 19

"Vega," I say, exasperated, and looking around to ensure I truly am alone, in terms of other human beings at least. "To what do I owe the pleasure?"

I would consider that a sarcastic remark, but my sentiment is the same as the others', Vega says. *I believe you should consider this moment a pleasure. You defeated and turned in to the police a malevolent force in the world. That's a great achievement; one you would have been proud of once.*

I don't say anything back, at least not yet. There's an aircon unit or a pump system nearby, providing a constant monotonous humming. I'm beside the hotel's gardens, in a damp brick terrace, lit by the dim orange light of the hotel rooms upstairs.

"First, it was Alessia who defeated and turned them both in to the police, I was just a tag-along," I point out. "And secondly, it would be nice to feel like I'm the master of my own destiny for one, brief time in my life."

Vega doesn't say anything, and I go on.

"He's right, though. I do still think about Aljarran, and all the other mistakes," I say, my voice wavering with emotion.

I think the way you're feeling is completely understandable,

Vega says. *For the first twenty-four years of your life, you were ruled by your heart condition and the resultant anxiety, always a passenger, never the driver. As soon as you acquired the nanomachine network – and become stronger than anyone in the world – you threw yourself into the most dangerous situations on the planet, and saved many lives, but by the same token, endured unintended consequences.*

I sit on a ramshackle brickwork wall – a layer of rainwater soaking into my pants – and speak.

"And the successes I did have – Charles Forrest, Silas McCaulay, and Rose Delissalt – they feel like someone else's. Hollow victories I was manipulated into making, on behalf of some other, scheming force. The CIA, Baynes, or frankly, you…"

I pause again, having some strange feeling – in the cold embrace of this dim light, uncomfortable humidity, and that monotonous humming sound – that I could be back in that subway train. I shake my head and purge the thought from my mind.

"I just want to feel like I can use these powers to change the world, and do it on my own terms."

There's another noise from somewhere – footsteps scratching against the moist bricks – and I dart up from the wall and to my feet.

"Kris?" a voice calls out, an impossible voice. One that I recognize, but from a long way away.

"Hello?" I call out.

A short, portly figure slowly walks around the corner of the building, and even though I recognized his voice, I can barely believe my eyes.

"Dante," I say with surprise, my voice echoing in the night. "You're here too!?"

"Oh, well, 'what's up' to you too my friend," he says, an irritated smirk on his face. He walks beside me, looking me up and down. "I flew out with Baynes."

"I'm sorry, I just didn't expect this to become a company outing," I say, and hold my hand out to him. He shakes my hand and leans on the wall next to me.

"Baynes said you objected to the money thing, and –"

"It doesn't matter," I interrupt him to say. "It's done. We did it, right? I'm taking the win."

"You don't sound convinced," he says with a bashful smile. "You didn't get your bad guy. I suppose that matters to you, doesn't it?"

"Yeah," I say. "We're slapping ourselves on the back for a job well done, and forgetting the real reason we're out here."

"We're listening in on the entire planet, Kris," Dante says. "We have 300 custom-made scripts scanning and translating 900 news wires in 150 countries. There ain't a single story about Paraguayan vampire movie fan clubs or cow exsanguinations in Belarus we don't read. The hunt is on, every single day. If he's out there, and he's still alive, we will find him."

I smile at him, and he goes on.

"It's true, we didn't get our bad guy, but we got a lot of other people's bad guy, and that really matters. There's a kid out there that won't take a bullet to the face because there's no wannabe vampire queen to sell that bullet."

"You're right," I tell him.

"You remember me saying about my kid brother?" he asks, stroking his bearded chin.

I nod at him.

"He's going to college next year. Law. I keep in touch with him the best I can, but every day I ask God to watch over him. It's a cruel, cruel world, and I'm thankful we're in the business of making it better."

He laughs and puts his head in his hands as though he's exhausted; I guess I haven't even asked him how the flight was yet.

"I mean, Jesus," he says, chuckling to himself, "there's a

vampire running around out there. There are nanotechnological superheroes and badass Italian commandos running after them. There are murderous arms dealers and genocidal cult leaders and drug lords and everything else. I think the world needs all the help it can get."

He stops chuckling and looks at me; his large, brown eyes tired but earnest.

"I guess the point I'm trying to make is that we're a team, and I'm glad of it. Sure, Baynes is a mind-numbing old jerk, but he's good at what he does, and this bounty money is going to ensure we can find Vincent, and do it quicker."

He holds his hand out, and I grab it in a show of brotherly love.

"Get some rest," I tell him. "We'll talk tomorrow."

He says his goodbyes and strolls away.

I don't feel that anger within me anymore. Have I always been such a sucker for pep talks? Or is it just that for the first time in years, I feel like I'm part of a family again, with all the tears and tantrums that come with it.

I push myself off the wall and go inside, hoping that for all his jubilation at making some money today, Baynes remembered to get me a room.

CHAPTER 20

I get a better night's sleep than I've had in a while, the only thing waking me being the caterwauling from a pair of drunk British tourists at 3 a.m., apparently locked in their own herculean struggle to hunt down their hotel room.

I jump out of bed and almost stand on the laptop Dante has apparently placed in my room. I take a shower and throw on yesterday's clothes, before going downstairs. There, I find Baynes and Dante digging into a breakfast of bread rolls and ham.

"Ah, our very own Rambo," is how Baynes greets me, as exuberant as ever. I wave my hand unenthusiastically and join them at their table.

"We've been looking into that name Delissalt provided," Dante says, making me wonder when anyone gets any sleep. "David Faye."

"Oh yeah?" I say, robbing a bread roll off Baynes' plate, an act that earns me an irritated glance.

"He's a real piece of work," Baynes says, watching me put the bread roll into my mouth and chew. "We're talking massacres, genocides, entire villages burned to the ground. Just the worst things you can imagine."

"Guess we don't like him, then," I say, flippantly. "What did he want with the blood?"

"We don't know that yet," Dante says. "If Delissalt is telling the truth, and he really did want wealthy people's blood, then we really don't know what to make of it."

"Some weird, religious thing perhaps," Baynes says, shaking his head. "Back when I was at the agency, we didn't take much notice of the Nubalayan civil wars, but you can usually trust those warlord types to be into some pretty hair-raising stuff. There was a guy we tracked who would charge into battle naked, he thought God made him invincible or something."

"Maybe I should test that out," I say, before taking Baynes' last bread roll off his plate.

"For God's sake, man, there's a buffet!" he cries, loud enough to draw glances from the table across.

"You don't think there's a possibility this warlord – this David Faye guy – is hiding Vincent?" I ask between mouthfuls.

"Doubt it," Dante says, crossing his arms, revealing the extensive tattoos on his forearms. "There's no Matriel presence in Nubalaya. In fact, there's barely any corporate presence. No resources, abject poverty, no water. The country's gone from British colony to dictatorship to civil war to democracy to civil war again."

Baynes stands up and wanders off in the direction of the buffet. When he returns, I see he's holding three bread rolls, one of which he throws onto my plate.

"There's no reason for Vincent to go there," Dante continues when Baynes sits back down. "It's a war-torn, starving, desperate nation. One of the poorest countries in the world. It's no vacation destination, and there's no Matriel laboratory there to burn to the ground."

"Well, then I guess that lead is dead," I say. Baynes

flinches a little as I say it – a tiny recoil into himself, that suggests to me there's something else on his mind.

"There is something else to discuss," he says, never making eye contact with me.

"What?"

"This is one of the most wanted men in the entire world," Baynes says. "He has a list of war crimes as long as my arm. He's a suspect in numerous massacres, and it's said he's stolen millions upon millions of dollars in a country where people are still starving. There are entire organizations founded with the mission of bringing this man to justice. He's the devil."

I wait for him to speak again, but he doesn't. He sits there with his hands on the table, looking me in the eyes expectantly.

"And?" I finally ask.

"Look," he says, reaching out to me with one conciliatory hand. "I know you're not going to like this, but please hear me out. If we find and capture this man, we'll be doing Africa – and indeed, the entire world – a massive favor. We'll be heroes. And then there's the bounty, a sum of –"

I stand up, sending the chair behind me screeching along the ground.

"Wait," Baynes says, "just sit down, will you?"

"Will you stop pimping me out to dodgy governments and police agencies?" I ask, probably a little too loudly. The next table along give me an odd look; I feel bad until I realize they may be that drunk British couple from outside my room.

"Kris, please, sit and listen to what we have to say," Dante says.

"What, you too?" I ask. Neither of them says any more – they just look at me with those pleading, puppy-dog eyes – and that couple at the other table are still staring at me. Slowly, I pull my chair back to the table from behind me and sit back down.

"With the kind of money they're offering for David Faye, we could radically step up our search for Vincent," Baynes says, slowly and cautiously. "I'm talking the hiring of special investigators. A sophisticated listening system, public campaigns in every major language. There'll be nowhere for him to hide."

"Man, can you really imagine me in Africa?" I ask. "I don't know anything about African cultures. I don't speak the language, whatever language it is. It's a big place, and I can't even drive!"

"We can create a convincing cover story for you," Dante says. "An American aid worker, something like that."

"Can you concoct an excuse as to why this aid worker carries a gun?"

"Hah, that's easy, you carry a gun because you're American," Dante says with a chuckle. "I'm going to send you some intel on this guy. I want you to read it and see if it doesn't change your mind."

"It's all on you, Kris," Baynes says, looking despondently at his empty plate. "If you don't wanna do it, we won't say another word about it. But, have a read of what Dante has put together. And then talk to us again."

"Fine, if it'll shut you both up, I will," I say, before rising to my feet again, and remembering a phrase from a news show I saw last week. "Mission creep, you know that term?"

"Mission creep, of course I know that term, I used to work in the CIA didn't I," Baynes says, with an amused look on his face.

"I liked the term; I looked it up, even," I say. "A gradual change in objectives in a military mission, resulting in a long, painful unplanned commitment. You guys, you're the mission-creep committee."

"Message received, Kris," Baynes says, crossing his arms nonchalantly.

And with that unwieldy, slightly awkward insult, I turn and leave.

CHAPTER 21

When I get back upstairs and to my room, I sit down at the desk – a small, dusty surface with mug stains so darkly imprinted you couldn't remove them with a blowtorch – and open the laptop I nearly destroyed this morning.

There's a small shaft of light escaping from the side of the closed drapes, illuminating a million particles of dust floating in the air. It distracts me long enough to forget what I'm doing, only remembering when the 'ping' of a new email drags me back to reality, and Baynes' latest bounty.

"Okay, one read through," I tell myself as I open the first of several documents Dante sent me.

The first thing I read is an account of the civil wars in Nubalaya, and a brief history of the country itself. A former British colony, it was granted independence in the late 1940s, sliding into a military dictatorship that lasted some twenty years of corruption and starvation.

Over the next few decades, the first Nubalayan civil war would break out – a brutal series of battles that would consume the entire nation – followed by a period of relative calm. Thirty years of a fledgling democracy, whereupon the wealth and wellbeing of Nubalaya began to increase again, albeit slowly.

An attempted military-led coup of the country's democratically elected government – as well as the assassination of the president – would plunge Nubalaya into another series of bloody conflicts, beginning the second Nubalayan civil war in 2006. A thirteen-year-long grinding war of attrition between two ethnic groups, seeing every major city devastated.

There was an uneasy ceasefire agreement seven years ago – a shaky peace that's persisted up until today – that officially ended the war, but didn't quite unite the country as intended.

As part of the ceasefire agreement – a massive, UN-brokered document, with more loopholes, cut-outs, and exceptions than a promise from Randall Baynes – parts of the country remained under autonomous control by rebel groups and local warlords. Nubalayan land in name, but almost lawless in practice.

Every picture I look at is the same: landscapes of devasted, bombed out shells of buildings, standing on the horizon like the sun-blasted skeletons of some horrible, prehistoric beast. Lines of refugees tens of thousands of people long. Children holding assault rifles. Men and women lying motionless in the dirt.

I stop clicking through the pictures and move onto the next document, a history of David Faye, who's suspected to be hiding in one of these areas, perhaps even leading one as a vengeful warlord.

The very first thing I read makes my jaw drop. David Faye was forcibly recruited into one of the Nubalayan rebel militias when he was merely seven years old. Even at that age, he fought without fear, rising to be an alleged captain at the age of twelve, and a colonel of an entire brigade – the so-called 'Avenging Angels' – by the age of fifteen. Today, he's thought to be twenty-three years of age, and mostly known by one name: warlord.

There's a picture of him as a thirteen-year-old boy. He wears loosely fitting, camouflaged clothing, and a beret on his head with a silver star. Despite his youth, he carries a rocket-propelled grenade launcher on his back, and seemingly isn't troubled by its weight. His face is slender and thin, and his neck wide.

He wears an uncertain expression on his face: stern and calculating, and yet still so very childlike, and tinged with a certain doubt.

The stories of his efforts within the militia are numerous, and gruesome. His platoon allegedly cut through the Nubalayan countryside like a wildfire, burning entire villages to the ground and salting the earth so no crop will ever grow. They massacred hundreds in every town; men, women, and children gone without a second thought.

I come to a particularly ghastly story of Faye's fighters finding a church, whose pastor was responsible for hiding the adjacent village's children from forcible conscription. Faye and his men murdered the pastor, found the children hiding within the church, and incinerated it, with the children locked inside.

"Jesus Christ," I say to myself out loud.

It's extremely grim reading, Vega says. *The use of children in the military during this period of human history sadly isn't uncommon. Typically, if you have a conflict in a country in which the population is young, and men of fighting age are scarce – due to the first Nubalayan civil war, in this case – warlords and militias will seek to recruit children to do the fighting.*

"Man, I had no idea," I say to him, clicking through another set of pictures. There's the church – a series of stone columns, blackened by fire and smoke – and beside them, row after row of black, burned bodies, mere scorch marks in the rubble.

I pull my face away from the laptop screen, feeling a tear forming at the edge of my eye. I manage to resist it, and after a minute of staring at a wall in solemn silence, I find the courage to look back to that screen, and the horrors that remain.

I pick up where I left off, reading the rest of David Faye's biography. The UN-brokered ceasefire deal didn't specifically mention child soldiers – a particularly shameful episode that international lawyers and Nubalaya's new powerbrokers wanted to forget – and so, many platoons like David Faye's went unacknowledged in the ceasefire agreement.

As a result, many of the warlords like Faye managed to slip through the cracks; many of the former child soldiers slipped into the shadows, joining criminal organizations or developing drug addictions to numb the pain, or they joined the various remnant militias in the lawless autonomous regions.

David Faye – unique in his own right as a child soldier turned warlord – is believed to live inside an autonomous region named Free Zimbala, where there exists a small militia still loyal to him.

The final document Dante sent me is a collection of photographs, which I almost can't bring myself to open.

After a deep breath, I do so, immediately seeing what appears to be a class photograph. Three rows of children, all with blank, vacant expressions on their faces. They can't be older than ten, but each of them holds a gun up to the camera, a grotesque mockery of what should be the happiest, most carefree time in a person's life.

I submit myself to being buried beneath an avalanche of gruesome, unforgiveable images. Mass graves: bodies stacked atop one another, ten feet high. The corpses of women bayonetted to death in an alleged initiation ceremony to Faye's platoon. A town square, whose uneven, sandy brickwork is dyed dark crimson by an earlier massacre.

Another tear forms in my eye, but this time I don't let up. I go on, until those tears are running down my face.

"I can't do this," I say to myself, moving the mouse to click away from the document again. Before I make it though, something catches my eye: a logo I recognize from somewhere. A large wooden crate – a shipment of ammunition, by the looks of it – stamped with the same mundane logo I saw Alessia stapling to Rose Delissalt.

"That logo," I say to Vega.

I see it, he replies. *It's the same one that appeared on shipping manifests that were affixed to Rose Delissalt's body. I would imagine her parents had a fake shipping company, under the auspices of which they exported arms and ammunition all around the world.*

"What was it, Alessia said?" I ask. "That those monsters would arm both sides in a civil war, and then stand back and watch?"

Something along those lines.

I close the laptop and go back to staring at that shaft of golden, dusty light, escaping from the side of the closed drapes; a purifying searchlight, dragging me away from the terrors I've just seen, and back into my world. My cushy, comfortable, complacent world.

I've spent days chasing bad guys in one of the wealthiest areas on earth. Even when I was held captive, it was in almost unimaginable luxury, on a multimillion-dollar superyacht. I know nothing of the sorts of suffering the people of Nubalaya have been through, my experiences in Aljarran and elsewhere merely scratching the surface of that kind of pain.

"David Faye, warlord," I say to myself, crossing my arms and rocking forwards and backwards ever so slightly. "What do you want with wealthy westerners' blood?"

I feel like there's a piece of this puzzle missing, and a great part of my last business dealings with the Delissalts left unfinished.

"What do you think?" I ask Vega.

You'd be going to a very dangerous land with almost no knowledge of the people, the language, the culture, and the customs. In addition, David Faye is an extremely dangerous man; he's proved that in his leadership of one of the most fearsome militias in the war, especially as he was himself a child. If you can find him – and that's a big if – he won't go down without a fight.

"And are there any reasons I shouldn't do it?" I ask, sarcastically.

The money would indeed be useful for your search for Vincent, Vega says. *It appears David Faye is responsible for a lot of death, destruction, and suffering, and he might still inflict more. In terms of their abilities to inflict large numbers of casualties in the world, David Faye and Vincent are alike. Vincent has the power, Faye has the experience and organization.*

"I must be out of my mind," I say, putting my head in my hands.

I keep my mouth closed and let silence reign, at least for a minute or so. A brief period to close my eyes and see the tear-filled faces of those bereaved mothers and enslaved children staring back at me; a remorseless veil of hurtful anguish pulled across my mind.

I reach for the cellphone on my desk, and click through a couple of times. There's a ring, and I put it to my ear.

"Kris," Baynes' nasally voice says, with a chorus of ambient chatter in the background. I guess he's still at breakfast.

"Get in, get him, get out, get paid," I say to him. "That's it right? No secret objectives? No complicating factors?"

"That's right," he says.

"Just the single, straightforward objective, and the chance to abort at any time if Vincent surfaces."

"We can arrange that," he says, the sense of smug accomplishment now evident in his voice.

I disconnect the call and throw the cell back onto the desk before rubbing my eyes again, hard enough to provoke a sharp pain, trying in vain to scrub those images from my mind. After a couple more minutes, I open the laptop again, and see a word written on David Faye's photograph, scrawled on it in black pen.

Warlord, Vega reads. *It seems an appropriately formidable name.*

CHAPTER 22

Baynes' mouth is leaking again.

Frantic words and aggravating phrases are spilling out of it. CIA terms and idioms I've never heard in my entire life – that make not a bit of sense – followed by fanciful tales of his experiences in Africa on agency business.

He talks about it fondly – like he recounts his college wrestling career – only the instances he describes are weird and mundane.

"And, and, and I suppose it was within that particular people's culture to brew up a red paste, a sort of thick, viscous, deep-red cream," he says, turning his head to look back at us from the front passenger side. "And the people would apply it to their faces and bodies, for cooling and aesthetic purposes I suppose."

Alessia is lucky enough to escape the brunt of this lecture by virtue of driving. Dante and myself – seated in the backseats – aren't quite as lucky.

"Only when my colleague and I came to apply the paste to our bodies did we realize something was wrong," he continues. "There was an itching, burning sensation. It grew until it was unbearable. We started to scratch the paste off our skins. People were talking, pointing, laughing at us."

"That's great Randall," Dante says in an optimistic, but not entirely present tone. I look across at him to see his face illuminated entirely by the light of his phone. I'm not sure he's even listening. Why didn't I think of doing that?

"Maybe a bit of friendly sabotage, Baynes," I tell him. "You know, maybe they didn't appreciate the presence of a couple of undercover spooks among them. Laced your red paste with some stinging nettles."

He laughs, banging his palm onto his thigh, taking way more pleasure in the thought of getting poisoned than he probably should.

"Good times, good times," he says, turning back around and looking to the road.

"You know, it isn't such a bad point though," I point out. "I'm going to walk out of an airport in deepest Africa, and into the dark unknown. I'll be mistrusted, feared, maybe even hated. How am I going to find the warlord without the co-operation of the community?"

"I've got something figured out," Baynes says, a threat as sinister as anything I've ever heard. "Just you wait and see."

Alessia drops the three of us off at Nice Côte d'Azur Airport, before saying a gruff goodbye and speeding off somewhere else, it being far too dangerous to put her on a plane right now, what with her being in a room with two dead cops just the other day. I, on the other hand, earlier changed my face back to the one I flew here in; the one on my fake passport.

Baynes and I say our farewells to Dante at the departures lobby, he being asked to go back to New York and resume the search for Vincent there. When he's on a plane, Baynes and I walk across a packed departures lobby, find a nook inside a franchise coffee shop, and talk over our next moves.

"I put the feelers out," Baynes says, perhaps using the

same feelers to prod a bagel around on a plate in front of him. "We've got a meeting with a man named Sunday Mufumba in Lushoto. His people will meet us straight off the plane."

"Okay," I say, waiting for an elaborate explanation that never comes. Instead, Baynes finally decides to pick the bagel up and take a bite. "Who is that, and where is that?"

"Lushoto is the capital city and the current seat of government of Nubalaya," Baynes says, in a self-satisfied tone that suggests he thinks I should already have known that. "And Sunday Mufumba is the Minister for the Interior."

"Minister for the Interior?" I ask.

"The government ministry responsible for internal security. Immigration, policing, all that fun stuff," he answers. "I suppose you could say he's the third or fourth most important man in Nubalaya's government."

"Right, of course," I say, putting any misplaced notions of interior design out of my mind.

"He's the man responsible for David Faye's largest bounty, by far. This is a job requested and quietly advertised by the Nubalayan government itself. Evidently, they wish to bring David Faye to justice."

"Why can't they do it themselves?" I ask, before remaining quiet as a man pulls a large suitcase past our table. "I mean, they could send the entire army after him. Why hire a westerner to do it?"

"I suspect we'll find that out soon enough," Baynes says. "What matters is that Mufumba, and hopefully, some of the apparatus of the Ministry for the Interior, will be able to provide some amount of support for us on the ground. Sure, a lot of people won't trust you – a dumb-looking westerner – and rightly so."

I cross my arms and look at him curiously. Am I supposed to be offended by that?"

"But," Baynes continues, "we'll have some level of support from the government, albeit covert support."

He looks back to his bagel before I see his eyes narrow with a certain sort of aggrievement, and he speaks again.

"Nubalaya was a British colony. A place where the natural resources were exploited; where the local population was subjugated and humiliated. In Nubalaya there's a longstanding mistrust of the western world, and it's easy to see why. It just makes me sick."

My jaw drops to about an inch above the ground. I'm so bemused I can barely even make a sound. Fortunately, Baynes doesn't notice – he's back to studying his bagel – and I don't have to explain how hilarious it is to hear a CIA man lament a wealthy empire meddling in everyone else's affairs.

He eats his bagel, while I turn my head and look out of the adjacent pane of glass, into the hectic lobby outside.

It's packed full of the precisely two types of airport traveler: the rushing, frantic type – a suitcase in every hand, a bag on every back, and a tense, strained expression – or the bored type – sleeping along a row of seats, or knocking back shots with increasing drowsiness.

Seeing people sleeping in the aisles – propping their heads up on their bags and burying their faces in books – brings me unwelcome flashbacks to the airport raid two years ago. I shake my head and turn back to Baynes before I find myself drowned in bad memories, and in the process, lock eyes with a wearied child, no older than ten, sitting at the other side of the coffee shop.

I think again of that picture of David Faye – probably the same age, but of vastly different experiences and traumas, or at least, I hope. Seeing him in that picture, encumbered by a weapon of war, and even knowing all the terrible things he's done in his life, it's impossible not to take the picture at face value: that of a child, forced to fight.

"It's weird," I say, looking back to Baynes, who's perusing the menu, his bagel long gone.

"What is?" he asks, looking up to meet my eyeline, before moving to adjust his collar with both hands.

"I've only seen one picture of David Faye," I say to him. "And he was thirteen years old in it. Granted, he had a rocket launcher strapped to his back, but he was still just a child. It's a strange feeling, traveling out to capture this bloodthirsty criminal, when the only mental image I can summon of him is from when he was a boy."

"Maybe this will help," Baynes says, reaching into his back pocket and taking out his cellphone. "The Minister for the Interior sent this through earlier. I was going to show you when we do the briefing, but you should see it now."

He holds out his cellphone to me, and on it, I see a grainy, imprecise picture of an adult man. Even with its imperfections, the picture is striking enough for me to reach out and grab the cellphone from him for a closer look.

He's taller, wider, and older, but I can see it's the same person, with the same slender, haunted face as the boy I saw earlier. He wears what appears to be a scuffed, blue tactical vest, and holds an AK-47 high in the air.

That's not nearly the most noteworthy thing about the picture, though. That would be the shape he's in: sharp, toned, tense muscles, rippling out of his dark skin. Bulging biceps, throbbing veins, and deep valleys between each muscle group. Every sinew looks like a coiled spring, ready to erupt.

Even with the imperfections of the picture his body is intimidating. He seems tall and slender, but everything that could conceivably bulge with muscle, does bulge with muscle. He's not unfeasibly massive and cumbersome like a bodybuilder. He seems taut and able; a man who's trained his body for blood-drenched violence.

"Jesus," I say out loud, before handing the cellphone back to Baynes' waiting hand.

"Yeah, I know right," he says. "All the famines in

Nubalaya didn't stop our warlord from getting his hands on a lifetime supply of protein powder, huh?"

I snort, making a pathetic attempt at laughter. That picture of him is still burned into my mind, almost irreconcilable with the one of him as a child.

"He looks strong," I say, the understatement of the day. "Strong, and dangerous."

I think about all my adversaries in the past – bumbling, overweight security guards or stern-faced goons – and lastly, Vincent.

"Perhaps he'll be the second strongest guy I've fought so far," I say to Baynes, an irresistible grin creeping onto my face. "The strongest, you know, human, at least."

I can almost feel myself beginning to relish the challenge. A brief departure from hunting a genetically modified vampire freak; a chance to test my mettle against cold, hard, human evil.

"They say he's possessed by a spirit," Baynes says, a wry smile on his face. "They say that there's a devil in him; an evil force that gives him the strength of ten men."

"Who's they?" I ask.

"His enemies. The families of his victims. The men who were wounded, maimed, and saw their colleagues murdered before their very eyes."

"Hmph," I grunt. "Wait until he meets me. He'll discover what superhuman strength really feels like."

CHAPTER 23

"It's hot," Baynes turns to me and says, a couple of drops of sweat already accumulating at his hairline. I nod back at him, feeling a veil of stuffy, ultra-humid air descend over me.

I follow him off the runway – a vast, empty concrete jungle, surrounded by reddish dirt with green, vegetation-filled hills in the distance – and through to the airport building. It's a small brutalist structure, appearing almost golden in the dawn light.

We wordlessly walk through the various lobbies and concourses, passing a number of stern-faced men in blue military uniforms, nodding at our passports as we present them. No one says a word to us until we get pulled out of a line by a smart-looking young man, wearing a suit and tie.

"You're the Americans?" he asks. "You're Mr. Baynes? Mr. Mufumba is waiting for you."

He moves a cordon aside for us, and we both sheepishly follow him down a series of corridors, and outside again, where there's a waiting car; a polished, black Rolls Royce.

"A nice warm welcome," Baynes says to me with a smile, as the young man holds the doors open for us. We both get in, and I'm immediately hit by that new car smell – the overwhelmingly conspicuous aroma of plastic and leather – and realize this must be a recent purchase.

"A mercifully cool car," I say back to him, feeling the cooler embrace of the AC as soon as the door slams shut.

We're soon speeding away from the airport, and I watch as the air traffic control tower disappears over the hills. We drive along a partially paved road – a battered, broken path of asphalt and red dirt, appearing almost like the surface of Mars – surrounded on both sides by thick, green foliage.

The leaves of long, spindly plants – bending and sharp like insect legs – reach out into the path of our car, as cars and trucks – some dented, some covered in red dust and dirt – pass by us in the opposite lane. A noisy flatbed truck drives past us, its bed packed with some thirty or forty men, all holding on for dear life.

We drive over a rickety metal bridge – a wobbly, shaky construction that vibrates and makes a horrifying noise as we drive over it. I look down, expecting to see a river below, but there's just tall, remorseless grass, every shade of green and yellow. Whatever water ran below here has long since dried out.

It doesn't take long before we come to the outskirts of a city – I see large tenement blocks in the distance, draped with flags and other colorful murals – and we're soon encircled by pedestrians walking alongside the car; men and women, boys and girls, walking with large, heavy-looking bags, or plastic containers of water on top of their heads.

There are small, shanty-houses in the road beside us – crude, but durable-looking constructions of corrugated steel and uneven plaster – and beyond those, I see a water pump, with a line of people waiting to use it.

"Man," I say, looking out into the road as a plume of red dust is kicked up by a passing truck. "This isn't what I expected Africa to look like."

"What did you expect?" Baynes asks as we pass the entrance to a massive scrapyard, populated by cranes that reach high into the air, and a gang of children who play with bits of errant junk beside it.

"I don't know," I say, realizing I'm betraying way too much about my lack of knowledge of the world. "I thought desert sands. Savannah. Camels."

Baynes laughs, before making a conscious effort to stop himself.

"Africa is a big place. This is sub-Saharan Africa, the climate is more akin to the jungles of Asia than the dry heat of northern Africa," he says. "It's hot, humid, and it'll rain."

I go back to the window and go on looking outside. We're stuck in traffic now – an unruly jam of dozens of cars and trucks, all making incremental movements and honking their horns – slowly inching past a busy marketplace, with stalls of fresh fruit, vegetables, and fish almost entirely hidden by the thick crowds of people.

I see their eyes follow our car – our polished, far too expensive-looking car – and feel something like a surge of embarrassment; a desire to look away, and pretend these windows are tinted far darker than they already are.

Some people laugh, some people point, but most people look up once, and then go on with their day's journey. I've only been in the country for an hour, but I'm immediately struck by how young a lot of people are. Fresh-faced women carrying foodstuffs, walking by the road; a line of children following an older man, all carrying back-breaking amounts of water.

"Mr. Mufumba would like to meet you here, in the streets," our driver tells us. I look across to Baynes who appears surprised – his eyes wide and expressive, as if he expected an invite to the presidential palace – before he sees me looking and wipes the look off his face.

We finally make it out of the traffic jam, and down another

street, flanked by a large military APC parked by the side of the road. I see military police surrounding it – men in green khakis, holding rifles by their sides – and another gang of children playfighting before them, pretending to shoot one another with wooden sticks.

The car slows to a stop beside a closed-up warehouse and another marketplace, this one thankfully a lot less busy. Our driver turns off the engine, before getting out and opening the doors for us with a tired smile.

There's an awkward, prominent gathering of men beside the road; a circle of a dozen men in black suits, and soldiers in green fatigues, never without a rifle. Baynes looks to the circle expectantly, and I see one man emerge from inside, looking at us with a large grin on his face, and walking directly to us, his hand outstretched.

"Mr. Baynes, Mr. Clark," he says, the newest name on my passport. He charges forward, brandishing his hand like an almighty welcoming weapon, and Baynes is the first to shake it; a vigorous, bone and socket-rattling handshake. "I'm so glad to welcome you to Nubalaya."

"Mr. Mufumba, it's an honor to be here," Baynes replies. "Thank you for inviting us to your beautiful country."

My hand is next for the welcome treatment, and I hold it out to him. He yanks my arm up and down – I have to engage the lat muscles in my back to stop him from rag-dolling me – and he follows it up with a slap on my shoulder.

"Good, good to have you both," he says, his voice booming and excitable. "God bless you."

He's a large man – heavy set, with a sizeable belly and broad shoulders – and around my height. He wears a gray suit with a blue shirt and no tie, and sunglasses that sit uncomfortably on his head.

The most noticeable thing about him, however, is the disfigurement. His head is large and rectangular, with a strong, square jaw, and hard temples that very abruptly join the top of his head. He's covered in pink scarring, running up the entire side of his face, and I get the feeling he's endured a lot of surgical intervention to get this way. Battle scars, perhaps.

"Let's walk," he says, as the circle of security around him loosens and parts to form a valley of stern, watching faces and wary bodies. "Lushoto is busy this morning, and school is out for summer, but I've got many things to show you."

We walk through the marketplace – far less busy than the one we saw before, this one seemingly a lot more conscious of our host's security – and its colorful stalls, with fruits and vegetables stacked neatly together. Children run between us, occasionally looking up with a smile and asking questions of me that I barely hear over the noise of the market.

I get a strange feeling, like this is all too unnatural, somehow. Every stall owner smiles politely, every kid that runs past seems joyous and carefree, every buyer milling between stalls is on a careful path, never staring too intently at us and our massive coterie of guards. It seems stage managed, perhaps a consequence of hosting the Interior Minister here.

Mufumba buys an apple from a stall, exchanging a handful of bills for it, before biting into it and turning back to us. I wonder what the purpose of this little walk through the salt of the earth sectors of his city is meant to serve, but I think I'll soon find out.

"These are the working people and the beautiful children of Lushoto," Mufumba says, holding his bulky arms out widely. "Everyone here was touched by the civil wars. Everyone."

He points at the woman behind the stall; a small woman with strained eyes, standing in the shadow of a plastic tarp.

"Mrs. Afa," he says, in his accented English, "you lost your husband and three sons."

She nods, a polite smile still on her lips. He turns to the

next market stall owner, an old man with grey, bristly hair on his head.

"Mr. Sika, you lost everyone, no?"

He says something in the affirmative, a shaky, hesitant voice I can barely make out.

"They say the war ended," Mufumba says. "But for a lot of people, it never did. It will never end. Everyone goes on living with the consequences, and our country limps forward, forever bearing the scars of the past."

He turns and walks again; Baynes and I exchange a glance before following, the three of us still moving within that circle of suits and soldiers.

We pass a few more market stalls – their custodians watching us go by with hopeful looks – until we make it to a silver plaque, beneath a tall, polished stone crucifix.

"This marketplace is the site of the February massacre," Mufumba says, very matter-of-factly. "Rebel forces, David Faye and his Avenging Angels brigade among them, murdered more than ten thousand people here. Women and children, the disabled and the old."

I look around, at the market stalls and the people sitting behind them, and the dusty paths surrounding the scene. It's hard to imagine this place stained with blood, it seems so full of life, so loud, and so vibrant. I can still hear the laughter and shouts of the children playing nearby.

"Here, at the site of this cross," he says, pointing to the crucifix and raising his voice to an emotional tenor. "There began a line of 10,000 people. David Faye and his ilk had them bayonetted, one by one. Any that tried to run were shot. Any that tried to fight were burned."

He takes a step towards us – his large, imposing frame standing squarely before Baynes – and takes off his sunglasses, revealing the scars around his eyelid, and a black false eye, shining like obsidian.

"I was a farmer back then, and I was brought here like the

rest. I ran and took a bullet to the side of my head. It tore through my face, destroying parts of my skull. It took years of treatment to correct. These are my scars, and these are my country's scars. And they will never heal."

He puts his sunglasses back on. I feel my heart beating angrily; the soil beneath my feet holds pain greater than any I can imagine.

"You must bring David Faye to justice," Mufumba says, looking me directly in the eyes. "Find him, capture him, and let our country try him for his crimes. He will get his judgment before the Nubalayan people, and then he will get his judgment from God."

I look away and back up to that crucifix, standing proudly.

"Mr. Mufumba," I say to him, "we'll find him, all right."

"Good," he says, a warm, jubilant smile creeping across his scarred lips. "Now, how about breakfast?"

CHAPTER 24

There he is, the big man, Jesus Christ himself. And he's looking down on us from above, with that stoic, sagely smile on his face; a smile that says I got nailed up there for you, and I'd do it again. At least, that's how I always saw it.

We're sitting in an expensive hotel dining room, beneath a humungous, tireless ceiling fan, watched over by a painting of Jesus, some six-feet tall. The table we're at could seat twenty-four people, but there's only Baynes, myself, Mufumba, and another man sitting here, with the remnants of his security standing around the sides of the room.

I'm told this hotel – the Saintly House in Lushoto – is the largest, most lavish hotel in the country; a building opened only last year to draw in rich tourists and businesses. I can't help but notice the corridors are empty, though, and the staff are quiet and desperately attentive to us.

Our voices boom and echo across the blank walls and polished floors, and there's a distinct lifelessness here, more like a mausoleum even than the mass grave we just visited.

Still, Baynes isn't overly perturbed. He's enjoying some

local meats and cheeses, brought around on a tray by a man in chef whites. I take a couple of strips of ham, but find I can't quite make myself eat them yet after visiting the marketplace, and all the grotesque history there.

Mufumba is speaking about Nubalaya, and his history as a farmer turned politician in the wake of the violence here, while serving us wine and delicacies. I'm not really listening, though; I'm trying to keep focused. I'm not in Nubalaya to be wined and dined; I'm here to bring a bad man to justice.

"I guess I'm still curious about one thing," Baynes says, looking to me in an expectant manner. "You have the entire police and military of the country at your disposal. Why does capturing David Faye require hiring outside help?"

"That is a great question," Mufumba says, with all the vitality and optimism of a consummate politician. "It is a complicated situation. The ceasefire that ended the second civil war was very important, but it was also flawed in its own way. It left many loose ties, and many questions unanswered."

He puts both his hands on the table and clasps them together.

"It was a bitter peace. Most combatants laid down their arms, but some didn't. Even now, small parts of the country remain under rebel control – Nubalayan in name, rebel-ruled in practice – and the ongoing truce is delicately balanced. We can't send troops into these regions, as we would risk reigniting the war."

He reaches underneath the table and slowly brings out a photograph, before sliding it along the table to us. It's the same one I saw earlier, of the adult, musclebound Faye.

"But," he continues, "if a couple of white Americans show up and abduct him, then we can blame it on your 'Uncle Sam', no?"

Baynes nods, a sly smile on the side of his lips. I'm sure he lives for these kinds of missions; cloak and dagger meddling in another country's business, only now he gets to do it in the name of his own, private agency, rather than the CIA.

"We believe David Faye to be in one of these autonomous, rebel-held areas. We believe he has armed supporters, and that children are amongst them. We believe that if you capture him and bring him to us, we can try him fairly, in a way that won't inflame tensions, and we believe we can unite this country again."

It makes sense, I suppose. The American-manufactured, razor-sharp scalpel, sent in to cleanly cut the warlord out of a sensitive area of the country. A job that a whole army – a blunt, forceful weapon of war – doesn't suit.

"There is one other thing," Mufumba then says in a tentative, hesitant tone. Baynes stops chewing and waits for him to speak. "We managed to assassinate someone close to him – a former general named Johnson Amun. This was six months ago, and it was, well –"

He pauses, quite uncharacteristically.

"Taxing," he finally says, shaking his head. "We thought it was a clean operation, but there was no hiding the fact that it was government troops that did it. There were riots in two rebel-held cities – the entire ceasefire almost boiled over – and worse, David Faye swore revenge."

I laugh, a short, loud snort, that gets every eye in the room trained onto me, like I laughed at a joke that wasn't a joke; a humorous overstatement, that wasn't so funny or overstated.

"Sorry," I say out loud after a few moments of awkward silence. "But he's just one man, isn't he? You're the whole government."

Mufumba smiles, a wide grin reaching across his cheeks.

"I applaud the strength of your conviction Mr. Clark," he says, "but he's not *just* a powerful man. He's an idea, and an icon to rally behind. To some sadly deluded people, he's a hero, who they'd gladly follow to their deaths. To others, he's a tyrant, who they would never, ever dare oppose. He's got a lot more power than just those muscles."

I sink back into my seat; I guess I should leave the talking up to Baynes.

"He's on the war path, and our time is running out," Mufumba goes on to say, clasping his hands over his belly and leaning back in his chair. "He and his men have raided two military outposts just this month. Stole hundreds of guns, hundreds of thousands of rounds. He's planning something, something terrible. And then there are the kidnappings."

"Kidnappings?" Baynes asks, his plate now empty, and his mouth back in service to the mission.

"Doctors, teachers, public service workers," Mufumba says. "Intellectuals of many stripes. The doctors are the ones we miss the most, however. David Faye and his forces have kidnapped six doctors so far. That's six doctors we no longer put to work in our hospitals."

"What the hell does this guy want with doctors?" Baynes asks.

Mufumba shrugs and opens his mouth to speak just as someone drops a stack of plates in the corridor outside the room. The sound echoes around the room – a ghostly, resonant smashing of porcelain – and he waits until the racket dies down before answering the question.

"We don't know. Maybe punishment for working under our new healthcare bill, or maybe he's just looking to ransom them back to us later. Or maybe he's planning something far more sinister. We don't know."

I think about that human blood – the blood of the wealthy, no less – stolen and sent directly to Faye, and now there are kidnapped doctors to add into the equation. Could Vincent be behind this all, somehow? And if he isn't, what is the warlord planning?

"Anything else?" Baynes asks.

"Just this," Mufumba says, before reaching under the table one more time. He pulls out another set of photographs, topped by a small, blurry polaroid, and slides them across the table to Baynes and me. "They say a picture is worth a thousand words, don't they?"

I grab the photographs – what feels like half a dozen printed pictures, held in place with a paperclip. I look at the first – that of a child, no older than eight. He has a big grin on his face, and large, expressive brown eyes. He's holding a toy train, and there are balloons in the background. I guess it's his birthday.

I show the picture to Baynes, who glances at it with a furrowed, confused brow. Mufumba makes a gesture like a wheel with his hand, an implicit direction to go on looking at the pictures.

I look at the photograph beneath it, and then the one beneath that. Two pictures of a young family – a husband and wife, and their two children, the boy depicted in the first photograph, and a smaller girl. The father wears a blue uniform, like a bus driver or the like, and the mother wears a colorful, traditional African dress.

The next two photos depict the father and son in the driver's seat of a train, with that rolling red arid countryside in the background. They look happy; a father and son, sharing one of those golden, childhood moments that gets photographed, blown up, and framed on the wall for years and years.

I unclip them from the pack and pass them to Baynes, and my eyes fall unpreparedly on the last photograph, a blurry, curious mess of colors and patterns that my eyes don't immediately recognize like the last few. There are vivid colors – red, blue, and a person, I think, lying face-down, and...

"Oh God!" I cry, my eyes finally recognizing the form in the picture. It's a body; a small body, in fact, perhaps a child's body, lying face-down, arms splayed out, on a dusty, bloody wooden floor. He's surrounded by blood – drying, congealing, dark-red blood – and his clothes are covered in it. I can't see his face, but I know it's the boy from the pictures.

I tear my eyes away from it – those horrific forms and colors lingering in my mind – and pass it to Baynes, whose reaction is a lot more muted: a snort, and a deep breath.

"The Daju family," Mufumba says, scratching the scars on the side of his face with one hand. "The father, a train driver; the mother, a homemaker. But today, they're all dead."

"Jesus," I say, before glancing one more time at that humongous portrait of Jesus himself, still staring down at us from above. "What happened?"

"The story we heard is that the father – while leaving for work one day – made a terrible mistake," he says. "He witnessed David Faye and his gang preparing to storm a government military outpost, just outside the border of the rebel-held zone. He was murdered in cold blood, as was his family."

I glance across the table at the photograph again, and see a toy train lying in the blood beside the body. It's a different color than the train in the first photograph, but the association is clear. I turn my head away just as Baynes begins gathering the photographs.

He makes sure to pass one to me after he's collected them: that of the father and son on the train. With a bit of hesitation, I take it from him and place it carefully in my pocket.

"These are the stakes," Mufumba adds. "This man – this warlord, this monster – will stop at nothing. He will keep fighting his war, and anyone who gets in his way – men, women, children – will perish."

He reaches across the table to us with his hand and clenches his fist.

"You must find him, and you must bring him to us,

because if you don't, there will be plenty more photographs like this."

I nod at him, feeling my heart racing; blood and nanomachines surging through my veins in hot, disgusted anger.

"Warlord, huh," I say, looking to Baynes beside me after a few quiet, poignant moments. "Let's get on with it."

CHAPTER 25

Mufumba – and his entourage – lead us downstairs and underneath the hotel itself to a mostly empty parking garage.

We walk past a series of grey, concrete columns – some daubed with spraypainted words, apparently left there from construction – and underneath dim white, fluorescent lights that swing gently when we pass them.

At the far side of the garage, we come to a white van. Mufumba stands beside it, glances back at us with a grin, and slaps the top of it, sending a metallic *thunk* echoing across the barren concrete walls.

"This is our gift to you," he says, with proud glee. "Inside you'll find everything you'll need for your mission."

It's a transit van, perhaps seven yards long, and more than a couple of yards in height. It looks in fairly good condition, despite there being a smattering of dirt in its lower reaches. On the side it bears a logo, in bright green lettering: 'NUBAL-AYAN SANITARY ACTION'.

"Sanitary, action?" I whisper to Baynes, who gestures back to me dismissively.

Mufumba leads us around the back, and one of his circle

of security rushes to the backdoors with a key. He opens it, revealing an expansive space within, and more equipment than I expected to see from the back of a plumbing van.

"Satellite internet, and mobile telephones," Mufumba says. "A choice of rifles and ammunition. Government IDs for both of you. And a holding cell, for when you capture the warlord."

I peer inside; the right side of the van is taken up by a desk, a chair, and a couple of laptops, all lit by a crooked spotlight above. On the left side of the van is a mostly empty gun rack, with just a silver handgun. And, beyond them both, a set of black steel bars: a prison cell.

"And there's one more thing," Mufumba says as his circle gathers behind him, seemingly ready to spirit him away from the scene as soon as he's done. "Our country is beautiful, but it's large. There's a lot you may not understand. So, we're donating the services of a guide. Dembe?"

From the depths of Mufumba's entourage – that circle of thickly set men in suits and khakis – a smaller man emerges. He's skinny and short, but wears on his face an expression of easy-going confidence that I could never in a million years hope to match.

"Dembe Mwebesa," he says, charging towards us with a handshake. "At your service."

We shake his hand – Baynes first, and then myself – before Mufumba speaks again.

"Dembe will travel with you. He'll answer any questions you have. He'll tell you if you're running into an ambush, and he'll get you out of any dead ends you find yourself in. He'll be perfectly discreet, and hopefully you'll come to find him to be invaluable."

I look back at Dembe, who smiles at me. He's young – he can't be any more than twenty years old – and wears a plaid shirt with the sleeves rolled up. I wonder how he got into this; is he a soldier, or perhaps a former resident of the rebel-held area?

"And if you need anything else," Mufumba says, crossing his arms, "you can call the ministry. But remember, our participation within this operation is secret. Once you get out there, into lawless, rebel-held territory, for the most part, you'll be on your own."

"Understood," I say, shaking his hand one more time. He again tries to eject my skeleton from my body with a vigorous handshake, and after giving Baynes the same treatment, he turns with his entourage, and leaves the three of us – Dembe, Baynes, and myself – alone with our new vehicle.

"Pretty cool huh?" Baynes says, turning back to the van as Dembe goes around the other side, letting himself into the front passenger side.

"It's better equipment than we've ever had before, I'll give you that," I tell Baynes, before noticing the giant green lettering on the side of the van once more. "Sanitary Action?"

"I mentioned to the Interior Ministry that it would be a good idea to disguise ourselves as a charitable aid organization," Baynes says, looking to the logo with a strange sense of pride. "Many developing countries around the world have substandard plumbing facilities, both in public and private residences."

"And?" I ask, and he goes on.

"Adopting the cover story of a toilet installation charity allows us to have a van, and explains why two American men are traveling to the most remote areas of Nubalaya. It's a worthy cause, too."

"I just hope we don't have to explain to anyone why our plumbing van contains guns, computers, and a prison cell," I tell him, my tongue firmly implanted within my cheek.

He smirks at me, and Dembe appears, walking back around from the other side of the van.

"I'm ready to leave whenever you are, sirs," he says, that infectiously confident smile on his face again.

"You don't need to call us that," I say to him.

"Aye, captain," he replies with a grin. His accent is a lot more American-influenced than the Minister's was. I wonder if he's another member of the generation educated on American sports and sitcom exports; a generation influenced by our relentless cultural reach.

"Shall we get on with the briefing?" Baynes asks, and we climb into the back of the van, and close the door behind us.

Illuminated by the dim light of the few spotlights in the van's ceiling, and the haunting blue light of the laptop screen, Baynes stands in front of those black steel bars looking like some vulgar haunted house employee. I sit on the chair, and Dembe leans against the closed back doors of the van.

"Okie dokie," Baynes says, clapping his hands together excitedly, his face lit in that devilish, cold blue light. "Let's talk about David Faye."

In his characteristically exuberant, and yet still so mundane way, he reveals the plan; we're to drive to the border of the rebel-held area, and then cross it. There, we have a meeting set up with someone loyal to the Nubalayan government, who'll hopefully be able to tell us David Faye's current whereabouts.

"And when we know where he is, we'll plan an operation to capture him," Baynes says, looking to me with wide, expectant eyes. "And, Kris, that's your department."

I nod, and give the thumbs-up.

"The border to the rebel-held area of the country where Faye is supposedly holed up – an area they call Free Zimbala – is an eight-hour drive," Baynes says. "We'll start that journey today. We'll each keep a satellite phone, and work together at all times."

I reach across the desk and pick up the satellite phone. It's bulky, heavy, and warm to the touch, but hopefully it'll survive a tumble or two.

"I probably don't need to tell you this," he adds, "but it's important we remain cognizant of each other's whereabouts at all times, as well as the location of our command post in this mission. David Faye will be dangerous, but so is the outside world, and you don't want to be walking alone across the African wilderness late at night."

"Stay aware of where you and the toilet van are," I say with a smirk. "Got it."

"It should be simple enough to get across the border and meet up with our contact," Baynes says. "Just a mere eight-hour drive, and if we run into any problems, I'm sure our friend here can solve them."

I look back at Dembe, who nods vigorously.

"Okay then," Baynes says. "If you're ready Kris?"

"I'm ready to kick this warlord's ass," I tell him.

"Then let's hit the road."

CHAPTER 26

I yawn – an almighty exhalation of breath that consumes me for a few seconds and makes my bones tremble within my musculature – before snorting loudly. I open my eyes to see Dembe in the middle seat staring at me, amused, while Baynes behind him smirks, and focuses on the road, leaning over the steering wheel like an elderly driver.

Was I just asleep? I don't remember dreaming – no horrific scenes of blood or gore or photographs of lifeless bodies – but the looks on their faces tell me I was gone.

"What time is it?" I ask.

The sky outside is darker than I remember it, a cold navy blue. The road ahead is paved with a beige, craggy form of concrete, full of puddles and potholes. To both of our sides the endlessly green, vibrant fields of jungle vegetation reign unfettered; tall grasses, small trees, and grasping vines that seem to reach out of the earth itself.

"Almost six," Baynes says. "We've been driving for six hours. You can go back to sleep."

"I don't think I was," I say, straightening myself up in my seat and rubbing my eyes.

"Right," Baynes replies in a sardonic tone.

Dembe looks at me with a playful smile on his face, before averting his eyes and looking back to the road. He's probably been told about the seasoned, nigh-invincible former spook and combat veteran, hired from America to take out the country's most feared warlord.

I'm sure meeting me – the pale, skinny guy, who can't ever win the battle to keep his eyes open on any journey longer than an hour – has proved contrary to his expectations so far. Hopefully I can capture Faye, and prove that American-made tools are the best.

Another hour passes – another hour of driving along a featureless straight highway, my sense of hearing relentlessly assaulted by a CD Baynes found in the glove box. The CD case has a bunch of French words on it, but I sure recognize the word Jazz, and recognize the symptoms of jazz.

Eventually I reach my limit; I push a button on the CD player, pull the CD out, and toss it out of the open window beside me.

"The hell are you doing?!" Baynes cries.

"Practice," I reply. "Disarming of a deadly device."

Dembe laughs; Baynes just shakes his head and goes on driving.

"You know, maybe if you learned to drive, you could control the CD player," Baynes says, still annoyed I took away his dinner jazz. "Imagine, a mysterious, world-renowned mercenary warrior, trusted to bring down the world's most fearsome drug lords and warlords, and he can't drive."

I ignore him and turn my attention to Dembe, sitting quietly between us like a child between a married, bickering couple.

"So, what's your story?" I ask him, moving the conversation mercifully on from the fact I can't drive.

"My story?" he asks, looking surprised that I bothered to ask.

"What brought you here?" I say. "How did you start

working for the Ministry for the Interior? For Sunday Mufumba?"

"I know Free Zimbala well," he says, straightening up his posture within his seat. "My family lived there, just before the end of the war. And now, school is done, I –"

"School?" I ask, cutting him off. "Wait a minute, how old are you?"

"I'm seventeen," he says with a nervous smile, a million miles away from his earlier confidence.

"Seventeen?" I parrot back at him, before trying to put a cooler face on my surprise. "Man, we're confronting a mass murderer here, is this your first job?"

"Not even close," he says with a sense of foreboding that I don't particularly wish to press him on. "I've been working since my age was in the single figures."

I feel like I should say something – some note of sympathy or pity or appreciation – but I say nothing. At his age I was embedded within a gaming chair, locked into videogame marathons. I knew nothing of work until I was eighteen.

"I speak all three official languages here, and I'm mixed ethnicity," he adds. "I'm part Kibali, part Uzimbe, on behalf of my parents' unlikely partnership."

"The two ethnic groups that primarily fought against one another in the first and second civil wars," Baynes clarifies.

"I like to think it gives me a unique view on the wars," Dembe says, before looking at the road ahead again.

"How so?" I ask.

"These wars, they call them the first and second Nubalayan civil wars, no? Everyone knows that's not even the full story. They were fighting tribal wars 300 years ago, before the colonizers ever got here. Land would change hands every time; one year's liberators would be the next year's subjugators. The British getting here just made it all worse; they favored the Kibali until it was better to favor the Uzimbe, and back again, depending on whose resources they needed to steal."

I lean back into the door beside me, listening to him intently. I didn't expect him to be so young, and I didn't expect him to speak so eloquently about all this. Then again, maybe I should have. After all, this is his country; he lived these wars.

"Capturing and trying David Faye will go a long way towards repairing relations between these groups and restoring peace, though," Baynes says.

"Sure, maybe," Dembe says, not wholly convincingly.

"You don't think so?" I ask. He takes a deep breath – his chest visibly deflating, like he's reluctantly deciding whether or not to reveal his true feelings – before speaking again.

"Look, everyone talks about good and evil. Everyone worships the same God. Everyone thinks what they're doing is right, and everyone thinks any cost is worth it in the end. They say David Faye did terrible things, but you know, so did a lot of people."

He takes another disconsolate breath and goes on.

"This new government, and this new Minister for the Interior – Mr. Mufumba – I'm sure he means well, but they always do. These politicians come out from their mysterious pasts – businessmen and farmers and generals we've never heard of – and promise us all these amazing things, but they're all scared they're going to be next against the wall, and that fear makes them do questionable things."

He pauses again, before regaining that confident smile.

"But this government are the ones who are paying me, so I'll tell you they're the good guys," he says.

I smile at him – a tacit show of appreciation for his joke – but it's clear he's cynical about our mission here.

"Our country is an uneasy balance of ethnic groups, armies, and cities," he says. "Right now everyone is at peace, except for some local lunatics like David Faye, but that won't last. All these 400-page ceasefires written by fancy European lawyers won't last. They're just a band-aid. We have bigger problems that no one cares to talk about; too much water under our bridge."

There's another uncomfortable silence that passes between us.

"You know, I can't speak of the politics about it all," I say, just as we hit a bump that rocks us all forward in our seats. "But I'm looking forward to getting my hands on this guy, and putting him in the dock. No one should do those sorts of crimes and get away with it."

Dembe looks at me with a guarded expression; slightly hesitant, and eager to remain respectful to me, but unable to resist a bitter strain of cynicism.

"Fine, by all means, put the warlord on the gallows," Dembe says, shrugging. "But everyone was touched by those wars in some way, and a lot still have blood on their hands. Our country's judge won't be in our courthouses, but in heaven. Only God forgives."

He looks away from me again, and back to the road. Baynes looks across at me, a blank expression on his face, before he too puts his eyes back on the road.

It's somewhat heartbreaking to hear Dembe talk like this – a cold, sober, cynical view of the future – especially from someone so young. I'm sure he's lost people too, though I feel I shouldn't ask him quite yet.

Then again, perhaps – in mine and Baynes' eager crusade to put this bad guy behind bars – the cold realism of the young man who spent his entire childhood in civil war is just what we needed. We might not solve any problems here, and that's okay. We'll just do our job and leave.

It's sunset now, the sky a deep orange, and the sun a dimming white, peeking from behind intersecting clouds. I join them and look to the road ahead, and our journey forwards along a bumpy path, to an uncertain fate.

CHAPTER 27

Just after nightfall – after the last slivers of light from the sun disappear over the horizon – we make it to the border to Free Zimbala, and the rebel-held territory.

There's a couple of Humvees parked by the side of the road, and a battered-looking armored personnel carrier with a gnarly looking, top-mounted machine gun – along with a flat tire – parked across a lane of the highway. Not exactly the US-Canadian border, but not too welcoming either.

There's a pair of men in dark-green camouflage fatigues that pop out from behind the APC – one of them seemingly drunk, the other cogent enough – brandishing rifles they helpfully keep by their sides.

Baynes slowly shows them the IDs that Mufumba provided us – supposedly non-governmental charitable-aid permits – and after a few words from Dembe in a language I don't understand, the sober soldier waves us through, while the drunk one continues to eyeball us like we're an unclaimed bottle at the far end of the bar.

We pass by unchallenged any further – our wheels crunching the dirt and gravel beneath them – and pick up speed again, the empty road ahead illuminated only by our headlights.

"We're early," Baynes says, looking at his watch. "The meeting with our contact isn't for another hour."

"See, this is why you're the driver." I look across to Baynes and say, "Do we go in there early?"

"No," Baynes shoots back. "Never meet a contact off-schedule. If you're early, they'll think it's an ambush. If you're late, they'll think you're hiding something."

We go on driving for another few minutes, until the boundaries of the town start appearing over the horizon; drab, single-story buildings, and uneven cinderblock walls, holding up jagged metal roofs. Far from the palatial grandeur of the newly built hotel in Lushoto.

Bayne slows the van down as we approach. We soon come to a crossing, and a town vibrant and full of life, even after dark. There's a set of market stalls by the road, a barbecue, and a selection of skinny-looking meats on kebab skewers.

"Why don't we pull in and get something to eat?" I suggest. Dembe nods his approval; Baynes is less thrilled to eat local, but he does as I ask, and pulls into a dusty sideroad by the edge of the market.

We all get out of the van and slowly make our way over. There's a persistent buzzing in the air; the sound of mosquitos all around us, and electric mosquito zappers close by. Those formerly green high grasses and reaching leaves of the countryside beyond are transformed in the night, now a black, unlit morass of strange hisses and noises.

A passing truck kicks up a cloud of dust into our faces as we view the foods on sale. Baynes goes for an avocado between two slices of pita bread, whereas me and my nanotechnologically iron stomach opt for the meat.

"The meeting place is nearby, just a few blocks away, we might as well wait here," Baynes says.

The three of us sit at a bench by the side of the road,

underneath a flickering orange streetlamp surrounded by a swarm of mosquitos and moths. We eat and exchange small talk – Dembe telling us of his schooling, and his hopes to get into engineering – and wait the hour out.

"Who is this guy anyway?" I ask. "This contact Mufumba set us up with?"

"Supposedly he's a former associate of David Faye," Baynes says. "Someone who runs a teamster office. You know, truck drivers and the like. A rebel warlord has to move a lot of stuff – arms, ammunition, stolen riches – and I guess our contact won't play ball with Faye any longer."

We quietly finish our meals, before Baynes feels compelled to begin filling the silence with one of his old stories. I get as far as him mentioning collegiate wrestling again before I rise from the table.

"I gotta take a leak," I tell them both, before walking away and back in the direction of the van. Baynes waves me away with a gesture of his hand and keeps talking, seemingly unwilling to grant Dembe a merciful reprieve from the torturous monotony of his story.

There are a series of backstreets, all of them accommodated by dirt roads, and populated by crude buildings composed of sheet metal and cinderblocks, the kind of house you build when your last one was reduced to dust overnight in the course of some awful war.

I keep walking, eventually finding another metal, rusted bridge, over a dried-out river. There isn't a trickle of water running – just a red clay riverbed, sprouting with yellow grasses, lit by a single floodlight above the bridge.

I get as far as stopping and looking around before I hear footsteps; slow, deliberate feet, flattening and snapping the grasses.

"Mister!" I hear – a high-pitched, childlike voice. I turn to see a child – seven or eight years old, perhaps – wearing a bright-red, but slightly stained replica soccer shirt. He's skinny and has a fearful look in his eyes. "Please, my mother has fallen down, she's not getting up, please help me!"

Before I can speak – ask him where, and how – he turns and runs off, down the creek below the bridge and along the dried riverbed. Suspicious, but now deeply involved, I look around one more time – seeing nothing but pitch-black countryside and the ramshackle buildings above – and follow him down the creek.

My feet slide into the clay – a muddy, possessive embrace that grabs the soles of my boots and doesn't want to let go – but I trudge on, seeing him round a corner beyond the bridge, wasting no time in rushing to whatever he's drawing me into.

I carefully make my way there, underneath the bridge – where the light splinters into tiny shards as it passes the metal grid above, like some primitive disco ball – and making it to the same corner I just watched the kid disappear around.

As soon as I plant my leading foot and turn my head, I instantly see that I've made a big mistake. There's no stricken mother lying in the grass. There's no paved street, or backyard, or water well where I'd expect to even find an adult. Instead, it's a lonely, beaten path, with dark bushes with grasping needles on both sides.

"Hey, what is thi—"

As soon as the words leave my mouth, a trio of figures jump out of the bushes. There's the kid from before – his eyes no longer desperate and fearful – and two of his buddies, just as young and conniving as he is. And what's more, they brought the tools for the job.

"Come on mister," the first kid says. "Dollars, now!"

He brandishes what appears to be an AK-47, its barrel and magazine highlighted by lines of rust, but otherwise in seemingly decent condition. He aims it at me, straining himself to hold it upright, it being clearly too heavy for him; a weapon of war, something a child should never, ever handle.

His buddies behind him run out to flank him on either

side – one holding a suspiciously plastic-looking handgun, the other aiming stones to throw at me. Together – their eyes watching my every movement, desperate to appear intimidating from behind their oversized weaponry – they make for a surreal sight.

I slowly put my hands by my sides, feigning like I'm going to reach into my back pocket. Their eyes follow my every movement, and I pause abruptly, before casually tugging the lapel of my suit jacket away from my body, revealing the silver grip of the handgun tucked into my waistband.

Their eyes suddenly fill with fear – an understanding that I'm not some clueless aid worker after all, but someone far more dangerous – and after a moment's hesitation, they shout something in the native tongue, and run away.

The first kid to meet me – the ringleader, judging by the size of his weapon – tries to keep up with his buddies, but the weight of the AK-47 causes him to fall flat on his face. In a cloud of dust, he climbs back to his feet and carries on running, leaving the rifle behind.

"Kids huh?" I say to Vega, walking slowly towards that rifle, being mindful of any further ambush.

Good, wholesome fun, Vega drolly says.

I bend to pick up the rifle and take a few moments to study it. It feels sturdy enough, but the aim is slightly crooked. I unload the magazine – finding it empty – and check there's nothing in the chamber.

"No ammunition, thank God."

What's that on the forend?

I look to the side of the rifle, holding it up to the scant light. There's a logo stamped there – three letters, FZA, followed by the smaller caption: Free Zimbayan Army.

"I guess this is property of the rebels here," I point out.

It's a shame you couldn't have caught up with that kid, he might have known something about David Faye, Vega says.

"You think?" I ask, before throwing the rifle far into the darkness of the bushes behind me.

If he's cunning and experienced enough to be organizing armed ambushes of outsiders, then you have to wonder where he got that sort of training. And of course, where he got the rifle, he replies.

I look ahead; the beaten dirt path is empty, the kids long gone.

CHAPTER 28

"This is the one," Dembe tells us, pointing to a large, square building on the corner of an intersection between two dirt roads.

One side of the building is entirely taken up by an old advertisement – an old, smiling man holding a soda can, now defaced with graffiti – and the other wall decorated by closed, rusted steel shutters. On the roof is a row of unlit, incomplete letters, once spelling 'logistics' perhaps, but now missing enough figures to be illegible.

We park beside it, and after rehearsing our cover story in case of unwanted questions – that we're a sanitary aid charity, meeting with our contact at the teamsters – Baynes and I get out, have Dembe guard the van, and walk to the office's entrance, just beside that garish, graffiti-ridden ad.

I push a button on the intercom, and we wait. After a few moments, I can see Baynes beginning to fidget in his stance, growing impatient. I push the button again and look at him; he looks back with a nervous smile, and straightens his collar.

"Maybe one more time," he says after half a minute. I reach forward again, push the button, and then knock on the door – a large, cast-iron door with a slit at eye-level – for good measure.

To our surprise – sharing a disturbed glance – the door falls open with the force of my knuckles, slowly sliding backwards on its hinges, revealing a quiet, dimly lit space.

"Huh," I murmur. "Well that doesn't seem ideal."

"Mr. Duran!?" Baynes shouts, before looking back to me with a far more alarmed expression on his face. I put my fingers onto the grip of my gun and slowly move inside, while Baynes lights the way with his cellphone flashlight.

Inside is a mess. What might once have been a mundane, tidy office, now looks like a bomb has gone off inside it. Filing cabinets are upended, loose papers fluttering in the breeze from the open door; desks lie upside down, their drawers strewn over the floor. Errant wires lie in a tangled mess around the floor, with no other electronic items to be seen.

"Something tells me this isn't how Mr. Duran keeps his office," I say to Baynes, who's far too busy surveying the scene to hear me.

"Duran!" he yells again, as I turn my attention to something else: something shiny, threatening, and conspicuous, sticking out of the wall.

"What's this?" I ask him, and he turns his flashlight onto me and the wall. Sure enough, there it is: a machete – some foot and a half long at least – embedded deeply within the plaster of the wall.

There's a trinket hanging from the handle – a glass skull – and a logo stamped on the side of the clean, shiny blade. I draw myself closer and see a familiar sight: that FZA logo from the child's AK-47.

"Someone left their steak knife behind?" I ask Baynes.

"It's a warning," he answers. "I don't know if the warlord got here first, and messed the place up as a warning to Duran, or if he caught Duran first, and then ransacked the place trying to find out about our meeting, but it's safe to say we've been found out."

"Yeah," I say, pulling the machete out of the wall. "Quite."

Baynes goes to flick a light switch, but nothing happens. I begin sorting through papers lying loosely on the ground, and being blown around the room, but it quickly becomes clear they're all useless. Irrelevant truck repair reports or details of industrial materials sent around the country. Nothing even remotely close revealing Duran, or Faye's whereabouts.

"Let's get out of here Kris," Baynes finally says, sounding defeated. "We'll go back to Lushoto, back to the Interior Ministry, and back to the drawing board."

"Right," I say, climbing back to my feet.

We slowly saunter back outside to the van, where we find Dembe sitting in the front, reading a soccer magazine. He lowers the driver's-side window as Baynes and I lean against the side of the van.

"What happened?" Dembe asks, politely.

Baynes and I make the most of the crude lamplight shining on us from above, and compete to see who can pull the most bitterly disappointed expression across our tired faces.

"Eight hours drive, man," he says, ignoring Dembe's question. I guess that's the true source of his disappointment: the wearisome drive. At least I eliminated our jazz problem, I guess.

"Yeah, it's rough," is all I can say in response. I look to Dembe – his head and shoulder sticking out of the driver's-side window – and shake my head. He gets the message – the hopeful smile disappearing from his face – and he quietly slinks back inside.

"We could stay here and sleep in the van," I say, tortured by the image of sharing that cramped space in the rear of the vehicle with Baynes – one of us cozying up to a rack of rifles, the other dozing uncomfortably in the cage.

He evidently finds the prospect as horrifying as I do, and he begins shaking his head. He says something, a tired stream of words that sail right past me, and I find my attention wandering down the block.

There's a group of kids playing at the very end of the block, by another junction in the road; I see them throwing something, and then cheering, laughing, or shouting madly at the result. Most of the kids wear muted colors – dark blues or greens or blacks – other than one: a kid with his back to me, and a bright-red, slightly dust-stained soccer shirt.

"Hey, did you hear me? Are you even listening?" Baynes asks. I look away from the gang of kids, and to his tired, frustrated eyes, and dreary furrowed brow. Then I look back over his shoulder again, and at that kid in the red, and his turn to throw.

"I think I need to go catch that kid," I tell Baynes, verbalizing the sudden, but strange-sounding impulse going through my head right now.

"What? What the hell are you talking about?" he asks, seeing me peering over his shoulder, and turning to look down the street at the gang of kids. "Those kids?"

"Yeah," I say, putting my hand on his shoulder and easing him out of my way. I hear him calling after me as I walk – asking the same bewildered questions as before – but I don't look back. I go on pacing towards the kids along a sidewalk pocked with weeds.

As soon as I get to within twenty yards, I see one of the kids – a taller, skinny kid, with frizzy black hair barely contained underneath a baseball cap – point in my direction. The boy in the red turns his head – a carefree smile on his face, right up until the point that he recognizes me – and then, without missing a beat, begins to run.

I sprint off after him, seeing him disappear around the

corner. The gang of his buddies forms a loose wall of sorts, protecting their game of dice – and their friend – and I push the taller one aside as he tries to block me off.

As I round the corner, I see that bright-red shirt sprinting through a gate beside two thick walls. I follow, running past a storefront lit by candlelight and a vehicle parked beside the road with two uninterested guys bent over the steaming hood, until I pass that gate and find myself in someone's backyard.

I look around; the yard is almost entirely bathed in darkness, with just a dim orange glow from a frosted glass window providing any light. I take a breath, and consider going back, until I see that bright-red shirt climbing and jumping a fence two more backyards along.

Racing over there, I vault the first fence easily – a sturdy wooden construction that barely wobbles as I lend my weight to it. The second is more difficult – a ramshackle chicken-wire fence, tied loosely to three steel poles stuck into the earth at odd angles.

I prepare to jump, but slip in the dirt – feeling that old, familiar pulse of panic – and instead hit it with the full force of my momentum, crashing through the chicken wire and landing harmlessly on my shoulder.

Hearing voices to my right, I turn my head to see a trio of women sitting underneath a backyard veranda, beside a lit grill, each sporting a greater expression of outrage than the last.

"Sorry!" I yell, picking myself up and resuming the chase, just as they start yelling fuming-mad words after me, and a small brown dog appears from the darkness, yapping at my heels.

I jump another fence, and find myself on another block, comprised of three burned-down houses and one shop with a closed, unevenly painted blue shutter. I take another breath and turn my head, seeing that bright-red flag of a T-shirt peeking out behind a trash can.

As quietly as I can, I approach the trash can and its suspicious hideaway. I hear the thunderous wheels and cacophonous engine of a truck in the road behind me, hiding the sound of my steps, and manage to approach the trash can.

I walk directly up to it, before kicking it gently with one foot. The boy jumps out – his eyes wide and full of terror at seeing me so close – and makes one last effort to escape, jumping into the road with his scared eyes still trained onto me.

"Hey, look out!" I shout, reaching forward and grabbing him by the collar. I pull him back from the road just in time for the truck to miss him, barely. The truck speeds on, showering us with dirt and mud, leaving a cloud of diesel fumes in its wake, taking my breath away.

The kid struggles and strains beneath my grip, trying to fight his way out of his shirt and my hand, but I seize him by the arm and lower myself to his eye-level.

"You know kid, I just saved your life," I tell him. "Settle down, I'm not gonna hurt you."

He stops fighting against me and takes a defeated breath. I look at him closer; he's definitely the kid who pulled the AK-47 on me; the wannabe gangster who could have helped himself to the seven whole dollars in my back pocket if he'd have been bolder.

"Alright," I say to him, as he stops fidgeting and stands perfectly still. "You want some money from me? You're gonna have to talk for it."

CHAPTER 29

Baynes sits on the third step of a slide, looking at me with the same confused, bewildered expression pulled across his face that he had when I first announced my intention to run across town and grab a child off the streets.

The kid sits on a small, rusted steel carousel, softly spinning himself from left to right, and back again. Every time he changes direction there's an ear-splitting metallic screech. It's the sort of sound you'd expect torturers to employ, only we're the ones supposedly asking questions here, not him.

"So, what's your name?" I ask him.

He hesitates, before looking at Baynes, turning his head to Dembe – leaning against a climbing frame – and then looking back to me. We're sitting in a mostly unlit playground. There's a deep circular depression in the floor partially filled with gravel. It looks suspiciously like a crater from long ago.

"David," he finally says. I can't stop myself grinning – a sly smile on one side of my lips – and I turn away from him slightly. What are the chances that this boy is the real David Faye, afflicted by some horrible reverse-aging disease? It's unlikely, but then again, in this world of nanobots and vampires, *anything* is possible.

"David," I repeat to him.

"David Olunga," he says, looking at us with those big, youthful and suspicious eyes.

"Right, nice to meet you again David," I tell him. "I'm Kris, and these are my friends."

He looks around at everyone, quite unenthused by their introduction, and probably still quite scared. He has chubby cheeks, a lighter shade than the rest of his skin tone, and skinny arms that hang languidly by his sides.

"I want to ask you some questions, and if you answer them, we'll give you all the American dollars you need to buy another soccer shirt, or a new bike, or whatever you want."

He nods, and changes direction on the carousel again; I see Baynes flinch from the noise.

"I want to know where you got that rifle from," I tell him. "The AK-47 you dropped when you tried to rob me."

"No hard feelings about that, kid," Baynes adds.

The kid – the younger David – looks between us one more time. Then he looks up to me with a calculating expression – his eyes riding off to the side, as though he's thinking of the largest number he can extract from us right now.

"Fifty dollars," the kid says. I glance over at Baynes, who slumps his shoulders, as if he can't quite believe we're being hustled by a child right now, before I look back to David and nod.

"Sure," I tell him.

"My uncle's friend," the kid says. "Me and my friends were playing at my uncle's next-door neighbor's house, and we found it there. We thought it was a toy, but when we found it was real, we thought we could make some money with it. All you aid workers usually cough up."

Cough up? He speaks in the vernacular of someone far more experienced in sticking up outsiders. I wonder how long he's been doing this, but that's a question another kind of aid worker should ask.

"So, your uncle's buddy, his next-door neighbor," I say, slowly and calmly. "That was his rifle you took?"

For a moment he appears amused, a cutting grin across his face, like I just asked a stupid question.

"He has a pile of them," he says. "He didn't even see me take it."

I glance up at Baynes again, who's smiling and nodding to himself, like we just won a prize on a scratch card. I gesture to him – rubbing an imaginary bill between my fingertips – and he hops off that playground slide, bounds over to us, and counts out fifty dollars, but refrains from handing them over quite yet.

"Can you tell us where this man lives?"

David the younger looks at the money he's earned, and then the rest of the cash Baynes is holding onto.

"Fifty dollars," he says. With a snort of proud, appreciative laughter, Baynes counts out another fifty, and hands the full hundred over to the kid.

He tells us the street name and describes the house. Dembe listens and shows me a thumbs up when he's done. He even gives us a name – Jonathan.

"You can go," I tell him. "Do me favor though, will you?"

He pushes himself off the carousel, before turning his head to me receptively.

"Don't tell anyone you spoke to us. Not your parents, not your teachers, not anyone. Can you do that?"

He snickers to himself – another sharp, cruel laugh directed at me and my naïve line of questioning. He stops himself as suddenly as he started, as though the cruel joke is on both of us somehow. Teachers? Parents? Perhaps he has neither…

"Yeah," he says, sullenly. "I can do that."

And with that, he takes his earnings and briskly runs away back in the direction of town.

"All right!" Baynes exclaims when the kid's out of sight. "That's great work, Kris. If he's telling the truth, this guy doesn't just have one ZFA rifle, but a whole stockpile of them. If we're lucky, he might be able to point us in David Faye's direction."

He stops himself, looking to Dembe before continuing his thought.

"With some, uhm, gentle persuasion of course."

"Why did he laugh just now?" I ask, seeing the smile drop from Baynes' face. "When I told him not to tell his parents or teachers. I mean, this kid pulled a gun on me tonight, so I don't exactly expect him to be an honors student, but he reacted like I was deluded or something."

"Plenty of children here don't go to school," Dembe says. "Life in Free Zimbala is tough. Forgotten in the ceasefire, no government programs, no international funding. As for his parents, a lot of adults died in the second civil war. Either killed in battle, collateral damage, or just straight genocide."

I think about what he said. I've seen a lot of children here – babies in their mothers' arms, toddlers running by the side of the road, middle-school kids playing in the streets – but not nearly as many adults. A nation of orphans, and entire piles of Delissalt-supplied rifles just lying around for the taking.

Dembe doesn't say anything more, and the three of us quietly leave the playground behind and make a slow walk back to the van.

CHAPTER 30

It's half past ten when we pull up to our newest person of interest's place, parking the van just down the block from his address.

We're in the next town over, having passed a small outpost of tents and bonfires on the way. The roads are better paved here, it probably being no coincidence we passed a convoy of military vehicles along the smooth asphalt.

Jonathan's street is a disparate, incongruous set of houses, each more eccentric than the last. There's a dwelling built from black and beige marble-effect walls – like kitchen counter surfaces – with a glass porch built in, and a church at the top of the street, boasting a tall, bright-blue neon crucifix, standing above the crooked telegraph poles and pylons that crisscross the block.

Jonathan's house – or at least, whoever's house our paid informant sent us to – is a wide dwelling whose roof is one long, sloped and welded sheet of rusted corrugated iron. The walls are painted in two halves – blue on the bottom, yellow on the top – and the pavement outside is sprouting grasses and weeds.

There's a small driveway too, and a truck parked on it,

bearing the logo and tradename of a repair shop. As I look closer, I see the same logo stamped on one of the windows of the property. It seems our gun stockpiler runs a repair business.

"This is definitely it," Dembe says, before sucking his teeth, provoking a sharp *clicking* sound.

"So how do we do this?" I ask, as Baynes leans over the steering wheel to get a better look.

"Given the inherent danger of confronting an associate of David Faye – especially one who apparently has stockpiles of weaponry – I'd recommend you infiltrate the grounds around the property, assess how many possible combatants are inside, and then adjust your approach accordingly," Baynes says.

"Sneak around, break in, count the bad dudes, put a gun to this guy's head," I say. Baynes, after rolling his eyes a bit, nods at me.

"If he's there alone, restrain him," Baynes says. "You know, your usual inimitable charm."

"Got it," I say, sliding my suit jacket off and hanging it on the back of the seat, before opening the door and quietly slipping out.

There's music coming from somewhere – an energetic, local style, with joyous singing and vibrant drums – and beyond that, the barking of a dog in the close distance. I cross the road – entirely free of traffic at this time of night – and walk around the side of Jonathan's house, a dirt-path alley.

He has a flimsy wire fence – probably as tall as I am – protecting a pile of scrap metal in the backyard. There are dented hoods with scratched paintwork, shiny hubcaps, and battered, broken bits of steel piping in one artfully constructed pile. No guns though; as careless as this guy is, he thankfully knows better than keeping his AKs outside.

After waiting a few moments – immersing myself fully in the ambience and the feel of the setting – I reach up to the heights of the fence, find a grip with my fingers, and quietly, slowly hoist myself over.

Landing as silently as I can on the other side – my feet touching down on a patch of damp grass – I negotiate my way around the pile of scrap, and make it across the yard, ducking down behind a wall, and a murky window above it.

Taking a deep, silent breath, I lift my head above the windowsill, and look inside. The window is covered with a layer of dirt and dust, and there's barely any light inside, other than what appears to be the flickering, inconsistent blue of a television or laptop, but I can make out a dining room, with chairs, a table, and piles of electronic devices topping each.

I keep low and clamber around to the next window, finding it entirely blocked off by a large, featureless bit of furniture inside. I hop across the backyard porch, and make it to the last window, and get what I came here for.

Inside is the source of that blue light – a flat-screen television, tuned into some local channel, sitting atop a chest of drawers. There are photographs on the walls – pictures of elderly relatives, perhaps – and a desk fan slowly turning.

In the foreground of the room, I see the silhouette of a man facing away from me, and the bright orange flame of a lit cigarette in his mouth. He's sitting in an armchair, and he's busily working on something, switching between a screwdriver and a set of pliers, and taking frequent puffs on his cigarette.

I reach upwards and push gently on the window. It's closed, but isn't securely shut, and I feel it rock slightly within the wall.

It's a single pane of glass, Vega says. *It's thin and doesn't weigh much. See if you can pull it open.*

"How?" I whisper.

Press your fingertips and palms against it; if your hands are sticky enough in this humidity, the glass will stick to your skin, and you'll be able to pull the window open on its hinges.

I do as he says, silently reaching up to push my palms against the cold glass, and leave them there for a moment. Then, as carefully as I can, I pull my palms backwards. To my surprise, it works; the window slowly slides out of its frame, far enough for me to stick a finger beneath it, and quietly prize it away from the wall.

I bet you never thought being so sticky with sweat would prove so useful, Vega says.

I hear the television, the man's breath, and the scratching of his screwdriver inside a metal appliance held on his knee. Every so often he laughs at something on the screen, and then goes back to his tools and his cigarette.

As quietly as I can, I climb through the window, coordinating my movements with a loud advertisement on the television. I reach for my handgun and pull it out of my waistband, aiming it at the man while making my approach.

By the time I make it to a creaky floorboard and give away my position – spurring him to straighten his posture and turn to face me – it's too late for him. He turns to find a stranger in his house, a mere yard away, aiming a shiny silver gun at his forehead.

"Easy now," I tell him. He doesn't seem to react; his curious, agitated expression seems locked on his face – panicked paralysis, perhaps – but the appliance he's working on falls to the ground with a loud *crash*, sending screws skidding across the floorboards.

Slowly, he puts his hands up – his cigarette still gripped between his teeth – and I get a chance to look at him fully. He looks like he's in his mid-twenties, though he could be older. His teeth are crooked, and his right hand bears a couple of circular pink scars; severe cigarette burns, or gunshots, perhaps.

"Jonathan?" I ask. He looks from side to side with his

eyes, before nodding silently, never changing the expression on his face. He looks way too calm to be held at gunpoint right now. "Anyone else here?

He shakes his head, and I take another step closer to him. He takes one final puff on his cigarette before letting it fall to the floorboard before him, and slowly puts it out with his foot. I gesture for him to turn around; he does so, and I restrain his hands behind his back with a pair of handcuffs I brought especially for the occasion.

He doesn't resist, flinch, or even make a noise. He carries himself with all the gravitas of a man who's been in this situation before. I lower him to his knees just in front of the armchair, and then – while keeping him in my sights – walk to the doorway to the next room; the one obscured by the furniture piece.

It's a small kitchen, with all the essentials: basic wooden countertops, a small oven, a refrigerator, and a pile of two dozen rifles, all in various states of disrepair. There are firing pins, magazines, stocks, loose bullets, barrels, and every other piece of a firearm you can think of, untidily stacked in plastic crates.

"Nice toys you've got here," I tell him. He takes a defeated breath and looks to me with a playful smile – a strange appreciation of my euphemism, and a show of defiance.

I call Baynes up on the satellite phone and tell him to join me inside. He knocks on the front door and I unlatch it and let him in, never once letting my eyes leave Jonathan.

"Is this our man?" he asks, looking at Jonathan, still kneeling with his hands bound behind his back.

"I think so," I answer. Baynes grins, adjusts his collar, and looks to the open doorway to the kitchen, and the guns. "Nice selection of toys he's got here!"

I shake my head and sigh, but he doesn't seem to notice. We sure could have seemed a far more intimidating duo if we didn't use the same lame phrases.

"I'm sorry my place is such a mess," Jonathan says with no small degree of sarcasm. "I wasn't expecting guests."

He's putting on a brave face; joking, smiling, and raising his eyebrows in reply to everything we say. He might be afraid deep down – a natural reaction to an armed home invasion, even with the cheesy one-liners – but if he is, he's doing a good job of disguising it.

"Don't worry about it, we won't be here for long," I tell him, walking over to him and kneeling so that I'm talking to him face to face, eye-to-eye. "We've just got some questions for you, that's all."

"Let me guess," he says. "You're going to ask me about *him*…"

CHAPTER 31

"Comfortable?" Baynes asks.

Jonathan is sitting in the armchair, his hands cuffed in front of him now, a concession we felt generous enough to give him, considering his calm co-operation so far.

"Yes, thank you," he answers. He wears a black sports shirt – one of those with smooth space-age fabric – and a pair of shorts. He's slender, but well-built, the contours of his muscles appearing through his shirt.

I hadn't noticed it until now, but he has a very affable expression; a perpetual smile, and a permanent soft light in his eyes, that'd be better suited towards working with children than working with firearms. He's far more well-spoken than I expected from a man with an arsenal in his kitchen, that's for sure.

Baynes and I stand at either side of him; Baynes stroking his chin, staring deeply into him, and I hold my handgun by my side, an ever-present reminder of the consequences of our host becoming suddenly unwelcoming.

"So, you said it yourself," Baynes says, taking his hand off his chin, and instead tapping on his temple with one finger. "The warlord. David Faye. You work for him, don't you?"

Jonathan leans back in his armchair, looking just as relaxed as he did when I first snuck in.

"Yes," he says; a simple, single word that perfectly answers our question, and yet one that shocks me.

I hadn't expected him to give it up so easily. In fact, I was worried we'd have to resort to more persuasive methods to convince him to talk. I have a horrible mental image of Baynes wielding a pizza cutter in one hand and a screwdriver in the other, while I try to hold both Jonathan, and the contents of my stomach down, but thankfully it seems it won't come to that.

"Okay," Baynes says, raising his eyebrows and glancing over at me, before looking back to Jonathan. I guess he's as shocked as I am. "Are those weapons his?"

"No," Jonathan replies. "This is Free Zimbala, it isn't illegal to stockpile weapons here. Every citizen of Free Zimbala is encouraged to bear arms to defend against government tyranny, when it comes. I run a repair business, and that includes repairing firearms."

"Right," Baynes replies. "And you provide those services for David Faye too, am I wrong?"

"You are not wrong," Jonathan says. "He's wanted by the illegitimate Nubalayan government on bogus, trumped-up charges. He needs firearms as much as anybody."

There's the right to bear arms, and then there's the stockpile of deadly weaponry – one that would put any good Texan to shame – in the kitchen here. But I keep that thought in my head for now.

"Where is he?" I ask, skipping the starter and getting right into the main course. "Where does he live? Where does he spend most of his time?"

"He doesn't live in any specific place," Jonathan says, as sweet and helpful as before. "He moves around. He camps out in the wilderness, or inside derelict buildings, or at the homes of trusted friends and supporters. He knows your sort is out to get him."

"Our sort?" I ask.

"Bounty hunters," he replies. "Mercenaries. Assassins hired by the illegitimate government. You're not the first, and you won't be the last."

"We just want to meet him," Baynes says with a sly smile.

"Oh, I'm sure you do," Jonathan says.

"Do you know where he is right now?" I ask.

"No, I do not," he says, before breathing a sad, dejected breath. The smile drops from his lips, replaced by an altogether more uncertain expression, like he knows the fun part is over, and he's about to do something he'll regret.

"How about the coming days?" Baynes asks, idly tapping his temple again.

Jonathan holds his breath; he doesn't seem to want to answer that one. After a few moments of uncomfortable silence, however, he speaks.

"Yeah, I know where he'll be," Jonathan replies, yet another admission – shocking in the ease at which he decides to give it away – that surprises both of us. "I know where he'll be tomorrow, in fact."

"Beautiful," Baynes replies, clapping his hands and then rubbing them together, like a crude caricature of a used car salesman who just sold the biggest lemon on the lot. "Where?"

"The train," he replies, leaning forward in his seat and looking Baynes directly in the eye. "Specifically, Nubalaya Railways Number 311, boarding here in Free Zimbala, going all the way across the country, and getting off the next day in the Mwanikan Republic."

"Mwanikan Republic," Baynes says, turning his head to the blank wall beside him, still tapping his temple. "That's another rebel-held autonomous zone, isn't it?"

Jonathan nods.

"Why's he traveling to another rebel region?" Baynes asks. Jonathan shrugs before putting that smile back on his lips, albeit half-heartedly.

"I'm the guy he asks to repair things from time to time," he says, coyly. "I'm not his secretary."

"But you do seem to know a lot about his travel arrangements," Baynes says.

"He makes that journey a lot, what can I tell ya," he says, before scratching his forehead with his bound hands.

Baynes takes out a notepad and begins scrawling down the info, occasionally asking Jonathan to restate something, or clarifying something else. I'm not at all satisfied though, and I can't quite accept this was so easy. David Faye is a bloodthirsty warlord; why would one of his own give him up so readily, without any kind of resistance?

"You're giving us this info way too easily," I say to him. "How do we know you're not sending us into a trap?"

Baynes stops writing, and looks across at me with judging eyes, as though he's back to being that used car salesman, staring daggers at me for mentioning the faulty transmission.

"If it were up to me, I wouldn't tell you a thing," Jonathan says, shaking his head.

"So why isn't it up to you?" I ask. "Why are you telling us where he'll be, if you're so sure we're out to kill him?"

"Because he told me to," Jonathan replies, his tone forceful and stern. "Because he said that I shouldn't risk my life for his sake."

He fidgets in place, his voice wavering with emotion, and he continues.

"He said that you Americans – you mercenaries – are cold and ruthless, and if I didn't give you everything you wanted, you'd kill me, and everyone I love. He said that you'd go to any lengths to get the secrets you're after, so I should just give it up before it ever gets that far."

He takes a deep breath, and stares indignantly into a blank corner of the room. I don't know if I believe it – a ferocious warlord, telling his followers to snitch on him to save their own skins – but given the conviction with which he said it, it's clear to me that Jonathan believes it.

"That's very noble of him," Baynes says with a sly smile.

"Isn't it true?" Jonathan asks. He looks to me. "What are you? Some former cop, turned mercenary? What, did you get sick of following the rulebook, so you came here to a lawless land to make a dollar that don't ask questions?"

He turns to Baynes.

"And you? Some former FBI or CIA suit, I bet? I've seen your type before – the way you talk, the way you carry yourself. I bet you've slammed a few detainee's heads into walls in your time, haven't you? Put a few jump leads where they don't belong?"

Baynes isn't fazed; he stands there with his hands on his hips, and that sly smile still locked on his face. Jonathan is right though: Baynes does look exactly like a cold-faced CIA suit, fresh out of a black-site torture pit. Hell, that's where I met him.

"You people always act ruthlessly," Jonathan continues. "You Americans, you westerners. You come to our lands and take without asking. And when we resist, you kill us. So yes, I'm co-operating, but only because I was commanded to."

I had something on the tip of my tongue, but it's gone now. It seems our reputation precedes us – the loud, brash, greedy Americans, taking everything we need down the barrel of a gun. I look to the gun in my own hand – a silver M92 – and wonder how much of that monologue was inspired by prior experience.

"Besides, it doesn't matter anyway," Jonathan then says. "Telling you about David's train tomorrow won't make a difference."

"Oh yeah?" Baynes asks. "And why's that?"

Jonathan leans forward slowly – never blinking or breaking his immutable cold stare into Baynes' eyes – and speaks.

"Because he'll kill you," he says, his tone cold and emotionless. "Both of you. With his bare hands."

"Jonathan, please," Baynes says. "Do you know how many times we've heard that?"

"And you've hunted down some pretty bad people, right?" he says back, the words spit with venom. "But, unless the rest of your army is waiting in the car, you're just two guys. Two white men with guns and chains."

He rattles his handcuffs around before him, his eyes and mouth wide, with a silly grin on his lips.

"You don't stand a chance. Most people in this nation – most who lived through the wars – have been to hell. David has been to the ninth circle of hell. He's pinched Satan in the nose, and climbed out to tell the tale. He's not a man; he's more than that. He's a survivor, and he'll survive you both."

I snort with laughter; a derisive, mocking sniff.

"I appreciate the concern, man," I tell him.

To that, he doesn't say anything. He just averts his eyes, leans back into a languid, carefree position in his armchair, and begins to laugh. A slow chuckle, that grows into an uproarious belly laugh.

We'll see who laughs tomorrow.

CHAPTER 32

"I suppose the good news is we're not going to kill you," Baynes says, as I pull Jonathan across the deserted road to our van. "We're not going to kill you, brutalize you, torture you, or maim you. We're Americans, we wouldn't do that."

I look at him with a dubious expression; has he forgotten his work at the CIA already?

"But we do need to keep hold of you for a bit," Baynes goes on to say as we walk slowly down the block. "Can't be having you running and telling the warlord that we've got an appointment booked with him tomorrow, can we?"

"I keep telling you, it won't matter," he says, as we make it to the back of the van. Baynes unlocks it, and I push a thankfully compliant Jonathan into the holding cell in the back. When the door is closed behind him, he puts his hands outside for me to unlock the cuffs.

"You know, you seem like a smart guy," I tell him, fumbling in my pockets for the key. "Why support this guy? This murderer, this warlord…"

I unlock it, and he pulls his wrists back, before going to his back pocket and bringing out a pack of cigarettes.

"Mind if I smoke?" he asks. I shake my head; it's a strange and amusing question, considering he's essentially our captive, but then I guess he is our guest.

He pulls out a lighter and lights his cigarette, before taking a long, tired drag on it; his face illuminated in amber as he does so.

"Like I said," he says, speaking with the cigarette still hanging limply within his lips. "He's a survivor."

He closes his mouth around the cigarette, and leans back in the cell, sitting down with his knees high, and his back against the side of the van. I wait for him to elaborate, but he doesn't; all I hear are the crickets, and the voices of Baynes and Dembe in the front of the van.

"That's it?" I ask, gripping the bars with both hands. "You'll work with a murderer, a man who's committed massacres, burned down churches, and slaughtered women and children, the most heinous acts imaginable, because he's a survivor?"

"Man!" he exclaims, spitting the cigarette out from between his lips as he does so. "We all fought in that war; we've all done terrible things! I was nine years old when they gave me a gun. Nine!"

He pants, clenching his fists beside him and staring into space, and suddenly I regret ever mentioning survivors.

"They gave me that gun, and they made me do horrible things, things I'll never forget," he says, his voice wavering. "They said, 'shoot this man, shoot that man,' the generals. The men with the devil in their eyes. And I did it! Because I was a kid, and when you're a kid, you're supposed to do as you're told."

He begins to sob; quiet, distressed breaths, and tears that he quickly mops up with the sleeve of his T-shirt.

"We all survived the war, but you know, we really didn't," he says. "We've got scars. Regrets. Terrors. And we live in this land that's still wracked with pain, and guilt. We're reminded of it daily."

He wipes his face one more time, and looks at me with two sad, bloodshot eyes.

"You Americans, you're pathetic," he says. "You have no idea. You consider the world your own, and don't have even the smallest understanding of it."

He pauses, taking a deep breath – his chest rising and falling – before continuing.

"David is the strongest man I've ever met. He's making amends, just like we all are. He represents the best of us – the children that were forced into that terrible war – and that's why I stand with him; that's why I'd die for him."

He turns away from me, and reaches around on the floor for his cigarette before finding it and putting it back between his lips. I don't say anything; I just pull on the cell door to ensure it's locked, and turn and leave him in the dim light of the spotlights, and his lit cigarette.

I slam the van's backdoor shut behind me, and then take a moment to think of everything he said. I let the words linger in my mind, his suggestion that the world isn't as simple as we Americans make it out to be; a world composed of many shades of grey, rather than morally impeachable blacks and whites. A world where children are made to fight.

I walk around the side of the van and to the front, seeing Baynes and Dembe waiting quietly in the front seats. Baynes sees me loitering, and makes an effort to open the door and jump out and speak to me face to face.

"How's our guest doing?" he asks, an insolent smile on his face. "Is he comfortable?"

"He'll be fine," I answer. "He's talkative, at least."

"Right, right," Baynes replies. "I'm going to get Dante to put some intel together on this train journey – times, number of cars, that kinda thing – and we can make a plan."

"Ya know, Jonathan said some things," I say to Baynes, catching him as he turns to open the driver's-side door again. He freezes as soon as I say it – his hand clasped onto the door handle – and waits for me to finish. "He told me about his past, being a child soldier and all. Choices that were made for him. Choices that were made for David Faye too."

I pause, before speaking again.

"He was a kid, and they made him this way. It wasn't his fault."

Baynes turns to look at me again. Even in the dim light – the flickering glow of a streetlamp overhead – I see a look of concern in his face, like he thinks I'm having second thoughts about all this; like we might not be able to get our hands on that big bag of cash at the end of the day like he hopes and dreams of.

"Let's get off this block," he says, opening the door and climbing inside. "We'll talk more in a bit. I've got some more information on the warlord that I'm sure you'd love to hear."

I follow him, going around to join Dembe – who regards me with an overawed nod – in the passenger side. Without a word, Baynes drives around the block, out of town, and rounds a corner ascending a sharp hill.

He drives around in the dark for a couple of minutes – disturbing a herd of cattle whose wide, black eyes stare back at us blankly, until they gain the presence of mind to run – and finally pulls up just before meeting the edge of a small cliffside, overlooking the town we just liberated Jonathan from.

The three of us get out, lean against the hood of the van, and look down at the town as the white light of the van's headlights peek out around our bodies. It's a patchwork of tiny dirt and asphalt roads, with colorful double- and single-story dwellings glowing amber in the streetlamps, and the occasional car or bike sauntering along quietly.

But further afield, I see something more: old craters in the road, full of dark, putrid water, and a burned-out apartment building in the distance, one façade entirely collapsed, and the other composed merely of concrete frames; the desiccated bones of civilization. Beyond that, there's an entire encampment of tents and mud huts. A refugee camp, perhaps.

From here, I see exactly what Jonathan was talking about: the scars of a nation. The visible pain of a country ravaged by war, rebuilding around skeletons left unburied.

"It's true," Baynes says, "this guy, David Faye – the warlord – he got dealt a bad hand. Most of the people – most of the children here – were dealt a bad hand."

Dealt a bad hand? The two of spades and four of diamonds I received at the casino the other night was a bad hand. I can't keep myself from looking over at him incredulously, but before I can protest, he speaks again.

"You know he's a former altar boy?" Baynes asks, an improbable smile on the edge of his lips. "Yup, he was an altar boy at his local church. A good, well-behaved, grade A kid."

Dembe flashes me a glance – high eyebrows, lips pulled to one side – that suggests he's heard this story before. He leaves his position at the front of the van, and slowly strolls to the edge of the cliffside.

"He was a sports prodigy even back then," Baynes continues. "Regional track and field star, soccer team, every sporting pursuit you can think of. He had four brothers, one sister, and two parents who worked hard and supported the family. David Faye won a scholarship to a school in Lushoto, everything seemed good."

"And then the war broke out," I say, interrupting him.

"And then the war broke out," he repeats. "His mother and younger sister fled the country as refugees. His father and siblings stayed behind in his hometown. They're all now missing, presumed dead."

I see Dembe begin to skim pebbles off the side of the cliff;

they land in darkness, making the slightest of sounds against the rocks below.

"David was stuck alone in Lushoto when the fighting started. He hid in empty buildings and stole food and water until one of the rebel forces picked him up."

Baynes turns to face me, half of his face lit in intense white light by the headlights beside us, and the other entirely shrouded within darkness.

"One of David Faye's favorite tricks was having people dig their own graves," Baynes says, emotionlessly. "Those that were strong enough to dig an entire grave were allowed to live and forced to join the fighters. Those that weren't strong enough to dig a whole grave were murdered, and buried in the graves they tried to dig. Entire bodies half-buried; legs and arms sticking out of the ground like crude gravestones."

"What are you saying to me?" I ask him, feeling a cold well of nausea at the depths of my stomach.

"That was his favorite trick because that's exactly what happened to him, when they found him living in the ruins of some building in Lushoto," Baynes says. "Even as a child, he was strong enough to dig that grave and survive. He's a monster this civil war created – a child, crudely sculpted into a killer – but don't forget, that doesn't make him any less deserving of justice."

Baynes looks away again, turning his head from the intense white light. A child, crudely sculpted into a monster. Again, I think of Vincent, made that way through no fault of his own, but necessitating a forceful response to stop him from killing more.

"He did terrible things, murder, massacres, genocide, and everyone believes he's fixing to do the same again," Baynes says. "He once was strong enough to dig one grave, and now he's strong enough to dig a million more graves. We have to stop him before he does so."

I look at him – his face stern and expressionless – and nod. "Then let's make this happen," I say to him.

CHAPTER 33

'm in that subway car again. And I know that I'm dreaming.

It's entirely empty; I see rows of empty seats with faded, threadbare fabrics, and a gray PVC floor, covered in scuff marks and stains from a million previous riders. I look around and see nothing but darkness beyond the windows.

It's eerily quiet; I can't even hear the engine. The car rocks gently, and tilts with an unseen bend. I don't know where I'm going, and I don't know where I've come from.

And then I see him, waiting for me at the end of the train car. My father, standing there with his fingers gripping an overhead handle. He's waiting for me.

Suddenly, I taste something like cigarette smoke – that familiar smell and taste that reminds me so much of him – and wake myself up. I'm face-down on the floor in the back of the van, using my own tired arm as a pillow, it seems.

I sit up, bending at my waist, and see Jonathan there, still captive within his cell, smoking another cigarette.

"You guys are a real sophisticated operation, aren't you?" he asks, sarcastically.

I rub my eyes and cough a couple of times. Last night I

opted to sleep in the back of the van, while Baynes and Dembe slept in the front. Sure, a luxury hotel suite would have been nice, but given the fact we're engaging in a cloak and dagger operation to abduct a warlord behind enemy lines in a rebel-held region that doesn't trust us, the van is our only option.

"Sorry to keep you there overnight," I tell Jonathan, my voice deep and encumbered with fatigue. "As soon as I grab a hold of David, we'll let you go."

He sniggers; that arrogant, snorting laughter, mocking the idea that me, a skinny American, could ever in a million years capture the warlord. I suppose that sitting down and explaining to him the trillion nanomachines inside my body would result in an even greater tide of laughter though, so instead, I just smile politely at him.

I slowly compose myself before jumping out of the back of the van into a glorious, bright, sunny morning, underneath a perfectly blue sky. Perfect weather to bring the warlord to justice, if I do say so myself.

I stretch out a bit, smelling the fresh air – untainted by Jonathan's incessant smoking – before walking around the side of the van and to the cliff side.

I see the refugee camp again, and a line of people waiting, looking so small they could be specs of sand delicately lined up in some indulgent art exhibition. I see fields of crops and pastures with grazing cattle, and beyond those, I see the forests – wild and green – encroaching and stealing every parcel of land that isn't settled.

When I turn to the driver's side of the van, the view isn't quite so expansive. Baynes sits there in the dark, his face illuminated by the laptop screen in front of him, and Dembe sits beside him, with his head tilted backwards and his mouth wide open, asleep.

I knock on the window gently enough to arouse a look of surprise from Baynes, who clumsily scrambles around in his seat while somehow keeping the laptop upright on his belly. After a couple of moments, he opens the door and jumps out, bringing the closed laptop with him.

"Morning," he says, sheepishly. "You surprised me. I guess I'm not so accustomed to seeing you awake so early."

"What time is it?" I ask, ignoring the implicit insult. He shrugs, holding onto the laptop with both hands, like it's a freshly delivered breakfast he can't wait to dig into.

"Seven, half past seven, something like that," he says.

I can't remember the last time I woke up so early. Even jet lag doesn't normally get me so bad. Something about sharing your quarters with a chain-smoking captive makes for a bad night's sleep, I guess.

"You're in good time though," Baynes adds. "Dante has been working from the other side of the pond. We've got a rough layout of the train, and I've put together a briefing, and something of a plan."

I rub my eyes, and aim something almost like a smile at him, before shielding myself from the sun's intense glare. The pair of us walk back over to the van and knock on the window – a lot more forcefully this time – waking Dembe up, who looks back at us with two attentive, bloodshot eyes.

Baynes stays behind to exchange a few words with him while I walk ahead, strolling along the edge of the cliff face until I find a bench of sorts; a rusted metal pew, overgrown with weeds, beside a wooden table, rotten and sprouting moss.

I plant myself on the bench – feeling it buckle a little under my weight – and wait for Baynes, who promptly joins me, still gripping that laptop.

"Beautiful day to bring home a war criminal, huh?" he asks, looking up at the perfect blue sky. I recall having a similar thought earlier, but hearing it out of Baynes' lips serves to remind me how ridiculous a thought it truly is.

"What have we got?" I ask.

He gingerly plants himself down on the rusted bench beside me, and gently positions the laptop on the table before opening it to a folder of saved pictures.

"I suppose this is like robbing a train," he says, with a playful grin pulling at the side of his lips. "Only, instead of stealing money or gold or whatever, you'll be stealing one of the world's most dangerous men."

I pat him on the shoulder and turn back to the laptop. Something tells me he's relishing the thought of this particular mission, with the intense sun, and the image and the romance of the train heist. It's like an old western movie to him.

With characteristic exuberance, he excitedly tells me about the train. It's a sleeper train, setting out from the east, and traveling the entire breadth of the country to its most westerly point, passing through Free Zimbala, and several other cities on the way. It terminates in the Mwanikan Republic, another rebel-held autonomous zone, just as Jonathan described.

"The rail network was put here by the British, and is very lovingly maintained by the Nubalayan people," Baynes says, with a sort of admiration he usually only reserves for the CIA, or Elvis. "The continued running of the trains was mandated in the cease fire agreement, even."

He goes on to explain in tedious detail the importance of the train network within the UN-brokered ceasefire – a train that runs between the various quarrelsome regions of the country with no overzealous border security. An important gesture of togetherness, intended to keep the country as one, guaranteeing freedom of travel to any citizen.

"A good idea, but troublesome it seems," he says. "This is how David Faye has been traveling between the rebel-held regions, perhaps organizing another uprising. Another civil war."

"Right," I say to him, hoping to prevent another ceasefire explainer. "So, when do I board this thing?"

"Around ten," he says, nodding to the laptop, and an eTicket Dante has emailed across. "You're in the first-class car."

"Putting some of those Monaco winnings to good use then," I tell him with snark.

"We're fairly sure that David Faye will have his own quarters on the sleeper car," Baynes says. "His own bedroom, his own bathroom, maybe even his own staff and attendants and security."

Squinting his eyes and furrowing his brow, he scrolls across a roll of pictures on the laptop – a small bedroom-like space with a bunk bed; a small bathroom, with a shower. A restaurant car, with neat tables for two and four, and waiters, and a staffed kitchen visible through a door beyond.

"Nice train," I say. "Beats anything we have back home."

"Like I said, these trains are the pride of Nubalaya," Baynes replies. "They're the country's circulatory system."

I look back at the pictures. I can see they're sourced from various tourist sites, social media posts, and travelogs. The sleeping quarters are small, tight spaces, furnished with fiberglass and varnished wood. The beds are each big enough to accommodate a single person. It's cozy, alright. But too cozy for an ambush? I don't know.

"Dante and Jude put together a rough floorplan," Baynes adds, clicking along to another document – a very crude illustration of where the walls, the rooms, the doors, and the tables are within each of the train cars. I train my eyes on it long enough for Vega to take it all in, and then nod at Baynes to move on.

"What's my move?" I ask. "Where do I board, and how do I get him off this train?"

"You'll board at a station an hour or so away," he says. "As for how you incapacitate and extract the target, well, that plan may have to retain an element of fluidity."

"An element of fluidity?" I ask, drolly. "You mean, I improvise?"

"In a sense." He leans back on the bench, provoking an unhappy *clang* from the rusting metals, and a very brief expression of panic about his face that I don't often see. "You'll be able to take a concealed firearm, and we can hopefully assume that he doesn't know what you look like. You probably won't be the only white westerner riding this train either."

He claps his fingers together, stretching them out. I rub my eyes again.

"Your satellite phone has a GPS tracker. I'll be able to follow your movements from the van, and follow the train accordingly," he says. "I'll also give you a long-range radio and headset. I'll be able to speak to you remotely, and we can arrange extraction in real time."

"Extraction," I repeat. "A fancy description for grabbing a war criminal off a train."

"The extraction itself might be more difficult," he says, tapping his finger against his temple in that nervous style of his. "I can arrange a distraction that will stop the train in its tracks; I'll have Dembe call in an obstruction on the line, it'll force the train to a halt, for a few minutes at least."

"Great," I say, feeling the day's first beads of sweat dropping down my cheeks. "So, all I need to do is hold him up, tie him up, gag him up, call you up, and then throw him off the train, where I presume, you'll be waiting with the van, correct?"

He nods, still tapping his temple, and rocking forwards and backwards in his chair ever so slightly.

"You know what he looks like, the shape he's in," Baynes says, somewhat warily. "He won't want to go without a fight. And make no mistake, he's a fighter. He's a fearsome, bloodthirsty criminal warlord, he won't be afraid to pull a gun on you and shoot you where you stand. Corner him, and he'll punch and kick and scratch and bite his way out. Whatever it takes to survive."

"So, I've got make it quick and easy," I tell him. "Sneak up on him, subdue him, and shut him up."

"Unless he's somehow been clued in already – and I doubt he has – you'll have the element of surprise, so use it," Baynes says, his tone assertive and confident in my abilities. "I'll be in touch with you throughout, and we both know that you're up to the task."

I nod, smiling at him and his gentle words of affirmation.

"We may only get one shot at this," Baynes says, as he pushes the laptop across the table to me. "If we fail to bring him in on this occasion, he could go underground. He'll disappear into his network of supporters and collaborators, and won't surface again for a long time."

"I understand the stakes," I tell him, looking at those pictures of the train's interior again. I click across a couple more times, until I get to that picture of the adult David Faye I've seen once before, the one with the intimidating, imposingly huge muscles, and the tendons and sinews straining out of his dark skin.

"You're just a stranger on a train to him," Baynes adds. "Keep it that way until the time is right."

I look into David Faye's eyes in the photograph: those cold, calculating, enigmatic eyes. Those eyes that have seen so much pain, so much horror. But soon, if I do my job, they'll see nothing more than the darkness of a prison cell.

"Just a stranger on a train," I repeat, as Baynes carefully stands up from the bench.

But I won't be a stranger for long.

CHAPTER 34

"Do you hear me? Over."

Baynes' voice rings out in my ear, a deafening and yet so monotonous siren that reverberates around inside my skull. I rip the receiver off my ear and speak into the mic hanging around my neck below it.

"Too loud man."

I find a volume controller wheel on the side of the headset. I turn it down and put it back to my ear, just as he finishes up telling me to turn it down, only in far more boring, agency-appropriate language that goes through me just as painfully as the high-volume blast.

I wipe the sweat from my brow and walk the twenty or so yards back to the van, where I find Baynes sitting behind the steering wheel, behind a pair of massive, ostentatious wrap-around sunglasses that he's evidently been hiding from me so far.

"Whoa, what's with the glasses, man," I say to him, eliciting a defensive, affronted look that I see even behind the shades. "You look like a welder, or like you just had cataract surgery. The Moth Man of Langley."

"You know, funny you should say that," he says, his face

lighting up again, the reflection of the sun in those damned shades blinding me. "I was posted in Beirut this one time, and –"

He goes on talking, and I tune him out, taking a deep breath and wiping yet another layer of sweat from my forehead. It's hot today; the low, stifling white clouds of yesterday are gone, along with the sweat-inducing veil of humidity. Instead, the sun hangs above me high in the sky, baking me in its dry, relentless heat.

We just made the journey here, a few hundred yards from the station, in a quiet hour of driving along dirt roads. After testing out the equipment – the headset, the firearm, the satellite tracker on the cellphone – we're almost ready to begin the extraction, if I can only extract Baynes from the reverie of his story first.

"Probably the largest concentration of moths you've ever seen, and I –"

"Are we ready?" I ask, cutting him off. He takes a deep, defeated breath, before looking down at the watch on his wrist.

"Five minutes," he says before looking back at me, blinding me with those shades again. "Oh, and I've got something for you."

He reaches behind his seat in the van and pulls out a black length of fabric. After shielding my eyes from the sun, I know exactly what it is.

"I don't know if it'll be useful," he says, revealing the motif of the ghostly face stitched there. It's my superhero calling card; my spook mask. "But, given we didn't explore a disguise, you might want to shield your identity with this."

It's true, I didn't have Vega remake my face around like I normally would. I didn't want to have the awkward conversation with Dembe about how I suddenly look terrifyingly different from the man I was last night. Sharing the previous night in the front seats of a van with Baynes was bad enough for him; surely the poor boy has been through enough.

"I'll pass," I tell him. "I need to remain casual, right? A business traveler in first class."

"Right you are," he says, putting the mask away behind him before leaning back, and semi-opening his mouth like he has something on the tip of his tongue. After a few moments, he looks behind him, ensuring Dembe hasn't quietly joined him in the front of the van, and he goes on to speak in a hushed tone.

"You know, don't you ever get tired of changing your face around like that? Don't you get tired of looking in the mirror and seeing another man looking back at you?"

I smile at him in pleasant surprise. It's a surprisingly deep question, by Baynes' standards at least.

"Sometimes," I reply. "It used to freak me out a lot more – the unrecognized man reflected back at me, the weird arrangement of bones in my face – but I spent two years pulling palm oil off trees in Asia with a face that wasn't mine. I got used to it, I guess."

"I've spent a lot of time in dangerous, distant countries, mostly under false names," Baynes says. "I've seen people lose their minds in those conditions. Friends, colleagues. When you live a lie, it's easy to forget who you really are."

I think of Charles Forrest, and that insane episode. Baynes takes off his shades and looks me directly in the eyes.

"I suppose what I'm trying to say is that we're doing this for the right reasons," he says, earnestly. "Sure, the money is good, but bringing the warlord to justice is the right thing to do, for the world, for Nubalaya, and for us."

He shields his eyes from a gust of wind, and the resulting shroud of dirt and dust kicked up.

"Again, the thing I'm trying to say is, I'm not losing sight of who we really are; who *you* really are," he says. "We're here because we need to get this guy. That's why you're here, that's the real you."

I think this is Baynes' manner of apologizing for the whole international money-grubbing mercenaries thing. I appreciate the sentiment nonetheless. I hold my hand out to him, and we shake hands.

"Let's go," he says, "the train won't be long now."

I go around the other side of the van and jump into the passenger side, and after a shout to Dembe in the back, he begins to drive. We pass a field of blank-faced cattle, chewing yellow grasses and watching us as though they already suspect we're up to no good.

We stop a block away from the station – a small, box-shaped building, with a red-tiled roof, and large, thick windows, stained entirely by dust. Beside it is a small parking lot, mostly empty, with a bunch of rusted steel girders reaching out of the dirt at strange, grasping angles, perhaps a new construction project, or an old one.

In the near distance I see the railway tracks snaking away into a sparsely forested valley, and beyond that, I see the wider wilderness; a featureless plain composed of dead trees and tall grasses. A whole lot of nothing, like the no man's land in this bitterly divided country.

"All right," Baynes says, leaning over the steering wheel, evidently ensuring no surprises are waiting for us. "When you get on the train, we'll drive out and let Jonathan go in the middle of the wilderness somewhere, close enough to a nearby town that he'll be safe, but far enough that he won't sound the alarm in a hurry."

I nod at him, and ensure the handgun is holstered within my suit jacket innocuously enough.

"After that, Dembe and I will follow the train along as best I can. Freeways, dirt roads, whatever I can get four wheels on," he says, putting those ridiculous shades back on. "When you have him, just call me and wait. We'll call up an obstruction and stop the train, and then we'll get him comfortable in the van and make our getaway."

"You make it sound so simple," I tell him, climbing out and slamming the van door shut.

"For you, it just might be," he says with an affirming grin. "But stay focused. Stay quiet, and then when the time is right, make your move. And more than anything else, be careful."

"The next time you see me I'll have a wanted war criminal tucked under my arm," I say to him with a wink. "Maybe I'll wrap a bow on him."

"I look forward to it. See you on the other side," he says, before speeding away. The van disappears into a cloud of reddish dust, and I walk on to the station.

The train station building is exactly as bare and economical as it looked from distance; a blank waiting room, painted green in aging, flaking paint, populated by a pair of wooden benches and a couple of women in dresses standing idly by, struggling not to stare at me.

I make my way through the waiting room and find myself at a ticket office. There's a man in a blue uniform smiling attentively enough, only not at me, but the desk fan before him that blasts cool air into his face, a luxury I'd pay any amount of money to enjoy right now.

I show him the eTicket on the screen of my cellphone, and he pushes a button on some device beside the hallowed desk fan, and produces a small paper ticket, before passing it to me and bestowing that attentive smile onto me for the first time.

Seems like a quiet enough morning, Vega says, as I take the ticket and slowly saunter over to the station platform. *Do you think you can keep it that way?*

I take a sharp intake of breath; a confident, unspoken reaction to Vega's question, puffing my chest out like the undefeated, cocksure alpha male of the pack.

In truth, I'm feeling perhaps the slightest bit nervous. I've willingly walked into the unknown countless times by now –

frantic, dangerous and thankless tasks, some I've succeeded in, and some I've failed in – but this feeling doesn't go away.

The adrenaline in my fingertips; the dynamite within my heels; the persistent heartbeat pounding on the other side of my sternum, reminding me it can all go so, so wrong…

But this time, I at least have one good thing on my side. I know my enemy, and the purest form of evil that he embodies.

I just need one chance, and he's mine.

A group of travelers gathering beside me on the platform wakes me from my daydreaming. I step across them to the edge of the platform to see a train oncoming – a blue engine, with white passenger cars following behind it, stained below by beige dust, and mud.

I can't see the end of the train – it goes on and on, following the meandering curve of the rails like a great white snake, disappearing beneath the horizon. I see more than a dozen cars so far, with no end in sight.

The engine car flies past me, bringing a dry, warm gust of air as it does so. When the train finally comes to a stop – some five or six white passenger cars already having passed – the gathering crowd behind me rushes to the doors.

I follow the crowd, and board the closest car – seeing a procession of curious faces staring at me from the dusty windows within. I'm sure I stand out like a sore thumb; a clueless white man, boarding a train in a place many Americans won't have ever even heard of, let alone vacationed in. It's like I'm a confused time traveler, here via teleportation malfunction.

As soon as I make the step across to the train, I'm greeted by a balding, middle-aged man in one of those familiar blue uniforms. He follows my hand expectantly, and I pick it up to show him a ticket, the sight of which provokes an excited smile from him.

"Good morning, sir, this way," he says to me courteously,

and immediately turns on his heel and begins walking away in the opposite direction. I take my cue to follow – enjoying one of the first VIP experiences of my entire life, in some of the most unusual circumstances – and soon find myself hurriedly following him down the train.

The first handful of cars are drab, joyless spaces: long, bright cars, composed almost entirely of grimy windows and painted cream walls. A long wooden bench runs perpendicular alongside each wall, and vertical steel poles stand at irregular intervals, making my guide and I dance around them and the standing passengers.

Some passengers – men and women; young and old; dressed up and dressed down – follow me along with their eyes as I walk, but mostly they keep to themselves. Mothers standing with bright-eyed children; men and women wearing various uniforms, reading books or listening to headphones. It reminds me of that subway train again, and Alfred Burden…

I try to put the thought out of my mind, and keep moving. I can't help but wonder how many – if any – of these people know there's a war criminal sharing this train; a butcher of men, women and children, who hungrily partook in tearing their land apart.

If they do know, would they even care? In my experience, most people just want to live their lives – putting food in the mouths of their children and clothes on their own backs – and try to stay out of the international affairs of spy agencies and malevolent rebel warlords. The virtuous indifference of the desperate worker.

We pass through eight cars like this, dodging poles and people and speculation until we make it through a doorway, and into a far more opulent, more visibly grandiose space. There's a bar to my right – staffed by a bored-looking bartender wiping glasses – and a set of empty bar stools, each a different, vibrant color of leather.

I walk on, following my guide through a very conspicuous set of glass panel doors – stenciled with floral patterns in gold paint – to a car I recognize from the photographs.

A restaurant, with a dozen small tables draped in pure white tablecloths, set with empty plates gleaming in the sunlight, and shining silver cutlery. My chaperon doesn't slow down – expertly brushing a heap of crumbs off a tablecloth with his palm without even missing a step – and we make it to the next car.

We step through another glass door, through a membranous black tunnel connecting the cars, and I find myself in a corridor of sorts, with a short series of doors to my right, each bearing a number.

"Number four, sir," my attendant says, before handing me a small, tarnished key. With an uneasy smile – the smile of a man not yet ready to accept luxury in his life – I take it from him, and he says a few words about our estimated time of arrival – 8 a.m. tomorrow – before promptly turning another ninety degrees and disappearing as quickly as we got here.

I take a look ahead – seeing a doorway, and yet another corridor beyond – before taking one last, guarded glance behind me, and unlock the door.

The train shudders into movement just as I get my foot in the door; a groaning sound permeates the train car as the wheels beneath grind into motion. I step inside and close the door behind me.

Seems homely enough, Vega says, as I scan my surroundings. There's a bunk bed – two single beds, one atop the other – and a large, wide window, out of which I see the red wastelands and green foliage of Nubalaya begin to accelerate by.

"Yeah," I say back to Vega. "It's a shame I'm not staying long."

David Faye is supposedly booked into one of these suites, Vega says. *He might be closer than you think; next door, even.*

"White tablecloths, floral patterns, silver knives and forks. It doesn't exactly scream the warlord's evil lair, does it?"

I suppose even war criminals enjoy fine dining, Vega says dryly.

There's a wardrobe beside me; a set of wooden doors, carved with those same floral patterns, and a desk with a teapot and a selection of cookies. There's even a print of a painting; a rolling landscape of green grasses and a distant waterfall, evocative more of Europe than of Africa.

The whole car is anachronistically decorated, like the set to some Victorian-era murder mystery movie. I don't know if Sherlock Holmes ever pursued a warlord on the Orient Express, but I can't help but get that kind of vibe from this place. It's like I'm awkwardly entombed in a Victorian time capsule, a weird remnant of British colonialism.

I look out of the window again to see a huge gang of children running along a dirt embankment beside the train. They're laughing, smiling, pointing, trying to grab my attention, but the train goes on accelerating, and they're soon left behind.

On some level, this whole car reminds me of that empty hotel where I met the Minister for the Interior. A lavish boondoggle, intended to attract rich tourists and businessmen; people like me, I suppose, only instead of building offices or datacenters, I'll be kidnapping bad guys.

"Well," I say to Vega, "I'd better get on with it."

CHAPTER 35

I head back out to the restaurant car, and take a seat at a table set for two. There are a couple new faces here; an African man wearing some sort of traditional shirt – full of vibrant, zigzagging colors – and an older, grey-haired westerner, entirely red-faced and looking like he's being cooked alive in his suit.

There's music coming from somewhere; a jaunty, happy little ditty with drums and trumpets, emanating from behind a closed door. It makes for a surreal backdrop to my mission.

A waiter – a slender man wearing a white shirt and black pants – files between the tables and holds up a finger to suggest he'll be with us soon, and I lean back in my seat, idly tapping a finger on the table in a displeasingly Baynes-like fashion.

"Excuse me, sir," a voice beside me says; male, deep, and Nubalayan accented. I turn my head slightly, expecting to see that white shirt of the waiter again, but instead I'm greeted by something else entirely. The dark, taut skin of a bicep, and a crisscross of veins straining out like a roadmap. I've seen that bicep before…

"Huh?" I mumble, looking up. I'm greeted by a pair of my own images again, reflected at me from a set of black sunglasses. But there's no mistaking the man behind them. It's him; it's David Faye.

"Can I ask, do you have a pen?"

His voice is deep and assured; polite, but assertive. He doesn't sound at all like I expected; the only thing I can think of is that he sounds like an airline pilot. A man whose voice conveys confidence and competence; a man trained to speak that way.

"A pen?" I ask, dumbly. "No, sorry, I don't."

He's motionless beside me, his hands clasped before him, quite inoffensively. Below his sunglasses, he smiles politely, his teeth gleaming like the spotless plates on our tables. He's clean shaven, both on his chin and his head, and he wears a necklace of wooden beads, and a neat, patterned polo shirt, from which his massive arms are struggling to be free.

It feels like an eternity; me sitting there, wide-eyed and slack-jawed, and he standing over me, poised and assured, like we're locked into some unspoken, ambiguous game of chicken. He's massive; perhaps six and a half feet tall, with proud shoulders that extend wide, like the wingspan of an eagle.

Does he know who I am? Has he made me? I'm wearing the same face I had when I collared Jonathan, but surely he couldn't yet have raised the alarm, let alone described me. Do I move first? Or do I wait for him to throw the first punch? He's still, but I don't doubt that he could spring into action at any moment, like a coiled rattlesnake…

"No problem," he says, slapping me on the shoulder with enough force to make my entire ribcage shudder. "Sorry to bother you."

And like that, the moment that seemed to last an eternity is over and he's walking to the other side of the car. He asks the man boiling to death in his suit the same question, before taking a seat at another table, and picking up a newspaper, like it was all nothing.

I take a breath – perhaps the first since I laid eyes on him – and slowly realize that my cover isn't blown after all. His attention is elsewhere – the newspaper, and a cup of tea on the table before him – and he hasn't looked at me since.

My heart is beating a furious rhythm; I can practically feel it in my teeth. There's something about sitting in the shadow of a fatally dangerous man-mountain – especially when you know that man is a cold-hearted killer, who's murdered tens of thousands of innocent people – that gets the heart racing.

The actual, far skinnier waiter ambles up to my table, and I inattentively mumble something about waiting to see a menu, never taking my eyes off David on the other side of the room.

He disappears behind the newspaper for a moment or so, before another man – shorter, wary-eyed, wearing a black shirt – walks up to him and begins saying something in his ear. He reminds me of Dembe; perhaps he's the same age, too. One of David Faye's former child soldiers, maybe.

Stay quiet, Vega says. *I'll try to record, isolate, and amplify the words he's saying.*

I do as Vega says, taking a deep breath and holding it, hearing only the distant chatter from Faye and his attendant, and the gentle *clank, clank* of the rails below us.

Sitting here a mere twelve feet away from him is a surreal feeling. He's just as intimidating and imposing as he was in the photograph – a tall, musclebound warrior, who looks barely human compared to the skinny teenager beside him – but there's also something placid about him. His eyes are hidden within his shades, and a casual smile sits upon his lips.

I look around; no one else in the car seems to be bothered

by his presence. The grey-haired old man still cooks inside his suit, and the Nubalayan guy begins to eat a soup dish. If they know they're sharing a train with a man who'd put Jack the Ripper to shame, they certainly aren't showing it.

Another eternity seems to go by until Vega speaks again.

Okay, he says. *I think I have something.*

I breathe again.

They spoke about room three, Vega says. *I would assume that is his quarters on this train for the night.*

Huh; he really is in the room next to mine. I stand up from the table, and without another glance in the warlord's direction, I make for the door, trying to cut as inconspicuous a figure as possible.

"Do you think he locked his door?" I ask Vega, after making it to the sleeper car, and checking there are no waiting bodyguards or kitchen staff loitering around.

You didn't, Vega notes.

I casually walk up to the door labeled 3, and after glancing in both directions, put my fingers on the handle, and push down. To my delight, it opens, and I push the door gently open to find it happily empty.

David Faye's room is much like mine – a set of bunk beds, a large, clear window to the outside world, and a wardrobe composed of two wooden doors, each with that ubiquitous floral patterning engraved thereon. He has no luggage; there's only a single, crushed can of soda that suggests he was ever here.

I put my hand inside my suit jacket, and feel the cold, sturdy grip of my handgun.

"No better time to do this than now, right?" I ask Vega.

I think so.

I look up to the top bunk, before reaching for the metal rungs of the ladder beside it and climbing up. When I'm in the top, I lay down flat, pull the sheet over me, and reach for my handgun. And then – lying there quietly in the top bunk, like the kid at summer camp who misses home – I wait.

"This isn't exactly how I expected this to go down," I whisper to Vega. "Hiding in a bunk bed, waiting for the big bad killer to finish his breakfast."

You're hidden, you're ready, and you'll be able to hold a gun to his head without raising an alarm, it's perfect, Vega says.

"And I can nap until he gets here," I sarcastically add.

I wait there, breathing slowly and listening for the telltale sound of footsteps outside. Every time I hear the *thump* of shoes in the corridor, I brace myself – tensing my shoulders and readying my trigger finger – but every time it proves to be a pacing waiter, or someone speaking in hurried tones down a cellphone.

"How long does it take a man of that size to eat breakfast?" I whisper to Vega. He doesn't respond. Either he doesn't wish to indulge me, or he genuinely doesn't know.

My eyelids start to get heavy, and I see the sunlight pouring in through the window disappear in an instant – the room engulfed in darkness – only for that same sun to fill the space again as soon as we make it out the other side of the tunnel.

I open my mouth to whisper another sarcastic comment to Vega when I hear footsteps again; hard, purposeful, heavy steps. I hold my breath one more time, and the door swings open, and the tall, tyrannical figure of David Faye strides in.

He strolls to the window, looking out into the vast, endless wilderness of Nubalaya, and I make my move. I gently aim the handgun in his direction, his wide chest impossible to miss. When I'm comfortable with my stance – still lying on the top bunk, the laziest secret agent in the world – I purse my lips, and whistle.

He doesn't react. At least, not at first. After a few fraught moments, I see his shoulders rise, as though he's filling his lungs with a breath he knows might be his last.

"Good morning, David," I say out loud, aiming the sights of my handgun directly at the back of his head. "I've heard a lot about you."

"Morning," he answers in that deep, calm tone. "You must be here to lend me that pen."

CHAPTER 36

"Put your hands on your head for me, would you?"

He hears me, and turns his head ever so slightly until I see the side of his eye, peeking out at me from beside his sunglasses. Seeing that I'm aiming a gun at him, he slowly does as I say, picking his arms up, and placing his hands on the top of his head.

"Who are you?" he asks, as I sit up and contort my body to throw my legs off the side of the bunk bed. "CIA? MI6?"

I snigger out loud, an amused, somewhat nervous chuckle. No one has accused me of being in the CIA for years. Hearing those words makes it clear; I'm truly back in the game.

"No," I reply, keeping the gun on him, and sliding myself down from the top bunk. "I'm independent. I serve justice."

"Sure you do," he says, with a smirk I see creeping across the side of his face. I hit the floor with a bump, and he doesn't flinch.

"We're gonna take something of a detour from our journey here," I tell him, stepping slowly closer, keeping my handgun trained on him. "We're gonna jump off this train early. I've got some friends I want you to meet."

He snorts with laughter. He's trying to remain cool and unflappable, a hard steel I-beam, unyielding to the pressure.

"And what happens if I don't want to go with you?" he asks. I feel my whole body tensing up; a provocative question, thankfully asked without any sudden movements, for now.

"Don't worry, you'll get off this train alive, so long as you do as I say," I tell him. "But if you don't, I can't guarantee I won't put a bullet in your head."

Slowly and defiantly, he begins to turn around. Gracefully, like a dancer, he spins on his heel, until he's facing me, and I'm confronted by my own threatening reflection in his shades again. I grit my teeth, snort a breath out of my nose, and take a step closer to him, pushing the barrel of my handgun against his forehead.

"I mean it," I tell him through gritted teeth, feeling a rising tide of anxiety within me – the prospect that he won't come along so quietly after all angrily rising to the forefront of my mind.

He begins to push his forehead against the barrel of the gun – the muscles and veins in his neck straining with the effort. I take a step back.

"What makes you think I want to get off this train alive?" he asks.

This is the part where I shoot him. This is the part where I pull the trigger, and put a bullet in that war criminal's brain; a nice, homey, warm place for the steel slug of a .45 ACP bullet to rest.

But I don't. I stare at my reflection in his shades, and hesitate, knowing that if I kill him now, there's no mission left. No justice, besides the knowledge that this cold-blooded killer will be dead. Perhaps that's enough; perhaps I should pull the trigger right now and end it all.

"Do it," he says, calling my bluff. I hold onto the handgun

ever tighter, and think to squeeze the trigger, but it's soon too late.

He moves sideways – a fast, indiscernible motion like the dazed blur of a passing train – and I feel my grip on the handgun evaporate into nothing. I see the silver metal of the gun flying through the air in front of me – batted out of my hands by my foe – and take another frantic step backwards.

He puts his fists up, his eyes still hidden behind those shades, and his jaw tense. I think to make a move for the gun – hopeful of evading his advance and getting my hands back on the only deadly tool in the room – but he pre-empts me. He charges across the space, and I feel myself smothered in his hands.

Suddenly, I hit the steel frame of the bunk beds, my back arching in pain with the force of the impact. His hands are across my face – his fingertips digging into the back of my cranium, his thumbs burrowing into my cheeks, trying to find my eyes – and I feel that cold dagger of panic, embedded directly into my chest.

I reach forward, grabbing his own head in my palms, and letting fly with my knee into his chest. I hit him once, twice, and then three times – feeling my kneecap bounce off his hard body like I'm kickboxing a fire hydrant – all while wriggling around in his grip, desperately trying to hide my eye sockets from him.

With the third blow, he lets go of my skull, and draws his fist back to throw a punch. I drop to my knees, and dive forward along the floor searching for that errant firearm.

"Where are you going?" I hear, just as I feel his grip on the back of my suit jacket. He pulls me up to my feet, and I feel a hammer blow to the small of my back. It knocks the breath and love of life out of me; a slow, droning agony that builds and fills me with pain and dread. I can practically hear my kidneys crying out.

I take a painful breath – my lungs shuddering in spasmic

pain – and fall to my knees. Then I see it: the silver grip of my handgun, sitting quaintly on the other side of the room. I stagger forward, reaching out, but watch helplessly as a black boot slams itself down onto my hand.

"You Americans," he says, as I growl into the floor in pain. "You can't live without your guns."

I pull my hand out from underneath his boot, my knuckles scraping across the sole of his boot, bringing a whole other flavor of pain.

"Come on, fight me like a man!" he shouts, as I clumsily find my way to my feet somehow, my hand still pounding with every heartbeat.

He puts up his fists again, and I put up mine, blowing another breath out from my gritted teeth. He feints a couple of times – two stance shifts, two tenses of his biceps, and two abortive punches – before throwing a jab that I narrowly dodge.

"Okay, you wanna fight," I tell him, as he throws another jab, one that I deftly avoid this time. "I'll give you a fight."

I throw a punch with every ounce of pained breath and every joule of nanotechnologically augmented power still in my body. He dodges; I glance his chin – feeling the tiny bristles of his shaved skin – and he catches my fist as I reel it back.

I pull, using all my might to extricate my fist from his grip, but it isn't moving. I'm entombed in stone, like my fist is his now. Out of options, I pull my left fist back and slam it across his face.

He staggers backwards slightly – his shades shattering into a dozen plastic shards that fall to the floor – but he doesn't ease his almighty grip.

In one furious, powerfully kinetic movement – like the catapult that flings the rock – he pivots his body sideways, and throws me by my fist into those wardrobe doors. I fly forward, hitting them with my face and chest, and yet I keep going, meeting yet another flimsy wooden wall – the back of the wardrobe – and break through that too.

When I finally do stop moving – meeting a hard surface, coughing up a cloud of plywood and plaster as I do so – I'm hit with another assault. This one loud, and shrill. A fearful scream. I shake my head and rub my eyes, before looking up to see an elderly woman standing in the corner of the room.

"Help!" she cries, as I look around to see myself in the cabin next door. There's a suitcase laid out, and a set of clothes on the bunk bed, and the poor woman standing here, her hands by her mouth in an expression of horror. He must have thrown me through the wall entirely.

I try to stand up, and hold my hands out before her in a pleading, conciliatory gesture, but find I have no wind in me, and no voice to speak. She charges past me, flinging the door open, and I'm despondent to see the massive figure of David Faye waiting in the corridor for her to pass.

"Here you are," he says, ducking slightly to fit underneath the doorway. I growl a guttural, animalistic noise at him, and throw my fists back up. He's removed the skeleton of his shades now; his eyes stare back at me, cold and calm, seemingly unfazed by the fight or the fact I had a gun pointed at him one minute ago.

He charges forward again, and I hit him with a punch, slamming against his forehead. He grunts in pain, but doesn't slow down, grabbing me around the neck, and forcing my head down to his chest level, before slamming his own knee into my cheek.

"Oof!" I hear myself cry – a sound that seems both distant and close by – and I fall sideways against the window, hitting it with the side of my face. I see the Nubalayan wilderness pass by – barren, dusty red hills; thorny, razor-like shrubs, and the unremitting sun – and can't help feeling it looks like heaven compared to *this*.

I feel hands at the back of my head again – almost a tickling sensation – and realize he's still holding onto me. I try to shove him away – pushing against that wide chest with both hands – but I'm not strong enough in this state.

He pulls his fist back, and rains it down upon me. I see it falling, like a flaming, rock-hard meteorite, with nowhere to go but the surface of my skull. I close my eyes, and brace for the impact…

CHAPTER 37

When it hits me, it doesn't feel like a fist, or like a flaming meteor. It feels like a cold splash of water, waking me up from some chilling nightmare.

I open my eyes and find myself in a darker space. The air is dark green, thick, and murky, and everything around me is slow going, like I'm submerged in molasses. Strange, silver shapes pass me, like fish swimming in a dark and grungy aquarium, and if I look closer, I see a larger mass there; a body, languishing in the mist.

At first, it looks like the body in the alleyway; the teleporter button I touched to get here. When I squint my eyes, and look a little deeper though, I see that it's me. I'm lying in the mist, and there's a larger figure standing over me. Imposing, frightening, and dangerous.

He was stronger than me. How can that possibly be? I'm a cyborg, he's just a man…

Kris, you have to wake up, Vega says, his voice somehow piercing the shadowy dimension I find myself in. *The nanomachine network is stimulating the production of norepinephrine in your brain. You were knocked out, but you're coming back around…*

I feel a strange sensation, like in this otherworldly realm I'm suddenly weightless. I'm pulled upwards, to another dimension, one of light and vibration. The sunshine pouring in from the window above me; the trembling *clank, clank* of the railway tracks below me.

I must be back, back in hell.

I snort, or cough, or snore or something – a rasping noise that I can't quite describe – while I shake my head from side to side, trying to clear the cobwebs from my vision.

I turn my head to see the humungous, titan-like figure of David Faye standing with his back to me. Beside him is the teenager from the restaurant earlier, and they both turn to look at me with wide, surprised eyes.

"Huh, thought I cracked your skull," Faye says, dropping his hands to his sides. "No matter."

The teenager alongside him holds something in his hands; at first it looks like a plate, but as my vision clears, I see that it's a gun. My gun.

Kris, you won't get out of this if you don't stand up and fight, Vega says, the voice in my ear imploring me to charge into the fire again. *You can fight, and you can beat him!*

Faye walks over to me – his black boots planting themselves just in front of my nose – and he reaches down to grab me.

"You're right," I murmur out loud, as Faye drags me groggily to my feet. "I have to beat him."

"What did you say?" Faye asks, his face now adjacent to mine. I stare into those cold, cool eyes one more time. They're brown, with large black pupils, and almost completely motionless. No fast movements, no bulging blood vessels; just two clear, cool openings to a soul who's seen this fight a million times before. A soul that has seen hell.

There's the loud sound of a metallic *click*. It's noticeable enough to make the warlord turn his head, and we both see his teenage buddy aiming the gun in my direction.

"No!" Faye shouts, instantly letting go of the collar of my shirt, letting me fall back against the window, where I lean uneasily. He charges over to him and grabs the gun: "Don't use this, get out of here!"

The teenager – a look of chagrin and displeasure on his face, like a chastened student – does as he's told, and leaves the room.

I make the most of the distraction, planting both of my feet firmly on the floor, and shaking my head one more time, provoking an almighty pain in my skull, but ridding myself of the dazed, hazy cobwebs at the sides of my vision.

I see him unload the magazine from the gun, putting it in the right pocket of his pants, before sticking the gun into his waistband. He turns back to me – his eyebrows high in his forehead, his eyes wide and expectant – and speaks.

"You gonna tell me who you're working for, or do I have to keep beating on you?"

I grin – tasting the acrid coppery taste of my own blood in my mouth – and walk towards him. I throw a punch, a hail Mary that he dodges, and another, that he doesn't. It hits him in the jaw, and I feel something like the sweet, agreeable crunching of bone and cartilage.

He stumbles backwards – two steps back, and drops to one knee – and I press forward. I throw another punch as he rises again, hitting him in the temple, sending a splash of blood across my face.

"Argh!" he grunts, dropping back to that knee. I feel myself blinking – his blood splashing around on the surface of my eyeball – and I put my hands to my face, rubbing my eye and wiping his blood from across my forehead.

When I get the blood out of my eyes and open them again, I'm met with another fist, hammering against my temple. It knocks me off my feet, but I seem to fall back into another's embrace. A hand cushions my fall. Only too late do I realize it's his hand; his fist, grasping the fabric of my suit jacket again.

For the briefest moment I feel like a ragdoll; a mere, weightless puppet, in the grasp of some massive celestial being. He throws me, and again I'm airborne before crashing into another wall, this time the white, featureless plaster partition beside the door.

My face breaks my fall again, hitting the wall and breaking through it in a choking cloud of plaster, before I land on my hands and knees in the corridor outside. I cough a couple of times, take a painful intake of breath, and look up to see that hateful, nightmarish figure advancing towards me again. And this time I run.

I scramble forward, crawling across the corridor floor on my hands and knees a couple of steps, before clambering to my feet, and running for the next car.

Blearily, I pass a waiter, wagging his finger as if to chide me, and then a man and a woman, who watch me with panicked eyes and open mouths. I look over my shoulder and see that the mountain is still moving; David Faye, in all his fearful intensity is pacing towards me still, a sadistic smile on the side of his lips.

My breath coming in ragged, painful wheezes, I make it through the next car, and keep moving until I get to another car entirely, this one far louder than the quaint corridors.

As soon as I push the door open, I'm hit with a blissful memory; a vibrant fragrance of a better time and place. It's a kitchen, and it smells like baking bread, and the bakery two blocks away from our house growing up, and the tired smell of the early morning, when my mother and I would pass it on our walk to school.

After a moment of appreciation, I put myself back in the present, and the throbbing, painful headspace I need to be in. I look over my shoulder again, and see him there, still pacing forward; the bloodthirsty warlord, trying to beat me to death.

"Hey! You can't be in here sir!" someone yells at the side of my face as I grab a knife – a large, shiny butcher's knife from a wooden block – and hold it above my head. I retreat, stepping backwards, sensing the kitchen staff behind me doing the same thing, and wait for my tormentor to make it through the doorway.

This kitchen is remarkably clean, considering it's confined to a train car. It's long and thin with countertops on either side, and a tiled black and white floor. There are cooktops with saucepans and ovens, and discarded crates with all manner of meats and vegetables, unusable in a fight like this.

Faye ducks under the doorway – his wide body blocking almost all the sunlight from the windows beyond – and advances towards me. I swipe the knife, a warning if anything, hoping to slow his charge, but he isn't fazed.

He puts his hands up and I swipe again, this time with a murderous butcher's intentions. I swing the knife in a diagonal motion, and he steps backwards. My eyes follow his, hoping to see the smallest note of panic at the prospect of being face-to-face with a knife-wielding kidnapper, but he's unflappable; his eyes flit between mine and the knife, ever cold and ever calculating.

I swipe again and he catches my fist, before bending my ring finger out and somewhere behind the back of my palm. I screech in agony – feeling something inside pop – and let go of the knife, which falls to the floor with a sonorous clatter.

Pulling back my hand, I clutch it close to my chest before looking around me for the next kitchen utensil that could save my life. I find a saucepan full of some deep-red liquid, and throw it at him, hoping it's on the boil. The saucepan merely bounces off him, staining his shirt with a tomato sauce, and those eyes still aren't daunted.

There's another bout of shouting behind me – terrified kitchen staff, bemused to be witness to a knife fight in their place of work – and I take the opportunity to run again, pushing past one of them and making for the door.

The next car is a darker, colder space. It's full of crates and bare sunlight, and after a couple more steps, I see that it's more a freight car than a passenger car. There's a wide freight door, through which the dry Nubalayan wind whistles and whips around the car, and a messy collection of boxes, all held in place by string cords and plastic tarp.

I keep running, making it to the freight door, and the wilderness outside that passes in a feverish blur. We must be traveling a hundred miles per hour – the repetitive *clank, clank* of the tracks below are barely intelligible now, having merged into one long, loud murmur.

I think of jumping out of the freight door – getting off this train, and giving myself entirely to the wilderness that flies past at an unfathomable speed, like the teeth of a buzzsaw – but I don't do it. I'm not ready to bail, not yet.

"Where are you going?" he asks, ducking under the oval doorway to the car yet again.

"You're a killer," I tell him, my voice raspy and hoarse. "You're a war criminal. You're gonna pay for everything you've done."

"Oh, you're one of *them*," he says. His cold eyes remain still, no twitch of the eyelid, no nervous look down, just relentless concentration and focus. He takes another couple of steps towards me, and I take a deep breath.

I throw my fists up and throw a trio of jabs to his temple. The first connects, and the second glances off him, before he ducks the third. I step forward, grabbing him around the neck and throwing a number of fists into his stomach with my other hand – one, two, three, four punches in quick succession, finding an unreceptive home in his hard abdominal muscles.

He pushes me backwards, and I spin myself around to

keep my balance. To my horror, he smiles at me; a small, confident smile that serves to defeat any notion I had that my punches hurt him. The assault I just laid into his body with every bit of nanotechnological strength I have was seemingly harmless.

My fists go up again, and I throw another couple of punches to his face, rocking his head backwards, only for him to reel forward again like a fairground whack-a-mole. I take one last deep, defeated breath – accepting my fate – and watch as he plants his leading leg in preparation for throwing a haymaker.

He hits me, hard. The impact knocks me off my feet, and I suddenly find myself face-down on the dirty metal floor of the car, coughing up a nightclub's cocktail of sweat, dust and blood.

As I feel his grip on the back of my jacket and my collar, I can't help but look outside and see the bright, dusty wastelands outside, blurred and flattened with motion, passing at breakneck pace. It looks almost peaceful, like still water.

Why can't I beat this guy? Why does he feel stronger than me? I'm not a normal man; I'm not a regular human. I'm a nanotech-augmented soldier, he's just a man. I'm electromagnetic fields and precision-cut carbon and nano circuits. He's flesh and blood.

Before I can find an answer to my questions, I feel myself moving again; falling, perhaps. The world is a dazed blur, no clearer than the wastelands passing outside. Suddenly though, the motion stops, and I slam down into a hard surface before reeling backwards.

It's the side of the car – the steel wall of the train car, now adorned with a dent roughly the size and shape of my head. I try to mumble something, and turn with my arm outstretched, either attempting to throw a punch, or trying to grasp a tentative hold of my surrounding world, even as it slips ever further from my grasp.

I blink, and see his face again: the tormentor, the warlord. Those malevolent, calm eyes. He punches me, once, twice, three times, twenty times, I lose count, and after the third, they don't even hurt. I'm not sure I even still possess the capacity to feel pain; I'm neither really here, nor anywhere else. My existence is a sheer cliff face, and I'm barely hanging on.

The bright, once hopeful sun goes down, and the entire car is bathed in darkness. I look at the warlord again and see a machine staring back at me. Polished, gleaming black metal skin, and emotionless, robotic eyes. He looks more like a robot – more a precision-engineered killing machine – than I ever did.

I feel myself sliding down a vertical surface and dropping to my face again. When I take a breath and pick my head up high enough not to taste the dirt on the ground anymore, the sun is risen again, and the breeze from the outside world on my face is heavenly.

Kris, you're still here, you still have some fight, a voice within me cries. Is it Vega, or some prodromal madness within me?

"God forgive me," another voice says. I blink – feeling the trickle of blood in my eyes again – and look up to see Faye towering over me as I lie beside the freight door. "Hush now."

I see him take my gun out of his waistband, before reaching into his pants pocket to retrieve the magazine. Forlornly, I turn my head, looking back to the outside. I could jump out of the freight door – jump off the train entirely – but I don't have the strength. I can barely lift my arm, let alone my entire body right now.

"God forgive me," he says one final time, pushing the magazine into the firearm. "But I must kill you now. You're a threat to me, and you're a threat to my children."

He aims the gun at my head, and I look back to the outside and see something coming; a helping hand, reaching from beside the tracks. I do the impossible – I pick up my arm and quickly thrust it outside, just in time to catch the gray vertical signpost passing the freight door, my dubious lifeline…

CHAPTER 38

Well, at least I'm not on the train anymore.

I feel like I'm lying down, perfectly horizontal, floating just off the ground. I'm moving faster than I can measure, but everything else is moving too; the ground below me whizzes by, like an eagerly revolving wheel. There's air rushing over me, and air rushing beneath me; an ethereal bullet, traveling effortlessly.

I see something above me too, like a rocket, flying roughly perpendicular to me. It's long, propelled forward by a jet of dark-red particles. It's my severed arm, accompanied by the trail of blood following it. It's faster than me too; quite the sight.

The back of my head is gently caressed by something, my hair ruffled, before I feel my whole body – a painful, cumbersome knot of limbs and bloodied stumps – slam into something hard and uncompromising. But I keep going, rolling along the floor, seeing the blinding sun above me turn to the dusky dirt and back again, over and over, like a pebble skimming across the dirt.

By the time I stop rolling – and painfully fill my lungs with a breath that feels like it could pop a hole in the side of my thorax – I'm facing upwards. The sun, bright and in the middle of the sky, fills my vision, and I summon every last bit of effort I have left to shield my eyes with my one good arm.

That was a close escape, Vega says. *Your right arm was severed at the shoulder by the signpost, if you haven't already noticed.*

"I have," I croak to him, before carefully exhaling, feeling a dribble of blood leave my mouth as I do so.

The force of your arm catching the signpost severed it instantly, but the same force dragged your body from the train. That severed arm saved your life.

"I should go find it," I deliriously tell him, closing my eyes to the blinding glare of the sun. "Take it home with me, have it stuffed and framed."

You need to stop the bleeding. The sandy ground beside you should suffice for now, so long as I can work to clot the severance in time.

I turn my head to the right and see the bleeding stump of my former arm for the first time, and a pool of dark blood accumulating in the sandy scrub. I cough a couple of times, and push myself over to my side before plunging the stump into the dirt.

Good, now don't move, Vega says.

"I'm not exactly in a hurry here," I tell him.

I'm in the midst of the Nubalayan wilderness, far from the sound of any human civilization. I can't see the train tracks from here, but they must be nearby. A sharp, hard stem of a troublesome shrub stabs me in the small of my back, and I hear a cricket of some sort chirping nearby.

The adrenaline still throbs around my body – the terror and the thrill of battle pounding a steady drum-beat inside my skull and knuckles – but I know that won't last forever. I can already feel the dull onset of the pain to come, like a grimly receding sea, an omen of some terrible tsunami.

"What was he?" I mumble, trying to keep my mind off the pain I'll soon be experiencing, but instead going back to the agony I suffered on the train. The pain that he gave me. The pain that shouldn't have been possible.

You have numerous fractures to your skull, and a bleed on your brain, Vega says, ignoring my dazed question. *You have lacerations to both kidneys, a ruptured spleen, and you have significant internal bleeding from multiple sites. There are potentially fatal blood clots in your lungs. Your C4 and C5 vertebrae are damaged, and you have more fractures and partial breaks in your bones than I care to mention.*

"Was he human? He wasn't human, was he?" I ask, wiping a sheen of sweat or blood or both from my forehead with my only hand.

I don't know. I will run an analysis on his blood and his genetic material as soon as your critical physiological functions are restored to a stable state.

"He was stronger than me, that's impossible," I say, letting myself sink into the sand and the dirt and the blood around me. "Is he a machine? Is he like me?"

The terrible thought suddenly enters my mind; what if he isn't human? What if he too is a host to the nanomachines? Granted a nanotechnological suit of armor by another wayward traveler from a different time and place?

I never considered the possibility before, but who's to say Vega was the only one they sent back? Perhaps there were multiple, and the child soldier David Faye was the first to play host.

"Nanomachines," I say, between fitful, pained breaths. "Does he have the nanomachines too?"

I don't make a lot of sense, but Vega knows what I'm asking.

No, he replies. *I can tell you that I detected no presence of nanomachines, nor any other futuristic technology during your fight. Any further analysis will have to wait.*

I take another breath and close my eyes again – feeling the dry, blistering sun on my skin – before remembering that it isn't just me and Vega out here. I reach into my jacket – ripped, bloodied, and covered in a layer of dirt – and take out the satellite phone Baynes gave me.

I hold it close to my face and see that it's undamaged, and miraculously still responds to me jabbing a couple of buttons with my thumb.

"It still works," I say, amazed. "I broke every bone in my body, but the phone still works. Maybe we should replace my arm with it."

Keep the stump of your arm pressed into the sand, Kris.

I navigate to Baynes' contact details and type out a short, hasty message, just as that tsunami of pain begins to appear on the horizon. This thing has GPS; he'll be able to find me, so long as he can off-road that van.

You're still losing too much blood, I'm going to have to induce unconsciousness to slow your heart rate and make you pump less blood.

"Do it," I tell him, closing my eyes for the last time and waiting to slip into a blissful sleep. "I'm tired of your company anyway."

Vega doesn't respond; I just feel myself sink deeper into the sand. Deeper and deeper still, until I'm entirely enveloped in darkness, and the world – and everything in it – shrinks to a grain of sand, and I slip away.

CHAPTER 39

I'm moving again.

I feel like I've spent my entire day in motion. Speeding across the country on a train; getting thrown through walls on the same train; making a very hasty, painful escape from that train.

Now, though, I feel sharp specks of dirt and sand grazing the small of my back. There's pain too. A lot of it, so much I can barely think of anything else. Just the motion, and the pain; my life, summed up.

I open my eyes and the brightness is overwhelming; a white veil of unbearable sunlight, laid over me like a death shroud. But it doesn't last long. In an instant, light turns to dark, and I reach up to rub my eyes with my one good hand.

There's another presence beside me too; a certain animalistic grunting, wheezing noise, and the cumbersome movements of someone exerting great effort. I look up to see a dark, grim ceiling, and a dim bulb dangling from it, and realize that I'm still moving; a pair of hands gripping me beneath the armpits.

"My God, how are you so heavy," I hear. It's Baynes, and

he's tragically out of breath. He sees my open eyes and speaks again: "You're alive? Are you with me? Can you hear me?"

I'm being dragged along the hard floor, and soon get the strange and humorous image of a particularly exhausted old donkey, dragging a broken plough across a field. Baynes lets go of me, and my head and shoulders sink back onto the ground with the wet slap of blood and sweat on concrete.

"I'm with you," I whisper to him. He appears upside down at the top of my field of vision; a sweat-drenched, red-cheeked Baynes, his normally so immaculately neat hair a torrid mess.

"What the hell happened to you?" he asks, in between sad, tired breaths. He sounds dismayed; I don't know if it was the effort of dragging me here, or just seeing me like this. "Did he have help? An entire gang of them? How did they throw you off the train?"

"He didn't have help," I answer, looking up at that dim bulb, hanging there perfectly motionless like the sun. "And he didn't throw me from the train. I jumped."

"You jumped?" he asks, his expression confounded, like he can't believe what he's hearing. This eventuality never cropped up in our plans, after all.

"Well, it was more like I got off the ride early. Pulled the emergency exit lever, shall we say."

He stands there above me, the same look of bemused shock frozen on his face.

"You look terrible," he finally adds, his lips barely moving, and his face still frozen. "You're covered in blood and bruises, and your arm…"

"What arm?" I ask him with a smile, just as that rising tide of pain overcomes me again, and washes the smile right off my face.

"Jesus, Mary and Joseph," Baynes says, only now beginning to shake his head from side to side. I can't recall him seeing me like this before. Sure, I've had my share of cuts and bruises, and cut off a finger in front of him, but I don't think he's witnessed an uncensored, bloody disarming mess like this.

I take a deep breath and try to push myself up to my elbow, bending at the waist. I get as far as my head and neck off the ground before Baynes gratefully steps in.

"Hey, here, let me get you," he says, putting his hands under my armpits again, and pulling me over to a harder, vertical surface, which I turn to see is a filthily stained concrete wall. He props me up against it, as I feel my battered and bruised organs inside my abdominal cavity jostling around, like blind drunk rednecks at a tailgater that turned sour.

After some gentle shoving and heaving, I find myself sitting upright against the wall with my legs splayed out below me, a worse-for-wear ragdoll.

"Where are we?" I ask, looking around. "What is this place?"

The walls are grimy and covered in rust stains. The floor is dusty and pocked with holes and grooves. It's a small room, empty, but for the out of place figures of Baynes and me. There's a large dark-red stain on the floor; at first I think it's my blood, only it seems to be dry. Someone else's blood from long ago, perhaps?

"The first empty building I could find," he replies, looking around at the same shadowy, cobwebbed corners as I do. "I think it was a wine shop, once."

I suppose that'll explain the suspicious stain.

"We'll stay here while you recover," he says, kneeling down beside me, crossing his arms. "If anyone shows up, we'll just wave our guns around and hope they're scared away."

"The American way," I say with another painful smile.

There's a silence that passes between us. This room is almost completely quiet. No humming or buzzing of fluorescent lighting tubes or wireless routers; just the dust and the dark. All I hear is my own ragged breathing, my lungs sounding like a set of bagpipes with a couple of bullet holes in them, agonizingly inflating and deflating.

"Does it hurt?" Baynes asks after a few too many quiet moments.

"Like you wouldn't believe," I say in reply, closing my eyes as I think of my severed arm again. It feels like my arm is still there, attached to me, only it's on upside down and inside out, with a curiously unbearable pins and needles sensation all along it. Phantom pain for an arm that'll soon grow back.

"He did this?" he asks.

I nod, flashing back to the train, and the hateful mountain advancing towards me at every moment. The great, unrelenting obsidian rock, unstoppable and uncompromising, beating me to every punch and impervious to my every blow.

"I don't know how, but he was stronger than me," I say, before spitting out a blood clot from between two loose teeth. Baynes is disgusted – I see his eyes squint and his jaw clench – but he doesn't look away.

"I thought that was impossible," he says, shaking his head again, his face frozen in another expression, this one a picture of dismay.

"So did I," I reply. "It's only Vincent, and his genetically engineered strength that can dole out a beating like that. I guess what they say is true: David Faye really does have the devil in him."

I say it with my tongue in my cheek and an abortive chuckle, but his expression doesn't change. It's true, though; I came up against a force that surely can't be human. A match for me, and more. At first, I thought I was the strongest man in the world, and then I met Vincent, and then I met David.

Baynes taps his index finger on his temple, before

standing up and pacing towards the corner of the room. He pauses there before turning again and pacing back.

"I'm, well, I guess I'm, I should say –" Baynes stammers, seemingly unsure of how to say it, or even what he's saying. "I think I should say that I'm sorry."

"You *think*?" I ask. He quietly sinks his head into his hands, before picking it up again.

"I put you up to this, didn't I?" he says, despondently. "This was my idea, bringing you across the world and making you go after that lunatic."

"Look, let's just cut out the, the –"

I interrupt myself, losing my voice to a coughing fit and hacking up a dismal lungful of congealed blood. I look up to see Baynes's face peering into mine, even more disgusted with the scene – and seemingly, himself – than before.

"We're going home," he says when I'm done hacking up the surface of my lungs. "We'll wait for you to recover, and then we'll get the hell out of here. We'll go back to the hunt for Vincent and forget this ever happened."

"Man," I say, before coughing a couple more times. I want to ask if he's at all curious about how the warlord could be so strong. I want to ask if he's really willing to give up on the quest to bring this guy to justice, especially after we've both learned how dangerous he is, and what he could be capable of.

But I don't ask him anything. I just keep coughing those blood clots out of my lungs.

"Are you okay?" he finally asks, as I begin wheezing like a rabid, dying hippopotamus.

"Can you get me a drink of water?" I croak.

"Oh, yeah, of course," he says, pacing back to the other side of the room. "I'll find you something, stay right there."

He vanishes into a dark doorway, and the sound of his frantic footsteps gets ever quieter until they disappear. I heave a couple of times, but I my coughing bout is over.

"Vega," I say, after enjoying a little silence, albeit too little. "What's going on, what can you tell me."

Your body is healing, but it will be a while before you're able to operate at optimum efficiency again, he says, rosy as ever. *Your arm will take a day and a half to grow back. Your internal organs will require twenty-four hours to return to peak performance. You'll make it back to 100% strength, but make no mistake, it was quite the beating you took back there.*

"Yep, I'm aware of that," I tell him, trying to keep as still as possible so that I'm not confronted by yet another pain to an organ I've probably never heard of. "What can you tell me about Faye?"

Well, thankfully that blood of his that landed in your eye was quite the bountiful sample. And you're right, he's not like other humans.

"Again, I'm more than aware of that," I say.

His blood is devoid of myostatin, a protein that regulates muscle growth. In ordinary, healthy humans, myostatin acts as a suppressor to prevent muscles from growing too large. The complete absence of that protein in David Faye's blood is a prime evidentiary factor for how he has such highly dense muscle mass and strength.

"What are you saying, that he's another genetically engineered specimen?" I ask, my surprise causing a big intake of breath that racks me with pain. "Is he another Matriel guinea pig?"

Not necessarily, Vega answers. *There's no evidence of gene editing and alteration. All of his genetic material appears to be in ordinary, plausible ranges for a healthy human being, with the exception of the gene that promotes the production of myostatin. Unlike Vincent, who had many obviously man-made alterations to his genes, all precision engineered to produce a very specific function and performance within his body, David has just one deviation.*

"So, he's a mutant?" I ask.

All humans are mutants, Kris, Vega says, drolly. *All human beings suffer innumerable mutations in their genomes, for better or for worse, at the point of their conception and indeed their whole lives. It's the very basis of evolution.*

"So, he's not a mutant, but a regular guy?" I ask, growing exasperated, and ever more pained.

No, he's clearly not a regular guy either, Vega says. *He's someone who has developed an extremely potent genetic condition. Like a freak sprinter whose blood allows them to distribute oxygen more effectively, or a champion diver whose lungs are that much more efficient than anyone else's.*

"Right," I say, feeling a slight bit of relief – and an equivalent amount of shame – knowing that the man who beat me until I was almost dead isn't a genetically engineered superhuman after all.

Of course, someone's upbringing is a case of nature versus nurture, your genetics versus your environment, Vega goes on to say. *Unfortunately, David Faye has undergone extreme forms of both. Raised in the most brutal war imaginable since he was a mere child, it's no surprise that he's such an effective and formidable fighter.*

I think of those eyes again – those cold, dark eyes, with no malice and no mercy – and the memory of him observing every punch he threw like he'd thrown it a million times before, and looking at me like I was just the latest in a long line of victims.

There's one more thing I have to tell you, Vega says.

"I'm all ears."

He isn't stronger than you.

Okay, now I'm *really* curious. I sit up a bit more, pushing my back higher against the wall behind me, provoking another cascade of pain.

"What makes you say that?"

I ran a kinetic force analysis, based on the relative damage to the nanomachines present in the areas of your body that took his punches, as well as the destruction of your bodily tissues.

My worst ever ass-beating, digitized and served back to me in a numeric report; truly, the future is now.

He's physically strong, for sure – by far the strongest you've come up against, with the notable exception of Vincent – but the raw power exerted by his musculature doesn't rival the sort of strength you can generate.

"You're telling me I should have kicked his ass?"

No, Vega thankfully says. *He's a seasoned warrior, a trained fighter, a survivor forged in the fire of war. He has more fighting experience than you; more familiarity in fighting for his life under pressure. But, with adequate preparation and self-belief, you could overpower him.*

I take another deep breath, a lot less painful than the last.

"I could beat him," I repeat out loud, my words echoing in the dark.

This isn't over. He isn't a demon walking the earth. He isn't possessed by evil spirits, or nanomachines, or genetically engineered to be a murder weapon made flesh. He's human; bone, blood, and a lot more muscle than usual.

I'm better than him. I'm a better fighter; I'm a better man. I just need to prove it.

I need to finish what I started. I need to do what I came here to do.

CHAPTER 40

"And finally, this one," Baynes says, throwing a weighty, colorful plastic package on the ground before me. It bounces, before deflating slightly, making a gentle *crinkling* sound. It's bread shaped, but beyond that, I have no idea. "I got it out of a gas station dumpster. Like the rest, it's a couple of weeks out of date, but you said you didn't mind that, so…"

I wave my hand, telling him he doesn't need to go on. Before me lies a veritable smorgasbord of expired and unappealing food products. Candy bars in ripped and torn packages; sandwiches in clingfilm wrap; bruised bananas and overripe avocados.

"Thanks," I say with a dubious smile. He isn't really listening though; his eyes are transfixed by the pink, glisteningly wet appendage stretched out by my side. My new arm, eighteen hours into healing. It's half the size it'll be when it's done, but I can already make out the fingers and thumb.

"Man, it's horrible to look at, isn't it," he says, his expression caught between disgust and morbid curiosity.

"That's my arm you're talking about, Randall."

He looks me in the eyes again, and we share an uneasy couple of moments of faux offense, before I grin at him.

"You get used to it," I say to him. "Imagine what it's like for me. I have to live like this, sitting idly by while raw hamburger meat oozes from my body."

I reach forward and grab a candy bar with a sense of urgency that seems to disgust him further. I can't remember seeing him eat at all this last day and a half.

In fact, I don't ever remember seeing him spooked like this. A man who once sat across the table from terrorists and murderers; a man who went undercover in countries hostile to the United States, where one wrong move would put him against the wall. He finally found his limit sharing a room with me and my disgusting right arm.

"How much longer?" he asks, meeting my eyes with his own. Still, I can see him tempted to look at the arm again, his eyes nervously struggling to stay still.

"Another eighteen hours," I tell him.

"Good," he shoots back. "Eighteen hours and we can get the hell out of here. We'll travel to Lushoto, go to the airport, and jump on the first flight we can get. We can forget about the minister, forget about the job, and forget about David Faye."

"This isn't like you," I say to him, pushing a deeply unpleasant chocolate bar between my lips and chewing. "Quitting, cutting and running, leaving a job half done."

"This isn't the agency, and we're not working for Uncle Sam anymore," he says, turning his back to me, finally escaping the sight of my new arm. "We don't have to risk our lives for the love of our country, or to save the lives of our fellow citizens."

"What about the citizens of Nubalaya? The children we see here every day?" I ask, my mouth full of awful, tasteless chocolate. "Don't they deserve to live free and peaceful lives? Lives free of the risk of getting forced to join this warlord's army, or finding themselves on the other side of it?"

Mentioning that one word – warlord – makes my skin tingle with pins and needles, and my internal organs gasp in pain. But pain is something I can handle; what I can't handle is the thought of David Faye being out there still, plotting to restart the civil war and immiserate millions.

"Kris, we didn't come here to improve the lives of the Nubalayan people," Baynes says, putting his hands on his hips. "We came here to capture David Faye, so that the government could put him on trial. We're not here on humanitarian grounds; we're bounty hunters."

"Don't remind me," I say.

"It's true, I'm sorry to say it, but it's true," he says, his voice sad and monotonal. "What was it you said? Mission creep?"

He paces to the other side of the room again, before pacing back. He dismissed Dembe yesterday, telling him our mission was done. I thought I stood a chance of talking him into pursuing Faye again, but while he's talking like this, I'm not quite so sure.

"We got ahead of ourselves. *I* got ahead of myself," he says. "I underestimated this entire mission. We should have a staff of five, at the very least. You and Alessia at the frontline, Dante, Jude and I providing support on the ground. I underestimated David Faye, and I almost got you killed. But I won't be doing that again. We're going home as soon as you're healed."

He paces around again. I can hardly argue with him. He's right, after all; we did underestimate David Faye. And he's right about one more thing: we won't underestimate him any longer.

"I don't know if I can do that, Baynes," I tell him as he paces back, his anxious face catching the dim light of the bulb. "I won't be able to sleep at night knowing David Faye is still out there, still breathing, still destroying. Just give me more time. Stay here with me for one more week."

He stops pacing and crosses his arms.

"No," he says, sternly. "When I found you out there by the rail tracks, I thought you were dead. You were covered in blood; you hardly had a pulse. I thought I'd be repatriating a body, and then I realized I couldn't do that, because Kris Chambers is already dead, he died on that subway train."

What is it with me and trains? Died on one, could have died again on the other. Maybe I should learn to drive after all.

I look up again at Baynes who doesn't seem to share my humor, though. If I didn't know him so well, I'd say there were tears forming by the sides of his eyes.

"Why did you disappear for two years?" he suddenly asks, a change in topic that I don't expect. "Why did you go and live in Asia under a secret identity? Thrash around at palm trees, or whatever you did?"

"Why?" I repeat, still unnerved at his sudden change in questioning. "Well, I guess, I didn't like what I'd become, you know?"

He stops pacing, and he crosses his arms ever tighter, like he's the vengeful principal at some high school for wayward teenage superheroes.

"I felt like I had no control over my own life. No agency. After the airport, and after, you know," I tell him, as he averts his eyes to the floor. "After we lost Jack, I felt like I was done. That I had nothing more to offer the world, and that the world wouldn't ever stop taking from me. Taking people I loved; taking chunks out of my sanity."

I take a deep breath, reeling slightly from the effort of dredging up unwanted memories, and go on.

"It took the knowledge that I was no longer the most powerful man in the world again to bring me back. Knowing that there was someone else out there with my strength – and knowing that he'd use that strength to cause pain and death and destruction – convinced me that I couldn't live in the shadows any longer."

"And now you feel the same way, huh?" he asks. "Now you've gotten the crap kicked out of you again and you're addicted."

I shrug at him, my newly regenerating arm still lying there on the floor, an ever-present reminder of what happened yesterday.

"I disappeared," he says, mournfully. "I disappeared plenty of times. Left my wife behind and assumed another identity, in Beirut or Moscow or Minsk or wherever. It was the job, right. But I never did it gratefully."

He puts a finger in between his face and his glasses and rubs an eye.

"I joined the CIA fresh out of college," he says. "I didn't like it at first. In fact, I hated it. I grew into it, of course, but I never realized until it was too late; I grew into it, but the CIA grew into me too. When I was young, the boys and I – Charlie Forrest too – used to look at the older guys and call them dead men walking."

He begins to pace again, before walking back underneath the dim lightbulb.

"The old timers; guys whose careers had reached a standstill, onto their third or fourth marriages, just going through the motions until a retirement they didn't want, and a pension they didn't need. Dead men walking."

"Jesus," I say, but he isn't deterred.

"We used to mock them. And then, we became them. My wife left me because I couldn't leave the job behind. There was always one more job, one more assignment, one more opportunity to save America."

"What are you saying?" I ask him. "That I need to find myself a wife?"

"No, that's not what I'm saying," he says, shaking his

head, perhaps offended by my flippant remark. "I'm saying you need to know when to call it quits. One more mission won't save America. One more warlord behind bars won't save Nubalaya."

"No, I know that," I tell him. "But David Faye? He's *my* guy. I can't let him go now. I want another chance to take him down."

He's quiet, but I can see he's worked up. His hands are on his hips, and his shoulders rise and fall with quick, emotional breaths.

"I never had kids," he says, throwing me another curveball that knocks the words off my tongue. "My wife and I, we tried, but…"

He pauses again, looking to the corner of the wall beside me, as if he can't quite finish the sentence. It's a painful memory for him, way more painful than I'd expected. Hell, I've known him all this time, for better or for worse, and I barely know anything about his marriage. Maybe I should have asked.

"Maybe if we'd succeeded in starting a family, I'd have learned to be better. Learned to be better at protecting those who depend on me, I don't know," he says, sullenly.

I look back at him with confusion. I don't know what he's trying to communicate to me; that he feels as if I'm the closest thing to a son, perhaps? He just shakes his head again and takes a deep breath.

"You have to know when to call it quits," he finally says. "Two years ago, you knew exactly. Now, though? I'm not so sure."

He walks over to the doorway, like he's about to leave.

"He's a killer, Kris," he says with evident regret. "He's a killer, and although you're many things – many great, brilliant things – you're not a killer. We leave tomorrow. No ifs, no buts. I won't put you in that kind of situation again."

And with that, he ends this strange spectacle and walks

out of the room. I hear the door slam shut behind him, and I'm left alone with my thoughts and my selection of expired treats.

I've never heard anything close to that level of emotional empathy from him before, he even seemed dangerously close to sounding like a human being. I'm quite shocked. It only took me getting beaten to within an inch of my life to get us there.

There's a strange feeling within me; part of me is relieved, and perhaps even a little heartened that he cares so deeply about keeping me alive. But I can't ignore the niggling doubt in the back of my mind – the burning, aching feeling that doesn't go away – that he doesn't believe in me anymore.

I put my hand in my pocket, and rummage around for the waxy, smooth surface of the polaroid I pocketed from the Minister's collection a few days ago. I find it and bring it out, before putting it to the dim light.

The father – the train driver in dark blue – and his son, both wearing hopeful, joyous expressions. The kid's first train journey, perhaps? I guess that doesn't matter anymore; they're both now dead, by Faye's hand.

My image as a superhuman – a man capable of beating any evildoer in this world – took a battering on that train, along with my body. It hurts. I feel I have a lot left to prove.

Maybe that's why I won't be leaving tomorrow. Maybe part of this is about my ego, my hurt self-image, and the realization that everyone in this world I care about will think less of me for this. They'll want to wrap me in bubble wrap and judge me by my looks again: a skinny, stupid mid-twenties kid.

He's wrong about one more thing, too: For better or for worse, I *am* a killer, and I'll prove it.

CHAPTER 41

Kris, if you're really serious about doing this, this is the time.

I open my eyes to darkness. Vega's voice, a hyper-technological alarm clock sent straight from the future, is pulling me out of a dreamless slumber and back into the cold, dark world.

Across the room, the dark, slender figure of Baynes lies beneath a dirty white sheet. He snores, loud enough to echo, but evidently not loud enough to wake me.

I slowly and quietly throw off the plastic tarp that's served as my bed sheet, before feeling my hips and elbows ache as I rise to my feet, the result of two nights of sleeping on this hard, uncomfortable floor.

After running my fingers up and down my new arm – my skin smooth, and my veins visible, even in the dim light – I clench my fist, stretch out my palm, and look to the doorway. Then I slowly sneak towards it, checking my pockets for the bare essentials – wallet and the satellite phone – and leave the sleeping Baynes behind.

There's another corridor out here, and a thick, metal door at the bottom of it, barely visible in this light. I gently push it open – it heaves and grinds on its rusted hinges but doesn't make enough noise to wake Baynes – and I step outside.

It's almost dawn; the sun isn't up yet, but the horizon is tinged with gold, and the deep black of the night is gone, replaced with an enigmatic dark blue. It's already warm and humid, an early clue as to how unbearable the coming day will be.

It's the first time I've left the building, a bland, long-abandoned rusted metal shack, with a sign out front that once presumably said 'Royal Court Wines', but now has a couple of letters missing.

There's a dirt road ahead, and another couple of buildings alongside it, but aside from that, this really does appear to be the middle of nowhere. I can't see the van – Baynes would have been smart enough to hide it – and there's no source of light other than the rays appearing on the horizon, so in the absence of better idea, I begin walking that way.

"Vega," I say, almost tripping over a stone by the side of the road, "talk to me; how do we find David Faye again?"

He was traveling to the Mwanikan Republic, another rebel-held autonomous area, Vega says. *I'm sure he still intends to go there, despite the hiccup on the train.*

I make it to the end of the dirt road, and a more carefully paved road intersecting it. Perhaps a couple of miles in the distance I see a gently dancing display of white headlights and red taillights, along with the quiet, low purr of engines and the sound of tires on sandy asphalt. A highway.

There's something else that may be of interest to you, too, Vega adds. *When I was recording and isolating the audio from David Faye's conversation with his fellow traveler on the train, a name came up. Akello Bayo.*

"Who is that?" I ask, climbing a sandy verge, making a beeline for the highway in the distance.

I don't know anything about him, other than his name and the fact that David was due to meet with him. Perhaps finding Akello Bayo should be your first port of call.

"Agreed," I say.

I walk another forty-five minutes or so, and the dark-blue sky becomes an overcast white so quickly I barely even notice it happen. I hop across patches of scrub, thorny vines, and treacherous crags in the earth that threaten to snag my ankle and force me back to Baynes' lonely wine emporium, but thankfully, I manage to avoid that fate.

I make it to the highway – a couple of lanes of traffic in each direction, with an ill-tempered truck or a beat-up car passing every few seconds – and take up a place by the side of the road, facing east; the rough direction of the Mwanikan Republic.

I don't even know where I am; the train carried me east until I made my early departure, far enough to carry me out of Free Zimbala, perhaps. But Nubalaya is a big place, a remorseless land of rainforest and savanna, dangerous beasts and fruitless nothingness. If I'm to travel to the Mwanikan Republic – to the other side of the country – I've got to improvise.

From the side of the road, I stick my thumb out, no doubt looking every bit as awkward and tragic as I feel. Here I am, a tired-looking white man in disheveled, dirty, slightly torn clothing, attempting to thumb a ride. I'd say I stick out like a sore thumb, but perhaps if I did, I'd be able to catch a ride.

Half an hour passes, and despite scoring some funny looks – a man behind the wheel of a semi laughing as he drives past, and a minibus full of children staring at me with wide, confused eyes – I don't get the ride I need.

Eventually, I begin to tire of the choking exhaust fumes, the putrid diesel smell, and the plumes of dust sent into my eyes by each passing vehicle. I reach into my back pocket and pull out my wallet, before taking out twenty dollars in four bills and holding them in my palm beside my outstretched thumb.

After a couple of near-takers – slowing, before accelerating again after getting a better look at the state of me – a box truck slows beside me and pulls up just a few yards ahead. I pace over there, and climb up to the passenger-side window to see an older man with a dour expression sitting behind the wheel.

"Where?" he says, a single, terse word, before scanning the rest of me to try and look upon those dollar bills again. I gently place my arm – and the bills – by the side of the window within his sight, and speak.

"The Mwanikan Republic, or as close as possible," I tell him. He doesn't react at first, before pulling his bottom lip over the top in a vaguely calculating expression. After a few moments, he looks back to my eyes and nods. I thank him, open the door, and climb inside, before putting the four bills on the dash.

He's an older man, perhaps in his fifties, with graying hair, and an entirely gray mustache, wearing a track suit. He doesn't say another word – wary of what he might learn about me, I guess – he just looks back to the road, pulling out onto the highway again.

I sit back, sinking into the leather of the passenger seat, and look around; there's a polaroid of a family above me – a woman, three children, and the driver – and a stack of books below my seat.

After a few minutes, I remember my manners and take out the satellite phone. I tap out a brief text message to Baynes.

I'm sorry buddy, I've already left, I write out. *I'm going to finish what I started with the warlord, and I can't waste any more time arguing with you. If you're still in, travel to the Mwanikan Republic and meet me there, but if you want to go home, I understand. Either way, I'll be seeing you soon. Kris.*

I pause, letting my fingers idly tap against thin air for a

minute. I look down, tap send, and turn the phone onto silent, knowing that he'll spend the entire morning trying to get through to me. He'll be able to track me on the GPS after all; if he really wants to track me, he can.

I take a regretful breath. I wish it hadn't come to this, but I can't have him by my side if he isn't one hundred percent committed. Maybe he really has come to see me as a son of sorts – a maladjusted, tortured, cyborg son – and sure, that's sweet and whatever. But it isn't what I need right now. I need to match the warlord for strength, and for coldness.

I won't get beaten by him again, and if Baynes worries that I will, I need to wipe that thought right out of his head.

CHAPTER 42

"Hey, hey, hey!" I hear, a deep, loud, but timid voice, wrenching me out of my slumber.

I blink and rub an eye, then look around. My driver looks at me before looking back at the road, and back to me again. He has a face like thunder, like I committed some great social faux pas in falling asleep in his hallowed cab. In fact, I don't even know what time it is; I could have been sleeping for hours.

"We're almost at the border," he says, before slowing and flicking his hazards on.

"Okay, great," I say, sheepishly rubbing my other eye. I watch the road as he pulls over, before looking back to me with an uncertain expression.

"You need to get in the back," he says. "There are soldiers, men who'll ask questions. Maybe questions you don't want to answer."

"Oh, yeah, sure," I stammer, before reaching for the door handle and hopping out onto the side of the road.

Shielding my eyes from a cloud of dust and dirt kicked up by the passing traffic, I go around the back with him. He pulls a chain by the steel shutters on the back of the truck, pulling them open with some effort, revealing a dark, pungent-smelling space. The reek from inside is strong and unappealing, but somehow familiar.

"Get in," he says. "I'll come get you when it's safe to come out."

I do as he says, climbing into the back of the truck. There are large burlap sacks at either side, and wooden crates further inside, full of God only knows what. The air is thick, and sticky almost, with the smell of some weird and exotic spices I can't quite identify.

I crouch between two sacks, and hear the shutters close again, plunging the entire space into darkness. Here, deprived of one more of my senses, and able to smell and taste nothing other than the contents of those sacks and crates, I suddenly recall the memory, lingering at the back of my mind.

"Hah, wow," I laugh to myself.

What's the matter? Vega asks.

"This is how I got smuggled into Aljarran, isn't it?" I say, with another chuckle and sickly intake of breath that I really could do without. "In the back of a truck, inside a sack full of reeking, unbearable spices."

You do have a taste for traveling in style, he replies, dryly.

I push my lips shut, screw my eyes shut, and bury my face into the collar of my shirt, trying to ignore the humid, painful air. The memory persists, too, and with it, a bitter feeling of regret and worry.

Two years ago, I went alone to Aljarran and changed the course of the country's future. What am I doing now? Have I learned anything? Have I learned nothing? Will I make the same mistakes?

No, I'm stronger now. Stronger of mind, and stronger of spirit. I won't make the same mistakes; I'm not crossing this border armed with delusions of grandeur. I'm not here to save a people; I'm here to bring one – just one – to justice.

I open my eyes and feel them burn, beset upon by those billions of particles of spice dust I'm sharing the back of this truck with. It's a weird place to be giving myself a pep talk, that's for sure.

Another half hour or so passes, and every bump and crag in the road we drive over rocks me, drawing yet another sickly intake of breath. By the time I feel the engine slowing to a stop, and the voices of the soldiers checking my driver's ID, I'm almost begging for them to open the door and fish me out. But that point never comes, and we drive on again.

The wheels below me go on turning, and I'm barely able to keep track of time. My eyes stream with tears, my lips burn, and my lungs feel like they're choking full of hot sauce. It's like I'm half-asleep in some delirious realm, part competitive chili cookout, part hell itself.

When the shutter slides up and open again – thankfully bathing me in a cleansing white light – I surface from between the two sacks of spices, and erupt into a coughing fit. I clamber out, rubbing my eyes with both fists, and jump out of the back of the truck before I'm even able to discern who's waiting for me.

"We're here," are the only words I can make out. I open my eyes – still wet with my own tears – to see my driver standing there before me, smoking a cigarette, hunched over the back of the truck. "Mwanika, or the Mwanikan Republic as they call themselves today."

"Thanks, man," I tell him, trying to sound sincere, but still agonized by the torture he put me through to bring me here. I reach into my back pocket, take out my wallet, and give him another bundle of bills, which he takes from me and stashes in his own pocket quicker than I've seen him move all day.

I look around and see we're parked beside a tall building – a granary of some sort – large enough to block out the sun entirely. Behind me there's a row of colorful apartment buildings – walls and balconies painted pastel reds and greens and blues – but seemingly no one home. The entire place looks deserted.

Above us is a tangle of wires threaded between buildings and wooden poles, more akin to a web laid by a giant, mechanical spider than the workings of a city's electric grid. There's a line of dark-green trees by the other side of the road, and a persistent wind that shakes the branches, and kicks a veil of dust into my hurting eyes.

The driver, without another word, pulls the shutter down and begins walking back to the driver's side. I reach out and put a hand on his shoulder, an effort to impart the sentiment that I'm thankful, but an effort he doesn't seem to appreciate. He pauses and looks back at me with aggravated eyes.

"Thanks for this, for everything," I tell him. He blinks. "Listen, I'm looking for someone. I have a name, and –"

He interrupts me, jerking his shoulder away from my hand and shaking his head as if to say he doesn't want to hear anymore.

"Don't," he says. "Knowing too much, that's a bad thing. I'm not interested in knowing what some lone American is doing here; I think we both know it's not going to be good, is it?"

I take a deep, disappointed breath – my shoulders falling, deflated – and he begins to walk back to the driver's side. As disappointed as I am, though, he's smart, and he's right. I look like trouble, I sound like trouble, and for anyone seen to be helping me, I'll likely prove to be fatal trouble.

I hear the door open, but to my surprise, I don't hear it slam shut, and the driver's small, tired figure appears by the back of the truck again.

"Here, go to this address, it's close to that crossroads," he says, scrawling a couple of words on a scrap of paper with a pencil, and then pointing down the block. "You'll find someone willing to talk with you, for the right price, at least."

He hands me the paper, and I take one look at it – '251

Khala Battery Park' – written in handwriting that's barely legible.

"Be careful here," he says, emotionlessly. "But I'm sure you know that already."

"Thank you for this," I tell him, and he waves a hand in some strange gesture – like he's batting away my words of appreciation – and walks back around to the driver's side, where I hear the sound of that door slamming that I've been waiting for.

Nice guy, really talkative, Vega says sarcastically.

"You could learn a thing or two from him," I tell him, whispering under my breath as the truck pulls away and drives off down the block. I rub my eyes one last time – shielding myself from the wind and the dust – and start walking.

CHAPTER 43

By the time I make it to the address on the paper, the streetlamps have begun lighting up, illuminating the dust, smog, and swarms of flies present underneath each bulb.

The address itself is a strangely lopsided structure; a mishmash of exposed brickwork, uneven plaster, and rusted steel, with no two roofs the same level, and no two walls the same color. It looks like a building that started small – a single room – and was extended over the years, by a series of different builders.

The most unusual thing, however, is the sign out front. Khala Dentistry Ltd; not exactly the place of business I expected to find myself in tonight.

"A dentist's office?" I mumble.

Prepare yourself to pull some teeth to learn the warlord's plans and whereabouts, Vega dryly notes.

I find a buzzer on the wall – a small doorbell-like button, along with a speaker haphazardly plastered into the brickwork – and push it. A voice almost immediately blares out of the speaker – a deep, crackling, male voice, shouting something I don't hear a single word of; just a litany of strange vowels and consonants, like a cultish ritual conducted via telephone.

"Uhh, hello?" I say, dumbly.

The speaker on the other side says one word; this one I know too well.

"American?"

I stand there, hesitantly wondering what to say in response, when I hear the door unlock itself. I push it, and find it receptive to my touch, swinging itself open. Without another word, I step through.

Inside is a grimly lit waiting room, and an empty reception desk. If this was a dentist's office once upon a time, it certainly isn't anymore. There are glossy magazines splayed out on a spacious coffee table; the dates when they were published are all from years earlier, though, and there's no sign of life from anywhere else, other than the distant *bump, bump* of bassy music.

I look around and see a single arrow painted in crimson on a cold blue wall. It points downstairs, to a basement area. I make my way over there and down the stairs, before turning my head to see the entire wall beside me filled with tallies.

Four straight lines, intersected by a diagonal line, hundreds upon hundreds of times over, all engraved within the plaster, like the visual diary of a mad man, or the count of something far more macabre.

At the bottom of the staircase lies a thick, cast-iron door, like the door to a bank vault or a fallout shelter. That music thumps ever louder, though; a pounding beat, like the unrelenting bass of the secret gathering of raver dentists, entering its 754th night without pause.

I push against the door, and with some effort, it slides open, scraping and squealing against the concrete floor. Beyond is darkness, but there's a throbbing, strobing blue light at the end of the tunnel, and the music grows ever louder.

With a trepidatious breath, I walk towards the light, and a circular window set within yet another door. Through the window I see lights – blues, reds, and whites – and human bodies, standing in close-knit groups.

"Yeah?" a voice beside me says, making me jump out of my skin. I turn to see a large man dressed all in black, sitting behind a counter. He looks a lot like a bouncer, and this looks a lot like a bar, with not a dentist chair or x-ray machine in sight.

"Yeah," I repeat to him, in the absence of anything more informative to say. "I'm looking for someone, I –"

"Go inside, don't make any trouble," the man says, gesturing to the door. I smile at him and go inside.

It's a bar, all right – a huge, spacious basement bar, illuminated in cold blue neon lighting, and kept alive by the sound of that bass pounding a dependable rhythm like a heartbeat, making every glass and bottle on every bar top and table tremble.

A quarter of the room is taken up by the bar – a curved counter, behind which three men shake up drinks and talk amongst themselves. There's large, ostentatious neon lettering around the walls – an array of combat-themed words and phrases – and a stack of empty spirit bottles set up like a target range.

The rest of the room is taken up with a series of tables and chairs, half of them occupied. There's a pool table in the corner, and a set of televisions with soccer games and other sports, along with a general, half-interested chorus of *oohs* and *ahhs* from elsewhere in the room, reacting to each play.

There's a logo too, partially obscured by a gang of biker-looking men: 'The Dentist's', the oddest name for a bar I've seen since my trip to Cleveland.

And yeah, about that gang of bikers: it hasn't escaped my attention that they're all Caucasian. Thick, beer-bellied, bearded men, covered in stifling leather and dark-green tattoos, more suited to some Nebraska truck-stop dive bar than a dentist's office in the most remote, war-torn corner of Africa.

In fact, the entire clientele here is dangerously eye-catching, despite my innate instinct to keep my eyes off them. There's the gang of Nubalayan men, passing a machete around and periodically erupting in loud laughter that exceeds even the bass in volume. There's a south Asian man, talking with the only woman here, watching a game of cricket on the TV, openly carrying a silver desert eagle in a holster.

I believe it's a mercenary bar, Vega says, his voice being the only noise I can hear over the sound of that bass. *Probably an organized crime-run establishment, populated by hitmen, cleaners, and former soldiers, gathering in a lawless place to discuss and find new work.*

I smile to myself and shake my head in amused disbelief. I can't believe these places actually exist. Then again, in a place like Nubalaya – a country still ravaged by the old civil war, and the many loose ties and unresolved feuds that come with it – it surely isn't too surprising.

Besides the odd gathering of suits on the train, it's the first time I've seen a group of professional westerners in Nubalaya. It only makes sense that they'd be here, looking for work in violence, rather than in construction or farming or medicine or any of the other sectors where this country needs aid. Exporting violence around the world. Hell, my hands are hardly clean, violence is why I'm here too; I suppose it's what we do best.

Go talk to someone at the bar, Vega says. *You're going to look suspicious, standing there gawking.*

I snort an aggravated breath, but can't deny he's right. I walk up to the bar, sidling up beside a man in a suit, flipping through pictures on a laptop, and an older white guy with a scar across one milky eye. He doesn't seem to notice me; he's transfixed on the soccer game on TV.

"Hey, can I get a drink?" I yell to a man behind the bar. He walks up, leaning across the bar and looking at me with two receptive eyes, until he senses something he doesn't like, and reels back across the counter.

"Why do you smell like ata rodo peppers?" he asks, his face contorting into a hurtful picture of mocking disgust.

"It's a long story," I tell him, drumming my knuckles against the sticky counter. "Beer."

He fetches me a bottle of beer, during which the man beside me with the laptop sheepishly stands up and walks away, evidently just as disgusted by the rancorous, spicy smell as the bartender. The scarred man beside me doesn't flinch, however. Perhaps the same battle that gave him that scar also took away his sense of smell.

"What's with the name?" I ask, as the bartender slides the bottle of beer across the counter to me, keeping his distance. "The Dentist's?"

"This used to be a dentist's surgery," the barman says, shrugging. "The owner was a dentist – he leased the old office upstairs – before he became a leader in the rebellion. He died in the war, and we honor his memory."

Just your typical mercenary bar named for a late dentist turned rebel insurgent leader. Of course, the classic; why didn't I think of that.

"How about the tallies outside? On the walls?" I yell to him over the pounding music. He leans over, still ensuring he doesn't come too close to me and my eye-watering aroma, and yells back.

"It's just an old tradition, goes back to the war," he shouts, the bass providing a martial drumbeat to his words "Every time a regular would make a kill, they'd add a tally to the wall. It's, you know, just one of those silly things."

"Right," I say, nodding, trying to keep the look of incredulity off my face. There are hundreds, maybe thousands of tallies out there. Either these boys are prone to bragging, or I'm sharing this bar with two dozen serial killers.

"You might rack up a couple of bodies tonight yourself; better hope none of these guys are allergic to pepper," the barman says, with a dubious smirk on his face.

"I need to talk to someone," I say to him, moving the conversation along. "I have someone's name, and I need to put a face to it."

He points behind me, and I turn around to see a man sitting alone in a booth, his attention not wandering farther than the number of empty shot glasses before him.

"Talk to him: Rafa," the barman says. "And take a couple of tequilas with you."

I have him get me those tequilas, and after settling the bill, I saunter over there, carefully carrying a shot glass in each hand. As I get closer, I see the man more closely; he wears thin wire glasses, perched uncomfortably on the end of his nose, and a T-shirt of some American death metal band. He's African, with large, drunk eyes, and a pencil tucked behind his ear.

"Hey, I heard you're good with names," I say to him. His lugubrious eyes follow the sound of my voice, rising to meet my face, but the rest of his expression remains unchanged, a vaguely amused smile. He looks like he can barely remember his own name, let alone anyone else's.

"Sure, I do names," he says in an accent quite different from anything else I've heard in Nubalaya yet. "For the right price."

I hold the shots of tequila out to him, and he nods receptively.

"That's a good start," he says, before kicking the chair opposite him at the table out. I sit there and put the two shots down. I carefully slide one shot across the table to him, but by the time I've taken my seat, he's already downed his shot, and he's reaching for mine.

"So, who do you want to know about?" he then asks, before downing the second shot in one rapid motion, placing the glass down, and crossing his arms in a professional, genteel manner, as though he's primed for business and didn't just imbibe a tequila double.

"Akello Bayo," I say across the table. Rafa smiles – a dubious, disbelieving smile – like I said something absurd or humorous, but as the moments go on, his amused expression evaporates from his face.

"Oh, no," he says, shaking his head and sinking his eyes down to the empty shot glasses. "No. No, no, I'm not getting involved in all that."

"Wha—?" I mumble, seeing him clumsily plant a palm on the table, moving as though he's trying to escape me and my dangerous line of questioning. "All that what? What the hell did I say?"

"Who are you?" he asks, still shaking his head. "You look like some yank tourist, you're no soldier, no mercenary. Why are you here, in a place like this, asking about a name like that?"

"I'm here for the same reason anyone else is here," I tell him, watching him fidget around uncomfortably in his booth, like an octopus out of water. "Just business."

"Are you out of your mind, or just stupid?" he asks, before finally calming himself down and quitting the fidgeting act.

"Just tell me who he is, and where I can find him," I say. "I'll make it worth your while."

"Okay, so you're stupid, you couldn't pay me nearly enough to get into that man's business," he says, his watery, uneasy eyes narrowing with suspicion. "And what the hell is that smell? Chili peppers?"

"You can't even tell me anything about him?" I ask, exasperated. "His looks, his job, his history?"

He uncrosses his arms and flails them around in a petulant, childish display, back to being that octopus again.

"And you get stupider still," he says through gritted teeth. "Everybody in this room knows the man. Everybody in this room knows his work, and his history. You don't exactly have to look very far to find him."

I stare at him blankly. What is he saying? That he's one of the sketchy-looking men in this very room?

He looks over my shoulder and gestures for me to look. I take a foreboding gulp and turn my head around, but rather than seeing a battle-scarred, 6'4" David Faye acolyte standing behind me, I instead see the blinding white light of a television bolted to the wall.

"Thanks for the shots, though," Rafa says. I hear him stand up and stagger away, but my eyes remain locked on the TV.

It's a news show, by the looks of it. There's a chyron running along the bottom, with headlines of the various things happening in Lushoto. In the main picture is a press conference of some kind; a bunch of reporters seated before a table with three men, all dressed in blue police uniforms, with a curtain bearing a police badge behind them.

In the middle sits a large, portly man, his two bear-like fists positioned on the table, and his face glistening with sweat. He talks quickly, his eyes flitting between his colleagues at either side of him, who themselves don't get a chance to speak. He picks questions from the gaggle of reporters in the crowd and laughs and jokes.

After a minute or so, the news show finally throws up a graphic with a name and job title to go along with the face: Akello Bayo, chief of police for Lushoto.

So *that's* why Rafa didn't want to get into his business. David Faye is meeting with the chief of police. A man who works for the Nubalayan government; a man tasked with keeping the peace, upholding law and order, and someone who presumably shouldn't be seen dead with the murderous, insurrectionist warlord, intent on restarting the civil war. And yet…

I stand up from the table, nod to the barman, and make my way outside.

I need to find this guy. By the flapping of my jaw, or the barrel of a gun, I'll take a seat with the police chief, and I'll politely discuss my concerns.

CHAPTER 44

'm inside a pizza oven, or at least, that's how it feels. I sense the slow, tantalizing trickle of a bead of sweat running from my hairline, between my eyebrows, and down the length of my nose.

We hit a bump in the road; a violent jolt, sending my face into the coarse fabric below me. I grimace, snort in annoyance, and find that the bead of sweat is gone.

I'm tucked up in the fetal position, inside the trunk of a car this time, sharing the space with a suitcase and a freezer bag full of pre-prepared curried goat meals that tortures my empty stomach with its smell. I barely have enough room to breathe though, let alone steal food from my gracious hosts.

Ah, yes, my hosts. Throughout my journey, I hear two twin children – a boy and a girl – laughing, fighting, and arguing in the backseat just behind me. In the front seats are a husband and wife; a nuclear family visiting relatives in the city, and the most unlikely people I can think of to agree to smuggle me back across the rebel border and to Lushoto, but people I'm grateful to, nonetheless.

The husband was only too happy to take my money, the wife slightly more troubled at the prospect of harboring a sketchy westerner, and the kids couldn't have cared less. The whole charade makes me wonder how I'd have reacted if my dad insisted on driving us to the lakes with some strange-looking, vaguely threatening stranger in the trunk.

Another uncomfortable journey, ill-fitting for a real-life superhero who's already saved human civilization once before, but if I can swallow my pride for a moment, I can admit it's practical, and gets me across the border without any questions asked. I guess it's just like Vega said, I travel in style.

I go on waiting, cramped up beside the curried goat, feeling the sweat drip off me with every bump and shudder of the vehicle. It's like being trapped in the womb of some monstrous robotic creature, ever trembling and jarring at the whim of a sputtering engine.

When the vehicle finally slows – when the kids in the backseat stop yelling at each other and start paying attention to the sights of the city – I'm almost in as bad a state as I was in the spice truck.

The engine ceases and the trunk springs open, but I'm not greeted by the welcoming morning light like I expected. I slowly rise to my knees and look around, seeing myself inside a grim, gray parking garage, surrounded by beat-up old cars and trucks, and a domineering concrete roof.

"This is it, end of the road," the father says to me, extending his hand to help me out. I grab his hand, and achingly climb out of the trunk, landing on my two feet with a painful jolt.

"Thanks," I tell him, wiping another few beads of sweat off my forehead.

I don't know the time, but I'm guessing it's around 10 a.m. Four hours ago, or so, I flagged down this blessedly generous family – and their slightly less generous car – on the outskirts of the last city, just after getting a late-night bite to eat and changing my face around.

"I don't suppose you can tell me where the police station is, can you?" I ask the father, as his wife walks around to grab the suitcase, eyeing me suspiciously. "The police headquarters, here in the city?"

He gives me a set of directions, never pausing to ask why I'd need directions to the police station of all places. I wave goodbye to them – the two kids joyously waving back to the strange, disheveled man who just climbed out of the trunk – and we go our separate ways.

I make my way outside, and to the bright, cleansing sunshine that I've missed so much, exiting the parking garage from a ramp.

There, I find myself thick within the Lushoto weekday morning; choking traffic, with cars impatiently chewing up any bit of free road they can find, and groups of men and women with bags of groceries and other stocky goods balanced on their heads.

What's your plan? Vega asks, as a tall gentleman brushes past my shoulder, clumsily trying to walk into the parking garage. *Are you going to turn up at the police station front desk and demand to see the chief?*

"To be honest, I haven't gotten around to thinking that far," I say back, thinking of all those hours I wasted in the back of the car, counting the beads of sweat dripping off me, when I could have been wasting that time talking to Vega instead. "Maybe if I mention the name David Faye, he might grant me a meeting."

Or maybe his men will take you outside and put a bullet in you, Vega says, giving me the far less optimistic view. *If this police chief is meeting an enemy of the state – the warlord – in rebel-held territory, you can bet that he's corrupted on some level. He might not take too kindly to you walking proudly in there, bragging that you know all about his secret dealings.*

"Maybe you're right," I say, looking across the street. I see that hotel where we met with the Minister – a tall, crystalline structure, a heady aberration in Lushoto's skyline – along with the beige, brutalist edifices of apartment buildings and office buildings that better represent the tone of construction here.

Go to the station and pretend to be a western journalist, putting a story together on the success of the post-war Nubalayan government, Vega suggests. *Find out if he's there, and if he is, if he'll be amenable to an interview. It's a long shot, but even if it doesn't work, you might find out his whereabouts.*

I walk on, past a gang of kids sitting atop a winding wall yelling for my attention, and a skinny, desperate-looking man attempting to show me a photograph of something or other. He takes a second look at me – at my creased, dirtied clothing – and quickly gives up his attempts to appeal to me.

I come to another large group of kids and teens, all kicking a soccer ball around in a public plaza, with a goal drawn in chalk on the side of a van. There's a line of motorbikes and mopeds waiting and watching impatiently for the ball to work its way to the other side of the square so they can drive through, and a refrain of honks and yells accompanies them.

I wait for the ball to get kicked past me – and the resultant crowd following it – before walking on, with a couple of kids almost running into me in pursuit of the ball. I see the smiles on their faces; their eyes transfixed by every bounce of the ball, and hear their voices, high-pitched and jubilant. Unlike the generation before them, they know nothing of war, *yet*.

I'm sure growing up here in Nubalaya isn't easy, but the lives of these children will get a hell of a lot harder if David Faye restarts that civil war. It's a cold, sobering reminder of the fragility of these kids' lives, and the fact I know there's a formidable warrior out there meeting corrupt officials and making dangerous moves, with uncertain intentions.

After another ten minutes of pushing and weaving my way past crowds of busy people and gridlocked traffic, I make it to the police station.

A strange, anachronistic structure, it's a tall building, flanked on both sides by smaller cubes. Its walls are entirely covered by windows; among them, two large circular ones, giving it the look of the head and shoulders of some crystal-armored giant, buried to the upper chest in the earth.

There's a row of empty police cars out front, and a garden of exotic trees I can't remember seeing anywhere else in this land. Beside it on either side is an apartment building, built so tightly snug that I can barely see a gap between them.

The sun shines brightly above the building, making it appear almost golden – the glowing fortress of law and order, and perhaps, a hive of corruption and sedition, and the frontier of David Faye's new civil war.

Time to find out.

CHAPTER 45

"Hi there, good morning, how you doin'," I say to the two uniformed men in front of me. One of them looks at me with a quizzical expression, with two wary eyes, like he doesn't see many awkward, overly cheery visitors at the front desk like this.

His buddy beside him glances at me, entirely uninterested, before looking back to his monitor. They both wear blue shirts with silver badges, and black pants with all manner of accoutrements, though I can't see holsters on either man.

Behind me is the unbearable sound of a handheld drill, and its drill bit squealing and screeching its way into a wall. There are two workmen, both wearing yellow hard hats and high-viz jackets, muttering between drill shrieks, and chain smoking.

The police station looks completely like a work-in-progress from the inside. There's a wide, wooden front desk that seems fairly immovable, but everything else is precariously hung on via nails or in a state of construction. Even the giant, ornamental police badge on the wall before me hangs askew, not yet bolted on.

"Yeah?" the suspicious, attentive one of the two policemen says. He sits before a notepad with a list of sorts, and a pen twitches between his fingers.

"I'm a reporter with WNRNW News, in the USA," I tell him, wondering if I overcooked that fake news station name, and added a couple too many letters. "I'm here to write a story on the police chief, Akello Bayo."

He looks at me unmoved – his face hard like granite – entirely unimpressed by my job title or the number of letters in my news corp. Finally, after a few seconds of awkward silence, that awful drill starts up again – a high-pitched wailing like the screaming of a banshee – giving me time to put my next bluff together.

"We're very excited to be writing a longform profile piece on the chief, and Nubalaya's impressive rise from civil war to lawful society," I tell him, trying to convey a sense of all-American enthusiasm in my voice. He still isn't moved though; he sucks his teeth and raises his eyebrows.

"Media inquiries go through the comms team," he says, before his buddy beside him leans in and mutters something in his ear that draws a smile from him. Then he wipes the smile off his face, along with any nascent warmness, and goes on: "If you need an interview booked, you'll have to take it up with them."

"Ahh, see, that's the problem," I say, before the drill blares out again, interrupting me. The man's expression doesn't change; he just stares at me, never blinking or giving me the slightest moment of encouragement. His eyes remind me of David Faye's, somehow.

The drill ceases, and instead, the loud *clunk, clunk* of a nail gun rings out. I take the opportunity to speak.

"Yeah, the problem," I say, leaning on the desk. "You see, I've got a very small window here. If Mr. Bayo wants that interview in print – an interview that'll be read by half of the east coast – he's going to have to meet me today. It's big, I can promise you."

His expression is still unmoving. Either he's entirely unwilling to facilitate his boss's media career, or he sees through my BS, even after I went to great lengths to procure clothes that didn't reek of spices.

"I'm sorry my friend," he tells me, dropping his eyebrows to a suspicious glance again. "You'll have to go through comms."

Dang. I'm not the silver-tongued confidence trickster Vega always expects me to be. That's definitely a skill to allocate more experience points into, the next time I get a leg blown off.

"Besides," the man says, as his buddy stands up from the desk and disappears down a corridor. "He'll be leaving in half an hour, and won't be back for a few days."

So, police chief Akello Bayo is here; I now know that much. I nod to the police officer, whose eyes slowly and warily leave me and focus back on the list in front of him. I turn away from the desk and think about my next move.

Maybe I wait, and hope to catch him on his way out of the building. I could tail him to his car, overpower him, and get the answers I need there. Then again, who's to say he won't walk out of this building with a bodyguard, and a driver, and a flirtatious secretary on his arm. It's a big building too, what if he takes a back door?

I realize I'm drumming my fingers against the front desk behind me still, barely aware I'm doing it. The guys in front of me are finished with the tools now, and seem content to smoke and natter on in a dialect I don't understand.

I look to the front desk again – drawing the officer's attention with my continued presence – and scan the area for anything else of note. I look down at the various papers, neatly arranged around the man and the empty seat, and see a floorplan for the new renovation, before letting my eyes linger on it long enough for Vega to take it in.

Police chief's office, upstairs, third floor, Vega says, apprehensively. *You're not going to do what I think you're going to do, are you?*

I chew my lip for a moment, still drumming my fingers on the front desk. Evidently, I'm beginning to annoy the police officer just as much as those power tools did.

"What's the matter, fool?" he barks at me, his eyes full of frustration. "I told you; you can't speak to him today, not without setting up a meeting, and for that –"

"Look," I say, leaning across the desk. Finally, the officer is daunted, and he reels back an almost imperceptible amount; the shallowest victory for me, and yet one I can build on. "I'm afraid I really, really need that meeting today."

I drum my knuckles across the surface of the table one more time before clenching my fist and swinging a punch – not too hard, but certainly not too soft – at the cop's cheek. Two of my knuckles connect perfectly, the impact jolting every bone in my hand and wrist, up to my elbow.

He lolls back in his seat – his eyes drifting to the back of his skull, and his mouth yawning open – before slumping forward onto the desk, his hands splayed out before him.

"Sorry, buddy," I say to him, feeling the aching imprint his orbital bone left on my fist. "You were maybe a little rude, but…"

I quickly remember I'm not alone in the room, and turn myself around to see those two workmen standing beside one another, a cigarette hanging limply in each of their mouths, and their eyes wide and fearful.

We share a few strange moments of complete stillness and silence until one of them drops the cigarette from between his lips, and the two of them seem to use that as a cue to scamper, the starting gun for their retreat.

They run, one after the other as though their lives depend

on it, the last man dropping his hard hat to the floor, which lands upside down and spins gently on the ground.

Well, you'd better hurry to the police chief's office, Vega says, in an unmistakably chastising tone, like I've acted just a little too rashly for his liking.

I see the police officer begin to stir – his back rising with frequent breaths and his fingers clawing against that notepad he found so enthralling – and get another idea. I turn back to the area the decorators were working on – a newly plastered wall and a partially installed skirting board – and grab the nail gun, left unattended on a bench.

"I need you to stay here," I say to the officer, nailing the sleeves of his shirt to the desk before turning back to grab the hard hat from the floor. I throw it on my head, and start briskly walking down the first corridor I see.

Walk to the end of this corridor, to the stairwell, Vega says. *Then ascend to the fourth floor.*

I walk on, my breath caught nervously in my chest, while swinging the nail gun by my side, hoping that if anyone sees me or sounds the alarm, I just look like the world's most out-of-place builder, rather than a cop-thumping invader.

Getting to the end of the corridor, keeping my head and my eyes trained forward and doing my utmost to avoid gawking into the offices visible beyond the windows and the open doors, I finally make it to that stairwell Vega was telling me about, just as I hear frantic shouting from the front desk area.

"Hey," a voice beside me says, just as I push past the door to the stairwell. I freeze and turn around to see two officers, both holding coffee cups, walking idly down the stairs. "You shouldn't be here."

One is tall, the other is short, and they're both wearing amused expressions, like they've never seen a skinny white guy in a shirt and suit jacket holding a nail gun before. Their badges shine in the stairwell's cold white light, and I'm already regretting what I'm going to have to do.

"Oh, sorry about that," I stammer, just as they make it to the bottom step. "I'm the architect, and—"

I throw a kick, sweeping the legs out from beneath the shorter one. He briefly takes to the skies, his feet leaving the ground and his hands flying out to break his fall, like a skateboarder careening off a halfpipe.

The other officer – the taller one – watches his friend lose his fight with gravity, before looking to me with panicked eyes and reaching for something concealed behind him. In a desperate effort, I reach forward, snatching him by the collar of his shirt, and slam him atop his buddy face first.

He falls – the two of them stacking like pancakes – and I'm able to see what he's reaching for: a firearm, holstered behind him. As soon as they both hit the ground – their bodies piling one on top of the other, provoking an oddly harmonic and synchronous *oof* sound from each of them – I throw a knee to the heads of both, hitting one, and then the other.

After that, the stairwell is quiet again, the only motion being the slow writhing of the bodies below me.

"Sorry, sorry, sorry!" I murmur, pulling one off the other by the collar, and laying them out beside one another. Then I take the nail gun from my other hand, and just like with the guy at the front desk, I shoot half a dozen nails into the floor, via the sleeves and sides of their shirts, carefully avoiding their skin. They're staying put, at least for now.

Brutal, but effective, Vega says. *I do have to question your fondness for power tools, however.*

I kneel down to grab the firearm from the taller cop, and rush upstairs. My footsteps echo out against the drab brick walls, and I hear the shouting from the front desk and the corridor below grow louder.

Here, across the next corridor, it's the final door on the right, Vega says as I make it to the stop of the staircase. A blinding ray of sunshine immediately hits me – I shield my eyes, seeing an open window and the flat roof of the adjacent apartment building beyond, with its washing lines and piles of plastic bags and other junk.

I pace through the corridor, seeing in the corner of my eye another set of windows to my left, and another busy office within, this one teeming with activity. People in white shirts with folders in their hands; computer monitors and bright, accusatory lights.

I don't turn my head; I just keep on walking, with my hard hat bobbing up and down as I go. Suddenly, a siren goes off – a shrill, head-splitting assault on everyone's ears – that makes even the bodies in the office clap their hands over the sides of their heads.

Taking the opportunity to move while my pursuers still battle the auditory assault, I run down the corridor and into a thick-set man, side-swiping him like a semi at an intersection. I spin myself around to keep my footing, and he tumbles to the floor, landing face-up.

I hop over his writhing, surprised body – a turtle struggling on its back – and make it to that door Vega told me about: the one labeled 'THE OFFICE OF THE CHIEF OF POLICE' in proud, gold lettering.

Something tugs at me; a brief, irresistible impulse to turn my head and meet the source of the shouting at the end of the corridor. I do so, and see a squad of three police officers, all holding firearms, and the first looking at me directly down the barrel of his gun.

I take a breath – a nanosecond's pause that feels like it could stretch to a lifetime – before throwing myself into the door ahead of me. It flies open – smashing against the adjacent wall behind it – and I plant two feet on the plush, carpeted floor within, finally at my destination.

CHAPTER 46

"Who are you!?" a voice cries out, deep, and yet so highly strung, loud enough to be heard even above the siren.

Before me is an ornately decorated room; varnished, spotless wood-paneled walls, and a large, semi-circular window looking out onto Lushoto's skyline. On the walls there are hunting trophies – large, fearsome heads of bucks and lions and tigers and bears – along with a strangely out-of-place painting of a motorcycle.

"What are you doing in here!?" he calls out again. He looks just like he did at the press conference: tall, round, and covered in a sweaty sheen that reflects the sunlight, and darkens his blue shirt at the armpits and collar.

He stands behind a large wooden bureau – like the president's desk, only filled with dainty ornaments and ivory horns and no papers in sight – with his fists clenched, but his arms flailing helplessly by his sides.

I turn away from him and reach for the door before slamming it shut. When I turn my attention back to the chief, he has his hand inside a desk drawer, fishing around for something he likely intends to threaten me with.

I dart across the room, making it to the edge of his desk before reaching across it and grabbing the back of his head with my hand. My fingertips feel the wet, bristly hairs on the back of his head, and using all of my nanotechnological might – strength that no doubt shocks him – I slam his head onto the desk.

There's a sonorous, echoing crash of flesh against hard wood, and the resulting tremble of every silly trinket decorating the desk; some falling to the floor and smashing.

"Oomph," he groans, before sliding backwards behind the desk and out of my field of view.

"Probably should have introduced myself first, huh," I call out across the room, before charging back to the closed door and the tall mahogany bookcase beside it. With one hand, I pull the bookcase down onto its side, completely blocking the doorway and sending the contents spilling over the carpet.

With the nail gun in my other hand, I then shoot a few nails through the wooden board at the back of the bookcase to either side of the doorframe behind it, jamming it in place. It's not exactly bank-vault tight, but it'll give me a few uninterrupted minutes.

Suddenly, the siren stops and all I hear are footsteps in the corridor outside, the occasional panicked shout, and the ringing in my ears.

I spin on my heels, turning to see the chief has risen above the desk again – blood spilling out of his nostrils – holding a thick, bright-red object in his hand. It's a fire extinguisher, and after staggering from side to side, he brandishes it like a weapon.

"Come on, man, let's not make this more difficult than it has to be," I say to him, grabbing the handgun I stole from the cop earlier – a black beretta – out of my waistband, and showing it to him. His expression changes from staggered anger to hopeless alarm, and he drops the fire extinguisher by his side.

"Who are you?" he says again, as I slowly make my way over to him, keeping the handgun very much visible, yet without directly aiming it at him.

"Nice photographs you've got here," I tell him, looking at the large array of framed photos on the expansive windowsill behind his desk.

There are at least two dozen: large black and white photos with thirty or more police cadets; vivid color polaroids of the chief and a woman, most probably his wife; and official-looking photos of him and various grinning, greying old men. Politicians and media figures, I'd guess. There is, of course, one notable absence.

"No photos of you and David Faye, I see," I say to him. He blinks, his mouth dropping open. "That's a shame. I've heard you two are thick as thieves."

"Me and David Faye," he says, more a rhetorical question than an attempt to deny association with him. He puts his hands to his head – his fingers rubbing along his temples – before looking back to me with watery, fearful eyes. "You're American? Who the hell are you? How do you know that?"

It's the third time he's asked who I am. I take a deep breath – hearing shouted voices from behind the makeshift barricade – and get to the point.

"If you want to leave this office," I tell him, holding the gun high in the air and aiming it towards his head, "then you'll stop asking the questions and start answering them. Why did you meet David Faye in the Mwanikan Republic rebel zone? You're a servant of the state, and he's an enemy of the state."

He looks to the barrel of the gun – the ambiguous black hole that could portend the rapid end of his life – and blinks again, before letting his top lip tremble, as though he has a whole lot to say, but dares not speak it.

"Chief, Akello, Mr. Bayo," I say to him, before chambering

a round and pressing the barrel of the gun against his forehead. "Talk, quickly."

"It's a bank robbery," he says, his nervous eyes darting between the gun and my face. "David Faye is robbing a bank, right here in Lushoto."

I look at him quizzically, squinting my eyes and furrowing my brow in perplexed thought. A bank robbery? Not exactly what I expected from the bloodthirsty warlord. I press the gun against his face again; his head reels backwards, and he talks.

"We made an agreement; he robs the Central Bank of Lushoto at an agreed time, in an agreed manner, and I ensure he isn't impeded by my police force."

"Hey! Chief! Hey! We're gonna grab an axe!" I hear among the frenzied, muffled screaming from outside the barricaded door, but I quickly focus my attention back on the chief.

"When?" I ask him, seeing his eyes dart from the blocked doorway and his would-be rescuers, back to the cold steel of the gun.

"Today," is his reply. "At 11 a.m., to be exact. You're too late to stop him, and I'm too late to stop him."

The time of day stares out at me from a clock on the wall, nestled between two repugnant-faced deer. It's 10:40; David Faye's bank robbery is a mere twenty minutes away. If I'm to catch him in the act, I've got to move quickly.

My eyes find the chief's again before I look behind him, and to the window. I can see the rooftop of the adjacent apartment building, with perhaps a yard to jump from here to there. All I'd need to do is smash the glass and leap across.

I hear more shouting from outside; hysterical insults and fanciful assurances that I'll be in cuffs, or have a bullet in my head soon enough. I hear the first impact of an axe swung against the thick wooden door, cleaving a path through my makeshift barrier inside.

But I can't leave yet; I've still got one lingering question.

"Why?" I shout at the chief, re-adjusting my grip on the pistol and pressing it harder into his skull. "Why are you helping him?!"

"Because I had to!" he shouts back, a bead of sweat running down his cheek. "Because my family was in need…"

I look past his shoulder again and see a photograph of the chief out of uniform, his smiling wife behind him, and two small children sitting on both of his knees. It reminds me of the photograph: the train conductor, his kids, and their grisly deaths. An entire nation's children, held to ransom by the warlord.

The chief backs away from the gun and I lower it to my side, just as another swing is made at the door, and the consequent crunch of steel into wood. I see a hole in the door, just above the toppled bookcase, almost large enough to aim a gun through.

Kris, the fire extinguisher, Vega says. *Shoot at it.*

I stare blankly at the chief for a moment – who looks back at me with two worried, reddened eyes – before pushing past him and reaching underneath the desk for the fire extinguisher, a bright-red canister, the size of a soda bottle.

I throw it towards the door, and when it finds a home in the stack of fallen books, I aim at it with my borrowed handgun and squeeze the trigger. A single shot – loud enough to make the chief flinch in the corner of my eye – hits the fire extinguisher, and a loud hiss fills the room, followed by a cloud of thick, choking white smoke. Now I don't even see the door.

Not wanting to stick around long enough to find out what fire extinguisher fumes taste like, I turn and aim a kick at the window. My boot breaks through the glass, and I elbow the remaining shards away before climbing onto the sill and looking at the jump ahead of me.

I wipe a layer of sweat off my forehead and bite my lip, thinking of the single, heart-stopping stride that separates me from this crime scene, and hopefully gets me started on my journey to another.

A jump from the frying pan, into the smoldering nuclear reactor meltdown.

CHAPTER 47

I shouldn't look down – I absolutely know I shouldn't look down – but the urge is irresistible. It's four stories, but from here – with the wind in my hair – it feels much further. An unforgiving drop to a dark, dirty alleyway. Quite the undignified end.

I steady my footing, and after a deep breath – hearing the door to the chief's office finally give way in an almighty *crunch* of timber – I jump.

With relative ease, I clear the gap, landing on my right foot upon the top of the barrier, some three inches wide, and jump to the flat roof below.

The force of my jump takes me to my knees, and the gravel that covers the rooftop tears its way through the fabric of my pants all the way to my skin, but I'm quickly up again, and as the hot, near midday sun beats down on me I break into a sprint.

I duck under a set of sheets drying on a line and beat my way through another set of clothes behind that, all while the distant shouts from the police station – and that white-mist-filled office – grow ever louder.

A gunshot blares out – a single *bang*, a warning shot

perhaps – but I don't look back. I duck beneath another row of drying sheets to find a small outbuilding just behind it; a structure only large enough to accommodate a dusty blue door, and hopefully, a staircase beyond.

The door is locked, with a handle that doesn't move an inch. I wind up backwards, before throwing a kick as hard as I can muster – the sole of my boot connecting flush with the surface of the door – and it flies open, taking me with it.

I grab the doorframe to stop myself from falling, my nails digging into the splintered plywood. It's a stairway alright – a single lane of steps, going down to an almost entirely dark space. I see dust particles hanging in the air, and a foreboding, musty smell that fills my nasal cavity.

Louder shouting from behind me – getting suspiciously closer, like my pursuers have made it out of the misty recesses of the chief's lair and are hot on my tail – convinces me that I've got to take the plunge into darkness. I run down the stairs, meeting a cloud of flies that I swat away, and in the pitch black at the bottom I find another door handle.

Finding this handle offers no resistance, I barge through the door and into a drab, dark corridor, and a veil of clammy heat that descends over my face like a death shroud. To either side of me is a row of doors – front doors to the apartments here – and at the end of the corridor, another door, conspicuous with its lack of letterbox and number.

I make a run for it, hearing my anxious heart beating in my ears for the first time. The adrenaline builds within me – the boundless energy in my step, the endless pit and swarm of butterflies in my stomach – and I wonder whether it's the desperate escape from armed police, or the coming confrontation with a bank-robbing warlord that has me feeling this way.

In no time I'm at the end of the hall, and push my way past the door to find another worse-for-wear stairwell. The steps are uneven and treacherous, the handrails warped and broken into sharp steel barbs, and there's a hole in the wall, through which the sun illuminates a shaft of dust.

I begin descending the stairs, making it to the story below before slipping on the bottom step and reaching out for the wall, knocking off a chunk of plaster with my clumsy effort.

"Hey!" I hear, a deep, furious word that repeats a dozen times with the echo. The unmistakable stern cadence of a cop. "Stop right there!"

If I'm not mistaken, I could swear that voice came from below me, rather than the corridor above. I freeze in some stupid pose, hesitating to make another move, lest I throw myself into the welcoming arms of another officer.

That voice is coming from downstairs, Vega says after a couple of fraught seconds.

I hear echoing footsteps – this time unmistakably from below – followed by another set of shouts from above; they're closing in on me from both directions. I make another move, this time darting behind the wall I just took a chunk out of, an open doorway, and another corridor filled with doors and apartment numbers and muffled talking.

"Oh man, I really didn't want to do this," I say to myself, sliding to a stop in the corridor, before looking both ways and taking a deep breath. I throw a kick at the door ahead of me – the very unfortunate apartment number 311 – and break it open with one effort.

It flies off its hinges, landing flat on the ground, and I quickly and uneasily walk inside. The air is thick with the smell of cooking – some form of spicy curry that takes me back to the spice truck – and I immediately find myself in a scant living room, with two leather couches, and a tapestry covering an entire wall.

From somewhere in the apartment, a scream sounds out – a long, primal, terrified scream – and I turn to see a couple of women – one old, one middle-aged, both brandishing pans like weapons – through an open archway to a kitchen area.

"Whoa, sorry, don't mind me!" I shout, passing through the living space and to another room; a blank and expressionless bedroom – with a yellow mattress tucked in the corner – and a glass screen door and a balcony beyond it.

I pull the screen door open and hop out to the balcony. I'm blinded by the sun and its relentless golden light, and feel its warmth on my skin before looking back to the apartment, and then down again.

I see the street outside, with its gridlock of bad-tempered traffic, and a couple of blue-clad cops running into the building, seemingly unaware I'm up here. I also see a balcony below this one – surrounded by a thin railing – and perhaps, an opportunity to give my pursuers the slip.

"God, what the hell am I doing," I ask myself, as I climb atop the concrete barrier around the balcony, and begin to hang along the other side of it, gripping the top of the barrier with every bit of grip strength I have. My fingernails dig into the coarse surface, and my legs dangle downwards.

You've been in worse situations than this, Vega says. *And if you're serious about intervening in that bank robbery, you'd better believe it's going to get even worse than this.*

I release my grip and drop myself to the balcony below. I land on my toes on its thin railing, swaying backwards in panic, before I manage to regain my balance and hop off it, breaking a couple of plant pots with my weight.

"You're not helping," I tell him, aggravated and jittery. I find the screen door ajar, and pull it aside, revealing a living space full of trash – crushed beer cans, putrefying fruit and vegetables – and inside, an old man slumped in an armchair, his eyes closed and his mouth open, apparently sleeping off all the fun he had with this stuff.

I swat at a cloud of flies, and battle my way through the piles of garbage as quietly as I can. A tower of beer cans falls to the ground, but my host doesn't stir, and I make it out of the room and to the apartment's front door.

"How long have I got?" I whisper to Vega, while putting one eye to a crack between the door and its frame. The corridor outside appears empty enough; dark and quiet, just how I like it.

There are seventeen minutes and nine seconds until eleven o'clock, Vega replies. *It's important to note that neither of us knows exactly where the Central Bank of Lushoto is. If you succeed in escaping the police and get out of this building, you'll have to find that out, before you even worry about apprehending David Faye.*

"I know, I know, I'll work it out," I tell him, before quietly opening the door and traipsing outside.

This corridor is much like the one upstairs, only darker and dingier. The smell from the apartment I just fought through follows me, as does the echo of my footsteps as I walk.

I get to the other end of the hallway, and a window hidden behind a set of dusty blinds. There's loud music coming from behind one of these doors – a jaunty, joyous little beat – that disguises the sound of my escape, and I make the most of it, parting the blinds and opening the window.

My fingertips tread across the grimy, dusty glass, finding a handle and pulling it open before I carefully look outside. It's a shadowy alley, separating this apartment building from the next. There's a dumpster directly below me, and beside that, a bunch of silver trash cans, and mercifully, no one around.

I climb onto the sill – the sweet, sickening stench of trash from below filling my nostrils – and take an unfortunate deep breath, before pushing myself off and taking the fall. I don't see my landing – I screw my eyes closed and hold my breath – but when I hit the plastic lid of the dumpster, I sure do feel it.

"Oof," I groan, landing ass-first on the dumpster, my head jerking backwards with the force of the impact. There's the pain – a deep, stony ache that goes around my entire body –

but after a couple of seconds, and when I regain my breath, it soon subsides.

I open my eyes and turn my head to look both directions across the alley. I see a distant line of traffic – cars moving at a snail's pace – on one side, and a more ambiguous, darker space at the other.

As I extricate myself from the garbage – slowly climbing out via the plastic lid that I've broken in two – I pull the cell phone out of my pocket. The first thing I see is the fact I have forty-three missed calls from Baynes, along with the most recent message.

'I'm coming to your location, don't go anywhere, and don't do anything!'

"Sorry Baynes, it's a little bit late for that," I say to the phone out loud, before thumbing my way to the GPS map app. I limp away from the dumpster – a dull ache resonating around my body, but no sharper, worrying pains – in the direction of the busy street.

The Central Bank of Lushoto is a fifteen-minute drive from here, roughly eastward. If I'm fast, and if I'm daring, I can make it there in time.

The temperature must be ninety or beyond – the air is thick and humid, and the sweat is already dripping off me – and running feels like the most unbearable thing in the world right now.

Skulking out of the alley, I see that the block is busy with disinterested people; men and women who are going about their day, with seemingly no knowledge of the fact I just held a police chief captive, or that I'm being chased by a squad of cops who want to beat my face into mush.

I see a truck passing in the farthest lane of the road – a large semi, with a long metal container on the truck bed – and after working out that it's headed east, I pace across the road and across three lanes of busy, ill-tempered traffic to get to it.

I sprint the last couple of yards, before hopping up onto a

rear wheel arch and grabbing a handle on the container, holding on for dear life. After I'm still, other than the onrushing breeze tousling my hair, I take a moment to gather my breath again.

"Can you memorize this route?" I say as the truck accelerates, and I try to focus on the map, and not the craggy asphalt below me whizzing past, or the strange looks from the driver of the moped behind.

I already did, Vega says. *I'll direct you in real time, if you're really dead set on throwing yourself into the middle of a bank robbery, led by one of the strongest, most deadly men alive, all while being pursued by the city's corrupt police force.*

"Stop it, you're making me sound like a badass," I tell him, slowly creeping my face out sideways to look at the road ahead.

He's right though, I've got to exercise caution; a lot more caution than I did the last time I fought him. I don't want to break any more walls down with my face, or get hammer-fisted into unconsciousness, or pull an emergency exit lever that happens to be a steel pole passing at 100 miles per hour.

"Why is he robbing a bank anyway?" I ask, seeing a line of cars up ahead, and realizing I might have to abandon my transport and run the remaining distance.

There could be any number of reasons, Vega replies. *If he really is planning a new armed uprising, then he'll need resources. Stealing money to fund arms and training will be a priority, and he'll be hoping to do it as cleanly as possible. No drama, and no casualties. It's likely why he made a deal with the police chief.*

"At least I won't run into the cops there," I say, just as my truck begins grinding to a halt in the traffic. I jump off the back and start running.

So, David Faye just wants his boring, drama-free bank robbery huh? Well, not going to let that happen; I'm gonna rain lead on his parade.

CHAPTER 48

I run. I run until the sweat drips down my face and into my eyes. I run until my lungs burn like I've spent the morning huffing gas and swallowed a lit match. I run until freshly squeezed lemon juice pumps through the veins in my legs, and my toes go numb, and my calves turn to unchiseled blocks of stone.

But I get there. The Central Bank of Lushoto, a large, beige building, composed of dark glass and strange horizontal bar-like edifices covering the windows – like they've historically had trouble with airborne bank robbers – and a giant, ornamental seal outside, bearing the name of the bank and a logo.

The sound of the city is relentless; the ever-present din of worse-for-wear engines, distant music, disparate chatter, and a hellish horn section provided by the tune of a hundred car horns. It sounds like a regular day; no gunshots, no screaming, no shouting.

I stop by a set of railings, a mere fifty or so yards from the bank, and stoop to catch my breath. After three or four painful, heavy breaths – sounding like I just got done smoking my way through fifty cigars – I talk to Vega.

"What time is it?" I ask.

It's 11:03, Vega replies. *The bank robbery will be in progress right now, I suspect.*

There's a couple of children standing near me, bouncing a basketball, but paying it no further attention. Instead, their eyes are on me, the red-faced, sweat-drenched westerner bent over by the side of the road. I'm not exactly inconspicuous right now; how do I insert myself into a bank robbery drama without anyone noticing?

I stand up again, straightening my back and wiping my forehead with the back of my palm, before walking the remaining fifty yards to the periphery of the bank.

The whole building is cordoned off from the public. There's a neatly painted steel fence that goes around the entire block – topped with sharp-looking spikes that yearn to taste human flesh – and by the entrance, a security barrier, with a curiously empty guard post beside it.

In fact, I can't see any guards around. No cops, no security guards, and no soldiers; just the strange, jailhouse bank building, standing alone in the otherwise busy city.

I wipe my eyes and squint in the direction of the lobby. I see the reception area, behind a set of gleaming glass doors, and a seemingly unmoved desk, staffed by two bored-looking receptionists. The whole area is empty; I see no tall, muscle-bound stick-up artist, and no AK47-toting robbers either.

"Do you see a getaway car?" I ask, looking to the street behind me, and the block beyond that.

No, there are no suspiciously parked cars nearby, and no cars idling with a driver behind the wheel as you'd expect from a getaway vehicle, Vega says. *It's possible that the getaway vehicle is already inside the building itself.*

"What? How?" I ask.

There's a basement parking garage beneath the building, it's signposted. Large banks send and receive money all the time. Armored trucks will come and go, and they'll most likely go downstairs to do it.

I turn my head to see a battered, dusty blue signpost for the parking garage, and secure access. There's a single road snaking around the building, presumably going downstairs.

That must be it, he won't be robbing pennies from the cashier's tills; he'll be robbing the secure underground vault.

I make my way to the security guard's outbuilding, a small, single-seat structure underneath a quaint little red-brick roof. It's empty, alright. There's a full mug of coffee beside a bank of four CCTV screens, apparently undrunk. No signs of violence, though; a pencil rests delicately across an arm of the chair, undisturbed by mortal struggle.

Kris, look out, Vega suddenly says, setting my eyes to swivel-mode. I hear a distant, roaring engine, much like the one I hitchhiked part of the way here on, and turn my head towards that snaking road to see a pair of armored trucks driving towards me.

I was hoping for a hand-to-hand confrontation – a big show down in a spacious bank lobby – rather than a frantic, nerve-wracking vehicular pursuit.

I take cover within the security hut, lowering myself behind the chair, knocking the pencil to the floor as I do so. I peek out from behind a couple of stickers on the glass and look at the trucks.

They're armored, alright – two vans that wouldn't look out of place in a SWAT-team arsenal, with thick-paneled metal, and a grill over the driver's-side window. They both bear the bank's logo, and the windshield is tinted black, gleaming and blinding me in the bright daylight sun, shielding the occupants from my view.

They're large, too, and no doubt full of David Faye's ill-gotten gains. Gold bars? Bags of cash? Whatever the payload is, it's hidden behind inches of thick, brittle metal.

The trucks make it to the security barrier which promptly rises, freeing their path, and providing the easiest escape from a bank robbery I can imagine. I guess the warlord did his homework and cloned the access fobs. I take my chance, and duck out of the security booth, before running to the passenger side of the first truck as it passes the barrier.

I hop onto the footrest below the passenger-side window – covered by a set of horizontal steel bars, just like the bank itself – and grab the side mirror to steady myself. Then I put my face as close to the bars as I can, and steal a glance inside.

There are two men; the one closest to me turns his head to look at me, the sweat-drenched, unkempt gremlin that just hitched a ride on the side of his vehicle. Behind him is a larger figure – taller, thicker, and cooler – who keeps his eyes on the road.

I don't need a pair of binoculars to see who it is; the adrenaline that fills the pit of my stomach can tell me that. I put my fingers across the handle to the passenger-side door, hesitate for a single lonely moment, and pull it, opening it wide.

As soon as I do so, I feel the wheels below me accelerate to a furious pace, and the engine beside me roar intensely. The occupant of the passenger seat – a slender man no older than twenty, wearing large, wide sunglasses and a thin, wispy mustache – opens his mouth to bark an insult I don't hear, and swivels his body to aim a kick at me.

I reach forward, grabbing his pants by the ankle cuff, and pull him out of the truck. He tries to grab onto something on his way out – the seat, the glovebox, my jacket – but he goes along for the ride, spilling out of his seat and into the road behind us.

The driver turns his head, and despite sporting a similar pair of flashy sunglasses – like the ones I broke against his face on the train – I recognize that chiseled, wide jaw, and the two thick arms holding onto the wheel. It's David Faye, for sure.

He wears a green uniform, seemingly a size too small for him – his biceps straining the fabric of the sleeves – bearing the logo of the bank, just like the truck.

"Hmph!" I hear him grunt, an agitated noise more suited to finding an unexpected speedbump in the road, rather than being carjacked by an unknown miscreant. Other than the noise, he doesn't react to my presence much. I have a different face and a new arm, after all.

One of his hands soon leaves the steering wheel as I jump into the passenger side, readying a punch with my right hand as I grip the glove box with my left. He jerks the steering wheel just as I go to throw it, putting me off balance, forcing me into the windshield. The side of my head cracks against it, but neither the glass nor my brain seems damaged.

"Stop the truck, now!" I scream at him, reaching into my waistband for the gun I procured earlier. As soon as he sees it – the black steel of the gun barrel in the pale, sweaty palm of my hand – he moves, reaching across the cab of the truck and seizing my wrist with his left hand.

I seem to seize up – his fingers digging into my wrist, his face curling into a snarl – and feel the same cold, deathly panic I experienced on the train. His strength – that barely human, myostatin deprived, mutant strength – takes me right back to the memory of eating those punches.

By the time I force myself to act – engaging my own cyborg strength, and the nanotechnologically augmented muscles in my lats – it's too late. He forces my hand and my firearm into the glass of the windshield, which breaks with an audible *crunch*.

I struggle against his grip, reaching forward with my other hand too in a slow attempt to turn the gun in his direction. Gradually, painstakingly, I overpower him, turning the gun to him, and sliding a finger behind the trigger.

Quickly, but calmly, he turns his head repeatedly, looking between me and the gun and the road. I look into his eye behind the lens of his shades, and we share a motionless, curious moment, like we impart some unspoken understanding between each other, amid our struggle. Does he recognize me, despite my new face? Does he recognize my strength?

He puts his foot down, jerking the steering wheel to the left and then to the right, and I fire; a couple of abrupt *bangs* blaring out in the cab.

My shots miss – they break his driver's-side window, sending tiny shards of glass to the road outside – and he puts a foot on the brake, bringing the truck to a sudden, violent stop.

I fly forward – my head crashing against the broken glass of the windshield, this time dislodging it and sending me to the hood of the truck. My handgun is gone – lost to the road – and my hand is empty.

I plant both palms on the cold metal of the hood, looking over at the drop to the asphalt before me. I move my ankles – feeling my legs thankfully still inside the cab of the truck – and push myself back in there, like toothpaste miraculously sliding itself back into the tube.

I hear the engine below roaring back to life, and when I duck under the front window again – the space where the windshield once stood – I see Faye still gripping the wheel with one hand, and winding up a punch with the other.

His giant fist hits me in the forehead, or in the temple, or at the top of my cheek, or perhaps all three. I reel backwards – the force of the blow disconnecting me from my consciousness long enough to mask the pain – and come back around to see the asphalt in the road, a frenetic blur.

I'm hanging from the passenger side, my head and shoulders upside down, my legs lodged beneath the passenger seat, barely keeping me attached to the truck cab. I see the ground whizzing by, six inches from my forehead, like the teeth of a buzzsaw, hungry to snatch the skin off my face.

"Oh no," I murmur to myself, reaching up to the side mirror with one hand, and the unbuckled seat belt with the other. I pull myself up, just in time to meet another knuckle sandwich, courtesy of my chauffeur.

For the first time, as that massive fist soars towards me, like the moon spinning through space, I see that he's wearing gloves; fingerless, black-fabric gloves. I have just enough time to close my eyes.

This time, I feel the pain; an unbearably sharp moment of agony, starting at the root of my nose and quickly reverberating into my skull, and my eyes, and the back of my mind like I just ran full speed into a brick wall.

I taste blood immediately, and open my eyes to see I'm falling again, and despite my best, desperate efforts – reaching hurriedly for something, anything, that I can dig my fingernails into – I can't stop myself from hitting the tarmac.

My shoulder blade hits the road first, followed by the rest of me – a short, sharp pain in my scapula, followed by a relentless, endless jolting to the rest of my skeleton, as I roll unimpeded across the road and two lanes of traffic.

I roll and roll, my knees and elbows taking most of the love, with a little reserved for the back of my head, too. When I'm finally still – when I fall out of the cosmic paint-can shaker I find myself in – the world is a blurred, sickening haze; an ever-moving kaleidoscopic landscape of amorphous, unfocused shapes, other than one, still visible in clear detail.

The truck. The armored van I just fell from – its passenger-side door still flapping open in the drag – accelerating away from me. I see it, burning a hole in my retina; the light at the end of my tunnel vision.

I pick myself up, peeling my limbs off the hot asphalt and shaking myself free of any of the splintered glass of unconsciousness still lingering in my vision.

The second truck passes me as I wipe my eyes and feel my nose, feeling a note of panic within me when I find that it's a lot flatter than it was before, and covered in hot, sticky blood.

I snort a thick, goopy trail of blood out of it, and start running.

That could have gone better, Vega says, unhelpfully. *You don't have any fractures, but you do have some pretty bad bruises that'll require rest.*

"It's not over yet," I tell him, my voice audibly different, what with my nose now being on the other side of my face. I see the second truck accelerating away, and with it, my means of catching up to the warlord.

I take a deep, painful breath, clench my fists, and run…

CHAPTER 49

Running is simple. You plant one foot down, thrust forward with the muscles within your thigh and calves, and then plant the next, all while pumping your arms like a madman, probably with some ugly, strained look on your face.

Running when you just got knocked out of a moving vehicle, however – running when your nose is broken to bits, and when every bone and joint in your body feels like it's been dipped in liquid nitrogen and smashed with a hammer – that's slightly more difficult. A roughly you-sized shadow of pain follows you in every step, never relenting.

My eyes, though – despite being full of watery tears, the side effect of that broken nose – feel fine. Great, even. And they're trained on the second truck, a few yards behind the first, accelerating away down a four-lane road, in the very middle of Lushoto's financial district.

Sprinting as fast as my bruised body can take me, I can see myself making up the distance between the truck and me. Every yard I get closer, I spit out another breath and harden my resolve, and I see those wheels turn ever faster. Every step hurts – every breath turns my lungs inside out – but I keep going.

It feels like a lifetime running across the Sahara – an all-consuming journey across some barren, torturous wasteland, all in service of reaching a destination that may very well be worse – but after a dozen more breaths, I'm almost within touching distance.

One more mad flailing of my arms, one more tormented thrust of my left leg, followed ever relentlessly by the grim specter of my own pain, and I'm there…

I throw myself forward, diving to grab the vertical handle on the back of the truck. I feel its cold metal embrace my fingers, and I hold on like my life depends on it, before easing the rest of my weight upon it and letting my feet glide off the floor, before planting them both on the rear bumper. I stand there, hanging on by a mere three fingers, while I catch my breath again.

"What's the best way of getting to the driver's seat?" I ask Vega between ragged gasps, realizing this isn't even the first time I've hung off the back of a truck today. I see the cars zoom past in the adjacent lanes, and bystanders watching with looks of wonder and concern, and very occasionally, amusement.

This truck is built to withstand hijacking; it doesn't provide a trustworthy footing to strafe along the side, Vega says. *Provided the van stays moving, your only option would be to climb along the roof.*

"I was worried you'd say that," I tell him, re-adjusting my footing on the slender bumper. After another few breaths – another few moments rebuilding the mental barriers I need, lest I realize what I'm doing is utterly insane – I climb.

I pull myself up via the handle and jump upwards, clawing my fingers into a groove on the very top of the van; a small gap, where the vehicle's back door meets the roof.

In a one-arm pull up that might look impressive to the car

behind, but feels painfully routine to me, I hoist myself up there, treading on the backdoor with my tiptoes until I can pick my feet up beside me.

I reach forward along the roof, using my sticky, blood-soaked hands to gain some purchase against the flat surface, and slowly pull myself away from the edge. I crawl forward, inching forth like a slug, leaving behind a thin smudge of blood as I go, while the wind whistles through my hair.

I watch the city pass by; tall buildings under construction, surrounded by massive cranes and dump trucks, and open-mouthed construction workers pointing in my direction. We pass a playground, full of rusted slides and overgrown grasses, and the sound of high-pitched shouts and laughter, and youthful wide eyes watching me cling on.

Through it all, I keep my eyes on the truck ahead – David Faye's vehicle – and see it weave in and out of traffic, slowing only to squeeze between two cars, or skid around a tight corner. He speeds through a red light – narrowly avoiding a crash – and the truck below me does the same.

Inching forward still – holding onto the side of the roof when we turn a fast corner – I make it to the truck cab, and the driver's side on the right. Wiping my eyes one last time, I swing myself down to the driver's-side door, clasping my fingers around the side mirror, and open the door.

Inside there are two men: the driver, a wild-eyed, aghast-looking man clutching the steering wheel tightly, as though it could be a weapon, and the passenger; a smaller man with frizzy hair and a backpack on one shoulder.

The driver takes a hand off the wheel, but unlike Faye, he doesn't have the presence of mind to throw a punch. Instead, he contorts his body sideways and readies a kick, hoping to knock me back into the road.

When he throws it – a weak, feeble kick with the sole of one boot – I catch his ankle, and pull him from the seat. He falls, tumbling forwards and out of the vehicle; a high-pitched wail leaving his lips as he departs.

I throw myself into his seat, inadvertently steadying myself with a hand on the wheel; a hand that abruptly steers the truck to the left, and we leave the road, scraping along a concrete barrier.

My passenger and I are thrown to the passenger side together – my shoulder hitting his chin, seemingly knocking him loopy and knocking the backpack off him – and provoking a loud, grinding sound of steel against concrete, as my brief period in charge of the wheel reshapes the side of the truck.

Kris, watch out, you're in charge of a heavy vehicle here!

Vega's words are enough to make me shuffle back to the driver's side and seize the steering wheel again. I turn it right – pulling us away from the barrier, and that earsplitting grating noise – and find two pedals by my feet.

"Man, I've never driven before!" I cry, before looking to my passenger again, slowly assuming consciousness. I reach over to the passenger-side door handle, pull it open, and he neatly falls out into the road.

It's an automatic transmission, Vega says, *so you don't have to worry about a clutch or gear shifts, but you do have to accelerate and steer.*

I grip the steering wheel ever tighter, before my right foot finds the taller of the two pedals. I press it down, and feel the truck begin to accelerate, and a grin creep across my face.

They drive on the left here, so you must stay in one of the two leftmost lanes.

I look out into the road ahead; we're still on that four-lane highway, speeding our way through Lushoto. I see David Faye's truck in the distance, tucked behind a couple of smaller cars, and to my right is a large semi-truck, with a bed of tightly wrapped lumber.

Carefully, I put my foot down a little more, picking up a

bit more speed, and some distance between myself and the massive truck beside me. I jiggle the wheel from side to side a little, trying to get a feel for its responsiveness.

This certainly isn't how I expected my first driving experience to go. I envisioned an empty parking lot, a mild spring day, and a calm and steady instructor. Instead, I'm careening down a busy road in a vehicular battering ram, in pursuit of a murderous bank robber, advised by my artificially intelligent invisible friend.

Apply the brake carefully, Vega tells me, as I accelerate dangerously close to the car in front.

I do as he says, taking my foot off one pedal and putting it onto the other, before turning the wheel and moving out of the way of the car in front. There's an ill-tempered honk of a horn behind me, and I look sideways to see a mirror completely askew, bent away from the road by my leaning all my weight on it earlier.

"I've gotta catch up to him," I say to Vega, before honking the horn another couple of times, and then wondering: in a city like this, does anyone even notice the sound of a horn?

And what are you going to do when you do catch up? Vega asks, as I hit the gas pedal again. *You've only just learned where the brake pedal is. You've got no knowledge of advanced pursuit techniques.*

"You're right," I tell him, my voice a flat, wavering murmur behind my broken nose. "But I've got to try, haven't I?"

We're out of Lushoto's neat and tidy financial district now, and into the slums; a densely built sector of the city, with the sides of the roads surrounded by parked vehicles and ramshackle merchant stalls. People selling knockoff DVDs from the backs of cars, and rows of dresses and vegetables and cellphone accessories lined up by the side of the street.

I keep my foot down and make up the distance to the next

car between our trucks – a small, white two-door hatchback – just in time to meet a ninety-degree bend in the road.

Faye's truck slows, deviates left, before making a wide turn right, narrowly avoiding a couple of motorbikes, and their irate riders. I see the back of his truck – the logo of the Central Bank of Lushoto, and his ill-gotten gains hidden within – disappearing behind another van, and know I have to catch up.

You're approaching with too much speed! Vega shouts in my ear.

I hit the brake, and turn slightly left, before making a wide right, but I overshoot it. I mount the curb – an almighty bump that sends me into the roof of the cab, hitting my head and compressing my neck – before I see the vehicle careering into a set of stalls.

I punch the horn and see a handful of people – their eyes wide and fearful, like deer caught in the headlights – diving out of the way. I jam my foot on the brake and desperately turn the wheel, and the truck slides sideways into a set of stalls, sending a colorful wave of fruits and vegetables flying. Reds, yellows and greens rolling across the road, only to disappear beneath my wheels.

A high-pitched screeching fills the air, a sense of mortal panic fills my belly. I feel another, curious movement; not just the slide of the truck, but another, more gradual change. I see the blue sky move sideways and realize that the truck is slowly toppling onto its side. I grip the wheel, and brace for landing.

With a painful jolt, the vehicle's body hits the dirt, and sends me tumbling to the passenger door. I hit my head on the glass, which duly breaks, showering me in tiny specks of tempered glass, like confetti.

When I pick my head back up, there's a plume of dust surrounding me. I cough repeatedly, rubbing my eyes and snorting another glob of blood out of my nose. There's a persistent, guilty ticking from the truck somewhere – an ever-present reminder of my failure here – and a clamor of voices and shouts from outside.

"Did I hit anyone?" I ask, between spluttered coughs and ragged breaths. I'm bathed in darkness; the windshield is seemingly resting tightly against a wall, or some other obstacle, and the only source of light is from the driver's-side window above me.

I could be mistaken, but I do not think so, Vega answers, a wave of relief passing through my body.

I stand up, planting my feet into the broken glass, and push open the door above me. Clambering out – my aching fingers finding some leverage on the door frame, I pull myself up to sit on the side of the truck, and look around at the scene.

There's already a crowd of people gathering. Men and women with quizzical, horrified expressions, two dozen of them, arranging themselves into a semi-circle around the stricken truck.

A long set of tracks in the dirt mark my path, along with bits of splintered wood, bent sheet metal, and torn, muddied fabric from the shop stalls, and those red, yellow, and green vegetables smushed into the ground. The road is twenty yards away at least; I really traveled some distance.

And speaking of distance, David Faye is nowhere to be seen. I straighten my back, climb to my knees, and look out onto the horizon with its many twisting roads, but he's gone.

So much for my driving lesson…

CHAPTER 50

Kris, you're forgetting something, Vega says, as that crowd around me grows ever larger, and I grow ever more awkward and self-conscious about sitting here, atop my throne of an upended truck, amid the horrendous mess I just caused.

"Huh," I murmur under my breath.

The backpack, Vega says. *The one that the passenger carried.*

That's right, the backpack. I didn't even remember that, but it could prove useful. I look back to the open door, and the dark depths of the truck's cab, before jumping back down there and fishing the backpack out from the footwell, by that broken window and the dirt.

I jump back up and climb back onto the upturned side of the truck, swinging the backpack around my shoulder, before shuddering forward, my balance briefly overcome by a spate of dizziness.

You're in shock, Vega says. *It's not serious, but you need to rest. Your body has been through a number of blunt force traumas, and your brain has suffered more than a dozen sub-concussive blows.*

"God preserve us, are you alright?" a woman asks – old, greying, with neat spectacles and a scarf around her head – offering her hand for me to take. Still dazed, having been shaken up more violently than a mariachi bands' maracas, I reach forward and grip her hand, and with her help, I slide off the top the upturned van.

My feet hit the dirt – my heel finding its way into the mushy remains of a tomato – and I stagger around for a few moments, before smiling to the woman.

Kris, there's also the matter of the gas tank you drove into, Vega says, in a low, ominous tone.

"Gas tank?" I ask out loud, before looking at the crashed truck once more, and behind it, the white, spherical metal gas tank, bearing a few triangular warning stickers, and one that I recognize well: *flammable*.

Gingerly, I take a couple more steps towards it, and see that the truck slid into it head-on, creating a large dent in the side. It towers over the windshield; no wonder I couldn't see out of it, a massive, crumpled mass of metal, but seemingly empty of gas, or otherwise not damaged enough to leak its contents.

"Whoa," I mumble, gripping the backpack on my shoulder ever tighter. "Close call."

As soon as the words leave my lips, a sudden, high-pitched hissing noise fills the air, like an ill-tempered anaconda. There's a murmur of concern behind me – the gathered crowd taking a collective step back, like they recognize the ominous nature of the sound too.

Kris, get everybody back, Vega says. I don't need to be told twice.

"Everybody," I say, turning back to that semicircle of people, and the old lady with the scarf over her hair, "get back!"

I hold my arms wide, barking the same words over and over, and watch as everyone's faces turn from morbid curiosity to mortal panic. They turn and run, and I pick up the volume of my voice, clearing the area.

Turning on my heel, and taking one last look at the wreck – the upturned truck, the crumpled globe of the gas tank, and all the surrounding debris – I see a ghostly, ethereal flutter in the air. A near-transparent wave of gas entering the atmosphere, like the hot air rising off a hot tarmac road in the height of summer.

And then, for the briefest moment, a white-hot spark, probably imperceptible to those who don't expect it. The gas tank – crumpled around the hood of the truck, painted a dirty, off-white – goes up in a massive ball of flames, and an impenetrable wall of scorching heat and deafening sound that sends me face-first to the dirt.

I find my hands buried in the mud, and pick them out to cup them around the back of my head. My ears are overcome by the high-pitched squealing of tinnitus, but I look up to see the entire wreck on fire; the truck and the gas tank both dwarfed by the bright orange fire, and above it, the black smoke that billows into the sky.

I pick myself up to my hands and knees and see the crowd, each shielding their eyes from the bright flames, or holding their ears, or burying their heads into another's bosom, but apparently unhurt.

My hearing comes back to me – the unbearable droning *eeeee* replaced by the rancorous sound of the flames in front of me – and I pick myself up to my knees. There's the sound of distant sirens, too. The fire brigade, or if I'm really unlucky, the police.

I turn to the road, expecting to have to gather my backpack and my shellshocked limbs and run. Instead, I squint my eyes, and see another vehicle entirely; not a cop car, and not the fearsome armored truck with a devilish, possessed David Faye behind the wheel, but one that makes me feel warmer.

It's the plumbing van; that eye-catching, absurdist clown

car, only instead of a cavalcade of children's entertainers waddling out, there's just Baynes. He opens the door, looking upon me with a bizarre expression: a frightful blend of concern, anger, and confusion.

He wears a blue shirt – one I haven't seen before – with his glasses balanced precariously on the bottom of his nose, and trudges towards me purposefully. With some effort, I climb to my feet again, just as Baynes makes it over to me.

"What happened? What exploded? Are you okay?" he bellows at me, before staring intensely at the flames. He grabs my shoulders and eases me to my feet, never diverting his stare from the wreckage, my latest masterpiece.

"Yeah, I'm fine," I say, my voice still sounding off-key.

"Your nose is broken," he says, looking back to me with concerned eyes for a moment, before looking back to the wreckage. "And you're staggering away from an explosion."

"Yeah," I repeat, "it's a funny story actually."

"I followed your position on the GPS tracker built into the satellite phone," he says, clutching me by the arm and shoulder, walking me slowly back to the van. "Then I saw a giant column of smoke on the horizon, and knew that had to be you. Finding you is easy; you're like the cowboy that lights a fire on the prairies."

I don't feel much like a cowboy; weren't cowboys supposed to be decent shots?

I shrug him off, and straighten my jacket, seeing the grazes and tears in my elbows and lapels as I do so. He puts his hands on his hips, and looks at me with that unimpressed, stony expression of his; the joyless principal, sent out to pick me up from a school trip gone terribly wrong.

I put another foot forward, continuing my slow march back to the van, when another loud blast goes off behind us. We both turn to see the truck enveloped in flames now, its secure doors blown open, and the contents on fire, much like the rest of the scene.

There goes half of Faye's stolen riches, Vega says, as Baynes looks back at me.

"What the hell was that?" he asks, holding a hand against his face, shielding himself from the glare of the fire, watching a descending rain of smoldering paper, blown out of the back of the truck.

"Money, I guess," I tell him, catching a flaming piece between my fingers, and waving it until the fire goes out.

It's not a bank note, that's for sure. It's a sheet of paper – or at least, the smoldering remnants of one – with ornate, intricate markings, like that of a dollar bill, but much larger, more akin to a stock certificate.

"Let me see," Baynes says, snatching the paper off me. He adjusts his glasses, pushing them up to the bridge of his nose, and reads the paper, flipping it over a couple of times. "It's from the Central Bank of Lushoto; a bearer bond."

"A bearer bond?" I ask, discounting the part I already know. "It isn't money?"

"Sure, it's money, in a way," he says, the tiniest of smiles creeping onto the side of his lips. "It's like a bond, but unlike most bonds these days it has no registered owner. It's just a blind IOU essentially; untraceable money. You don't see these much these days."

David Faye wasn't stealing money, or gold bullion, or the blood of the wealthy this time. He was stealing bearer bonds. I don't know exactly what that means quite yet, but it's one more piece of a vastly incomplete picture. I push the half-burned paper into a pocket.

"I'm sorry to repeat myself here Kris, but I do have to ask," Baynes says, putting his hand back on my bruised, hurting shoulder. "Why did I find you beside the flaming wreckage of a bank truck full of bearer bonds today?"

I blow a labored breath out of my mouth, and look back to that crowd of people; some of them are speaking into cellphones, others talking between each other, pointing fingers at us.

"I'll tell you in the van."

CHAPTER 51

"Please, tell me you didn't rob the bank for some ungodly reason," Baynes says, steering past a broken-down pick-up truck by the side of the road. Just seeing that steering wheel is bringing back bad memories. We've been traveling in silence for a whole minute, and it's the first question he's asked me.

"Man, of course I didn't rob the bank," I tell him, blowing another exasperated breath out of my mouth. "Why would I rob the bank? The bank in an impoverished African nation?"

"Why would you be standing next to a flaming bank van in that case?" he asks, a question he's asked me three times now, but probably a fair one. "What, was the money truck already on fire when you thumbed a ride?"

"It was him, David Faye," I reply, before sinking lower into my chair as two police cruisers pass in the opposite lane, their lights and sirens blaring. "He and his men robbed the Central Bank of Lushoto. I managed to hijack the second of the two trucks he used for the getaway, and, well…"

I don't finish the sentence; the mere words seem to make my skin crawl, those bruises throbbing with conspicuous, remorseful pain. I think he can work out what happened though: that I had my first driving experience today, and it didn't go well.

"Your driving skills made the truck explode, I think I understand what happened there," he says after a few tense seconds. "So, you got into an explosive vehicular chase with the warlord. Anything else you want to tell me about?"

"Well, I suppose there's the police station, and the chief, and the—"

"I'm sorry, the chief? The station?" he says, increasingly agitated. Another police car passes us in the opposite lane, and Baynes takes another look at me – sunk cautiously into my seat – and shakes his head. "I guess I'd better take the side streets."

He takes the next turn, and maneuvers us into a busier, single lane of traffic; a dirt road that languishes in the shadow of an apartment building, with no blaring sirens or flashing lights, or the prying eyes of cops hunting a man of my description.

"The police chief was working with the warlord," I tell Baynes. "They'd arranged to keep the cops off the bank robbery long enough for him to make his getaway."

"How'd you find that out?" he asks.

"I had to persuade him to tell me," is all I say in reply. Of course, Baynes knows exactly what I mean by that.

"But why bearer bonds," Baynes says, digging his fingertips into the steering wheel, and leaning over it, speaking to the road. I can't tell if he's aiming that question at me or searching his own mind.

"You said it's untraceable money, right?" I ask. "Maybe he's stealing them because they can't be tracked and he can spend the money however he wants."

"That's right, but that isn't my question," he says. "The question isn't why is David Faye stealing bearer bonds; the question is why is the Central Bank of Lushoto *printing* bearer bonds? And how does David Faye know they're there?"

I lean back in my seat, and leave the drudgery of the rhetorical financial questions to Baynes.

"It doesn't make sense. Bearer bonds are banned in most countries now due to corruption. Money laundering for criminal gangs, or corporations looking to evade paying tax. The last time I even heard of bearer bonds was a decade ago; some corrupt Central American government using them to pay a drug smuggler gang off."

I wondered how long we'd take to dredge up memories from Baynes' agency past. Mercifully, he doesn't go on for long.

"Basically, all I'm trying to say," he says, after a couple of minutes of almost indecipherable speech, recounting those agency memories, "is that no country needs to print untraceable funny bucks these days. The only reason you'd print them is because they're easy to steal."

"So, what are you getting at?" I ask him. "That the bank printed them especially for David Faye to steal?"

"Either that, or they printed them especially for someone else to steal," he adds, tapping his fingers on the steering wheel. "And David Faye stole them first."

I turn away from Baynes and the road ahead, and instead look out of the window beside me, and the streets of Lushoto. We're far outside the city center now; those construction sites, apartment buildings, and glassy towers are long gone.

Instead, a shantytown of smaller, impoverished housing stands at each side of the road. Houses built from mismatched shapes of bricks, topped with rusted steel roofs. A school composed of shipping containers, half-buried in the red, muddy earth. A water well, built upon a concrete altar, and a line of sullen people halfway around the block.

A group of kids kick a ball around in the dirt behind a fence, but on a closer look, I see that it isn't a ball at all; it's a set of beanbags taped together, in a rough ball shape. They don't wear shoes, and their clothes are dirty and tattered. And it isn't a mere fence, but a set of tall, jail-like barricades that seek to keep the children contained. An orphanage, it claims to be.

It's hard to believe Nubalayan government even has the resources to print untraceable, easily stealable money, let alone the idea that someone would want to do it. Maybe we have it all wrong; maybe it's some corrupt bank official, or some easier way of procuring international aid, but it sure doesn't look good…

"And now, what do we have," Baynes says, as I look back to him. "David Faye still has a truck full of bearer bonds, and half of the payload has gone up in smoke. He's amassing quite the collection of stolen oddities, isn't he? Bearer bonds, the blood of the wealthy."

"Money to fund his new civil war," I add, before struggling more with the next part. "And wealthy blood to feed his army of vampire aristocrats? I don't know."

He bites his lip before pushing his glasses up the length of his nose again, and adjusting his collar.

"We might have a hard time relaying all this back to the Minister," he says, completely deadpan. "His chief of police is working with the enemy; his central bank is missing all of its crooked cash, and you turned his city into a giant, open-air barbecue."

The Minister, I'd almost forgotten about him. Strange to think we're here in Nubalaya at the behest of a government paymaster; I've been entirely motivated by a singular desire to get my hands on the warlord. I guess having your face and body beaten to pieces by a war criminal will do that; revenge, and a desire to prove myself by any means necessary.

We go on driving for another hour or so, making it out of the city and out of the impoverished outskirts, to a place where there are red badland plains on one side of the road, and the ever-encroaching rainforest on the other, its dark, ambiguous vegetation swaying in the wind.

Baynes takes a right turn, slowly driving us along a long-forgotten gravel road, barely visible among the tufts of tall green weeds that have almost succeeded in reclaiming it to nature. The canopy of the forest looms over us, and before long, I can't see the midday sun.

Deeper within the forest, we come to a rusted metal bridge over a ravine; every beam a different shade of filthy brown rust, completely unrecognizable from its originally painted color, and barely even recognizable now as a bridge.

I think to ask him if he's going to drive across that thing, but to my relief he goes off the road, and to the ravine underneath it; a sandy, craggy dark place, where the sun doesn't shine.

"We'll sit here until the heat dies down," Baynes says, carefully reversing the van into the ravine, directly underneath the bridge. He turns the engine off, and I hear the rusted metal above us croak and strain in the wind.

I sink back into my seat and cross my arms. Suddenly, I realize I'm breathing through my nose again; it's healed already. In fact, it no longer hurts to exist anymore.

"And you know," Baynes says after a minute or so of silence, continuing a conversation that apparently never started. I guess he's got something on his mind. "I have to tell you, Kris, what you did back there is not cool."

"Not, cool?" I repeat.

"Running off into the night," he says, tensely. "Ignoring my calls, my messages. Going out there alone, without any help, without any support. Going out there to track down the warlord, and doing it on your own. You could easily have been killed. Hell, by the look of that whole wreck, you almost were."

I sit there, my arms still crossed, breathing deeply and quietly through my nose. This is the part where I get scolded by the principal, I suppose.

"You didn't believe in me," I finally say to him, after a few moments' pause.

"What?" he shoots back.

"You didn't believe in me," I say again. "You thought he was stronger than me. You thought I wasn't up to the task, that he'd kill me, and maybe kill you too."

I sound like a petulant child, but I think I'm right. He didn't believe in me. He saw me take a beating and wanted to call the whole thing off. He wouldn't have taken 'I can' for an answer.

"I had to prove myself," I add. "Sure, it was stupid; *I* was stupid. I shouldn't have left you like that. But you've got to understand, I had something to prove, and today I think I did. I didn't catch the warlord, but I did burn half of his ill-gotten gains, and got a hold of this too."

I use my foot to pick a strap of the backpack up, picking it up out of the footwell. I unzip it, finding a bunch of garbage – empty junk food wrappers and scraps of paper – as well as a cell phone that lights up to the touch.

"Seems like a lead, right?" I ask.

He doesn't respond. He just looks at me with a dubious expression, one I can barely make out in the dark. Maybe on some level he understands: David Faye isn't your regular bad guy, and I'm not your regular good guy either.

"I'm sorry," I sincerely say after a few more quiet moments, the only sounds being the sounds of the forest, and the metallic groan and intermittent tapping of the bridge. "It won't happen again."

"I know," he says, resignedly. "After all, it's not like I'm in charge, is it?"

He takes a loud breath and takes the cellphone from me, before carefully thumbing his way through it.

"Besides, this talk is the easy part," he says. "We've still got to update the Minister."

CHAPTER 52

"He said he'd be free at two o'clock," Baynes says, his face contorted into one of bafflement and strenuous effort – his eyes squinted almost closed, his mouth wide open – while he taps away at the laptop; the perfect *middle-aged man tries to use technology* face.

He taps a few more times on the laptop's keyboard, before adjusting the screen slightly. I sit back, and blow a bored breath out of my mouth. We're sitting in the back of the van, illuminated in cold, sterile white by the ambient lights above us. Before us is a blank, black screen, awaiting the arrival of the minister.

After a couple more taps, and an annoyed grunt from Baynes, the minister's head suddenly appears on screen; massive, square, and scarred, occupying most of the frame.

"Mr. Mufumba," Baynes says, courteously. The Minister doesn't say anything, at least at first. The quality of the video link is pretty bad – parking in the deepest, darkest rainforest beneath a rusted bridge isn't great for reception – but I can see he isn't in the welcoming mood he was in when we first met.

"Mr. Baynes," he says, his voice crackling with the poor audio quality. "Have you got some things to tell me?"

He wears a grimace on his face, and I can see a sheen of reflective sweat on his forehead. He looks anything but cool. In the background, I see a very ornate setting, like the sitting room of some mad sultan's palace. There's furniture upholstered with fine patterns and golden trimmings, and paintings on the walls.

Baynes chuckles – a curious, nervous snort – before answering.

"Well, we've made some progress," Baynes says, "and we've had some setbacks, and—"

"Setbacks!?" Bufumba yells back, the small laptop screen struggling to contain his massive, intimidating head. "You blew up half the town! The entire city is on edge now!"

I think half the town is a bit of an exaggeration. It was a singular gas tank. Still, I think better of pointing that out right now.

"There was an attempt made to apprehend David Faye," Baynes says, in the most passive voice I've ever heard. "The attempt was not successful, but we were successful in procuring some other items that may still lead us to him."

"The Central Bank of Lushoto was emptied out!" Mufumba yells, his great, ruddy face shuddering within the frame of the picture. "All that money, gone! All that money, that could have been used to build hospitals, or put books on shelves in our libraries, or trained up new teachers to fill our schools. All that money, either burned up, or in the hands of terrorists!"

He goes on like this for a bit longer, occasionally clenching his fists beside either side of his chin. He's angry, that's for sure, but there's something strange about this performance. He's barely mentioned the focus of our mission: the warlord.

"You've messed up!" he shouts. "The both of you, you're

idiots. Bumbling, doddering fools! You've really screwed this up. Explain to me why I shouldn't have you both arrested…"

Baynes launches into a very technical, very dull explanation of the various international treaties and geopolitical concerns that would make arresting us both a big mistake, but there's something else on my mind, and on the tip of my tongue. Something that I can't quite resist spitting out, despite the fine line Baynes is trying to tread.

"Bearer bonds," I say, taking advantage of a brief pause in Baynes' speech. My words are met with silence; I hear the bridge creak above us again, a tense undercurrent.

"What did you say?" he asks, narrowing his eyes and tilting his head slightly.

"It wasn't money that was in the trucks. It wasn't money that David Faye robbed from the bank," I say, my tone unmoving. "It was bearer bonds."

Another silence. I see Mufumba moving, his head bobbing up and down in place, as if he's nervously adjusting his posture, or as though if we were sitting across a table from him, he'd be preparing to throw it over.

"What are you trying to say?" he barks at me at last. Baynes doesn't move, but I think I see the side of his eye twitch.

"I'm sorry, I was just pointing it out," I say. "You said it was money that he robbed, I'm just clarifying, it was bearer bonds, not money. There's a difference, isn't there?"

He's quiet again, but his eyes are aflame with anger. A crease in his forehead twitches, and he slowly raises a hand to wipe the sweat from his scarred face. Then, as abruptly as he appeared on our screens, he reaches forward and terminates the video link without another word.

I hear Baynes breathe deeply, before stroking a hand through his stubble. He doesn't speak though; he seems content to live in the awkward silence for now.

"Well," I say after it becomes unbearable, "that was weird."

"Weird?" he asks, quick as a shot. "Sure, weird, let's go with that."

"What would you suggest?" I ask.

"I think it sounds like we're fired," he says.

"Do you think those bearer bonds are his?" I ask, letting my imagination run away. "Untraceable, corrupt money he was hiding for a rainy day? Or perhaps he's in league with the warlord now, and they were supposed to split that money?"

I think back to those angry, spiteful eyes; a desperate and indignant reaction at the simple mention of the contents of those trucks.

"Hell if I know," Baynes says, probably just hoping to end my wild suggestions. "But what I do know is, we're stuck."

"Stuck? How?"

"He's already threatened to have us arrested," he goes on to say, before closing the laptop. "We can't just turn up at an airport and jump on the next flight. He might have guys waiting for us, guys who aren't there to wish us a sweet farewell."

He puts his head into his hands, rubbing his fingers through his hair, before resurfacing and looking back to me.

"I think we've unearthed something big here," he says, tapping his temple with one finger. "Bigger than David Faye, and bigger than the bounty. A live grenade, inside a can of worms, inside Pandora's box, inside a smoldering bank truck. I think we know something we shouldn't."

He doesn't say the words with his usual excitable panache. Instead, he seems despondent. We're stuck here in the middle of Africa, having quite possibly turned the government against us, as well as the murderous, superhumanly strong warlord. We can't leave, and neither can we complete our mission. We know too much.

I take a deep breath before jumping to my feet and making for the exit.

"Where are you going?" he calls after me.

"I'm going for a walk," I tell him. "I need to clear my head. I'll be nearby this time, and I'll have the satellite phone. Don't worry."

I open the van doors and jump out, hiding Baynes' bitterly aggrieved face as I slam them shut.

Hiking underneath the rusted bridge, stepping through the grasping grasses and between tall, twisting tree trunks, I make it to a path of sorts; a clearing in the forest, roughly wide enough for one man to walk down, where the grass has died, like death himself has walked it.

I walk on, pushing branches and massive fern leaves out of my way, finally making it to a paved road, almost entirely reclaimed by nature. There are tufts of grasses rising out of its crags, and white painted markings, stained green by the ways of the forest.

Following it along, I come to the husk of an old building, now just four gray brick walls, and a fallen roof, through which the roots of a nearby tree reach. Beside it is a large, paved area, permeated by moss and bushes growing through its ancient, fading asphalt.

The road goes on, and there's a break in the tree canopy above. I feel the warmth of the sun on my skin again, and the breeze through my hair. I keep walking until finally I make it to a larger building, hidden in the tree line. Three stories, entirely covered in patches of moss, and strangled by dark-green vines.

Despite its more recent greener makeover, I can see burn marks on its gray remains; huge, black shadows that reach upward, the scars of a ferocious fire. Inside are blackened beams, almost worn to dust, along with the thick, browning roots of a nearby tree.

This was a town, once upon a time. Former civilization,

now reclaimed by nature. It has a haunting beauty – a dark, enigmatic tale to tell, where the slow whispers of the forest are heard louder than the charred ghosts of the humanity that used to live here.

I take a seat on a fallen tree trunk, never moving my eyes from the ancient ruins before me. The smell of earth and damp moss is carried on the wind, but every once in a while, I think I sense a hint of ashes.

"Vega, what do you think about all of this?" I ask him. "Bearer bonds? Cans of worms?"

It would seem to be quite the complication, he replies. *Someone printed a bunch of untraceable, anonymous riches, and David Faye rode in and stole them. And, for whatever reason, the Minister is incensed by the situation, as well as by you pointing it out. He never explained himself fully, but his reaction was surely worth a thousand words.*

"Do you think that money, those bearer bonds, were his?"

Perhaps, or maybe connected to something unseemly he's involved in, if Baynes is correct in saying the only reason those bonds would be printed is to facilitate an easy theft. Of course, then the question becomes: how come David Faye stole them?

"When did this become so—" I say, searching for the right word, before seeing the grasping roots from a thick, tall tree in the near distance: "deep."

You came to a remote, war-torn African nation, looking to capture a dangerous warlord, Vega says. *It was never going to be easy.*

I stand up and think to make the walk back to the van, but as I do so, I see something in the corner of my eye; something unusual, that stands out even in this dystopian setting of burned-out buildings and wild, unfettered nature.

A tall stack of tires, some seven or eight, all placed very deliberately atop one another, coming to maybe five feet in height. Beside that stack there stands another, and beside that another, and another. Seven in total.

Black stacks of tires, conspicuously placed there like strange sculptures. Quiet, motionless and dark figures, standing there in the street. I walk closer and hold out my hand to rub my fingers along the rubber. It's tough and brittle, like it's been burned or has stood here so long as to have degraded in the elements.

Suddenly, I'm seized by the impulse to look inside the stack, into the hole in the middle. I lean over and see only darkness at first; the black rims of the tires and the lack of light overhead conspiring to create a black hole.

There's something else, though: a dark debris right at the bottom of the stack. It looks like coal; a filthy black pile of rubble, like someone tried to start a fire here, and beside it, a globe of sorts, with a visible crack within it, and two holes.

It's a skull; a charred human skull. And next to it, a long, charred bone, like one of the bones in your legs. It's a pile of human bones, sitting comfortably at the bottom of this stack of tires. Someone was forced to stand in the middle of this stack, and then burned…

I step back and rub my fingers across my forehead, before covering my mouth with the same hand and taking a deep, gasping breath. I'd bet there are bones at the bottom of those other stacks, too. Seven charred skeletons; seven agonizing deaths.

I think to try and do something – to topple the stack of tires, and its obscene symbolism – but then I realize that there's almost nothing I can do. Do I dig a lonely, mass grave in the dirt with my bare fingers? No, these remains must be identified and buried with dignity, something I can't do.

After a couple of minutes of thought, I wipe a tear away from my eye, and go on walking. I leave the old village behind, with its skeletal buildings and those horrifying monuments to murder. I resume that strange, deathly path, and slowly make my way back to the van.

Vega's words echo within my mind: *it was never going to be easy.* I always told myself that I didn't expect it to be easy; that I'd come here and keep my eyes on the prize: the warlord. That I wouldn't be arrogant enough to come here and think that my superpowers could change the country.

But staring into that stack of tires really did hammer the reality home. I'm powerless; powerless to help, powerless to provide, powerless to solve anyone's problems but my own. Compared to this country's troubled history, and its tortured memories, and its unburied corpses, I'm small. There's so little I can do to help, even if I tried.

Despite that, I still have my mission, my own personal focus, my own burning resolve. David Faye; the war criminal, the murderer, the tyrant, the warlord.

I don't care about the Minister, and why those bearer bonds were printed. Hell, so what if he is trying to steal from the people; they can – and will – figure that out and have their justice. It isn't my fight.

I can't help those poor, sad souls whose bones still sit within those grotesque monuments. But what I can do is strike a blow for the many that were murdered by David Faye, and the other war criminals.

I can defeat the warlord.

CHAPTER 53

Chili peppers. Hello again, old friend.

After my experience in the back of that truck, I could never fail to pick them out of a line-up. An entire basket of light red and orange, shriveled little peppers, probably more than 200 of them. I can't smell them from here, yet in the back of my mind, I know exactly what they smell and taste like.

We're parked by the side of the road, on the side of a massive hill. The road – a barely paved asphalt path, broken up in all places by crags and gravel-filled potholes that rock you around in your seat – winds up and around this hill, snaking up it in hairpin turns and uphill drives.

It's terrifying to look down – almost a sheer drop to the next hairpin turn below us – and the sides of each road are marked by jagged skid marks in the mud, or in one place, a burned out husk of a mini-bus.

The spices are part of a roadside shop, and even then, it isn't much of a shop. An old man, pushing a trolley packed-full of those vegetable-filled baskets, like some hill-side air steward. He makes eye contact with me and smiles, as though he fervently believes I'll ever touch another chili pepper in my life, ever again.

"Dante's on the phone," Baynes shouts to me. I turn to see his face and half of his body leaning acrobatically out of the back of the van. "Come on!"

He disappears back into the van, and I slowly trudge my way over there.

Last night we slept in the van, underneath that rusted, swaying bridge, deep within the Nubalayan rainforest, Baynes in the back and me sprawled across the three seats in the front.

The Minister isn't taking our calls, seemingly still upset that I had the temerity to point out the difference between stolen bearer bonds and stolen cash. We still have no idea whether we're free men, or if at any minute Mufumba's men are going to swoop in and throw a pair of not-quite-so-fancy bracelets on us both, or perhaps just put a gun to our heads and be done with it.

I stride up into the back of the van, and throw the doors shut behind me. Baynes is waiting there, perched attentively on a little chair, sitting before the blank laptop screen. His eyes are as excited as ever, but there are large, purple bags under them, a symptom of a rough night's sleep.

"He was here a minute ago, let me just—" Baynes says, before unveiling the same *middle-aged man uses technology* face I saw yesterday, tapping idly on the keyboard.

Dante's face suddenly appears on the screen, his hair slightly messy, and his eyes sleepy and languid. I wonder what he's been putting himself through to look like that, until I remember that the time back home is six hours behind – 6 a.m. – and he's likely worked for us all night.

"Baynes, Kris, good morning," he says unenthusiastically, before closing his eyes in a blink that goes on for way too long. I see the office behind him – that gray, unappealing space beneath the vape shop, and see the slivers of morning light, barely making it through those thin, grimy basement windows.

"Dante, how's it going with that cellphone?" Baynes asks.

Yes, the cellphone, the one I dug out of the backpack that I managed to rescue from the flaming wreckages of both the bank truck and our hopes of capturing David Faye that afternoon.

There's a passcode on it – a seemingly insurmountable obstacle to us reading it – so we used some computer program to clone the contents, and send it to Dante. I guess this is what he spent all night doing; it's good to have friends in sly places.

"It wasn't easy," he says, rubbing his forehead with one hand. "But I managed to construct a copy of the firmware and use an old exploit to get past the passcode."

"And what did you find?" Baynes asks.

"I've put a file together. I'll send it your way," he says, before putting a large paper coffee cup to his lips, and drinking. "There's not much related to the man you're seeking, this David Faye fella, but there's some interesting stuff in there regardless."

"Interesting?" Baynes asks. Dante doesn't answer right away, and Baynes evidently gets impatient. "Interesting how? You found the missing Watergate tapes? Another angle of the JFK assassination?"

"Interesting in that we've uncovered a location," Dante says, putting the coffee cup down and taking an annoyed breath. "Social media accounts and search engines have logged the user's locations in real time. There's a place the user of that cellphone has visited, time and time again, for a few months now. Somewhere you'll probably want to check out."

I cross my arms and breathe a quiet, disappointed sigh. I wanted something *more* than this; co-ordinates and credentials to David Faye's inner sanctum. Detailed information as to his whereabouts, as logged diligently by one of his deputies. Perhaps some chatter about his secret allergy to shellfish, or some other outlandish advantage I can gain over him.

"What's the location?" Baynes asks, tapping his temple with his finger again. Someday I'll figure out why he does that.

"It's a school," Dante says. "Or, rather, a former high school. It was built just before the civil war by an international charity; it's the largest of its kind in Nubalaya. I guess they might be using it as a headquarters of sorts. From the data I've managed to extract from the cellphone, that former high school is exactly where the user came from to do the bank robbery."

Huh, that's more like it; a base of operations, and a chance to find David Faye sitting atop his vibrating throne, or whatever the hell he lives like when he's not committing acts of terror and larceny.

"I managed to retrieve a couple of months of talk within some encrypted group chats," Dante then adds, his voice still tired and detached. "Most of it seems coded somehow, like they know there's a possibility that someone, someday might be eavesdropping. They speak in single letters and numbers, and emojis and pictures, and David Faye never participates."

"Smart," Baynes says.

"But," Dante says, "I did discover something hidden in those group chats, something you'll love."

Baynes looks at me with tired, but hopeful eyes, and we look back to the laptop screen, like two old nursing home residents enraptured by the final moments of a daytime game show.

"Blood," he says, "I think I've found that stolen blood; the blood from the private clinic in Monaco."

"Where?" I ask.

"In that former high school building," Dante says, a smile

creeping onto his face for the first time. "There's a discussion among the cellphone's owner and a few others, and they talk about receiving a shipment of blood, and the best ways to keep it refrigerated."

"Sounds tasty," Baynes says, with a wicked smile. "Thanks a lot for this Dante. Get some sleep."

"One more thing," I interject, holding my hand up like I'm in class, before putting it back down again. "Speaking of all this blood, do we have anything on Vincent? Any sightings in the wild?"

Dante's face loses the tiny amount of vigor it had; the lights in his eyes go out.

"No," he replies, sounding like the whole worldwide search for a living vampire has him decisively beaten. "There have been no sightings, no credible leads, nothing."

I lean back in my chair before nodding at him appreciatively. We say our goodbyes, and that big, gloomy, tired face of his disappears. Baynes blows a tired breath out from his inflated cheeks, and turns to me.

"So, we found the blood," he says, enthusiastically.

"We found the blood," I repeat.

Baynes reaches forward, taps another couple of times on the laptop's trackpad, and finds that dossier Dante emailed to us. He clicks through a series of pictures; satellite images of the former high-school the warlord's men have been frequenting, as well as on-ground images of the surrounding area.

It's a huge area; several large, multi-story buildings, car lots, and what appears to be an overgrown sports field. Despite the size and the investment that evidently went into it, I can still make out blackened craters in the pavements, piles of rubble beside the buildings, and holes in the roof. The scars of war.

"No pictures from inside the school," I point out, before feeling a little silly that I'd even think to ask.

"I guess the wonders of satellite imagery only go so far," Baynes replies, drolly.

"So, we're doing this thing, right?" I ask him, rubbing my fingertips together.

We haven't really spoken about David Faye since yesterday. We don't know if that bounty is still up for grabs, or even if our mission is still ongoing. Our supposed boss refuses to speak to us, ever since we discovered his bank was printing some dubious currency. After the bank raid fallout, we don't even know if we can leave the country without getting thrown in jail.

The only motivating factor for me to pursue the warlord now is because it's personal; because I've seen all those mass graves, all those war scars across the country, and all those orphaned children. But it just so happens, that's a hell of a motivating factor for me.

"Well, we've nothing to lose but our lives," Baynes says, dispassionately. "Who knows, perhaps we get lucky and capture this guy. Perhaps we somehow manage to bring him back to the capital, and then plead for our bounty and our flight out of here."

"That's more like it," I tell him with a playful grin.

"It's not like we have any other option," he then says with a shrug. "Either we finally succeed where we've failed twice before, and capture one of the most dangerous men in the world, or we hide out here, get arrested, and then put on trial for blowing up half the town."

"I mean, it wasn't *half the town* was it?" I ask him sarcastically, thinking of the Minister's wild accusation.

"I'd better get to work," Baynes says, holding up a dubious open palm; an apparent invitation for me to high five him. I do so, and he smiles before turning back to the laptop.

We found the blood. I don't quite believe it; I never thought we'd manage to track it down. If nothing else, while I'm throwing my fists into David Faye's face, I can ask him a quick question about why he stole it, and maybe solve that mystery.

I look at the laptop screen, and the satellite images that Baynes flips through again. So what if I didn't learn about David Faye's secret shellfish allergy? What was I going to do, take him out for sushi?

I might have learned something else, something better: I might have learned where he lives. And besides, I've got another idea…

"I'll be right back," I say to Baynes, who grunts in acknowledgement, never taking his eyes off the screen in front of him. I open the van doors and climb out, stumbling out into the mid-afternoon sun.

To my relief, that old man with the ramshackle trolley, and its many baskets of fresh food items is still there, still looking to the passing traffic with hopeful eyes. I can't imagine how he made it up here to the hillside at his age, but I'm very glad he did.

I walk up to him, spy those peppers, and pick one up out of the basket. That familiar smell – that sickly sweet, muddy smell – hits me immediately, and my fingers almost itch to the touch.

"Do you want to buy a bag?" the old man asks me with a toothless smile, before giving me the price in the local currency.

"No," I reply. "I only need one."

CHAPTER 54

"Buddy, you really, *really* need to learn how to drive."

Baynes words are said with tedious venom; a bored, and yet so spiteful tone, like he hates me for what I've put him through, even as he's lost his mind to the sheer mundanity of it.

That's right, it can only be the eight-hour drive west to Free Zimbala, once again.

"Considering the last time I got behind the wheel, it ended in an explosion and a great, smoking wreckage the whole city could see," I say back to him, "I thought you'd be begging me not to drive again."

He doesn't say anything; he just leans further forward, looming over the steering wheel like he's come to hate it, and wants nothing more than to throttle it. Better the steering wheel than me, I suppose.

At least we're nearly there. The mid-afternoon sun slowly fell beneath the horizon, and the deep blue sky gave itself over to a fast-moving procession of gentle, fluffy clouds, which themselves began to darken. Now, it's pitch black, and tiny splashes of rain appear on the windshield.

After another couple of minutes of driving, we make it to an old train station, alongside a set of badly rusted rails, out of service since the war, by the looks of things.

The station itself has long been emptied out; even the window frames are missing. It's merely four walls and a sagging metal roof. Someone has scrawled 'FREE ZIMBALA' on the side in spray paint, too, alongside other revolutionary messages.

Behind the empty husk of the building though, I see a winding dirt road, overcome with wild, unkempt vegetation, and beyond that, I see the high school; a set of large, rectangular buildings, decorated with small and irregular windows, some of which are boarded up, along with a bunch of smaller classrooms, all connected by corridors and walkways.

It's upright, it's enormous, it's unexciting, and it's unimaginatively built. It's a high school, alright. Curiously, the floodlights that surround it – bright white lights, like those trained on a football field, or a prison yard – are switched on, fully illuminating the building. Someone is home.

"I want to ask you one more time," Baynes says, parking the car beside the overgrown railway, and turning off the engine. He turns to me, his eyes tired, and sincere. "You're sure about this?"

I wish he hadn't parked so close to the railway – even seeing those rusted tracks, and the tufts of grasses and stinging nettles growing inside the ballast brings back painful memories – but I won't back out now. That stolen blood – just like my own spilled blood – brought me here, and I'm not going back without a fight.

"I'm sure," I say to him. "Time to look the devil in the eyes again."

We go through our plan one more time: I sneak into the

building and he remains behind the wheel, in a pre-agreed location. We don't have a headset anymore – that was thumped off my head on the train – but I still have a miraculously still-functional satellite phone. If I get into trouble, I can call him.

Likewise, I haven't got a gun. Finding one on site is a priority, unless I want to do the whole thing with my bare hands; yet another mission on hard mode, I suppose.

We have no up-to-date indoor floorplan, and no pictures of the inside of the building at all. I could walk in there and find David Faye and one hundred of his baddest pals smoking cigars rolled from the bearer bonds and sipping bloody Marys mixed with that stolen blood.

Or it could be completely empty. It's the great unknown, and yet again, I'm throwing myself into it.

I hold out my fist – a tacit, awkward invitation for Baynes to bump it – and after giving me a dubious look, he moves his fist into mine. He wishes me luck, and I reach for the door handle, putting my fingers on it and hesitating a couple of seconds – seeing those train tracks again – before opening it, and getting out.

My mind is still awash with grim foreboding and painful memories; scars left by my prior encounters with the warlord, even though my skin is unblemished. My heart beats a nervous rhythm inside my ribcage, and the hairs on my arms stand up, as though I just locked myself in an industrial freezer and there's no one around to hear my calling.

Before I know it, I've made the entire walk over the grassy wasteland beside the old station, and I'm standing directly before a tall, silver fence, whose spotless steel glints in the ambient glare of the floodlights. I put my hands on it, feeling the clean, cold metal.

"This fence is new," I say to Vega.

Someone is newly conscious of security here, he replies.

I find a foothold in one of the hexagonal loops, and begin

climbing over. The fence barely sways as I climb it, and after carefully navigating the coils of barbed wire at the top, I hop over it and jump to the other side.

Be careful, Vega says. *Stick to the shadows, and away from the floodlights. There aren't any visible sentries, but the premises are large, and you could easily walk into a trap.*

I do as he says, sprinting across a freshly cut lawn to a shadowy outbuilding – something like a janitor's office – far from the glare of the nearest floodlight.

There's a boarded-up window beside me – I can't see inside, but I can smell something familiar. Not blood, or gunpowder, or any of the things I'd expect to smell at the warlord's base. It smells like fresh paint.

I look out onto the remaining distance between my position, and the largest of the school buildings – a massive, beige sarcophagus, laid flat across the earth. It's missing a couple of siding panels, and there's a growth of moss along its walls, but aside from that, it looks in good shape. No holes in the walls, no craters in the earth, no scars of war.

In fact, all those blemishes I saw in the satellite photographs – taken a mere six months ago – are gone. Someone's spent a lot of effort to make this complex habitable again.

After taking a breath – an attempt to steady my nerves – I make the sprint from my position to the school building, sticking to an unlit avenue between two old soccer fields, the sound of my footsteps disguised by the grass.

I make it to the schoolhouse in a matter of seconds, basking in the shadows cast between two columns, and look down the entire length of the yard – an asphalt lake, lit by damp white light.

"Well, I'll be damned," I say, looking to a partially dismantled truck, parked by a set of closed doors.

The bank truck, Vega says. *It looks like they're scrapping it and removing any identifying features.*

The Central Bank of Lushoto logo on the body has been spraypainted over in blood red. The wheels are missing, and the truck itself sits upon a set of breezeblocks. I bet they were smart enough to take the bearer bonds out of the back, too.

I hug the wall, walking slowly and quietly along the length of the building, and stop when I make it to a set of doors, once composed mainly of glass, but since boarded with thin plywood. The handles don't move, but I find the plywood more accommodating, and manage to pop it out of place far enough to unlock the door from behind.

I slowly push the door aside, revealing a dark corridor, stretching almost as far as I can see. There are doors on either side – entrances to former classrooms – and the pervasive smell of fresh paint. A warm orange light spills from one of the open doors; somebody's home.

As quietly as I can – traipsing on the toes of my boots – I begin walking. I tiptoe past empty trophy cabinets, and dusty photographs still pinned to the walls; classes of thirty smiling high-school kids, and a soccer team lined up before a set of lustrous silver cups.

This whole school was built by donations; a well-intentioned effort to ensure these kids had a bright future ahead of them. Instead, the civil war broke out, those children were forced to pick up weapons, the school was bombed out, and a monster with fresh blood on his hands -and stolen blood in his refrigerator – moved in.

I make it to that open classroom doorway, with its sole orange light illuminating a long rectangle across the floor. There's a sound, too; a very quiet, very gentle tone, repeating over and over. A dial tone.

"'Allo?" a voice says, carefree and youthful, thankfully not talking to me. I look into the classroom through the crack between the door and doorframe, and see a man pacing up and down inside an empty room, speaking on a cellphone in a local dialect I don't understand. He wears a black sleeveless T-shirt, and cargo shorts, and he's unarmed.

    I wait until he turns his back to the doorway, and then hop past it, continuing my way quietly down the corridor. No need to raise the alarm yet. Sure, I can unleash a torrent of violence with ease, but ending one is far more difficult.

CHAPTER 55

That smell of fresh paint grows ever stronger as I reach the end of the corridor, and a door propped open at the bottom of it. I squeeze through the doorway and find myself inside a building site.

The walls are still wet with new paint – I see them glistening white in the dim light – and the room is full of wooden crates, and bulky, ambiguous structures, hidden underneath foam blankets. In the corner, a murky window lets in a few silver shards of light from the courtyard outside.

"What is this place?" I murmur to Vega, treading across the spotlessly clean tiles on the floor. I run my fingertips along one of those foam covers, and gently pull at it, unveiling a fume cupboard, and inside it, a box of test tubes, brand new.

A laboratory, Vega says. *All new equipment, too.*

"What are you building, David?" I whisper.

There's no smoking gun, yet. No half-finished dirty bomb lying around; no textbook lying open on a chapter titled *How to Grow Anthrax*, but he's obviously putting something dangerous and unsavory together here.

Still, by the strange circumstances of my so-called *gift* I've seen many illicit laboratories in my time – nefarious workshops run by homicidal madmen and diabolical schemers – but there's something missing. It's distinctly intermediate; no cowering scientists, no barrels of illegal, flammable chemicals. Dare I say, I've seen better.

I leave the room and head to the next, which I recognize immediately as a former cafeteria. There's a distant racket – the loudly persistent purring of an engine – and a set of long tables and benches, some of them still littered with empty plates and unclean cutlery.

The room is huge; tall ceilings and rows upon rows of tables; a mess hall that'd suit any emerging insurgent army, or terrorist training camp. I even find an unfinished jigsaw puzzle: a pride of lions, lying before a half-eaten animal.

Following the sound of the noise, I come to a thick metal door with a circular window inset within it, and beyond that door, a fully stocked kitchen. Industrial ovens, rows of gleaming cooktops, and a cavernous sink, full of soap suds and dirty plates.

Someone's half-way through doing the dishes, Vega says. *Perhaps you shouldn't disturb them.*

"You're right, but I want to know what that racket is," I tell him, as that humming engine grows louder. I smell something other than paint for the first time – diesel, drifting in from a window left slightly ajar. A generator, I expect.

Beside that window is a walk-in refrigerator door, shiny, chrome, and sitting on a set of thick hinges, like a bank vault. I quickly walk over there, and with some effort, pull the handle and slide open the door.

It's dark, right until the point where I take my first couple of steps inside and a motion-sensor catches me, flooding the room with a cold, blue light. There are boxes of the usual items you'd expect from a kitchen of this size: bright-colored fruits and vegetables, as well as stale-looking bread that barely moves when I touch it.

My attention is captured by something in the corner, however. A stack of white, plastic crates, with rounded edges and reams of writing on the sides of them in block capitals, like warnings and disclaimers. I get closer and make out the language – French – along with a yellow biological hazard warning sign.

I don't think you need to open those boxes to know what's in there, Vega says.

"The blood," I say. "We found it."

I examine the boxes, and the intact plastic seals on them. They're cold – he's obviously gone to a lot of trouble to transport them, store them, and refrigerate them – and completely unopened.

"Looks like he hasn't gotten around to cracking the blood open yet," I say. "Saving it for a special occasion? Christmas treat?"

He's certainly stockpiling it for a reason, Vega says, ignoring my sarcastic comment.

"But, why?" I ask, leaving the blood, the bread, and the freezer behind, and walking back to the kitchen. "Why go to all that trouble to pay for the blood to be stolen, only to stash it here, next to a batch of zucchini and that moldy bread?"

There is a simpler explanation, Vega says, before another noise disturbs the both of us; an echoing laughter from beyond the kitchen, in the cafeteria hall.

I rush to the door, and carefully edge my face closer to that round window inset within it. I see four figures darkening the entrance to the cafeteria, standing in a rough semi-circle. They're chatting, laughing, pushing each other around without a care in the world. They don't know I'm here, yet.

"I need to get out of this kitchen," I whisper to Vega. "Someone's coming back for these dishes, I know it."

There's another doorway inside the cafeteria, a few yards away, Vega says.

I turn my head and look across the way, seeing that

doorway he's talking about; a bland, gray door, unremarkable and invisible if it wasn't for the fact that it might be my only means of escape.

As slowly as I can manage – careful not to provoke a telltale creak from the hinges – I push the kitchen door open, and when I'm convinced those guys are too enraptured in their horseplay to see me, I slide myself out, keeping low, and rush to the door.

It's a small door, barely big enough to accommodate my frame. It looks exactly like the access door to some secretive part of the school; the dark and dingy pit where they'd throw the bad kids, or maybe just the staff room they tried perilously hard to hide.

I open it, and with one final look over my shoulder – confirming I haven't been seen – I go inside.

Rather than being confronted by anything particularly sordid, I'm met with darkness, and the vague, unlit outline of a staircase. I close the door behind me – encountering a small creak, but nothing that'll get me caught and cooked alive in those ovens – and slowly tread upstairs.

The taste of dust and decrepitude in the air is overwhelming – I finally found the first part of this complex that hasn't had a fresh renovation, it seems – and when I get to the top of the stairs, I step into moonlight.

There's a hole in the roof, and below me, a bunch of pots and pans laid out, collecting water. There's bird crap too; lots of it, whites and grays and browns littering every surface. I trudge forward slowly, past the hole in the roof, and disturb a couple of pigeons, who flap around, and fly for another spot in the rafters.

My hand finds a wooden handrail, and I part a series of black, dirtied curtains in front of me to discover a walkway, accompanied by lengths of ropes and metal levers. I turn my head to see a large painted backdrop of a cityscape – with skyscrapers and a round, yellow moon – stained and faded by years of exposure to the elements.

I'm in the rafters of a theatrical stage, it seems; one that hasn't been used for years. I keep walking along the wooden walkway, until I come to a rope that seems sturdy enough to hold my weight, before reaching out and climbing down it, still surrounded by those black drapes keeping me shrouded in darkness.

My feet hit solid floor again – treading the wooden floorboards of a stage, angled so slightly upwards – and again I hear voices. I can't see anything – the black curtains on a rail above me hide my form from the rest of the room – but I think I can make out laughter, and footsteps.

I drop to my knees and begin crawling across the floorboards, underneath the drapes. When I hear a familiar voice though – boomingly loud, and coldly self-assured – I freeze in place. It's *him*, I just know it's him: the warlord.

"This is it, right?" I hear him ask, while holding my breath. "In these bags? All the material we asked for?"

"Yes sir," another man replies, in a notably different accent. European, perhaps. "All here, present and accounted for."

I'm still surrounded by warm, flowing fabrics – the drapes that lay across the stage – but I feel anything but safe. My heart races – I can practically feel it in my teeth – and I'm briefly transported back to that train, and those giant fists raining down on me again. The hurting; the shame of defeat, the agony of losing that arm…

No, I won't be intimidated. Not this time. I clench my fists, take a deep, quiet breath, and very carefully resume crawling forward beneath the drapes, finally reaching the end of the stage, and a sheer, meter-high drop beyond.

It's a huge, empty hall; an assembly hall, doubling up as a theatre, it seems. There's a flat, dusty floor – overlooked by a row of highly set windows, letting in a trickle of moonlight –

and a stack of plastic chairs at the back of the room. There are four columns – thick, vertical beams – built in a square shape.

And in the middle of the hall – standing exactly in the middle of those four columns, dead-center of the space – there are two figures, facing one another. One is a small man, wearing all black and a baseball cap – a man I haven't seen before – and the other is the tall, muscular figure I know so well, standing with his back to me.

He wears a colorful and tight short-sleeved shirt, full of traditional African patterns, and black pants. I can't see a gun on him; the only deadly weapon he appears to possess is his own body.

Beside them both is a row of black sports bags; I count eight in total. I can see the bags are wide and bulky, and packed full of something. Money? Drugs? Weapons? I feel like I'm intruding on some sordid exchange; David Faye is clearly buying the contents of those bags, but what are they?

From my vantage point – hidden partially beneath the black drapes – I see him hand something over to the man in the cap; an envelope, perhaps. They shake hands, and the man in the cap turns and walks away, leaving the bags behind.

I slowly reach behind me and into the back pocket of my pants, pulling out that single chili pepper I bought earlier today. I crush it in my palm, and slowly and meticulously rub it across my fingers and knuckles, only stopping when it completely disintegrates. The smell is overwhelming, and practically brings tears to my eyes, but now I'm ready for a fight.

A door slams shut in the distance, and I see David Faye bend to look at the contents of his sports bags. He unzips one of them, rifles through it, and then zips it back up, apparently satisfied with what he finds.

I close my eyes for a moment, taking one last, affirming deep breath, and slide myself off the stage. My feet hit the floorboards with an echoing boom, and I see that wide set of shoulders of his tense up before he looks over his shoulder to see me.

"David Faye," I say out loud, my voice echoing a dozen times across the empty walls and drab ceiling. "The warlord."

It's time to dance with the devil once more.

CHAPTER 56

"I've seen you before," he says, crossing his arms and nudging one of the sports bags out of his way with his foot. "You were in that truck with me, after the bank job."

My brief flirtation with the art of hijacking a moving vehicle; something I'd rather forget. I haven't changed my face since then, so it's little wonder he remembers me. I see there's something else about his expression though, a certain skepticism. He remembers me from elsewhere too.

"It was you on the train, too," he says, before turning his body to face me. "Your face was different, but I recognized you on the truck."

I remember looking him in the eyes, and seeing the seedlings of recognition there, like he knew the only man audacious enough to attempt that hijacking was the same man who'd ambushed him on the train.

"How'd you know it was me?" I ask, as he continues slowly walking towards me. His jawline tenses up at my question, and his right eye twitches.

"It's your smell," he replies. "Your scent, your weight, your strength, your habit of wildly swinging your fists; all passion and no practice. You're not a normal man, I can tell you that much."

I put my fists up, tasting a bitter, spicy tone of chili pepper carried through the air as I do so.

"An American mercenary, with an ever-changing face," he says, his arms still crossed; his thick, veiny biceps straining against the fabric of his shirt. "And they have the nerve to say *I* do witchcraft."

He stops a couple of yards away from me and just stands there, the immovable mountain.

"You should be dead," he says in an inquisitive tone, narrowing his eyes at me. "I saw you leave that train. No one could have survived that."

"What's in the bags, Dave?" I ask him, changing the subject from my own mortality, and trying to ignore the fear rising within me. I'm stronger than him; I'm smarter than him. I can defeat him, and I will.

"A man who changes his face, like the snake sheds its skin," he says, ignoring my question. "A man who survives certain death, like the devil himself. I don't care to find out what you are; I only care about how you got here."

He uncrosses his arms, slowly and purposefully, never lifting those searching, piercing eyes from me.

"And how did I get here?" I ask.

"By God's plan," he says, before I see his shoulders fall with a breath, and he strides towards me.

I hold my fists high and stay on my toes, deftly strafing out of his way. He aims a wide-angled punch – a sharp scythe that whistles past my ear – and I barely manage to dodge it, backing away from him, trying to use as much distance as I can gather.

His eyes – those deep, dark and intense windows to a brutal soul – watch my every movement, never flinching and never wavering. I keep myself calm, even as he strides towards me again, pivoting to throw a kick, which I step over.

He leans forward on one foot, preparing to throw a right hand, while keeping his left menacingly low. I take my opportunity and jump forward, hitting him with a jab that knocks him slightly off balance. He takes his eyes off me for the first time, shaking his head, and moving one hand to his mouth.

"I'll ask again," I say to him, as he puts his eyes back on me. "What's in the bags? What is this place? This former school, what are you building here?"

"You're weak of soul," he says, his tone deep and emotionless. "Weak of soul, weak of mind, and weak of spirit."

He steps forward again, throwing a barrage of punches that I dodge left, and weave beneath. He throws a wild right that I back away from, and he instead hits one of the columns in the center of the room, knocking a huge wooden chunk out of it. I'm quicker than him; I'm proving that to him here. And soon I'll prove that I'm stronger too.

His jaw tenses again – the first telltale signs of annoyance in his otherwise unflappable countenance – and he feints with a kick, before throwing a lightning-fast jab to my chin. It glances off me, but knocks my head sideways, and I don't see the next one coming.

He crashes his fist against the side of my head, hitting me square in the temple. The impact immediately staggers me – up becomes down, and down becomes somewhere beyond the stars – and before I know it, I'm falling again.

The scant slivers of moonlight, and the stray strands of the floodlights outside seem blindingly bright in their intensity – like I'm lying on a surgeon's table – and I feel the cold, hard ground beneath me, catching my desperate fall.

My eyes readjust, and I blink to see the warlord's feet, and his thick, steel-toed boots staring me in the face. I plant my fists into the ground, and try to push myself back to my feet, but I only get as far as Faye's waiting hands.

He grabs me by the back of my collar, and clubs me across

the face with one of those huge, meteoric fists. I barely even feel the impact this time – I seem to lose a couple of seconds in the melee – and the next thing I know, I'm facing him.

I try to throw a fist, but watch helplessly as it sails past his temple. He grabs me across my waist – his thick arms snaking across the small of my back like the roots of a tree, tunneling beneath the earth – and lifts me off my feet, as he begins to squeeze me in a bear hug.

I lose all the breath in my lungs – every bit of precious oxygen wrenched painfully out of me – and feel loud *pops* and *snaps* throughout my body; ligaments and tendons breaking under the tension. I screw my eyes shut and see myself in a vice; my body squeezed relentlessly, mercilessly.

I'm drowning in a sea of pain – a dark, smothering lake of thick mud, sinking without trace – when I manage to catch a whiff of that chili pepper, and remember the fact my fingertips are coated in it…

Delving deep into the pit of my stomach, rousing every last fire and impulse from my nervous system, I find the tiniest sliver of strength I have left; I open my eyes, and jam my fingers into his eyes. My thumbs scratch at the corners of his eyes – my fingertips scraping at his nose and eyelids – and when I see him screw his eyes shut in pain, I punch him in the lip.

He staggers backwards, and eases that vice-like grip just the smallest amount, giving me the opportunity I need. I hold my fist high up in the air, and bring it down on his forehead as hard as I can muster, like I'm playing some death-defying version of fairground strength tester.

He drops to one knee, and my heels make it back to the floor. I take a breath – a vital, lifegiving breath – that wracks me with pain, but fills me with a strength I never knew I'd feel again. I cough a couple of times, fight away the temptation to vomit, and look back to the teary, streaming eyes of my opponent.

I extricate myself from his grip, landing another two punches to his face, and spinning backwards on one heel, as he grabs his eyes with both hands. He bats away at me blindly, throwing useless, hopeless punches, before rubbing his eyes again, trying to regain the use of his vision.

"You're strong, David," I tell him, my voice hoarse from the fact he tried to squeeze my soul out of me a moment ago. "But you can't handle spice like I can."

I stride towards him and hit him with everything that I've got: a right hand that I wind up, swing in the widest, most brutal angle I can, and hit him square in the side of the jaw. I feel the impact of this one, alright; my wrist buckles painfully – my knuckles crunching against the bones of his face – and he flies backwards, landing on his back.

Feeling myself filling with pride and joy, and hate, and the yearning to seek revenge for all of that pain I felt, and all of those harrowing stories of murder and suffering, and those charred bones in those stacks of tires, I jump atop him.

Kneeling over him, I throw a bunch more fists; relentless, heartless blows, bloodying his eyes and mouth. Each punch I rain down provokes an almost intolerable pain in the bones of my wrists and knuckles, but the impulse to keep inflicting this pain – this retribution for everything both I and this country have been through – is too great for me to stop.

I see him barely consciously trying to squirm away – to turn his head from the blows, or to wrench his body away from mine – but I don't let him. I hit him again, and again, and again.

Eventually, he stops moving; his face, once unblemished, now covered in blood, and his eyes thick with swelling. There's a huge laceration over his eyebrow – a yawning chasm, pink in the middle – that spews blood out like a faucet. I stop myself – more to catch my breath than out of reverence for my own pain – and climb off him.

"I'm stronger than you are," I pant, my breaths ragged and triumphant.

He stirs a little, his shoulder twitching, and his hand moving slowly to his face, shuddering as it goes, but it's clear that he's in no condition to fight back. I win.

I slowly and painfully climb to my feet, before dry heaving a couple of times – my body's effort to put all my internal organs back in their starting places, back before the warlord's attempt to re-arrange them. Then, I look behind us, past the pool of blood that's accumulating below his eye, and the marks our boots made in the dust.

Those sports bags – the large, bulky black ones that sit in the middle of the room – grab my attention. I walk over there, kneel beside one, and call out to him.

"What's in the bags then, David?" I ask him, moving my trembling fingers to the zipper. "What's worth getting pummeled to a bloody mess for? What's worth dying for?"

I unzip it, and something large and bulky immediately falls out. It's colorful, glossy, and heavy, and I go to catch it as it falls. It's a book; a large, heavy book.

Reaching into the bag, I pull out another object, a similar size, and just as heavy. Another book; a science textbook, in English. I rub my fingertips across my forehead quizzically, and go to pull out another, this time a math textbook.

"What is this?" I say out loud, vocalizing my confusion. I pull out another book – a primer on IT systems and databases – and open it, looking inside the pages for hidden compartments or spaces, but find just pages. Hundreds and hundreds of pages about computers and programming.

I scramble to my feet and turn to the next bag, before dropping down beside it and unzipping it. I pull the bag open, and see that it too is full of textbooks. Math, biology, French language, English literature, physics. I pick up another book and open it upside down, shaking it.

Nothing falls out; there's nothing inside it but words and pictures. It's just a book.

"What's worth dying for," I say again, asking myself the question more than anyone else.

He's not setting up a terrorist training camp here; he's not building some launchpad to build the rocket that'll start the next civil war.

He's setting up a school…

CHAPTER 57

"Get on with it, will ya?" I hear a voice from David's direction say, followed by a groaning, hellish gargling noise. "You're here to kill me; well, I don't fear death."

Picking my head up out of the book, I look over to him and see him lying there on his back, with blood still draining from the laceration in his eyebrow.

"There will be no death," he says, his voice pained, but resolute. "Just a beautiful second life in heaven, with my creator."

He launches into the recital of a bible verse – one I recognize from my father's endless radio sermons - and tries to pick himself up, bending from the floor at the waist.

"Books," I say to him, walking over to him again and kneeling beside him. "There's a bunch of schoolbooks in those bags."

"Huh?" he grunts, before backing away from me a yard, pulling himself along by the palms of his hands until he makes it to one of those supporting columns – the giant, vertical beam he took a chunk from earlier – and props his back up against it, with his tree-trunk-like legs still splayed across the floor.

"What is this place?" I ask him. "What are you building here?"

"What does it look like?" he barks back at me. "It used to be a school, and it will be a school again. We're rebuilding it."

"Why?" I ask, still shocked by the mundanity of my discovery.

"Why?" he repeats back at me, just as baffled as I apparently am. He tears a strip off the sleeve of his shirt, and puts it to his eyebrow.

"The blood – the blood you had stolen from Monaco," I stammer. "Why? Why did you steal it?"

He shuffles around uncomfortably, dabbing his eyebrow with the scrap of fabric in obvious pain.

"Why does any free republic need blood and medicine?" he asks, another rhetorical question. "We need it for our clinic. We need it for blood transfusions; for the many ill of sickle cell anemia, and HIV, and a hundred other diseases that plague us."

"The blood of the wealthy," I say to him, leaning forward, my hands out in a near pleading gesture. "You requested the blood of the wealthy."

He looks confused again, and perhaps – underneath all that blood and swelling – he's offended by my line of questioning; like I'm asking foolish questions.

"Would you prefer we stole the blood of the poor?" he asks. "Would you prefer we stole from desperate hospitals, in impoverished areas? I wanted to steal the blood from Monaco, from a clinic that could afford to get some more."

Suddenly, I seem to remember Vega saying there was a simpler explanation for the boxes of blood that sit in that refrigerator. I've been so consumed by this pursuit of Vincent, and stories of vampires and blood-drinkers around the world that I lost sight of what blood really is: the life in our veins.

"Why are you here?" he asks, wrapping the length of fabric around his forehead, a makeshift bandage. "Why are you trying to stop our work here?"

"Because you're a murderer," I tell him, my voice unsure and wavering. "You're trying to restart the civil war; you're stealing money from the Bank in Lushoto to fund your militia. You'll conscript children, you'll kill thousands. You're the brutal leader of the Avenging Angels brigade. You're the warlord!"

My words echo a thousand times across the lonely walls and ceilings; a deafening, repeating series of accusations that the very building itself seems to want to contradict.

He doesn't react at first; he just smiles – or maybe grimaces – showing his bloodied teeth.

"I hate that name," he says, with a deep, wheezing breath. "Warlord; everything I wanted to leave behind."

"But it's true, isn't it?" I ask.

Suddenly, I hear footsteps echoing loudly from down the hall. A gang of Faye's men appear – fresh-faced, outraged, yelling insults in my direction. They see their warlord on the floor, bloodied and beaten, and then their eyes fall onto me.

I jump to my feet and hold my fists up, but as soon as I see the guns in their hands – held close to their bodies as if they're scared to use them, but deadly nonetheless – I relax my arms, and drop them carefully to my sides.

They aim at me – one of them closes an eye, aiming for me – and I brace for the coming storm; the ensuing hail of bullets that'll tear into my flesh and perforate my organs and split my bones asunder. The storm of gunfire that'll bring me untold pain if I'm lucky, and if I'm unlucky, kill me instantly.

"No!" David yells out, before saying a couple more words in the local dialect. The men look at him, confused, before lowering their guns. "No more blood will be spilled here."

I turn to him, my mouth hanging open in surprise and relief. I quickly remember my fight on the train with him, and his vociferous refusal to allow his buddy to pick up and fire a gun at me.

He yells a few more words to his men, and couple of them disperse – running away down a corridor – while the other pair hang around at the edge of the room, vigilantly and aimlessly.

"The police chief, Bayo Akello," I then say, jabbing my finger in his direction. "You threatened his family, that's why he met with you, why he was willing to betray his country, and—"

"I saved his family!" David shoots back. "Some kidnappers captured them from a national park, and I had my men rescue them. Chief Akello was grateful to me."

"You locked all those people in that church and burned it to the ground. You murdered untold thousands; made them dig their own graves," I tell him, clenching my fists in anger once again. Just because he's sparing my life for now, I'm not letting him off this hook. I take the photograph out of my pocket; the one of the train driver. "You killed this man, and his family."

He leans forward, and I slowly creep closer to him. He looks at the photograph held between two of my reddened, spice-stained fingers, and I think I see a light of remembrance in his eyes.

He turns his head, looking to those two goons he left idly standing at the edge of the room, and shouts a couple of words to them. One of them nods, before taking one last, mistrustful glance at me, and running away down the corridor and into its darkness.

"Him? His name is Howard, Howard Daju. He's fine," Faye says to me, before coughing a couple of times, and dabbing at his cut eyebrow again. "I bet he told you we killed him, didn't he?"

"He?" I ask.

He moves his hand to the back of his pants, contorting his

body slightly as he does so, his thick shoulders rising and falling with each breath. With one hand, he pulls something out of his back pocket; a wallet, in black leather. He opens it, and slowly takes out a picture of his own.

"I always keep this photograph with me," he says, holding out a small, faded photograph in my direction, folded once and fraying at the edges. "I hold onto it so that I'll never forget."

I slowly approach him and take the photograph. It's a black and white photo of a squad of pre-teen boys dressed in military uniforms, perhaps twenty of them, sitting by the side of the road. There's a burned-out car in the distance, amid the barren, harsh wasteland of Nubalaya that I've come to know so well.

David Faye – far younger, but immediately recognizable on account of his height and musculature, even at that age – is visible in the front row, and the other children stand around him. All the kids are armed with assault rifles, and some carry massive-looking grenades on their belts, and others, those thousand-yard stares you see in old war photos.

Right at the front, though, sitting beside David, is a much older man; an adult, wearing a black beret, with several silver stars stitched onto it. He's in his late thirties, wearing a severe expression and military fatigues, stretched across his portly body. He looks like the squad's adult leader.

There's something strangely familiar about him. I can't explain it, but I get the same feeling looking at the older man in this picture as I do when I look at myself in a mirror, or catch a reflection of myself in some shiny surface.

"At first, we just called him the General," David says, as I go on studying the photograph. "He was that and more to us. Our general, our leader, our hope, the only adult we knew, the only adult we felt we could trust. The man we were prepared to die for. The man who a lot of us did die for."

He dabs at his eyebrow again, as another trickle of blood runs down his jaw and his neck.

"I wasn't the warlord, I wasn't the one who recruited all those children; who led those massacres, and the destruction of villages and all of those atrocities. I'm not the one who poisoned those children's minds," he says, his teeth gritted with anger. "He did! He was the warlord!"

I look back to the photo, and the man's strange, oddly familiar face. I've never seen that face before, so why do I feel like I know him? All the children in the photograph – David Faye included – seem to gather around him with such reverence in their eyes. How come I've never seen him until now?

"After a year on the road, a year at war, I learned a lot about him," David says, his voice wavering for the first time, like he's recounting memories far more painful than the beating I gave him. "I learned his true name: Eric. But you'll know him by another name."

As he says it, the photograph begins to tremble in my fingertips. I can't stop looking at the man's eyes; they elude me, somehow. And then, like a bolt of lightning, struck directly to my brain, I get it; I do know the man. Like me, he's changed his face, but he'll never be able to change those eyes.

"Sunday Mufumba," he says. "The Minister for the Interior of Nubalaya. He's the man who sent you to capture me, isn't he?"

I look back to the photograph. He's right; his face is entirely different – smaller, with no pink scar reaching down one side of it – but those eyes are unmistakable. I get the same feeling every time I see a new face of mine in the mirror.

Mufumba didn't bring us here to eliminate a dangerous warlord, bent on restarting the civil war.

He brought us here to clean up his own past, and some inconvenient truths: *he* was the warlord…

CHAPTER 58

"That scar on his face," he says, before threading the needle through his own brow, slowly and painfully pulling the suture through it, and stitching it tightly closed. "What story did he tell you?"

David Faye sits in the same position – his back square against the wooden column – while one of his men holds a mirror out in front of him. An open first-aid kit lays beside him, and I watch the squeamish process of him stitching himself up, repairing the damage my nanotech-enhanced strength did to his genetically freakish body.

"I don't know, something like he used to be a farmer, and he was brought to the marketplace in Lushoto with 10,000 others; the February massacre," I say, remembering what Mufumba told us about his scarring. "He said that you and your troops tried to execute him; that he was shot in the head in a botched attempt at an execution."

David averts his eyes from the mirror and looks to me instead, a sly smile on his purple, swollen lips.

"Well, he's right about one thing," he says, before looking back to the mirror and making another stitch with the needle.

"He was present at the February massacre, but he isn't being honest about which side of the gun he was on."

He makes another suture, followed by a short grunt of pain.

"There was a battle in the final months of the civil war," he says. "The government forces had us pinned down, under siege inside an old office building in the middle of Lushoto. Me, Eric, and many of my old brothers in the battalion."

He takes out a set of scissors from the first-aid box, and cuts the suture off, having stitched the length of that laceration.

"We had a handful of ammunition left. They were shelling us, blowing massive chunks off the building. It seemed hopeless; we were sure we were going to meet our Lord in heaven," he says before looking back to me, his eyes full of anger now. "Eric, though, wasn't so sure about that. He was worried he'd be captured. Put on trial for the world to see."

He puts two fingers to his temple; a rudimentary gesture that means only one thing.

"He stood before us and put a gun to his head, and he pulled the trigger," he says, gravely. "But he didn't die. He damaged his skull badly, disfigured the entire side of his face, and put himself into a coma, but he didn't die."

I think of the Minister's scars; a crisscross of pink, bumpy scarring all the way down his face, that shiny black false eye, and the unnaturally square shape of his head and jaw. He's had a lot of surgery, alright. An entire facial reconstruction, in fact. It seems I'm not the only one who can change their face to assume another identity.

"All of my brothers were killed or captured during that siege. I'm the only one that managed to escape," he says, wistfully. "Eric, our dear general, and the man we swore to die for, was taken to hospital and nursed back to health; his entire face reconstructed, so that only my old brothers and I could recognize him. And then the UN rolled in and forced the ceasefire agreement onto us. The war was over."

He looks at himself one final time in the mirror, ensuring the stitches are tight, before politely gesturing for his follower to take the mirror away.

"Eric still had something to offer, though. He had a new face, a new identity, and he knew where all the bodies were buried; after all, he buried them. He made a deal with the new government: he'd reveal the names and whereabouts of all the former rebel forces – a chance for the new people in charge to settle some scores – in exchange for a government position."

"Minister of the Interior Sunday Mufumba," I say. He nods.

"There's no new civil war," he says. "Because the old one never really ended. It's just a colder, shadow war now, rumbling on in tit-for-tat killings and score settling. That's what this all is: Eric is trying to give himself a new name, while eliminating everyone who knows his older one."

I'm sure the bearer bonds have a role in this too; another inconvenient truth we happened to stumble upon.

"I took a different path," David then says, beginning to pick himself up from his seated position by the column for the first time. "I was taken in by another survivor, an old teacher of mine, from before the war. I was sixteen years old, and I'd already seen unimaginable horrors by then. I was little more than a feral animal, but he saw the good in me. He taught me to read and write again, and taught me that I'm worth something in this world."

He manages to get to his feet – all six feet five of him – and stretches his arms out widely.

"My old mentor, Johnson Amun," he says. The name rings a bell; I think Mufumba told us about him, way back in the briefing.

"I've heard that name," I tell him. "Mufumba told us he

was a general, and that they had to assassinate him for the sake of national stability."

Faye looks back to me with incredulous, hurt eyes. He scoffs – snorting derisively – before putting his fingers to his lips and teeth, evidently checking what's still there.

"They murdered him," he says, between gritted teeth. "But they didn't mean to. They wanted to kill me instead. He was just collateral damage. I would have been happy to live my life in the shadows and put everything behind me. But they killed the person closest to me, and so I took up a weapon again."

He takes a step towards me, somewhat menacingly. I climb to my feet, and put one foot forward, defensively, unsure as to his intentions.

"I'm not anyone's warlord," he says, his voice stern and resolute. "I'm not trying to start a new civil war, and I'm not trying to kill anyone, other than one man."

There are more footsteps down the hall – a decisive, echoing pair of marching bootsteps – and we both turn to the source of the noise. Two men approach, one of them the man Faye dismissed earlier, and the other a familiar-looking man in dirty blue overalls. He's in his thirties, with tired eyes, but a wide smile. I think I know who it is.

"My God," I say, putting my hand to my mouth in a dumb-looking show of shock. "I know you."

I reach back into my pocket and pull out the same photograph I showed David a short ten minutes ago. That photograph of the father, Howard Daju, and his son on the train. I stare into it, and then at the man in the blue overalls once again.

"You're Howard Daju," I tell him, and he smiles awkwardly, before looking to David with a confused, perturbed expression, once he sees that he's bruised and covered in blood. "I was told you were dead. I saw a picture of your bodies, you and your wife and your children…"

"What?" Daju says, even more distressed than before. He frantically looks between me and David, his face full of panic, apparently somewhat unappreciative of the fact a crazy westerner is claiming to have seen pictures of his dead family.

"Your wife and children are perfectly fine," David says to him, and he seems to take a deep breath of guarded relief, though he doesn't take that look of panic off his face. David looks back to me and speaks: "You've been hoodwinked. You saw a faked photograph. I didn't kill Howard, or his family."

He's right; the man who Mufumba claimed had been brutally murdered – his blood-soaked body lain face-down alongside his wife and children – is standing before me, unhurt. I think of the supposed kidnappings of doctors and other professionals Faye had undertaken; could it be that they weren't kidnappings after all, but defections?

"Howard here works on our rail system in Free Zimbala," David says. "He's living here in the complex, along with his family. He's a skilled worker and a valued part of our project. And as you can see, he's far from dead."

Howard looks around and nods sheepishly, before disappearing back down the corridor he came from. David takes another step towards me and holds his large hand – still stained with blood – out to me; a handshake.

"I don't want to fight you," he says, his eyes partially obscured behind his purple, swollen eyelids, but sincere, nonetheless. "Do you believe what I tell you?"

This man – this massive, dangerous, and intimidating man – who I've spent the last week dreading the very sight of is graciously extending his hand to me. This man who I've viewed with fear and hatred and fury, this man whose name I've spit with the same scorn as I would the devil himself, is asking if I believe him.

And I think I do.

"Yeah," I say to him, slightly dazed from the avalanche of crushing revelations that just landed on me, but at least willing to reward the fact he seemingly made Howard Daju rise from the grave tonight with a handshake. "I do."

I shake his hand, feeling his warm, tough skin on mine for the first time out of desperate, mortal combat. I feel something like a surge of electricity; a strange infusion of adrenaline, perhaps my body's subconscious reaction to being so close to a man who inflicted all that pain on me.

We part hands, and he snorts a thick spurt of blood out of his nose. One of his men brings him a change of shirt from somewhere, and he slowly peels off his blood-soaked shirt, its vibrant colors stained in dark crimson.

His body is like that of a manically obsessed bodybuilder's – that much I knew already – but I see scars, too. A circular wound like a bullet hole by his shoulder, and a set of straight, narrow lash scars on his back. There isn't an ounce of fat on him, owing to that genetic mutation of his, and those scars lie over his round, taut muscles like valleys in the earth.

"This project, this state within a state, this Free Zimbala," he says, waving his arms widely, before putting the new shirt on. "This was the dream of my mentor; that we can have a state free of the corruption that men like the so-called Minister Mufumba bring. Now that my mentor is dead, it's my duty to see it through."

He walks over to the stage, and I follow him, stopping when he jumps up to sit on the edge of it. He sits there, surrounded by those long black drapes, and goes on speaking.

"That's why Howard, and Martin, and Tariq, and Gideon, and everyone else in this complex follows me. Not because I'm a tyrant, or some rebel warlord. Not because I have magical powers, or that I'm some devil among men. It's because I'm doing something people want to believe in."

"What about the bearer bonds?" I finally get around to asking him. "Why did you rob the bank?"

He grins – that ever-present coolness still visible beneath all those facial wounds.

"Oh yeah, *that*," he says. "Those bearer bonds were part of Eric's retirement fund. He couldn't just steal cash from the central bank. Cash has serial numbers, it's hard to steal. Instead, he printed a bunch of bearer bonds, made some deals to exchange them for money with some old friends, and almost got away with it."

"Almost," I repeat.

"I learned about them when I rescued the police chief's family from those kidnappers," he adds. "I couldn't let him steal from my country like that. I set out to rob them myself, and police chief Akello was only too accommodating. Of course, I'd have two truckloads of cash to spend on schools like this, rather than one, if it wasn't for you."

He still wears a slight grin. I smile back, uneasily, and cross my arms defensively.

"Yeah, I suppose I should say I'm sorry about that."

"You were hired to capture me or kill me, weren't you?" he asks. I nod. "You were only doing what you thought was right: removing an evil presence from God's earth."

"The things he told us," I say, averting my eyes from his, and uncrossing my arms to clench my fists before me. "The stories we heard, of the civil war, of the brutality, and of you, I –"

"I'm sure a lot of what he told you was true," he then says, his voice despondent. "He was there to see it all. He told us what to do; who to aim at, who was coming to kill us, who we had to kill to survive. He put a rifle in my hands when I was seven years old."

I lean against the stage and listen to him.

"I fought, I went to battle, and I fired that gun, because the only adult I thought I could trust told me to. I saw all my old classmates die – everyone who Eric forced into our army; everyone he gave a weapon – and I stayed living. Eventually I thought it was God's will that I was so strong; that I kept standing where others fell. I still do."

I see tears at the edges of his swollen eyes. He puts a hand up to dab them away, before looking at me, and shaking his head.

"But now I know that all those terrible things we did – that Eric made me do – was the devil's work. I was seven years old, and I was already a murderer, and what crime is worse than murder? For that, every day, I try to make penance before I meet God."

"Right," is all I can think to say, a simple affirmative word to answer all of his soul searching. Is he good? Is he bad? Or is he a good person who started his life by being made to do a lot of bad things? Does any of it even matter, in the end?

What crime is worse than murder, he asks? Perhaps murder by another's hand. Perhaps influencing others to murder your enemies; poisoning the minds of children to commit the crimes you believe are below you.

There was an entire generation here born into the worst war imaginable. An entire generation of children that were born into madness; an entire generation that look to God to be their judge, because man will never be up to the task.

I'm about to open my mouth to say something a lot more insightful when I feel a subtle buzz in my pocket. My satellite phone, and the spook on the other end, worrying that I'm six feet under by now.

"Look," I say to David, taking the cellphone out of my pocket. "I have support here. Just one man, but I need to update him on – well – all of this, I guess."

David grins and gives me a massive thumbs-up, before pushing himself off the stage and walking to join a couple of his followers. I look to the cellphone, see a bunch of messages from Baynes, undoubtedly going out of his mind from worry in the back of that plumbing van.

Pushing the call button, I put the phone to my ear, and barely hear a single dial tone before he answers.

"Kris, how's it looking from the inside? What's your status?"

My status? How do I explain that I finally beat my nemesis, only to find out he isn't the warlord after all?

"Well, let's say I found out some things about David Faye," I say, looking over at the blood-stained shirt of his that still lies on the floor.

"Beautiful, are you out of the building?"

"No," I answer. "I'm still here."

"Is David Faye with you? Did you manage to apprehend him?"

"Yeah," I say. "But—"

"But what?" he quickly interjects.

"But… it's complicated."

CHAPTER 59

"Sunday Mufumba. That son of a god-damn—"

David waves one of those massive paws in front of Baynes' face, derailing the train of words coming out of his mouth almost immediately.

"Hey, let's not take the Lord's name in vain," David says, making Baynes quickly close his mouth.

Baynes hasn't quite adjusted to the fact we're sharing a room, a table, and indeed, a meal, with the fearsome David Faye quite yet. His eyes keep drifting over to him, watching him vigilantly as though his biceps could explode at any minute.

We're sitting in the building's cafeteria – the wide-open, echoing space full of tables and benches – eating a hastily prepared meal of potatoes and salad. I don't bother asking if our meals were refrigerated next to the stolen blood.

David hungrily eats his meal, albeit slower than he ordinarily might. I see he's chewing on one side of his mouth, while one of his eyes is swollen shut altogether.

Baynes, on the other hand, has barely touched his food. He's been too deeply engrossed in everything David has told him: the Minister's former identity, the explanation for the stolen blood of the wealthy, and the robbing of the bearer bonds, and the rebuilding of the school, and everything else that wrecks our bounty mission.

He even insisted that David bring the poor guy from the photograph – Howard Duja – to us once more, so he could verify with his own eyes that the evidence the minister supplied to us was false.

Now, he just sits beside me at the table, cutting a dejected, frustrated figure. I can't tell what disappoints him more; the fact he's learned we were lured here under false pretenses by a genocidal, corrupt politician, or the fact that we'll never get our hands on the bounty now.

"Man, I should have listened to my intuition," Baynes says, taking his eyes off David again, and putting his head in his hands. "Stay out of Africa; that's what we used to say at the agency. It always gets messy in Africa."

"Sorry to disappoint you," David says to him, a dubious expression on his face. Baynes surfaces for a moment and looks over at him, and for a moment, I think he's going to apologize, but he just sinks his head back into his hands.

"Well," Baynes says from within his hands, "we should go."

"What? That's it?" I ask. "Go? Now? We only just figured it all out."

He slowly picks his head up out of his hands again and rubs his eyes. When he opens them and looks squarely at me, I see that they're tired and bloodshot.

"I think our work here is done, don't you?" he says. "We've got to figure out how to cross the border and get home."

"Excuse me, but I have to ask," David says, as Baynes' eyes dart suspiciously to his massive, conspicuous frame once more. "Is your work here *really* done?"

Baynes doesn't answer; he just narrows his eyes at our host dubiously, wondering what he's getting at.

"You still have a contract in place, don't you?" David asks. "You still have to capture the apparently notorious warlord, and bring him to the Minister of the Interior."

"Huh? What are you saying?" I ask him.

"Do your job. Complete your contract. Take me to Eric," he says, coolly and decisively, crossing his arms.

"So, you want us to pretend we captured you?" Baynes asks.

"I know Eric; I spent the formative years of my life with him. He won't be able to resist meeting me face to face. I bet he'll insist on you taking me directly to the palace."

"The palace?" I ask, before thinking back to our videocall with the disconcertingly giant, angry head of Mufumba, and the ornately decorated backdrop behind him. It certainly wouldn't surprise me now to learn that when he's not trying to convince foreigners to murder his enemies, he's lounging around inside a palatial throne room.

"On the outskirts of Lushoto," David says. "It's a former British Colonial mansion. When he agreed to become Minister, it was one of his first requests. I have no doubt in my mind that he'll ask you to take me there. He'll want to kill me himself."

"What, you're saying we let him?" I ask, bemused.

"You gave me a pretty convincing beating," he says, tilting his head, showing off the full extent of his facial injuries. "Put me in a pair of handcuffs, and anyone would believe that you did your end of the bargain. But here's the thing; the handcuffs you put me in don't necessarily need to be locked."

"So we wheel you into his palace like a trojan horse?" Baynes asks, a dry smile on his face. "Then what? You do another bout of surgery on his face with your bare fists? Cut him up into little pieces and mail one to each corner of the country?"

David tenses his shoulders and raises on eyebrow above his swollen eye. Baynes pauses, before going on.

"Why should we facilitate your revenge fantasy, buddy?" he asks. "We're talking about the assassination of a government minister here. Then you're only a couple of bloody steps from declaring a coup. Civil war."

"There will be no new civil war," David says, unwaveringly. "Nubalaya can't take another conflict; we have much still to rebuild. No, what I want is to be put inside a room with Eric, alone. I want to right this wrong; to remove this cancer from my country. After that, I'll return here, to my home, and continue my duty."

"And what do we do when we see you on our television screens, announcing a new dictatorship in Nubalaya?" Baynes asks, still prodding away at him, more courageously than before.

"I can't just sit in his seat and call myself the new minister. Outside of autonomous areas like this, I'm still a hated man," David replies. "The so-called Minister has had seven years to malign my name; to call me the spawn of Satan himself, to say that I'm the warlord who disfigured this country. Seven years to put all his crimes on me."

Baynes' eyes – formerly full of daring and incredulity – drop to the table.

"Take me to him, and I'll end this," David says, knocking on the table before us with his fist. "This country will finally be free of Eric, and his lies."

I turn to Baynes, whose expression is characteristically guarded, but whom I know is tempted by the idea; an opportunity to strike back at the corrupt politician who sold us a bunch of lies and threw us into an unnecessarily dangerous situation with a genetically freakish superhuman.

"What's in it for us?" he asks.

"Not much, I have to admit," David says. "I can guarantee you safe passage across the border to a neighboring country, and I can offer you the chance to feel good about effecting real change in Africa. I bet you CIA types don't get to experience that too often."

I smile to myself, trying hard not to laugh. Baynes' face remains cold and stern, but even he can appreciate that one, I'm sure.

"What do you think?" he says, turning to me. I keep the smile on my face and shrug, a tacit admission that I'll go along with it, if Baynes is willing. He crosses his arms and leans back on the bench, his lips pressed together stiffly, like he's just finished sucking a lemon.

"All right then," he says after a few moments' pause. "I mean, we did say we'd capture and deliver David Faye."

He takes off his glasses and rubs his eyes again. I can still smell the spice wafting off my fingers.

"You're sure he'll have us deliver you straight to him?" I ask David, who nods silently. "Will he have security?"

"Oh yes, he'll have security," he says. "Armed, capable men, seconded from the Nubalayan armed forces."

I see Baynes shifting around uncomfortably in his seat. The presence of badly paid armed goons isn't quite as intimidating a prospect for me, though.

"They won't be a problem," I say to David's evident delight. He grins widely, his smile reaching from ear to ear, with his teeth still stained slightly by blood.

"So be it," Baynes mutters under his breath. "We came here with aspirations of providing some amount of justice. I suppose this is the best we're going to get."

A small, twisted form of justice, bent 180 degrees out of shape from what we sought in the first place. A justice that demands we put one man in a room with another, on the unspoken understanding that only one of them will leave.

But given everything we've learned, it's the only justice that seems right.

CHAPTER 60

"Mr. Baynes, I've been told you bring good news."

Mufumba's voice is wary, but polite. I look to David, who shares the cramped space in the back of the van with us. He tries not to react to the sound of Mufumba's voice – loud and garbled by the poor quality of the phone's loudspeaker – but I see his jaw tense up; the ligaments straining as he grinds his teeth.

"We sure have, I'm sure you've seen the evidence we sent already," Baynes says to the cellphone, his face lit in ghostly white by the spotlights above us. "The warlord, packaged and ready for delivery."

Packaged? Delivery? I see Baynes' face contort uncomfortably after saying those words. I guess they sounded better inside his head than they do outside of it.

"Splendid!" Mufumba crows on the other side of the line. "You'll be bringing him to an official government residence in the outskirts of Lushoto. I'll have the directions sent to you."

David looks at me knowingly, and mouths something to the effect of *I told you so*. The grandiose palatial residence we'll be wheeling our trojan horse inside, I expect.

Last night, after eating the sad remnants of our meals, we

staged a picture of David, battered, bruised, bound and locked up in the cell in the back of the van, and sent it on to Mufumba. After that, we rested, and made the journey to Lushoto earlier this morning. By the time we got here, Mufumba was practically begging for us to call him back.

"Are we bringing him directly to you?" Baynes asks, his conniving eyes drifting to mine. "I wouldn't want to allow him any opportunity to escape."

"I wouldn't have it any other way," Mufumba announces, triumphantly.

Baynes ends the call and looks to David and me with a sly smile on his lips.

"He really is stupid enough to fall for this," he says with some amount of surprise.

"It's not stupidity," David says, "it's hubris. He's lived in the lap of luxury for so long he's forgotten what it feels like to be at war. The fear, the excitement, the pain."

"War?" I ask. He leans against the side of the van, crossing his wide arms. His eyes are still bruised and swollen, but he's still a fearsome sight.

"The civil war, I told you it never really ended," he says. "But today, it will. With Eric – or Sunday Mufumba, or whatever he wants to call himself – the final impediment to true peace still stands."

Baynes looks between us both, before nodding to himself, and wiping his mouth with the back of his hand.

"Let's get on with it then," he says.

David changes into that blood-soaked shirt he was wearing yesterday – completely rigid with dried blood – and we put a set of the thick, reinforced handcuffs that came with the van on his wrists, without locking them.

I push the door of the van's tiny jail cell – barely big enough to fit David's huge frame – closed, and move to lock it.

"Huh," I murmur out loud as I lock the cell door. "Here I

am, a white foreigner, putting a black native in chains. It doesn't feel good, you know?"

"I'm sure it doesn't," David says, his face between two bars. "But consider this, a week ago you tried to shoot me in the head. I think we're making progress."

I smile at him, bid him a short farewell, and go to join Baynes in the front of the van.

We drive for another hour, and I watch the busy city of Lushoto pass me by, gradually growing sparser and quieter, until it feels like we've crossed back into the jungle itself. The road grows coarse, eventually becoming a dirty track in the grass, and the sky above us disappears behind a tall canopy of stifling trees.

We make it to a break in the road – a series of box-like buildings set in a line alongside it, as well as a tall, mean-looking wire fence, topped with unwelcoming barbed wire. If I didn't already know we were headed to the minister's residence, I'd believe this was a surreptitiously hidden military base.

A deep-green military Humvee blocks off the road, and three bored soldiers stand beside it, clutching their rifles and following our van intently.

"We've got the goods," Baynes says to one of the soldiers, who goes around the back and signals for us to join him. We do so – hearing the impossibly loud jungle again as we walk – and open the backdoor of the van, revealing the massive, bruised frame of David Faye, who plays his part by gyrating in his cuffs, and yelling some epithets in the local dialect.

"All good?" Baynes asks, to which the soldier licks his lips and nods. We get back in the van and the other pair of soldiers moves the Humvee, and our drive goes on.

We suddenly find ourselves outside of the jungle again; that canopy above us gives way to the white, overcast sky, and the trees and vines and bushes on either side of the car are gone, and a neatly trimmed green lawn lies in their stead.

There are occasional flower beds, with brightly colored tulips and roses, and white gravel paths cut into the grass. I see a large, white house in the distance, too, standing on a small green hill like a gleamingly clean, entirely conspicuous castle. It looks no less out of place than a dishwasher on mars.

"I guess this is the place," Baynes says, as the house draws nearer. It's a wide mansion, comprised of two floors with wrap-around balconies on the highest. Every window is an archway, every doorway is paneled in immaculate white, and every roof is neat, gray slate. It's a strange white elephant, standing in the thick rainforest.

It looks like it could be a museum to the various British colonial atrocities committed here in the previous two centuries, or the mansion of some ancient, half-mad family of robber barons. Instead, I know it's the palatial residence of the minister, at least for now. It's beautiful and indulgent.

We slowly drive up to the mansion, and a marble courtyard just in front of it. There are four draped-off statues present, all standing on four rather new and expensive looking plinths. I don't know who the statues depict beneath those drapes, but I bet I could make a decent guess.

Another two soldiers wearing green fatigues and rifles slung across their backs greet us at the courtyard, and ask us to turn off the engine and step out of the van. We do so, just as a familiar voice emerges from the direction of the mansion; a pleased, booming loud voice, like someone delighted to find his Christmas has come early.

"Gentlemen!" Mufumba yells, his disfigured face grinning from ear to ear. "Welcome to my office!"

Office? I see no cars parked, besides military vehicles, and no bored or distraught-looking workers with ties slung around their necks like nooses, on cigarette breaks, surely the visible symptoms of an office.

"Mr. Mufumba," Baynes says, trying to echo his enthusiasm, and holding his arms wide. They commit themselves to a bizarrely mistimed hug-and-chest-bump combination that leaves Baynes looking visibly uncomfortable. "We've got him in the back."

Once more, we all gather around the back of the van – Mufumba's large, portly figure, standing between Baynes and I – as I open the door.

There David sits, his knees close to his chin, in the dingy darkness of the prison cell. Rather than turn the air blue with performative swearwords and threats though, he doesn't say anything. He just stares – a cold, penetrating stare – directly at the minister.

Mufumba himself has a small smile on his face – a nervous, wry grin at one side of his mouth – and I get the feeling he doesn't quite know what to say. A strange, cagey silence passes between them – the unspoken appraisal of all those years of war and hurt and manipulation – all while David still stares at his former general with eyes that could burn a hole in him.

"Shall we take him inside?" Baynes finally asks, just as the silence becomes unbearable. Mufumba is rocking forwards and backwards slightly on the spot; a tiny action, one of excitedness or nervousness or perhaps both, and one that's only too apparent in the otherwise motionless quiet.

"Yes," he says, putting that enthusiastic grin back on his face, before yelling to the two soldiers nearby, who rush across to us and aim their rifles at our pretend prisoner.

David still doesn't speak; he lets his eyes do the talking. The laser-focused, unbroken stare that conveys just a small amount of the agony of the civil war, and the terrible things this man made him do, and the bitter vengeance he'll undoubtedly soon seek. Despite being behind those bars, he's undaunted.

"Let's go inside," Mufumba says, "it's time to end this."

CHAPTER 61

"Nice place," Baynes mutters under his breath. I can't tell if he's being sarcastic or not.

Baynes and I walk side by side, with David's hulking form in front of us, his hands still suspended in those unlocked handcuffs, with the two soldiers on either side of him, their rifles pointed nervously in his direction, and Mufumba behind us.

The interior of the mansion is just as I'd expected: like the set to a movie biopic about a mad dictator. Every surface seems to be fringed in gold; every wall adorned by a painting or ornament that manages to be more obnoxious than the one that preceded it.

Below our feet is a fluffy, elegant red carpet, and on the ceilings above us are a series of sophisticated chandeliers, each hiding a single, dingy lightbulb inside. The walls are painted a pure white, but they too betray nails, newly installed wooden beams, and filled-in areas where recent maintenance has been attempted.

There's a large, wall-sized painting of Mufumba, standing proudly in military regalia – scar and disfigurement and all – and in the background, a smaller group of men, one of which

I recognize from the photo David showed me. It's Mufumba – or Eric as he was known – before the bullet and the plastic surgery, an underappreciated little easter egg in his self-hagiography.

I feel like I'm walking the timber halls of Charles Forrest's jungle getaway again. What a weird and unsettling final mile for David Faye to walk, if it really were to be his final mile. A sick parade through the various riches and corruptly gotten gains of the man he once called a father figure. A man who immersed him, and the country, in hell.

"Into here," Mufumba says, making a karate-chopping action to the left. "This room, here."

He jumps to the right of our little prisoner conga line, and we follow him, the soldiers bringing the still quiet David along at the end of their rifles.

We walk through a large open doorway into a circular room, which chiefly reminds me of the oval office. There are three huge windows, through which I can see a verdant garden, and a large desk in front of it. Everything else – the large armchairs positioned in front of the desk, the cabinets in the corner – is similarly painted with gold.

I guess this is the 'office' Mufumba spoke to us about. It's a strange place to stage a score-settling showdown and summary execution of a political foe, but then again, I wouldn't have expected anything less from a shape-shifting warlord.

"Thank you, thank you, gentlemen," Mufumba says, as one of the soldiers kicks the back of David's knee, sending him to a kneeling position in the center of the room. I clench my fists, holding a breath inside me for a beat too long, and wait for whatever comes next.

"Firstly," Mufumba announces, as one of the soldiers locks the door, "I have to thank our American friends here. Without them, we might never have succeeded in bringing the notorious warlord David Faye to justice."

The two soldiers look to us with wary, guarded expressions, before each flashing us a small smile. I'm sure providing rapturous and affected applause to foreign mercenaries isn't part of their job description. Mufumba, on the other hand, claps heartily, the surreal sound of his singular applause echoing around the room.

David still hasn't made a sound, though. His eyes have barely left the minister – drifting occasionally to the armed soldiers – with his arms still suspended behind him in a pair of unlocked handcuffs.

"Your reward money will be coming to you," Mufumba says to Baynes. "We'll have our people talk to your people, you know how it is."

Baynes nods, and keeps up his polite smile.

"And you," Mufumba says, looking to David at last. He approaches him slowly and cautiously, one foot in front of the other in a defensive posture, as though he's worried David might burst from those handcuffs at any moment; a very valid concern. "I've waited a long time for this."

"It's been a while, hasn't it?" David asks, his bruised, slightly swollen eyes still locked on the minister. "It's been a long time, Eric."

Mufumba doesn't say anything; he furrows his brow and purses his lips, sucking his teeth like he's thinking of the perfect retort. I see sweat forming on his forehead already. He's so close to removing the last, problematic link to his deadly past life, and yet he can't seem to find the words.

A few tense moments pass – I sense Baynes beside me nervously shifting his weight between his two feet – and Mufumba evidently decides he doesn't want to confront the past after all.

"Give me a gun," he yells at one of the soldiers, who abruptly unveils a handgun from a holster, and puts his rifle down while he hands it over.

Mufumba clumsily grabs at it, turning it around in his

palm. In a split second, I turn my head to see the other soldier distracted – his eyes occupied by the gardens beyond the windows, and his rifle pointed harmlessly down.

Panting a quick breath, I quickly plot my footwork, and then look to David, who takes his gaze off the minister at last, and knowingly meets my own eyes. He winks at me, and I take my first step.

I throw myself at the distracted soldier – three quick steps towards him – building up enough momentum to make it to him before he can turn his head, and shoulder-barge him completely off his feet. He flies backwards – clutching his rifle with one hand – and I jump atop him and bring a fist down upon his face.

He goes limp beneath me, and I pick up my fist to see his eyes rolled into the back of his head. I hear a commotion behind me – a loud struggle of limbs and shouts and cries – and I turn my head to take it in.

The scene is like a renaissance painting. David is standing tall, holding the soldier's rifle with one hand, and that handgun Mufumba was clumsily handling with the other. The soldier himself lies on his back, unmoving, and Mufumba is on his knees, dazed, and clutching his face.

Baynes, on the other hand, stands there in the exact same place and pose as he did before this momentary storm of ultraviolence broke out. He has his hands on his hips, and a taciturn, almost bemused look on his face, like he'd have appreciated a warning.

"Wha, wha—" Mufumba groans, holding his nose with both hands. I take a circle of trusty duct tape out of my pocket and get to restraining the soldier below me, before moving onto the next one, lying barely conscious a couple of yards away.

"Hush now," David says to Mufumba, pointing the handgun at his head. "That's what you always said to us, isn't it?"

Mufumba rocks sideways, but in his eyes, I can tell he's coming back around. He focuses on David, not with the wary nervousness he had about him once, but with a desperate, mortal panic; the look of the mouse, frantically scurrying to escape the cat. All flight, no fight.

"Don't want to hold the gun? Hush now, child," David says, his voice wavering with emotion. "Don't want to sleep in the cold? Hush now. Don't want to fight any more? Hush now."

"Mr. Baynes, Mr. Clark!" Mufumba shouts, his panicked eyes flitting between us energetically. "What are you doing? Help me!"

Baynes crosses his arms and looks away from the minister.

"You asked us to deliver him to you," Baynes says, his tone stern, but his eyes still looking away from the stricken man. "And that's what we've done. No more and no less."

"You idiots! You imbeciles!" he yells, entering the anger stage, before looking back to us with panicked eyes again. "The money! You fools; you won't get the money if you let him kill me!"

Baynes looks to me – a modicum of hurt in his eyes – before looking back to the corner of the room, and breathing a long, theatrical sigh.

"Oh yeah, the money. Don't believe I haven't thought about it," he says in a yearning, wistful tone. "I've thought about it long and hard."

David seizes Mufumba by the back of the collar of his shirt; the sweat is dripping off him now. He looks between us still, his anger subsiding and his expression softer now.

"Twenty million dollars!" Mufumba yells. He looks between us with wide, bulging white eyes. "Thirty! Forty million dollars!"

"Guess I'd better leave this room before I start getting tempted," Baynes says to me with a smile, never looking at

Mufumba this whole time. "Have your reunion. I'm sure you boys have got a lot to catch up on."

Baynes starts to walk in the direction of that giant doorway, the only way out of this room. I look back to David, whose gaze is still transfixed on Mufumba – his gun pointed against his forehead – and turn to join Baynes in taking my leave.

"Hey! You!" Mufumba yells. I pause and turn back to him, to see him staring at me from the corners of his eyes. "Mr. Clark! You'll take the money, won't you? Come on now!"

I cross my arms. I've got no intention of taking his money. I just want to be done with this whole thing; out of this land, and back to chasing *another* mysterious, morally ambiguous superhuman around the world.

Still, I can't resist imparting a final word to the minister; a man who lied to get us here, lied about his own past, and soon faces a very overdue reckoning.

"Hush now," I say to him, looking at those pleading eyes one more time – no doubt seeing an entire history of deceit and evil flash before them – before leaving him to his fate.

CHAPTER 62

"Forty million dollars."

Baynes has said those three words some five or six times now, most often combined with a forlorn closing of the eyes, and a shake of the head.

"Still, he wouldn't have been good for it," he then adds. "He'd have promised us another couple of zeroes if we waited long enough. We'd have never, ever seen the money. Not a shiny dime."

He's said that a couple of times already too, a post-hoc rationalization; him telling his avaricious subconscious that refusing to take the war criminal's tainted, stolen money was the only option.

To my utter non-surprise, he shakes his head again, and I blow a bored breath out of my cheeks and cross my arms. We're sitting beside a truck stop in the middle of nowhere. There's a gas station, a paved road, and two endless sides of the same forest, running perpendicular to the road.

It's blisteringly hot, with a sticky veil of humidity covering every pore of my skin, and the sweat lashes off me, forming an uncomfortable clammy layer underneath my clothes. In short, the exact weather I'll remember Nubalaya by.

"Forty million," Baynes says again, shaking his head and putting his hand to his eyes.

We're waiting here for David, and his promise to get us across the border and out of the country.

The soldiers guarding Mufumba's residence didn't exactly stick around to defend their boss's legacy. When we announced we'd taken the house, they downed their arms and split, rather than give their lives to avenge the minister. An uncharacteristically clean end to a messy week.

Of course, I've no idea what happened between Mufumba and David. Baynes and I agreed to keep ourselves in the dark, and stay the hell out of it. David needed to remove his former general – and the man who made him a murderer as a child – from that lofty position of power. Mufumba needed to answer for what he did. And we didn't need to be involved.

I see a red car going over the hill, its hood and bumper fringed with rust and silver scratches in the paintwork. As it approaches, it slows, and comes to park beside us. Only after the cloud of red dust it kicks up settles do I see David's massive frame climbing out of the passenger side.

"Well, this is it," he says, leaning against the roof of the car, his elbows splayed widely across it. He slaps the roof: "My friend here will drive you through an unwatched area of the border."

I look into the driver's side and see a man – no older than David himself – looking straight ahead to the road, with his hands on the wheel.

"What now?" I ask. "For you, I mean."

He wipes his forehead with the back of his palm and shrugs slightly.

"I'll go back to Free Zimbala and finish the work I started there. Finish the school, try to make something of this country," he replies. "I don't know how long the ceasefire will prevail. I don't know if we'll return to war again, but I do know it's far less likely without men like Eric in positions of power."

"You won't fight again?" I ask, more a plea for no more political assassinations and bloodshed than a real question.

"No, no more fighting," he says with a deep breath. "My name is dirt. Seven years of propaganda, seven years of half-truths from the Interior Ministry has seen to that. There are few places in this country I can be seen in public. But, you know, that isn't the end of the world. Maybe I'll leave the continent, maybe I'll live in the shadows."

He looks up the road, and then down the road, and then back to me.

"All I have to say is thank you," David then says, smiling courteously. "I know you were brought here under false pretenses, and put on a wrong course. It took a lot for you to realize that course was wrong."

I side eye Baynes beside me who with the slightest of movements, probably perceptible only to me, mouths *forty million* with his lips. To be fair, I can't argue with the sentiment; I lost an arm back there, and almost got beaten to death. A very costly course-correction, but one I'm very glad we made.

Baynes crosses over to David's side of the car and shakes his hand.

"It's been educational," he says, his voice tired and monotonal. David slaps him on the shoulder, a blow that seems to stagger him, his body jerking forwards clumsily. I guess David doesn't yet realize that Baynes and I aren't made of the same stuff.

With an awkward, sheepish smile, and quick adjustment of his collar, he gets into the back of the car, and David looks back across the roof of the car at me.

"No hard feelings?" I ask, gamely. "You know, for all that

fighting we did. The black eyes, the spilled blood. I bet you had a lot of explaining to do on the train."

"No," David replies with a chuckle. "It was God's plan that we fought each other, and it was His plan that we reconciled. Nubalaya is a far better place for it."

"Right," I say. "God's plan, huh."

"There is one more thing," he says as I start to walk to the car. I stop in my tracks and lean against the roof adjacent to him. "I don't usually mean to question him, but there is one more facet to God's plan that I don't understand."

I think I know what he's going to ask me.

"You wear the face of a person yesterday, and the face of an entirely different person today," he says. "You survive a fall from a train that would kill another man. You're the only man in the world who can beat me for strength, yet you're half the size of me."

He leans across the roof of the car.

"What are you?" he asks, his eyes full of trepidation and unease.

"It's a long story," I say after a deep breath. "A story I shouldn't get into right now, but when you're done building your schools and your clinics and whatever else you've got on your plate, look us up, and I'll tell you all about myself."

He nods, purses his lips, and reaches across the roof of the car with one hand. I shake his hand, and with one final look – his expression caught between genial gratitude, and wary uncertainty – I open the door and join Baynes in the back of the car.

The loud hiss of the forest gives way to the driver's tinny car radio, and some rap song, apparently in another language. We speed away and I look backwards, and watch the massive, statue-like figure of David Faye grow ever smaller in the distance, until he disappears entirely, and all I see is the road, and the impenetrable green of the forest.

"What a bust," Baynes says. I don't hear him at first – the

driver's music drowns him out – until I replay it in my mind and think about each word.

"What?" I ask after a few too many moments, turning to see him.

"How long have we been here? I lost track of the days," he says. "But what I do know is this whole escapade was nothing more than a massive waste of our time."

"You think?" I ask.

"What?" he shoots back, his eyes full of surprise that I'd even question it. "We came here to pursue a possible lead on Vincent and secure a massive bounty; a bounty that would have made our little vampire hunt far easier."

His cheeks begin to turn red. I don't know if it's the mention of the money again, or the fact that this car's suspensions are shot, and every annoying bump in the road sends us flying towards the ceiling.

"Instead, what did we find?" he asks, a question I open my mouth to answer, but don't do so in time. "Pain, blood, sweat, and tears."

He's talking like he's the one who had his skull pounded into dust by a genetic freak.

"You lost an arm, for crying out loud," he says, and I nervously glance at the driver in front, who thankfully is still nonchalantly focusing on the road and his soundtrack. "You could have bled out and died right there in the dirt. And for what? So we could go home empty handed."

He petulantly turns his head to look out of the window, as if that's the final word, and the entire matter is closed.

"I dunno," I say after a minute or so of silence. He turns back to me, his expression tired, but combative. "I feel like it was a success. Maybe our largest success yet."

He tilts his head incredulously, like he's forensically analyzing me for signs of sarcasm or insanity.

"A success?"

"Sure, a success," I repeat.

"Did you forget we saved civilization a couple of years back?" he asks, provoking another quick look in the driver's direction.

"We did, and think about the cost," I reply, remembering Jack's lifeless eyes, staring coldly into me. He doesn't say anything; he lets his eyes drift downwards mournfully. I go on: "No, this time we came to a distant, mysterious land, learned a little, took a bit of a beating, and then learned a little more. In the end, I feel like we helped."

"But we didn't do anything," he says, scratching his temple, and then combining that with the typical tapping of his finger there. "Sure, we gave Faye a lift into the minister's residence, but do you really think he wouldn't have made it there himself, eventually? It's not like he was shy about using those fists of his."

Don't I know it; I can close my eyes and still feel the force of them, raining down from the sky and battering chunks out of my face. Baynes stops tapping on his temple, and looks back outside.

"I don't know," I say after a few more quiet moments between us, filled by the radio. "So what if we didn't do more? So what if we didn't bring the all-singing, all-dancing American intervention show?"

He turns back to me with scorn in his eyes, correctly detecting the attack on his beloved CIA.

"We stood back, heard the full story, and decided that justice was a greater reward than the bounty. It feels like we actually helped, like I can be proud of this one, unlike all the other times I've gone to a distant place and made a massive, craterous mess. It's a happy ending, somehow."

He scoffs – I see his shoulders rise with a breath and a sneer – and shakes his head.

"What's the moral of this story?" he asks.

"God, I don't know," I say. "Don't go bounty hunting.

Don't think there's an easy buck to be made inserting yourself into other people's business."

"Or don't go messing around in Africa," he adds. "I should have known that from my previous life."

I guess there's no getting through to him; he's unable to comprehend a world in which the happy ending wasn't enforced at the pointy end of an American stick, and there was no juicy carrot waiting for us at the end. We were the bad guys, at least at first, and he won't ever truly understand that.

"You know what, though?" he says, chuckling to himself. "You really did a number on him back there."

"Huh?"

"David Faye," he says, smiling impishly at me. "Those bruises, those stitches. You beat him. One of the most dangerous men on the planet, raised in the fires of the worst war imaginable, and you beat him. He's a born killer, but you're something greater than that."

"Yeah, right," I say back awkwardly, looking to the driver again, who's still focused on the road.

"I'm sorry for ever doubting you back there," Baynes says. He smiles at me – an affirming, amiable smile – and turns back to his window, going back to watching the trees flash by.

Readjusting myself in my seat, I turn to my own window, and feel something sharp jabbing my thigh through my pants.

I slip my hand into my pocket and pull out that polaroid photograph of the train driver and his son; the very people Mufumba insisted were dead, complete with another gory, fabricated photo to 'prove' it. The poor man we demanded be paraded around in front of us to prove his ongoing mortality.

I look at the photograph again, and into their cheerful eyes. It's like they've been on some great journey in my mind; a sad and violent death, followed by a surprising rebirth and a second chance at life. That man – Howard Daju – his son, and his family are alive, and with them, there's still hope for Nubalaya.

CHAPTER 63

I see those hordes of people waiting in the arrivals lounge. Chauffeurs holding large placards with formally spelled names on them; families waiting for their mothers or fathers; husbands waiting for wives or vice versa. There are smiles, there are tears, there are professional, curt greetings.

And then there's Alessia, standing to one side of the hall, almost invisible behind the crowd. She's leaning against a column, wearing funereal black, and as soon as she sees us, she slowly picks up her eyebrows – her eyes remaining still and caustic – and begins to slow clap our arrival.

"Another job well done, fellas," she says, her tone dripping with sarcasm.

"Shut up," is Baynes' only remark as we step past her and begin walking out of the airport.

"Thanks," I say to her when Baynes has forged too far ahead to hear us. "I think the whole trip was kind of worth it."

She turns her head, her expression one of quizzical, pleasant surprise.

We make it outside the terminal, and I'm embraced by the cold welcome of the east coast. The hairs on the back of my neck stand up, and I'm taken aback by how good it feels to escape that sweaty blanket of sub-Saharan heat and humidity.

I breathe the air – that thick, smoggy upstate New York air – and close my eyes, and savor the moment. There's nothing quite like an intercontinental pummeling to make you miss home.

We get into Alessia's rental car and make the drive home, a three-hour trip, mostly in silence so far. Baynes is in the back and sleeps almost the entire way – his mouth occasionally sagging open, a yawning chasm – but unusually, I find I'm not tired. There's still too much on my mind.

"Aren't you going to drive one of these days?" Alessia asks, some half hour away from Enderton. Her tone is uncertain; maybe she's decided to break a couple of hours of silence to taunt me over crashing that bank truck in Lushoto, or perhaps she doesn't know about that yet, and she's sincerely asking the question.

"I'll get around to it," I say to her. "I have to learn, first."

"Get one of us to take you around a parking lot sometime," she says, earnestly. "Get some miles behind you, get to know what a steering wheel feels like."

I guess she is sincerely asking the question. She evidently doesn't know I've already got a mile or two behind me, as well as a great blazing inferno.

"Don't I need a license?" I ask. "Pass the driving test, that sort of thing?"

She turns away from the road and looks at me like I said something incredibly stupid.

"What's the point?" she asks, grinning to herself. "You make yourself a brand-new face every other day. You're legally dead. What, do you wanna get a new social security number too?"

I blow an annoyed breath out of my nostrils. I guess she has a point.

"Just get behind the wheel sometime, it'll do you some

good," she says, clearly unaware of the flaming consequences of the last time I did that.

"Yeah," I say, embarrassed. "Maybe another time."

"I was meaning to ask you," she says after another couple of breaths. "You said this whole Nubalaya thing was worth it. I can't help but notice we didn't get the bounty, so what did you mean back there?"

"Oh, yeah, that," I say, leaning back in my seat and looking out across the freeway. "I dunno, I feel like we actually made a difference in that country, despite doing almost nothing at all. Hell, at first, I think we were the bad guys, and by the end, well, I'm not sure we quite did enough to make ourselves the good guys, but—"

"Kris, that isn't how it works," she says, interrupting me. "There are no bad guys, and there are no good guys. The world is a kaleidoscope of different shades of gray. And those shades change, after every bullet that's fired, after every death and every birth. Every day."

I'm sure she's said something like this before; some cynical effort to make me see the world as she sees it. Still, yet again, maybe she has a point.

"I went there looking for David Faye; the warlord," I say. "When I found him, I thought I'd meet a bad guy, but not just any bad guy. A devil; an evil man."

Alessia keeps her eyes on the road, but I see her raise an eyebrow.

"Instead, what I found was that he was just like me," I tell her. "A man with strength he didn't ask for, given to him by chance, and some cruel lessons in how to use it. Someone who tried to escape it all, only to get dragged back in."

"Dio," she says, followed by a few more words in Italian. "Another superhero?"

"No," I reply. "Human. Just about."

We go another couple of minutes in silence.

"He had a lot of regrets. But I guess we've all done

things we regret," I tell her, keeping my mind away from Aljarran, and the subway train, and Jack, and all of those padlocked pandora's boxes, full of all the memories I can't revisit.

"Oh, don't I know it," she replies, in a curt tone that tells me that's the end of our discussion.

David Faye was a special child, born with a unique strength, and forced into a brutal war. Immense pressure and oppression and torment was his making, like a blood diamond. He did terrible things – things no child should be made to do – because he was powerful enough to survive.

Even now, he's still trying to survive; trying to be strong where others are weak, trying to be a light where his neighbors live in darkness. If he deserves a second chance – a chance to put the memory of those terrible acts behind him, a chance to be *good* – then I do too.

By the time I'm out of my highway-induced reverie we're back at the office. Alessia parks beside that vape shop – the Vape Megastore – and its collection of grimy windows where its walls meet the sidewalk. Our office.

There's a figure standing outside, with his hand to his ear. He's wearing a grey sweatshirt and black track pants, and a shock of black frizzy hair, a little longer than it was when I saw him here before. It's Dante, and as soon as he sees Alessia's car, he puts his hand into his pocket and jogs over to us.

"What the hell does he want?" Alessia asks as I roll the window down.

"Does no one want to answer their god-damned phones?" he shouts, exasperated. Baynes wakes up behind us, jolting forward like he's been painfully wrenched from a more pleasant place.

"Huh?" Alessia grunts, putting her hand into her pocket and picking her cellphone out of it.

"We got a lead, an hour ago," Dante says, a small smile

creeping onto his lips, before he remembers how aggravated he is, and he grimaces once more.

"A lead!?" Baynes barks, roaring back to life as though he didn't just spend three hours soundly asleep. "What lead?"

We haven't even made it out of the car yet, and we're already discussing the next fun way for me to get myself Swiss-cheesed by bullets, violently un-armed via high-speed locomotion, or more optimistically just drained of all my blood by a psychotic teenage killer.

"A superhuman," Dante says, the smile back on his face now. "Or at least that's what the folks on social media are calling him. Real lurid stuff."

"Another rich, deluded wannabe bloodsucker?" I ask him.

"No, you're gonna want to read this," he says, pulling up his cellphone and scrolling his thumbs along it.

"Can you perhaps give us the shortform summary?" Baynes asks, after a couple of awkward moments of silence, other than the still-ticking engine that Alessia soon turns off.

"An armed gang attacked a Matriel Pharmaceutical facility in Arizona," Dante says, excitedly. "And get this, videos recorded at the scene show the leader getting hit by bullets and shrugging them off like paintballs."

"Arizona huh," I say, thinking it over. I can't deny I'm feeling the thrill of the hunt too though. "Was it Vincent? What was he doing there?"

"His face isn't clear in the video," Dante says, "but they're saying the gang fought security at the facility and made off with a bunch of sensitive items. There's no more information yet, but it's the best lead we've had."

"Pack a bag!" Baynes yells, fumbling to remove his seatbelt. "We're going to Arizona."

Alessia mumbles a bunch more words in Italian. I turn to her and see her sunglasses have slid to the bottom of her nose, and her unimpressed brown eyes are staring back at me.

"I guess I'd better turn the car around," she says, nonchalantly. Still, I see a sly smile on the side of her lips. Our greatest chance to track down Vincent yet; her best chance of avenging her old friends.

"Kris, what do you think?" Baynes asks, having finally extricated himself from the seatbelt.

I look back at him, and that irrepressibly enthusiastic expression of his. He hates languishing in the basement below a vape shop just as much as I do. From vampiric arms dealers to genetic freaks to corrupt, warmongering ministers and back to vampires again. I feel like a freshman at the college I never went to; there's no such thing as a quiet weekend anymore…

"Sounds to me like we're already an hour late," I tell them. "Let's get a move on."

AFTERWORD

The story continues in The Gift book six: DUPE

They say he's the Second Coming; that he's immortal. Is he really a heaven-sent prophet, or is he just someone else's dirty work?

Kris Chambers and the team have only just returned home when news of an armed attack on a pharmaceutical facility becomes lurid national news. A grainy, handheld video of a burning hole in the side of a secure facility, and a mysterious, shadowy figure taking numerous bullets to the chest, only to rise again and fight.

Their most fruitful lead takes them to Colorado, where a devoted follower – a so-called disciple – is incarcerated in supermax federal prison. With no other options, Kris sneaks into the prison, intending to speak to him man-to-man.

He soon hears tales of a formerly paralyzed conman, blessed with the miraculous ability to walk again and superhuman powers. A man who inspires perfect loyalty from his followers, and the shamelessness to call himself the Second Coming.

But is he really an incarnation of a god? Is he an immortal, avenging angel, sent to rally the meek and purge society's evildoers, or is he still the same con man he always was?

With the both the cops and Matriel hot on Kris' tail, it's going to be a wild ride...

Thank you for reading; please leave me a review if you have the time, and follow me on Facebook to hear the latest news about the sequel.

Printed in Great Britain
by Amazon